THE
Dead OF Winter

THE
Dead OF Winter

David A. Crossman

Down East Books
Camden, Maine

Copyright © 1999 by David A Crossman
Cover illustration copyright © 1999 by Jim Sollers
ISBN (cloth) 0-89272-445-5 ; (pbk) 0-89272-476-5
Book design by Eugenie S. Delaney
Printed and bound at Versa Press, Inc., East Peoria, Illinois

5 4 3 2 1

Down East Books
Camden, Maine
Book orders: (800) 766-1670

LIBRARY OF CONGRESS CATALOGING-IN-PUBLICATION DATA

Crossman, D. A. (David A.)
    The dead of winter : A Winston Crisp mystery /
by David A. Crossman.
        p.   cm.
    ISBN 0-89272-445-5 (hardcover)
    ISBN 0-89272-476-5 (paperback)
    I. Title.
PS3553.R5728D42   1999
813'.54—dc21   99-16369
                                              CIP

My wife and I were in a little pub in Castle Combe, England, talking out the plot of this book so it would be clear in my mind as I started writing. All of a sudden we noticed that conversation at the tables around us—which had been robust—had ceased. All eyes were upon us, and for an instant we wondered what we'd done. Then, of course, we realized that they thought they were overhearing a plot to murder some poor soul. This is for them, and others who see the mysterious in the mundane. P.S. They'll never find the body.

My heartfelt thanks to my editor, Barbara Feller-Roth, whose efforts, together with those of Karin and Alice, have succeeded in making me seem both cogent and literate. Tough job. Good work!

SEPTEMBER 3, 1935

THE STORM THAT HAD BEEN THREATENING all day finally broke, as if someone had run a filet knife along the bulging underbelly of the thick black clouds. Bandy Wiley stared out the window, the driven drops of rain on the glass creating the illusion of tears on her face. "Who was them kids? Do you know?"

Her brother, slumped in the overused sofa, stared into the empty fireplace and grunted.

"What?" said Bandy, turning from the window.

"I didn't say anything," Willy snapped. "I don't know. I never seen 'em before. Summer kids."

"You think they saw anything?"

Willy sucked loudly at his can of Carling Black Label. He didn't reply.

"You think they saw?" Bandy repeated, her voice rising with anxiety.

"Shut up, will you," Willy snapped sharply. "How'm I s'posed to think with you blabberin'? Just shut up."

"*Me* shut up?" Bandy wailed, her anxiety rising. "*Me?* Who was it dug the hole while you was pacin' back and forth moanin' like a baby? Me shut up? If it wasn't for me, she'd still be bangin' 'round in the back of your truck. You friggin' fool . . . you ignorant . . . I s'pose that was *your* idea of a plan."

Willy's lower lip quivered and tears puddled in his eyes. "I didn't mean for it to happen, Ban. I was just playin' around, you know. Like I do. You seen me a hundred times with girls. You know. Just playin' around. Foolin', is all."

Bandy's anger subsided. Her older brother wasn't retarded, but he didn't miss it by much. All her life she'd been getting him out of scrapes. But nothing like this. She'd done the first thing that came to mind. But was it the right thing? If only their father were alive. She turned again to the window and stared at the streetlight on the corner. "See what you get when you fool around?"

Willy was on the verge of sobbing. He buried his head in his hands and spoke through his fingers, his voice mucousy and wet. "She was just teasin', too, Bandy. She teased back, like they do."

"I doubt it," Bandy replied. "She wasn't like that."

"Then she said some awful things," Willy replied upon consideration.

"Well, you prob'ly had it comin'."

"I just give 'er a little push," Willy said in his defense. "I didn't know she was so close to the edge of the deck."

"You just give her a little push," said Bandy, turning to face him. She fastened him with her dark eyes, full of fear and rage. "You don't know your strength. People are always tellin' you to leave them alone. All you done your whole stupid life is push people around. You can't do that, Willy. Everybody's smaller than you. You can't—"

Willy had dug his fists into his cheeks and was peering at her over them, his knuckles stained with tears. Bandy fell to her knees in front of him. "You know that, don't you, Willy? You know now, don't you? You can't ever let somethin' like this happen again. Not ever."

Unable to restrain himself any longer, Willy burst into a storm of pathetic sobs. "I won't, Ban. I won't. I swear." He threw his arms around his sister's neck. "Don't say nothin', Ban. Don't tell nobody."

"Don't you worry 'bout it," Bandy replied, stroking the back of his head with her dirt-caked palm.

Bandy had no idea what the legal consequences of his crime might be, but given the hand that life had dealt her and her brother so far, it wasn't hard to imagine him strapped in an electric chair. That wasn't going to happen. She'd see to it. She seized the lucky brimstone that hung on a string around her neck, raised it to her lips, and kissed it three times: once for Willy, once for her, and once for the soul of Cailey Hall.

"Come Thursday you'll be back on your ship." She laughed a hollow laugh in his ear. "When it comes to gettin' away from somethin', the merchant marines beats the French Foreign Legion all to pieces, don't it?"

Willy buried his head between her breasts and quaked silently in her arms, soaking her blouse with his tears. "I'll take care of everything," Bandy assured him softly. One way or the other, she'd been taking care of him ever since their father died when she was eleven and her brother was sixteen. Their mother had run away long before that. It didn't matter that she'd gone only to the other side of the island; it might as well have been another planet for all they'd seen of her since. Bandy folded Willy into the shelter of herself. "Don't you worry," she crooned.

For a while they clung to each other, suspended above a gaping chasm that could be filled only with prayers. But Willy and Bandy hadn't been raised to pray. So they twisted and cried, with nothing but echoes in reply.

At last, Bandy seized Willy firmly by the shoulders and pushed him to arms' length. Then she lifted his chin until their eyes met. "Willy, you can't come back to the island, you know. Don't you ever, ever come back."

"But I won't see you!" This realization tore a renewed torrent of tears from the young man. For a long time his sobs echoed from the walls of the little clapboard house by the cove. "What am I gonna do without you?"

Bandy had no tears. Embracing her brother with all her might, she questioned the darkness with her eyes, whispering to herself beneath Willy's sobs: "Who *was* them kids?" She clutched the brimstone and made a wish against them.

CHAPTER

1

OCTOBER 16, 1970

THE BODY IN THE WAVES moved to the rhythm of the ocean, erratic in the aftermath of the recent hurricane. It mesmerized the tall, hard-faced woman as she stood on the bluff overlooking the little cove, staring through thick glasses, her mouth opened in a scream that never came. Horror had stolen her breath away. Not that there was much body left, just leathery skin–draped bones dressed in the remnants of clothes long out of fashion. A tangle of long dirty-blond hair floated on the water, surging back and forth with the angry push and pull of the surf. There were no eyes in the gaping skull, but the water that was pooled in the sockets reflected the sun, which now and then peeked through the scudding clouds, giving the illusion not of life but of restless death.

There was no one else on the moor—a nervous glance or two had told her that. For a moment she stood wringing her hands, scanning the horizon for any sign of a lobster boat. It was October; they were usually all in by this time of day. In the far distance she could make out the sails of a schooner receding south, fleeing winter in Penobscot Bay for the warm waters of the Caribbean.

She slipped once or twice on the seaweed in her haste down the ledges to the shore. Pulling up the legs of her dungarees as she went, she waded into the ocean, pulled the sodden remains from the surf, and draped them over her shoulder, fighting the impulse to be sick as the frigid water drained from the corpse and down her neck.

OCTOBER 28, 1970

"Really, Annie, I insist. If you can talk Paul into coming here for the holidays, I won't have to go to all the bother of closing up the house while I'm away. You'd be doing me a favor." Kitty's words oozed welcome, but her eyes, as she stared through the window at the harbor, were full of the coming winter. "What? Margaret? Of course. Bring her along." That would mean opening the north bedroom. Cal wouldn't like that. Nuisance. "How cozy. She must be such a comfort after . . . after all you've been through."

For a while, early that fall, it had seemed that Anne was losing her battle with depression. According to her husband, she'd spent most of her time in bed, benumbed with pills. Lately, though, she'd shown signs of improvement. He thought she was up to the trip, but, because of the recent friction in their marriage, she wouldn't take such a suggestion coming from him. She'd have to think it was Kitty's idea.

"You know I'm right, Annie," Kitty prodded gently. A mild thunder shook her heart. If she could talk the distraught woman—her oldest and dearest friend—into accepting the offer, everything would be all right. Everything would be perfect. "It'll do you a world of good to come back to the island. You know how peaceful it is. Quiet. Just what the doctor ordered."

Anne was hesitating.

"You won't have to lift a finger if you don't want to," Kitty continued. "Cal will take care of everything." A lot of good Cal was lately—nervous as a cat, jumping at shadows, and stalking the night like a distracted specter. Still, she was competent with her chores. If she could hold on through the holidays; Paul thought that would be long enough. "What do you say, my dear?"

Anne's initial resolve was crumbling audibly.

"I won't take no for an answer, you hear?" Kitty persisted. "As far as I'm concerned, it's settled. If you need me for anything, I'll either be at the house in Alexandria or the cottage on Aruba. We'll keep in touch by phone.

"You just come and make yourself at home for as long as you like—a month, at least. As long as you want. Pardon? Oh, I'm sure Paul will see the sense in your getting away for a while. I'll talk to him if you like. Certainly can't hurt, can it? Do you a world of good, dear. A world of good. Mind you, I'd warn Margaret she won't find much companionship on the island in winter. Not much mental stimulation to be found after Labor Day, if you know what I mean. Only the local people.

"What's that, dear? Oh, yes. Of course. You'll have no end of rest. It's like another world out here. The occasional hiker and whatnot, but no one to bother you." Kitty drew the final arrow from her quiver and fit it to the string. "I think it would be good for Paul, too. Don't you? A little time away together could be just what you need to sort things out."

Kitty listened intently, but her eyes didn't move from the harbor. "You leave him to me, dear. I'll call him at work. No, no. Don't trouble yourself. I've got the number of the State Department around here somewhere. They'll track him down for me.

"All you have to do is show up, and leave everything else to me."

DECEMBER 27, 1970

Augustus Knight didn't like Penobscot Island. In particular, he didn't like the islanders.

Those who loved him best would have said he enjoyed not only the perquisites and privileges of his position as chancellor of the university but the subtle obeisance offered him by his fellow academics, a deference that, he imagined at some unspoken level of his psyche, was tendered not so much in consideration of his position as in recognition of a manifest superiority that his character betrayed, a superiority that islanders were too dull to comprehend.

Far too socially aware to give voice to such sentiments, he nevertheless entertained them—and heartily—as, with his hood pulled tightly over his face, he made his way solemnly up Main Street, past the little knot of gossiping natives outside the post office, on his way to the Bermann estate. Of course, they would talk about him when he was out of hearing. What else had they to talk about?

Within the insular world of academe Augustus had no difficulty maintaining the conceit that his was a larger world where issues of lasting consequence were scrutinized and dissected by intellectual giants whose resolutions were to be distilled by the social machinery and spoon-fed to the populace for the betterment of humanity.

Outside the bubble, however, among people who could repair outboard motors, knit nets, and gather the necessities of life from their surroundings, that conceit could only be buttressed by a running interior dialogue designed to demonstrate, to his own satisfaction at least, his intellectual superiority.

Such a display would of course, if given tongue, be wasted. Should he turn and skewer the populace—among them the ferry attendant who offered him a cigar as he stood heaving his breakfast over the railing, and the supercilious restaurant worker who had given him directions to the Bermann estate—with but a sampling of the intellectual pyrotechnics of which he was capable, they would stare at him blankly, too thick to realize they had been made asses, too primitive to know they stood in the presence of a higher, albeit beneficent, power.

The liberal conscience of his better self battled halfheartedly against the arguments that formed, of their own volition, to the rhythm of his footsteps. What were these thoughts other than harmless amusements with which to exercise his brain? By the time he reached his destination, he had suppressed the niggling whispers of inferiority sufficiently that he was almost eager for the interview with Johnny Bermann, an equal.

Knight's part of the upcoming dialogue had been carefully framed on the drive from Orono to Rockland and between bouts of seasickness during the crossing. He stood for a moment by the cemetery at the head of the dirt drive descending to the Bermann estate and turned the delicate network of phrases over in his mind. He must be careful not to invite suspicion. His solicitousness after his old schoolmate's health must seem genuine. Paramount. Only in passing would he make reference to the upcoming election and his aspirations. An aside. A caprice? No. A duty. Yes, a duty. Johnny would appreciate that. It would demonstrate how much he'd changed. He had become chancellor, after all.

Of course, no direct reference could be made to cheating at school all those years ago. Remember how foolish we were in those days? he'd say, with a brief, lighthearted laugh in punctuation. Of course, things were different then, weren't they? *We* were different. We've learned so much over the years. We've learned what's important, haven't we? We must put childish things aside. A Biblical quote. Perfect. The inference of penance. Well, I just wanted to know how you are. You're writing a book, I understand. Don't introduce the topic too soon, he reminded himself; say it in passing. A simple "by the way," perhaps after the second cup of ginseng tea. That would be appropriate. Scholarly. Unless, of course, Johnny brought up the book first. Oh? Really? What's it about?

That would work nicely.

Once Knight had the information he needed, he could respond accordingly. He'd worked that through as well.

Lost in thought as he mechanically strode toward the house, he was almost surprised by the sound of his knuckles rapping on the door.

There was no reply.

"Johnny?"

A frigid gust of wind blew up from the bay and slapped his cheeks. He tugged the drawstrings of his hood a little tighter. "Johnny? Are you home? It's Augustus . . . Auggy Knight."

Still no reply. He rapped again. There was a shuffling sound on the other side of the door, then a slow, deliberate lifting of the latch as the door swung open, revealing a version of Johnny Bermann with whom Knight was not familiar. Disease had sapped his vitality, and his eyes seemed to echo the crypt.

"My God!" Augustus exclaimed involuntarily.

There would be no tea.

DECEMBER 28, 1970

"Listen to that wind howl," said Matty. She lifted the shade on the solitary window in Winston's room and peeked out into the blindness of snow. "All I think about is them poor little animals out there, tryin' to find somethin' to eat."

Winston knew she'd feed them all if she could—bake them thick, steaming berry pies with juice oozing through little geometric slits in the crust and over the sides of aged, chipped graniteware pie pans. She'd bring them inside and make them drink hot tea and cranberry juice and eat scones dripping with butter. Then, when they were done, she'd tuck them into little beds, for which she'd stitched the quilts herself, and make them stay there until spring.

That was Matty—a name that was, to Winston Crisp, synonymous with home and welcome. And optimism. Most of all, optimism. Not long ago she was the only one on the island who thought he'd live another day.

He didn't reply to her observation about the weather, but she wasn't surprised. He hadn't replied for months. "He's doing so much better," she told Esther Poole every day at the post office. Today she'd had something new to report. "He's makin' these little noises down in his throat that sound almost like words. Well," she amended, reining in her enthusiasm, "little gruffles, anyway. Is that a word, 'gruffles'? That's what it sounds like to me.

"Doctor Pagitt says he's through the worst of it, comin' out've the coma like he done—praise the Lord." She thought for a second. "Well, he doesn't say that—I do. I s'pect he thinks he did it all himself." She chuckled. "Anyway, I don't imagine he'll ever take up the bicycle again—not that he should've been on one in the first place at his age—but he should be up and around come spring. . . . Summer anyway."

Things couldn't have been better for Matty. Since his recovery from the coma she'd had an invalid all her own, someone to tend to who couldn't talk back. If Winston looked as though he needed his pillow fluffed, it got fluffed, with no argument. If she felt a chill, Winston got an extra blanket or two. If she was a little warm—well, at Winston's age, there was no such thing as too warm.

"Come spring, I expect," she'd repeated a little sadly. Not that she'd mind having him up and around again, reading her the poems he'd written that every editor in the free world seemed to regard as a personal insult. She loved his poems. They rhymed, and she could understand what they were about. And they stirred up real feelings—a smile, a tear. What was wrong with that?

But once he was master of himself, she knew he wouldn't let her fuss over him anymore. He'd say, Now Matty, three pieces of pie is all I can eat. He wouldn't want hospital corners on his sheets, because he liked to kick his blankets out at the end. She couldn't understand how he could sleep that way, with his bare feet sticking out, and why he never froze to death. But he wasn't going to court disaster on her watch. As long as he was immobile, she'd put socks on his feet and make sure they were tucked in nice and warm, just the way she liked hers.

When she was in his room, she talked a blue streak as she puttered and straightened and dusted. Ostensibly it was to keep him company, but beneath the level of admitting it to herself, she kept up the chatter to keep the ghosts at bay. Ever since the night last summer when that young woman had gone screaming down the stairs and out into the night like a banshee, the room had been full of her presence. Clean as Matty might be, even she couldn't expunge the residual horror from the blue-flowered wallpaper. The very doilies, witness to the surreal nightmare of the events that led to Crisp's near death, reeked with a dark, unnameable madness.

The sound of Matty's words also drowned out the persistent inner voice that whispered it had all been her fault: She should have known; she should have reacted faster. Never mind that she'd saved his life. It should never have gotten so close—not under her roof. Not to her Winston.

It had been a very near thing. Near enough so no one in town mentioned Crisp's name aloud during the early, breathless stages of his convalescence for fear that such mention would remind the angel of death that he'd left a job unfinished. Even now, five months later—with the "Professor," as Crisp was known to the townsfolk, well on his way to recovery—when conversation turned to the deaths of Mostly Sanborn and that poor redheaded girl whose body was found frozen in ice, voices automatically fell to just above a whisper. Better safe.

Crisp watched Matty appreciatively as she made her customary rounds of the room, dusting where there was no dust, straightening what wasn't crooked, and in between patting her blue-gray hair that she imagined errant, or mindlessly pinching the pleats in her apron and pressing them into respectable ridges between her thumb and forefinger.

He had a surprise for her. He cleared his throat. She stopped and turned attentively, thinking he might need something. "Winston?" she said. "What do you want, dear? Do you want the paper and pencil?"

He cleared his throat again. "Matty," he said. His voice was ragged and hoarse, but there was no doubt about it; he'd spoken her name. The effect was impressive: Matty's fingers froze in midworry. Unprecedented.

"Winston?" she breathed in disbelief, taking a tentative step toward him. "Did you say something?" She had to be sure it wasn't just wishful thinking.

"I believe I did," said Crisp with a creaking smile. There were pops and crackles in the words, but that was to be expected of a mechanism so long unused.

The look on Matty's face was worth the price of admission. She sank sideways into an old white wicker chair that complained loudly of its sudden, unexpected burden. "Winston," she repeated. "Praise the Lord."

"Amen," said Winston simply. "Merry Christmas—a little late, I'm afraid."

Unwonted tears overflowed Matty's eyes. She buried her face in her dust cloth, and for two or three minutes her body convulsed silently to the cadence of her emotions.

"So I told her, 'You know what, Missy?' I says. 'God give animals just enough brains to keep 'em fresh.'"

Joel Philbrook laughed at his joke. So did the other old men gathered around the potbellied stove, as they had a hundred times before, ever since last summer when Joel had a dispute with the young hippie with the "Love Animals, Don't Eat Them" button on her peasant blouse. Entertainment was hard to come by on the island in winter.

Outside the hardware store, two industrious young boys were shoveling narrow paths in the deep new snow. It was light and powdery and shoveled easily, but the fierce southwest wind, swirling indecisively, whipped it back in their faces, no matter which way they heaved it, and stuffed it down the necks of their shirts.

"How much you payin' them boys to rearrange the snow?" said Harry Ames. He took a long, loud sip from a thick green glass Coke bottle and drummed his rope-worn fingers impatiently on the game board, making the checkers jump. "You gonna move, Bergie?"

"It ain't my move," Bergie replied calmly through the overhang of his thick black mustache. He took an expressive pull on his old meerschaum pipe. "It's yours. I been waitin' five minutes."

"It ain't either my move," Harry contended. "I moved this little fella"—he rested a bony finger on one of the ancient wood pieces—"from here to here." He repeated the move. "Instant replay, just like on Wide Worlda Sports."

Bergie tossed a wicked wink at Drew, who was stoking the fire. "And I moved this one over here, mister man."

Harry saw at once that he'd been wrong, but he wasn't about to admit it. "You didn't neither," he sputtered. "Did he, Drew?" This appeal directly to the owner of the worthy institution bypassed the lesser judges seated in the semicircle, most of whom had already begun to snicker.

"I can hear the gears slippin' all the way over here," said Bergie, tapping his temple.

"Well, I guess it's a familiar sound," Harry retorted. "Must keep you up most nights."

The tide of laughter turned and washed up on the shore at Bergie's feet. Harry, a nervous bundle of eccentricities fueled by prodigious amounts of carbonated caffeine, was an easy target, but once in a while he gave as good as he got. He took another determined sip of Coke. He would have won the battle if only he'd left it alone. "Did he move, Drew?"

Drew emptied the ash pan into a beaten old scuttle. A scattering of live coals poked their head through the ashes and made faces at the world. "Don't ask me. You two been sittin' there so long I was about to put price tags on you."

Joel chortled. "I doubt you'd get much for 'em, Drew."

"Sure I would. Sell 'em as scarecrows."

Everyone but Harry laughed. "Cussed fools," he said. He leveled a malicious glare at Joel. "Why don't you go back up to East Haven where you belong?"

The barb hit home. Of course, Joel had lived on Penobscot Island for more than seventy years, since he was six weeks old, but there was no disputing the fact he'd been born on East Haven. Some things are beyond debate.

"Wind's fillin' them paths up fast as them boys can shovel," Pharty observed from his seat near the window. At nearly eighty, Pharty had earned a seat closer to the stove, but he preferred to sit near the door. From there, through the huge storefront window, he had an uninterrupted view of Main Street and enjoyed describing the comings and goings to the others. He did it well.

Inwardly Harry repented of his comment, but it would remain an unspoken sorrow. He moved his checker.

A hand-painted '37 Chevy pickup pulled into the parking lot across the street and stopped in the lee of the massive stone eagle that had been erected to commemorate the island's glory days, when granite, not lobsters, was king. A heavily bundled figure squeezed out of the cab, fending off the wind-heavy door.

"Here comes Stump," Pharty announced. "Better hide the silver." He'd have said that no matter who was coming.

Drew fluffed the faded green corduroy cushion in Stump's worn wood chair near the fire, then took the stained porcelain cup from its hook on the chimney and filled it with hot, strong coffee.

"He'll be wantin' that," said Moochie. "Wind must go through him like an old fence. How old is he now, anyway?"

Drew, who kept the town records, knew that Stump would be ninety-two next week, on January 4, but that was privileged information so he kept it to himself, as he did a lot of things.

"Too old to be drivin'," said Harry. "And that truck's older'n mud."

Drew brushed off a short three-legged stool and tucked it under the chair, just the way Stump liked it. "I don't guess he's apt to do any more damage than these teenagers you see tearin' 'round here most nights."

"Don't drive fast enough to bend grass," said Joel.

Harry ignored them. "In this weather, too. And two-thirds blind."

"Oh, don't worry 'bout it," said Pharty. "He could drive around the island blindfolded anyhow. Here he is." The door latch clicked. As the door swung open, the wind gave Stump a final nudge over the threshold. "Well, look what the cat dragged in," said Pharty. "What're you doin' out on a day like this?"

"Thought I'd best come keep an eye on you youngsters. Make sure no one was sittin' in my chair," Stump replied as he took off his coat and hat and shook them over the stove.

"Hand 'em over," said Drew. "I'll hang 'em up."

Stump handed them over, settled slowly into his chair, and retrieved his coffee cup from the stovetop. "This fresh, Drew?"

"Better than that," said Pharty. "It's free."

Stump sipped loudly and sighed. "It's mostly stopped snowin' now," he said. "Just blowin' around." He took inventory of the others in the store. "Not much point openin' on a day like this," he said. "All you're gonna do is attract riffraff like this that sits around all day drinkin' your coffee and cheatin' at checkers." He took another sip of coffee, the level of which rose a drop or two as his eyebrows melted into the cup. "Looks like you been gettin' around this mornin', young Joel."

"Me?" said Joel, shifting onto the other cheek. He'd forgotten his cushion. "What do you mean?"

"You was up at Everette's place this mornin', wasn't you?"

Joel was caretaker for a number of the summer "cottages" tucked among the trees on the north coast of the island. Most of the houses, which were built in the last century by well-heeled bankers, industrialists, and tycoons from Boston as places to stow their families during the timeless, idyllic Maine summers, were now owned by doctors, lawyers, and the nouveaux riches. They were all of the same mold: huge edifices of twenty to thirty rooms, most with a boathouse, a guest house or two, and various attendant outbuildings, all dressed in perfectly weathered cedar shingles with perfectly weathered white trim and with windows perfectly framed with dark green shutters.

Over time the island had embraced the grander buildings with thick, fragrant tendrils of juniper and majestic stands of spruce and birch that nuzzled them on all sides. The secluded bowers shielded them from the cruel winds and kept time at bay. Most of the lesser buildings—abandoned for years, their uses forgotten—the earth had thoroughly invaded. Over the years, shoots of grass and snaking vines had patiently and relentlessly pried board from board, exposing crooked rows of hand-forged nails so the salt air could get at them. Against the earth's bosom the boards had moldered and rotted and mingled with the rich, dark soil. Home.

"What would I be doin' up to the Everette's place?" said Joel. It crossed his mind that this might be one of those days that Stump wasn't altogether present and accounted for.

"That's what I was wonderin'," said Stump. "Said the same thing to Alby."

Alby was Stump's grandson-in-law. "What's he got to do with anything?" Joel wanted to know.

"He was up to the house this mornin'. Said he was comin' across the Thoroughfare from East Haven and seen a light in the window up there. Figured you was workin' for a change."

Joel looked quizzically from Drew to Pharty as if to confirm that they heard what he heard. "There couldn't be no light up there," he said. "I ain't been up there since October. Neither's anybody else. 'Sides, the power's off."

Drew wasn't so sure. "Saltonstahl's place was broken into last year. Remember? Took all their booze."

"Serves 'em right for leavin' it up there all winter," Harry judged.

"You think somebody broke in?" Joel said worriedly. He was supposed to be checking the place at least once a month. That's what he was paid for. But things were so busy all winter, what with one thing and another. And there'd been a lot of snow. That made it hard to get in and out.

"I don't know," said Drew. "It happens."

Stump tapped his cup on the stovetop, indicating his desire to have it topped off. Drew complied with a smile. "All I know," said Stump, "is Alby said he seen a light when he come across the Thoroughfare this mornin' and he figured it was you up there."

The words hadn't been absorbed by the fragrance of turpentine and wood smoke before Joel had his coat on and was out the door, slamming it behind him. The old ship's clock, proudly bearing the name Millberry's Magnesia etched in frosted glass on the door of its cabinet, witlessly carved away a few more seconds of life in even slices.

"The Everette place," said Harry, taking a final pull at his empty Coke bottle, refreshing a thirty-five-year-old memory. The words dislodged a fragment from some craggy fissure in his mind. "They never did find out what happened to Cailey Hall, did they?"

"Disappeared," said Drew, settling himself into his seat beside the fire.

"Disappeared," said Harry. He snapped his fingers, but they didn't make a sound.

A stinging wind assaulted Joel's face and ears as he stepped from the nice, warm cab of his Jeep, slammed the door, and high-stepped through the first of a rank of drifts that stood between him and the Everette cottage. The snow had stopped, but the sky—low and darkening as day shut her eyes—threatened more. Once through the drift, he stopped and looked up at the house. Rows of curtain-less windows stared blankly back at him. No lights. That was a relief, though it was hard to fight the feeling he always had, that there was an entity in the house, a presence, watching him through those dark, empty rectangles. The feeling was especially pronounced at the moment.

"Alby was seein' things," he assured himself aloud. "Probably two sheets and a pillowcase to the wind. Must've been, crossin' the Thoroughfare in weather like that." Nevertheless, as long as he was here, he'd double-check the doors and first-floor windows.

It was then, lowering his eyes in appraisal of the next drift, that he noticed the footprints. "What's this?" he said.

Of varying depths in the undulating snow, the indentations had been rounded by the wind but were still sufficiently defined so that three sets were obvious: two headed toward the house, one coming away. He stared down into the nearest set. A sudden gust of wind sent a ghost of snow into his eyes, and he shivered involuntarily. A quick glance to the west told him that weather was on the way. "Somebody's been here, all right," he said. It helped to begin with the self-evident. "Not long ago," he ventured. "Two come in," he declared. "And one come out," he surmised. "Somebody's still here." That summed up the evidence.

In the two minutes it took him to decide what to do next and make his way to the house, the wind picked up and began filling in the footprints. Soon there would be no evidence that anyone had been there, himself included.

He climbed the little porch at the north end of the house and tried the door. Locked. He felt through his pockets for his key, then realized he'd left it in the Jeep. He knocked sharply and waited. There was no response. He knocked again, harder this time. "Come on, I know you're in there," he bellowed, to which there was an even more pronounced silence.

"Probably dove out the window on the other side," Joel speculated aloud. *He* certainly would have, had he been in the intruders' place. He didn't need to go inside. All he had to do was make sure there was no damage, find out how they'd gotten in, and close it up.

He pushed his way through the drifts eddied in the lee of the house, then stood on tiptoe, cupped his hands around his eyes, and pressed his face to each of the kitchen windows in turn. Everything was covered with dead flies, of course. Junie Phillips would sweep them up in spring when she came to open the house. Otherwise, the room was orderly and neat. He could see through to the windows overlooking the Thoroughfare. Thick draperies of snow obscured the mainland from view. Five minutes, he thought, ten at most before the storm hit. "Good six inches comin'," he forecast.

He plowed on. Next was the big bow window of the dining room, which he couldn't reach flat-footed. He'd need something to stand on, which wouldn't be hard to find if the carpenters had been as careless as usual when they reglazed the windows last fall. They probably had left some loose staging, or a five-gallon caulking bucket tossed up against the house somewhere. A few kicks at the snow, however, revealed something even more substantial: the sawed-off stump of the weigela he'd pruned last spring, a good two feet high. Perfect.

He reached up and grabbed the window ledge with one hand while the other found a solid hold among the remaining branches of the bush. After kicking the snow from the stump, he rested his foot on the step so conveniently provided and pulled himself up high enough to get his eyes and nose over the ledge.

Despite the reflection, it took no time to see that things weren't as they should be. The large Nantucket blue–painted dining room table, which had been covered with a sheet, as had the rest of the furniture in the house, had been uncovered. The sheet was folded on the sideboard, and the flies had been swept up into a neat pile in the corner.

A faint flicker drew his attention to something even more startling—a candle, burned to the stub, guttered in its own juices. As he watched, it died. Its soul rode a wisp of smoke to the ceiling and was gone. The table was set for two with an assortment of the imperfect odds and ends of china, silver, and crystal that were common in the summer homes. A bottle of wine stood unopened on an island of lace in the middle of the table.

Attempting to cup his hand around his left eye for a better look, Joel rested his elbow on the window ledge and redistributed his weight. As he did so, his foot slid off the slippery stub of branch, and he tumbled into the snowbank in a heap, his head missing the stump by sixteenths of an inch. Slightly dazed, he sat there for a moment, trying to sort things out in his seventy-six-year-old brain. "Yessir," he said. "Somebody's been here."

He picked himself up and whisked the snow from his collar, then plodded through the drifts to the next set of windows, those of the sitting room. Here the ground dropped off, and there were no convenient branches or even so much as a paint can to stand on. That meant he'd have to climb to the porch through the waist-high bank of snow at the foot of the broad steps. He swore. Already he was cold clear through, and he was going to be colder before it was all over. Still, someone had gotten in somehow, and it was his job to find out where, then nail it, or shut it, or lock it, or whatever he had to do to keep it from happening again. Then he'd have to make a report to Luther Kingsbury—and tell the Everettes. He wasn't looking forward to that.

"What in hell would anyone be doin' up here lightin' candles is what I want to know," he asked aloud as he plowed up the steps. Whoever it was, he'd love to get his hands on them and give them a good shake. "'Til their teeth rattled," he said to emphasize his thoughts.

The same wind that had piled snow at the bottom of the steps had swept the porch clean. At the top step Joel stamped his feet.

The leading edge of the squall was halfway across the Thoroughfare now, pushing a stinging wind before it. Not a quarter of a mile away the snow was falling so thick he couldn't even see East Haven. The nine miles back to town would seem like fifty on roads already slick and, despite perpetual plowing, choked with the residue of previous storms.

At least it was easy to see into the house from the porch. The windows were wide and high, and there were lots of them. There was nothing out of order in the sitting room, though the sight of all the chairs draped with sheets made him think of the time he'd stumbled into the morgue when he'd gone to visit his Aunt Lorraine over at the hospital in Rockport.

On the other side of the room, through the open doorway, he could see the dining room table. Other than the table, the candle, the sheet, and the flies, nothing was out of place. The windows and the porch door were all secure.

At the front of the house, separated from the sitting room by a wide wood archway, was the living room. A cursory glance indicated that nothing was amiss, but he couldn't see much because of the reflection. Stepping up to the big window that overlooked the bluff and the Thoroughfare, he again cupped his hands around his eyes and surveyed the room.

Only one thing was wrong: The sheet on the chair nearest the window bulged unnaturally high, as if it had been thrown over somebody who was sitting there. Joel laughed aloud at the notion. Half a second and he'd remember what it was they'd put there that made it look that way.

Then he saw the shoe.

Overheated by the excitement, an icicle overhead squeezed a single, frigid drop of water down his neck, and it carved along his spine like a knife.

"**H**ELLUVA SHOCK THE OLD MAN HAD," said Jerry Oakes. He absentmindedly picked up a few herring, then tossed them back in the bait box and brushed a handful of salt over them. "He come in for supper last night lookin' 'bout like this." Jerry picked up one of the dead fish by the head and shook it.

Dickey Wentworth struck a safety match under his thumbnail and relit his corncob pipe for the fourth time in five minutes. The pungent smell of overburned Holiday tobacco drifted around the shed on thick blue clouds. "Good thing he didn't have a heart attack," he said, somehow managing a thoughtless epithet every second or third word, as is peculiar to coastal dialect. "He had one about two years ago, didn't he?"

"Stroke," said Jerry. He should know. Joel Philbrook was his wife's grandfather and had lived with them going on eight years, since Sissy, their youngest, was still in the cradle. "His heart's pretty good."

"Well," said Dickey, "I don't care how good a person's heart is, seein' somethin' like that would give it a good kick."

"Somethin' like what?" Harm Gregory, the new arrival, entered stomping. Thick chunks of crusted snow abandoned their hold on his green wool pants and splattered on the floor. The counterweight on the door—an old blue glass toggle filled with sand and attached to a rope and pulley—tugged the door closed with a solid thud and rattle. Harm threw back his fur-lined hood and shook the snow from his unruly copper-colored bangs. "Ain't it some nasty out. Colder'n a whore's heart."

"Mornin', Harm," said Jerry. "You ain't haulin' today, are you?"

Harm tossed an incredulous glance at the lobster buyer as he unzipped his coat. "Not likely," he said. "You'd sooner find me in church than out in that smoke." For a moment the six eyes at their disposal stared out the dirty window at the harbor. Salome's veils of fog drifted in and out among the few lobster boats that hadn't been hauled out for the winter in a graceful, deadly dance set to a music beyond human hearing.

"That's what I figure," said Dickey. "Nature's way of sayin' it's a good day to stay inside and bend some spruce bows. I bet I lost fifty pots this year," he added, exaggerating, as lobstermen did everything but their income. "Time to start trawlin' anyway. Them bugs stop crawlin' come Christmas."

"Fourteen below up to my house," said Harm.

"Fourteen? Really?" said Jerry. "It was closer to zero down to my place."

"What time?"

"When I got up. Five or so."

"Sleepin' in, was you?" said Harm.

"Well, I didn't figure there'd be any rush goin' on down here," Jerry explained.

"It's come down a few degrees since then," said Harm.

Dickey counted nine heaping spoonfuls of Chock Full O' Nuts into the percolator. "Zero's all you have to say," he said. "Below that, you're just nit-pickin'. Don't s'pose you want coffee, Harm?"

" 'Course I do."

Dickey added a few more spoonfuls.

"What was you sayin' 'bout heart attacks?" said the new arrival as he warmed his hands over the oil-drum stove.

"We was talkin' 'bout what happened to Joel last night."

"Joel Philbrook?" asked Harm, looking at Jerry. "He have a heart attack?"

"I'm surprised you ain't heard. Figured it'd be all over town by now."

"How could it be?" Harm objected. "It's only eight o'clock. News don't spread that fast 'til the beauty parlor opens." He laughed.

"He didn't have a heart attack," Dickey said before Jerry could respond. "He found a dead body up at Everette's. Under a sheet."

Harm turned his gaze to Dickey in disbelief. "No." He looked at Jerry for corroboration. "A dead body?"

Jerry nodded. "Yup."

"Whose?"

"Johnny Bermann's."

"Johnny Bermann?" Harm propped an empty lobster crate on end, drew it closer to the fire, and sat on it. Steam rose from his black rubber hip boots as the ice melted in puddles on the floor. "At Everette's?" Jerry nodded. "You don't say?"

The Bermann estate, just outside the village on the wind-battered eastern shore, where Johnny had made his home since moving back to the island a year earlier, was about as far as you could get from Everette's, at the affluent north end of the island. His family wasn't native, but they had a history in town, even if a doubtful one. That made them more than just summer folk.

"What was he doin' up there?"

"Havin' a picnic with some woman, to hear Joel tell it," said Jerry.

"What woman?"

Jerry shrugged and explained about the footprints, the table setting, and the body.

"Any woman desperate enough to meet somebody in an unheated house in the dead of winter is a woman I wouldn't want to meet out behind the fish house," Dickey observed.

"Wasn't unheated," Jerry replied. "They had 'em a fireplace up there. One've them Franklin stoves like they got up to the Legion Hall. They had that fired up."

"Hell," said Dickey, "that won't do no good. Them things draw all the heat right up the chimney. Pretty to look at, though, if you open the doors."

"It was nothin' but ashes anyway by the time Joel got there," said Jerry.

Harm was more interested in the body than the woman, real or imagined. "Under a sheet, you say?"

"Some curious, ain't it?" said Dickey, approving the bewilderment in Harm's eyes.

"Beats all."

"That ain't all that's curious," said Jerry, with an inscrutable curl of the lip.

"What?"

"Well," said Jerry, situating himself in his chair a little more leisurely than necessary, "Joel saw the shoe—"

"You said that," said Dickey impatiently.

"Just wait a minute," said Jerry, with a cautioning tilt of the head indicating that the information could be withheld indefinitely. "What I didn't say is one of 'em was on and the other was off."

"One of what?" said Harm, maintaining his stoicism with effort. "One of the shoes?"

"And socks," Jerry added.

"He was barefoot?" said Dickey.

"Not both, just one."

"One foot was bare?"

Jerry nodded sagaciously. "The other one had both a sock and a shoe on, and it was all shriveled up."

"Shriveled up? You didn't say nothin' 'bout it bein' shriveled up," Dickey complained.

"I just did."

Harm sensed that Jerry was holding something back. "What else?"

Jerry hesitated a moment, his black eyes sparkling with morbid fascination. "His eyes was open wide . . . and he was cryin'."

"Was cryin'?" said Harm. "You mean, he'd been cryin' before he died?"

"Nope. I mean when Joel took Luther Kingsbury and Doc Pagitt up there and uncovered the body, there was tears runnin' down his face."

"Maybe he wasn't really dead," Dickey theorized.

"Oh, he was dead, all right."

Harm had a hard time swallowing that. "Dead and cryin'?"

"Dead and cryin'," said Jerry matter-of-factly.

"What else?"

"Nothin'," said Jerry. "One shoe off and one shoe on. Dead and cryin'. That's all."

"What do you think, Doctor?" said Matty as she hovered over his shoulder. He was shining a light into Crisp's eyes, which Matty couldn't understand. His eyesight was fine. "What do you see?"

"I see," said Pagitt, clicking the little penlight off and slipping it in his pocket, "precisely two eyes." He chuckled and winked at Crisp. "You're one lucky man, Professor," he said. "You've been coming back to life in bits and pieces all this time. Most people who've been through what you've been through, it's the other way around."

Crisp smiled sardonically. "Have you treated many people who've been through what I have, Warren?"

"Can't say I have," Pagitt replied. "Not and lived to tell about it." He turned to the proprietress. "You were right, Matty. When I didn't think he'd have a snowball's chance in—"

"Doctor!"

"Haiti," Pagitt amended on the fly. "Anyway, you never gave up." He looked at Crisp again. "Much as I'd like to take credit for your recovery, Professor, I've got to say it's more likely that this woman nagged the Almighty 'til He was forced to toss you back."

"Like the widow and the judge," Matty agreed.

"Who are they when they're home?" asked Pagitt.

"It's in the New Testament," Crisp explained. "A parable that Jesus told about a woman who went before a judge demanding justice and wouldn't leave until she got it."

"What'd he do?"

"He gave in," said Crisp, the corners of his eyes crinkling along lines unused to laughter.

Pagitt picked up his thick down jacket and put it on. "I'd've tossed her in jail." He pulled on his hat. "Matty, don't you go making him talk all at once. The larynx is a muscle. So is the tongue. They need time to get strong."

"Is that why he talks like he's got a mouthful of marbles?" she asked in a confidential whisper.

"That's right." Pagitt picked up his bag and opened the door. "You comfortable, Professor?"

Crisp turned his good ear toward the doctor. Fine, he meant to say. His mouth moved, but no words came out.

Matty shot Pagitt a worried glance. "Doctor?"

"It's all right. His voice will come and go like that 'til those muscles get used to working." He patted her on the shoulder reassuringly. "I'll look in again this evening. If everything's okay, I don't think you'll need to be calling me anymore, Matty. At least, not if good things happen. The way things are going, I expect he'll be trying to get on his feet before long. You see to it he holds the walker when he does. Okay? His legs have about as much strength as soggy spaghetti."

Matty quivered enthusiastically in assent.

"See you later, Professor."

Crisp turned his neck stiffly toward Pagitt. "Only socially, let's hope."

Pagitt laughed politely as Matty walked him down the stairs to the door.

"Is there anything else?"

"Pardon?"

"Is there anything wrong I should know about Winston?"

"Not that I can think of," said the doctor thoughtfully. He'd known Matty long enough to know she often took a roundabout way to the point.

"I mean," Matty continued, tapping her temple, "is he all to home, do you think? I remember back when this all . . . that night you told Luther Kingsbury you was worried that if Winston lived, his mind wouldn't be all there."

"Oh, no. I'd say there's no problem. I was worried about a lack of oxygen resulting from his paralysis. Doesn't seem to have happened. Whole thing's a miracle as far as I'm concerned, I confess." Pagitt sat on the parson's bench by the back door and began pulling on his boots. " 'Course, you should know better than anyone. He's been writing notes to you for a while now, hasn't he?"

"That's right," said Matty.

"Did he write anything to make you suspect he wasn't the brightest marble in the bag?"

"Well, no. But I just didn't know what to expect." Matty took Pagitt's plaid wool scarf from the hat tree and wrapped it around his neck. It was the first time she'd really looked at him that morning; her attention had been on Crisp. "Why, Doctor, you don't look well. Are you all right?"

Pagitt smiled a long-suffering smile. "I was up pretty late last night."

Matty prided herself on not being a gossip, so if there was any currency in being the first to have a bit of news, it meant nothing to her. However, as a concerned citizen . . . "Somebody call you out? Nothing serious, I hope."

Pagitt knew he'd made a mistake mentioning a late night. "Oh, well, it all comes with the territory, I guess. Part of the job," he said noncommittally. He opened the door, admitting a gust of wind that came in and took a large bite of the summerlike warmth from Matty's back hallway. She pulled the collar of her sweater together at her neck.

"You've done a good job, Matty," said Pagitt, wanting to get off the subject as quickly as possible. "You missed your calling."

"Oh, now," said Matty with a self-deprecating giggle. "I don't know about that."

"Just see he gets plenty of fluid and rest and, like I said, don't try to make him talk too much. Or *eat* too much. Chicken broth will be fine. Okay?"

"Of course," Matty replied. "Don't you worry."

Pagitt, emerging from the warm cocoon of Matty's home into the brittle midwinter morning, yawned.

"So, what time *did* you get to bed?" Matty ventured. There was nothing to lose.

Pagitt looked at his watch. "Haven't been yet," he said. "Good-day, Matty. Take care."

Matty was still fretting an hour later. "He looked like death warmed over," she said to Crisp. She'd made him a midmorning meal and brought it to his room on a tray.

"Did he say what was wrong?" Crisp found an indefinable pleasure in the sound of his voice as it echoed in his ears.

"Not for love or money," said Matty, revealing a little more of her frustration than she'd intended. "Just that he'd been out all night on a call."

"All night?" Crisp thought aloud. "Perhaps a delivery? Anybody expecting that you know of?" If she didn't, no one did.

"That's what I thought at first," Matty replied, compressing her right eyebrow, which, owing to the dynamics of her physiognomy, caused the other to arch. "But there's nobody, as far as I know. Hildy

Bickford is due in two months or so, and Samantha Dyer had hers last week—six weeks early if you count back from the wedding." There was no judgment in the observation; it was simply a point of interest. "I saw Hildy down to Irma Louise's yesterday noon. She looked healthy enough—women in that family have babies without stoppin' to lie down—so I doubt anything's gone wrong with her."

How anyone would subject an unborn child to the fumes inhabiting Irma Louise's House of Beauty and hope to deliver a healthy infant was beyond Crisp's comprehension. He watched as Matty sliced a fresh peach into his steaming oatmeal. He wondered where she got fresh peaches in the dead of winter. "Well, I'm sure you'll find out what's going on when you go to the post office."

Secondhand news, thought Matty unintentionally. "Now, you tuck into this little bit and finish it up." She fixed a napkin under his chin.

"Honestly, Matty," Crisp protested, "I just finished breakfast two hours ago."

"That was two hours ago." She held up her hand to bar further argument. "Doctor's orders. He said you were to have plenty of fluids."

"Fluids, Matty," said Crisp, holding up his teacup. "*This* is a fluid."

"Oh, for pity sakes, Winston, you can't have tea without a little something to go with it. Anyone knows that. Goes without saying. Now, you stop fussing. Do you need anything else before I go out?"

"I'm fine," Crisp yielded. "You run along."

Matty turned to leave.

"Matty?"

"Yes?" she called from halfway down the stairs.

"If there's anything from a publisher . . ."

That was the first thing he'd written when he came out of the coma he'd slipped into that awful night. Made sense it would be at the top of the list now that he had his tongue back. "Not yet. Don't worry, you'll be the second to know." She added under her breath as she continued down the stairs, "And if they're just more rejection letters, I'll burn 'em with the rest, which is better than they deserve."

Crisp waited until he heard the front door close. A moment later he heard Matty out on the porch, exchanging greetings with her new neighbor, Gerty Sanborn, who had moved into the garage apartment across the dooryard.

Crisp set the tray on his bedside table, threw aside the covers, and looked at his legs, which stuck like a scarecrow's from his pajamas. "Well, old fellas," he said, "may I have this dance?"

Slowly and carefully, ignoring the loud, persistent complaints of his joints, he maneuvered his legs over the side of the bed and bent his knees until his stockinged feet rested on the floor. He closed his eyes a moment, absorbing the delicious sensitivity—however painful—of his extremities, so long moribund.

Resting one hand on the bedside table and the other on the bed, he pushed and dragged himself to a more or less upright position. Cautiously, one handhold at a time, he let go, willing his reluctant muscles to unfold as he stretched himself to his full height for the first time in a very long time. He was eighty-one years old. In the last five months he had been locked in a freezer to die, lost two toes and one finger to frostbite, been poisoned, wrestled with madness, fallen in love with a dead woman named Amanda Murphy, and, as he lay paralyzed in bed, been attacked by a crazed, syringe-wielding killer.

But here he was, against all the odds—and his own expectations—alive.

Planting his feet solidly on the floor, he stretched until his very sinews seemed to tremble and his bones creaked in their sockets. He could still reach the ceiling; though the effort exacted a price, it was worth the pain. He had resolved to accomplish two things this morning even if it killed him, two things he'd been planning a long time. First, come hell or high water, he was going to reach the window and look outdoors. He had developed an obsessive need to see something new. His eyes were fatigued by the day-after-day sameness of his bedroom; he knew the name of every book in the bookcase and could recite their authors alphabetically. He'd counted the cracks in the ceiling plaster, the tufts of cotton on his bedspread, the holes in the lace trim on the lampshade, and the flowers on the curtains and wallpaper. It was time to fill his senses with the greater world.

Second, he would smoke his favorite pipe; it sat with the others in a wood rack on the little table in the corner where an ebony box held his favorite tobacco. Next to the box was a pack of matches.

Odd how much his toes hurt, even though they weren't there. Surprising how two such tiny, unheralded appendages had played a seemingly critical role in balancing him all these years. He was unsteady in their absence. It brought to mind the time when he was seven and had lost both his upper front teeth. That night, unthinking, he'd tried to bite into an apple, and absolutely nothing happened. Why one thing should make him think of the other, he had no idea. But it did.

Where do one's parts go when they predecease the body? Does there exist on the outskirts of heaven some kind of holding room for the odd bits and pieces—arms, legs, fingers, toes, artists' ears, and lovers' noses—that make a premature appearance in the hereafter, to be rejoined (seamlessly, one supposes) at the resurrection?

He had time for such thoughts: The nine-foot trip to the window took nearly three minutes. It incorporated various modes of transportation: a cane to help him to the walker, and the walker to get him to the window. Of course, with muscles the consistency of raw squid, there was no way he could make it back to the bed under his own steam, which had been his intention initially. There'd be nine kinds of hell to pay when Matty came back and found him sitting next to the window—which he had managed to open an inch or two, just enough to feel the breeze and smell the cold—and smoking, to boot. But it was a price he was willing to pay. If she killed him, she killed him.

Having filled his pipe, he lit it and drew pungent smoke deep into his lungs, which responded with blissful convulsions.

Hacking and coughing, he opened the window a little wider to spit when something caught his eye. A truck had pulled to a stop on the other side of the common, and four men—Joel Philbrook, Charlie Williams, Luther Kingsbury, and Nate Gammidge, the county coroner from Rockland—were moving something—a body, by all appearances—from the truck into Charlie's funeral parlor. The tableau reeked of déjà vu, roughly prodding Crisp's shiver mechanism to life.

"Amanda?" he whispered hoarsely.

CHAPTER

3

➤

"YOU REMEMBER ALL THAT BUSINESS about Old Man Bermann, don't you?" The speaker was Sadie Mitchell. It was Tuesday morning and, as usual, Ginger Foster and Emily Minot had gotten together at Sadie's house to knit bait bags. Thursdays—variety being the spice of life—they did pot heads for lobster traps.

"'Course I do," said Emily, rhythmically weaving the big wooden shuttle through the web of nylon twine. "Least I know about it. They've got this book up at the historical society tells about him. We're none of us old enough to remember it firsthand, I hope."

"No, well, you know what I mean. Wasn't that some awful, runnin' him off the island like that?"

"I don't know Old Man Bermann," said Ginger, closely inspecting her knots.

Sadie looked at her friend incredulously. "I keep forgettin' you're from up Ragged Island."

Tiny Ragged Island was stapled to Penobscot by a hundred-year-old iron and granite bridge. As a result, natives on both sides no longer considered it a proper island but more of a peninsula. Nevertheless, despite the fact it was only a fifteen-minute ride from downtown, it maintained a distinctly separate identity, primitive and remote.

"Old Man Bermann . . . What was his name, Em? Somethin' foreign. Siegfried or—"

"It was Oscar," said Emily.

"Oscar? Was it?" Sadie replied thoughtfully.

"Oscar's not foreign, Sadie," said Ginger. "One of my nephew's cats is named Oscar."

"Why would any sane person name a cat Oscar?" Sadie wanted to know.

Ginger reminded them that the boy's mother was from away.

"Oh, that's right, too," said Emily. Enough said. "Anyway, he was Johann's father."

"They called him Johnny," Sadie clarified, her voice booming from the close walls and the low ceiling of her kitchen. "The son."

Emily knit a little faster. Many things may be beyond her reach—she found talk of politics and international affairs particularly tiresome—but when it came to island history she was something of an authority, especially when it came to the Bermanns. "My Grampa Roberts worked up there," she reminded them. "Oscar's wife was named Ingrid. Swedish, I think she was. Died while they was here, tryin' to give birth. Baby died, too. They're buried up at Robert's cemetery, practically in their dooryard. Not long after, Oscar packed up Johnny and left. 'Course Johnny was only a baby when that happened."

"Johnny—that's this one?" said Ginger, with a nod in the general direction of Everette's and the north.

Emily nodded.

"Poor man," said Ginger. The others bowed their heads over their work for a moment in silence. The net stand creaked as they pulled their knots tight, making an irregular counterpoint to the ticking of the clock on the wall and the water that cackled in the kettle on top of the cast-iron stove.

"He come back to the island for a while in the thirties. I remember that," said Emily.

Sadie didn't remember that. "Who brought them back, the Old Man?"

"No, no. Oscar was dead by that time, I imagine. Johnny come alone. He was some good lookin', Mother says. 'Course I was too young to notice at the time. But he ain't too hard on the eyes now."

"Wasn't," Sadie said.

"Wasn't," Emily agreed with a sigh. "He took the boards off the windows of the old place and moved in."

"When was that?"

"What's the old place? Everette's cottage?" Ginger interrupted.

"No, no. The Bermann estate," Emily said in response to the second question. "That would've been 1935. The summer I had my first period is how I remember," she replied to the first.

Sadie had been upending the ash cans of her memory and coming up empty. "He just come for the summer that time?"

"I guess," Emily concurred. "Like I said, I didn't much notice at the time."

Ginger was confused. She put down her knitting and wrestled with a contentious bra strap. "Then what was he doing up at Everette's?"

"That's certainly a question, my dear," said Sadie. She put down her netting, pushed back her chair, and went to the stove. "And I don't think we've heard the half of it. Who wants more tea?"

"Yes, please," said Emily.

"I don't think I'll have any more," Ginger demurred. "Ever since I had children, all I need to do is look at liquid and I have to go."

"Oh, don't get me started," said Sadie. But it was too late; she was started.

For the next fifteen minutes the conversation followed a some-what erratic course, from bladders to children, husbands, medical procedures, the breakup of the Beatles, the fact that nobody exchanged baskets of candy on May Day anymore, and reminiscences of old boyfriends.

"Speaking of boyfriends," said Emily, "my Aunt Jane was sweet on Johnny." This was the point she'd been trying to make. It gave her a personal connection to the tragedy and some small share in the perverse glory reflected by such a connection.

"Is that so?" said Sadie. She tied off a net and applied her Zippo lighter to the knot, watching carefully as it turned from brown to black, then burst briefly into flame, which melted the ends firmly together. She blew it out. "Janie's only four or five years older than you, isn't she?"

"Six."

"Six? That would put her at about seventeen at the time. Well, I didn't know that. 'Course I was only nine, so I don't sp'ose I'd've noticed in the first place."

"Oh, well, they wasn't an item exactly," said Emily. She'd never said any such thing. "But they might've been if not for Lou Ann O'Connor."

"Now, that name's familiar," said Sadie. "Where do I know it from?"

"She summered here a few years, right up 'til '41 or '42," said Emily.

"Oh, that's right. Now, wasn't she connected with the Everettes somehow? Stayed up there, didn't she?"

Emily's fingers stopped what they were doing. "Did she?" She knocked around silently in her archives for thirty seconds or so while the clock, the kettle, and the shuttles kept time. "I believe you're right. Now isn't that a coincidence? In fact, that's where she stayed, up at their place. She was a friend of one of the Everette girls—that's Kitty Emerson." She leaned in Ginger's direction. "Kitty and her husband, Dr. Emerson, bought Captain Hill's place out on James Island. 'Course, he passed away not long after, the doctor did."

"Kitty Emerson was an Everette?"

"That's right. One of six children, and their names all began with 'J.' I don't know how their parents ever kept 'em straight. Catholic, don't you know."

"Kitty don't begin with 'J,'" Ginger protested.

"Kitty's a nickname," Sadie explained. "I forget what her real name is, but I know it begins with a 'J.' Just like all of 'em. That was about the time Cailey Hall went missin'." Sadie stopped netting and massaged her fingers.

Ginger exhibited a renewed interest in the conversation. "Missing? Who went missing?"

Emily didn't drop a knot. "That's right. I'd almost forgotten. Cailey was cook up there, wasn't she?"

"Kitchen help," Sadie corrected. "They had their own chef come up from Mass'chusetts."

"What do you mean she went missing?" insisted Ginger, who had stopped netting altogether. "Missing where?"

"If they knew where, she wouldn't've been missin', Gin'," said Emily.

"You know what I mean," said Ginger, who, with an aggressive up and down thrust, skewered a row of diamonds in the mesh she'd been working on. "How did she go missing?"

"Nobody knows," said Sadie. "They turned the island inside out lookin' for her. We was all involved in the search, wasn't we, Em?"

Emily confirmed that statement.

"Didn't find nothin'. Some kept lookin', off and on, all summer long. 'Course they was lookin' for a body by that time."

"Well," said Ginger a little breathlessly, "I never heard that before."

"Long time ago," said Sadie.

Emily nodded. "Probably fell overboard and got caught in the undertow. She'd've been halfway to Nova Scotia 'fore you know it. Wouldn't be the first someone from the island took that route to Canada. Not by a long haul."

Sadie agreed.

"Anyway, as I was sayin'," Emily continued, "young Johnny fell for Lou Ann O'Connor like the walls of Jericho. I must admit— don't tell Janie I said this or I'll deny it—but compared to Janie, who wasn't what you'd call painful to look at, Lou Ann was . . . well . . ." She thought better of finishing her thought. "Less said soonest mended. I'll say this, though. She was about the prettiest girl *I* ever saw. Not that I'm any judge."

The boat had gotten too far from the wharf for Ginger's liking. "Back up a minute. You said the Old Man—Oscar—was run off the island. What for? What'd he do?"

Sadie unwrapped a new skein of twine and tied one end to the spindle on her side of the net stand. "That was durin' the war. The First World War."

Emily nodded. "I always did feel sorry for that man, even though I never knew him. Mother spoke of him often. Like I said, Grampa Roberts—he was mamma's father, she said aside to Ginger—he worked up on the estate, so she used to spend a lot of time up there. Said he was the nicest old man. Generous, too. Kept thirty or forty men employed up on the estate after the quarries closed, buildin' things that didn't need to be built, 'til he had his own little town up there 'fore long."

"Then why did he get run off the island?" Ginger reiterated.

"He'd moved here to the island in about 1915, straight from Germany," Emily explained. "Had a wicked thick accent."

"So? There were a lot of immigrants about that time, weren't there?"

"Swedes and Italians, yes," said Emily. "Germans, no."

Ginger stared in disbelief. "You're saying they run him off the island just because he was German?"

"You have to remember, it was during the war," Sadie reminded her.

"There was an awful lot of propaganda in them days," said Emily. "You remember how they put all them Japanese in prison

camps during the Second World War, even though they was American citizens."

"Fear," said Sadie.

"That's right. Same thing with poor Mr. Bermann. That accent just didn't go down well with some folks at the time. Started with name callin', 'Bermann the German,' —things like that. Then one thing led to another, the way they do, don't you know. He held out almost two years, but when they started readin' off the names of the dead up at the flagpole on Memorial Day—'bout 1917 that would've been—well, things started to get out've hand after that. Even the women joined in, so my mother says, like the whole war was Mr. Bermann's fault. Called him a spy, they did. Folks started talkin' 'bout signal lights flashin' in the middle of the night and secret tunnels bein' dug from the house to the shore. Next thing you know, there was a couple of mysterious fires up at the estate.

"He asked the gov'ment to send some troops out to guard his property. His family, too, I should imagine. But that was right toward the end of the war, and they couldn't spare the manpower.

"Grampa Roberts was the last employee who stayed up there. Mr. Bermann give him the keys the day he left and told him to keep it ready 'til after the war. Then he went off to New York."

"And he never come back?" said Ginger. She was a good ten years younger than the other women, and that much further separated from the events described.

"Just like Charlie on the MTA," Sadie replied.

Emily drained the last of her tea in spite of Ginger's bladder. " 'Bout 1923 or '24 Oscar Bermann wrote Grampa Roberts and told him to board the place up. He did, and that was that."

"All them pretty little outbuildings up there just weathered and started to fall to pieces," said Sadie, sighing sadly. "They had little weather vanes on each of 'em indicatin' what they were. There was a horse on the stable, a pig on the sty, a rooster on the henhouse. They got some of 'em up at the historical society."

"And the gardens," said Emily. "Those beautiful gardens.

Mother has this old hand-tinted stereoscope of 'em. Not like anything this island's ever seen."

"All gone?"

"Nothin' but weeds."

"I've never been up there," said Ginger, having taken a minute to absorb all she'd heard. "So, Oscar never came back, nor did anybody else 'til Johnny in the thirties?"

"That's right," said Emily.

"I thought things were confusing up to Ragged Island. My head's spinning," Ginger replied thoughtfully. "I think I will have some tea, Sadie." She turned to Emily. "So, whatever happened to Lou Ann O'Connor? I take it that nothing ever come of her and Johnny."

"Don't seem so," said Sadie. "She kept comin' long after he did. I wasn't but thirteen or fourteen last time I seen her. Like Em said, that was '41 or '42. She could've fallen into a hole since then for all I know."

Once again a thought-heavy lull wrapped itself around the pendulum of the old clock and swung slowly back and forth.

"He was a history teacher, wasn't he?" Sadie asked. It was the kind of comment intended to lead to a neat tying off of the topic.

Emily rocked in her chair and nodded. "Some college down in New Hampshire, I seem to recall."

"What do you 'spose brought him back to the island after all that time?" said Sadie. Weave and pull. Weave and pull. "Johnny, I mean."

"I heard he was workin' on a book 'bout old Oscar," said Emily. Weave and pull. Weave and pull.

"Sad," Ginger thought aloud. "And to die crying. I can't think of nothing sadder than that." Weave and pull. "All alone in a big, strange house." Weave and pull.

"I tell you what I'd like to do," said Nate Gammidge as they placed the body of Johnny Bermann on the frigid granite slab. Nate hadn't been able to get to sleep last night after Doctor Pagitt's call.

THE DEAD OF WINTER ➤ 49

He caught the first boat to the island and was taken to Everette's, where they'd left everything the way they found it, in accordance with his wishes. The few possibilities he'd managed to formulate during his disturbed night had fallen apart in the face of the evidence. "I'd give my back teeth to get Crisp over here."

"Doc won't let you?" Charlie Williams removed some rubber gloves from a glass-fronted drawer and stuffed his hands into them.

Gammidge shook his head. "He can't even talk anyway. And Matty'd just as soon shoot me as let me bother him with something like this. Still, I bet he could make more sense of this mess than we ever could. Me anyway," he amended.

Luther Kingsbury could understand. He'd taken the job of constable as an alternative to lobstering, which made him seasick, and carpentry, which he hated. For the first three years it had been pretty much a piece of cake, his duties confined mostly to enforcing the curfew, patrolling Main Street twice a night, keeping the drunks out of harm's way, and hauling the hippies out of Boon Quarry when they couldn't resist the urge to go skinny-dipping. Then two murders turned up last year, almost three. And now this. What was the world coming to? "Sure is a strange way to die. Can you make anything of it, Charlie?"

At Gammidge's request, Charlie and Pagitt—who had gone to attend to some other patients—had conducted a minute examination on site at Everette's. Charlie had folded back the gray wool blanket and looked at the body. He shook his head. "I don't know if even Crisp could make much of this, I don't care how long he was in the CIA."

"NSA," Gammidge corrected. "The National Security Agency."

Charlie grunted. "Whatever." He reviewed the evidence out loud. "Post-mortem lividity in the feet. That's to be expected. *Rigor mortise* isn't complete, 'course that don't tell us much in this cold. Half the people in town might be dead, and not know it 'til spring. No visible wounds. No cuts. No breaks in the skin. No sign of any kind of struggle. Just these bruises on top of his knees."

"And tears in his eyes," Gammidge said, as if the undertaker needed reminding.

"And the tears," Charlie echoed. "I've never seen anything like it. Far's I can tell, there's no reason this fella shouldn't get up and go to the dance down at the Pier this weekend. 'Cept he's dead." Charlie straightened up. "Glad I don't have your job is all I can say."

"Why couldn't it just be a heart attack?" said Kingsbury hopefully. "Plain and simple."

Charlie said what Gammidge was too polite to. "Then he took off one shoe and one sock, draped a sheet over himself, and died?"

Luther had forgotten that. Maybe there was something to be said for carpentry. "Why do you think his foot's all shriveled like that? Looks like my wife after she gets out've the tub."

"The other one's the same way," said Charlie.

"The other foot?" said Gammidge incredulously. "The one in the shoe?"

Charlie nodded. "Shoe's as dry as a bone, though. Besides, there wasn't any water up there. It's shut off for the winter. 'Member that toilet?"

He remembered. It couldn't be flushed, and the smell had been overwhelming. "He must've been some sick," said Kingsbury. "Both ends."

Charlie's attention was suddenly drawn to the corpse. "What's this?"

"What?" said Gammidge, leaning over Charlie's shoulder.

"I hadn't noticed this. His wrists are slimy." Charlie ran a finger over the slippery residue until his rubber glove unexpectedly adhered to something on the skin. "And sticky."

"Sticky?" said Luther, curiosity quickly overcoming his revulsion. "Where?"

"All around the top of his wrist," Charlie replied. He checked the other arm. "Here, too. Same thing." Bewilderment pushed his forehead into a series of wrinkled arches. "Now, what do you make of that?"

"Doesn't anybody die normally out here?" said Gammidge. He looked helplessly from the dead man to Charlie, then to Luther, whose returning look was, if anything, even more helpless than his own. Gammidge sighed and pulled himself up to a sitting position on the counter.

Charlie was preoccupied. He sniffed his gloved fingers. "Ivory."

"Ivory?"

"Soap," said Charlie. He stuck his finger under Gammidge's nose. "Smell."

Gammidge complied reluctantly, his expression instantly expressive. "No mistaking it," he said.

Kingsbury took a turn. "Ivory, all right. It's the only thing Maggie uses," he said. "You ever seen a woman who cleans soap?" he added.

"Cleans soap?" Charlie and Gammidge replied in unison.

Kingsbury nodded adamantly. "When it blows."

Charlie and Gammidge traded questioning glances. Kingsbury deduced that his comments begged explanation. "All this talk about soap just reminded me of it, is all," he said. "We live way up on the hill, you know. Nothin' between us and the weather. Maggie don't like weather. She goes kinda crazy around the house. When it blows, she cleans. And I mean cleans. I come into the bathroom once during a good sou'wester and she was cleanin' the soap."

The questioning glances continued.

"When it rains she bakes like some kinda demon. Puts Betty Crocker right in the shade. I like comin' home durin' a good rainstorm." Kingsbury squinted narrowly at the wrists of the corpse. "Soap, you say?"

Gammidge shook his head as if to break a trance. He wanted to laugh but wasn't sure he should—he could never tell when island folks were pulling his leg—so he just sort of choked instead. "What I want to know is how did he die?"

"Heck if I know," said Charlie. "Like I said, he shouldn't be dead. If it wasn't for the sheet draped over him, and his wilted feet, I'd say he just had a heart attack and died."

"So he's got wilted feet," Luther protested. "Can't somebody with wilted feet have a heart attack?"

"Not 'til you tell me why he's *got* wilted feet," said Gammidge.

"And the tears," said Charlie, more to himself than the others. "I've never seen anything like that." He raised his weary eyes to Gammidge. "Somebody must've killed this man."

"Seems that way," said Gammidge. Charlie nodded reluctantly. "Or if they didn't, they had some mighty strange ideas about what to do with a dead body."

They stared at the earthly remains of Johnny Bermann, but the remains told them nothing. "The way I figure it," said Gammidge at last, "is he was meeting somebody up there. A woman, what with the wine and all. And I'd say they arranged this meeting and he had one thing in mind and she had somethin' else. You find that woman," he concluded, "you found the one who done it."

"Maybe we should get Alfred Hanson out here," Kingsbury suggested, eager to abdicate the investigation to the attorney general's chief medical examiner.

"He isn't there now," said Gammidge. "He rode the McKenniston case right up to Washington."

"Washington?" said Charlie. "What's he doin' there?"

Gammidge didn't know. "Somethin' at the Justice Department, seems I recall."

"Don't that beat all," said Kingsbury, "when it was the Professor done all the work."

"Well," said Gammidge with resignation, "it was Hanson who let him. He ought to get credit for that. Besides, that was a different kind of case than this is. The only reason the attorney general's office got involved in that case was because of Senator McKenniston. Nope," he concluded, "this is local business. Looks like we're going to have to figure it out on our own."

Gammidge ended with a prayer. "I wish Winston was here."

CHAPTER

4

"DOCTOR PAGITT!" said Matty in alarm as winter blew the door open. Once he was safe inside, she tossed herself against the door and slammed it shut. "You look like Hades after a fire sale. Come in and sit down. What have you done to yourself?"

"What a day," Pagitt replied wearily. He removed his scarf and draped it over the hat rack. "How's our star boarder?"

"Physician, heal thyself," said Matty.

Pagitt laughed weakly. "I'm okay. Tired is all."

"I've seen livelier faces starin' up from a bait box," Matty declared. "You haven't slept all day, have you?"

There was no point in denying it. "Part of the job sometimes," he said, holding up his hand as she inhaled to protest. "I took your advice this morning, though. Soon's I got home I had Jennine make me some beef bouillon, then I stretched out on the love seat for a nap.

"You know how they say if you want it to rain, all you need to do is wash the car? Well, if you're a doctor and you want to drum up a little business, all you've got to do is lie down for a minute and someone will call with an emergency."

Matty tried to appear uninterested as she helped him take off his boots. "Someone had an emergency, did they? Wasn't Hildy Bickford, was it? She's not due for a while yet."

"No, it wasn't Hildy Bickford," Pagitt replied. "It was a woman who's staying out at the Emerson's place for the holidays. Mrs. Emerson's not there."

This was news to Matty, who prided herself on knowing everyone's comings and goings. "She's not?"

Pagitt padded after Matty in his boot socks as she went to the kitchen and poured steaming water from a kettle on the stove into a cup. "Nope. She left four or five days before Christmas. Gone to spend the holidays with relatives, I gather—down in Washington, or thereabouts. Meantime, she's letting these people use the place. They're old friends, I take it."

"What's their name?"

"Quindenan." Pagitt selected a tea bag from among the selection she offered.

"What?"

"Quindenan. He's in the government somehow. Not an ambassador but something like that. No sugar, thanks. I like the name. Quindenan. If I ever get around to writing my book, I'm going to name my victim Quindenan."

"Oh, mercy. You're not writing books, too, are you?"

"Who else is?"

Matty remembered her oft-spoken pledge never to tell a soul about Crisp's poetry. "Oh, just seems like everybody is, that's all. Must be somethin' in the air."

"Well, I don't guess I'll ever actually get around to it. I always used to think there was a book in me screaming to get out." He sighed.

Matty looked at him over the rim of her cup and smiled warmly.

"Not screamin' so loud anymore I guess," she said.

Pagitt smiled.

"Well, that's a lucky thing for your Mr. Quindenan, I'd say," Matty observed with a chuckle.

"How so?"

"He doesn't have to end up a victim."

They laughed the comfortable laughter of old friends. They'd known each other as long as they could remember. Truth be told, there was a time when Pagitt had been pretty sweet on Matty. Of course, in a town as small as Penobscot, everyone's likely to have been sweet on everyone else at one time or other. "Anyway. There's Mrs. Quindenan—her name's Anne—the woman I was called up to see, her husband—he's on the mainland on business—"

"So soon after Christmas?" Matty interrupted, disapprovingly.

"His name is Paul, I think," Pagitt replied, thinking that no one seemed to notice that he worked through the holidays, though they'd surely notice if he didn't. "And there's the daughter. Pretty young woman. Bluest eyes you've ever seen." He massaged his chin. "I don't recall her name right off."

Matty leaned close to him across the table and lowered her voice. "What was Mrs. Quindenan's problem?"

Pagitt tipped his head and shrugged one shoulder. "Nerves, I guess. She was wound up like a cheap alarm clock. Couldn't get anything out of her."

"She called you?"

"No, it was Cal who called, but the daughter was behind it, I gather. She was worried."

"Cal? Is she still keepin' house for Mrs. Emerson?"

Pagitt nodded. "Yes. Cooks, too."

"She still works for you, doesn't she? Cleanin' up at the medical center?"

"Oh, yes. Just two days a week now. Cheryl Williams has taken over most of the job since Cal started full time out there."

"Cal's a good cook," Matty reflected. High praise indeed from the island's best, Pagitt thought. " 'Course, you have to keep her from the cookin' sherry."

"Unfortunately," Pagitt agreed. Cal was a lone drinker, and although he'd never actually seen her drunk, he'd seen the morning-after effects many times. Hers was not a unique problem on the island.

"Did Cal or the daughter have any idea what the mother was upset about?" Matty wanted to know.

Pagitt removed his tea bag and wrapped the string around the spoon and pulled it tight, squeezing a few concentrated amber drops into his cup. "Not really. The daughter took me aside before I left and told me her mother had been acting strange."

"Strange?"

"Well, for the last few days she seemed happy and excited, is what she said. Like a kid before Christmas. Had been for a few days."

"She wasn't happy by nature, then?" said Matty, concerned.

Pagitt shrugged. "Then all of a sudden she changed."

Matty leaned closer in confidence. "You don't suppose it was . . . you know . . . ," she said, trying to drag the term from him with her eyebrows. "Women's problems."

"Menopause?" said Pagitt, trying not to seem amused. "Oh, no. I shouldn't think so. It came on too abruptly, and no one expected it. Anyway, whatever brought it on, the woman isn't talking, that's for sure. Says she doesn't know what all the fuss is about, and that she's fine."

"But she's not?"

Pagitt lowered his head and looked at her knowingly through his eyebrows. "It doesn't take much of a doctor to see that. Her vital signs are pretty good, but her face is the color of pollack and her eyes are bloodshot. I'd say she hasn't been sleeping well, if at all, and she's as nervous as a bug in a birdcage.

"The daughter said she went out yesterday, sometime after the first storm pushed through—"

"Late morning," said Matty, giving the event a chronological context.

"Thereabouts, I imagine," Pagitt agreed. "Anyway, she was all right. Excited, like I said, but all right. But when she came back, the daughter says, she was a different woman. Went and locked herself in her room and didn't come out 'til ten or so last night, pasty looking with sweat on her forehead, the daughter said. She thought she must've come down with the flu. She was going to call me, but her mother wouldn't let her. Margaret, that's her name."

"Whose? The daughter's?"

Pagitt nodded. "You know," he said a little dreamily, "she's one of those women that's like a painting."

Matty begged his pardon with her eyes.

"You know, almost too pretty to be real."

"How old a woman are we talkin' about, Doctor?" said Matty, underlining the subject in remonstrance. She was a little alarmed.

"Oh, I don't know. Twenty? Twenty-five? Frankly, I have a hard time guessing the age of women. Could be anything. However, since the mother's probably in her fifties . . ." It suddenly struck Pagitt how Matty was looking at him. "Oh, Matty, don't be foolish."

"Foolish about what?" said Matty. "I don't know what you're talkin' about."

"She's just a child, for pity sakes," Pagitt objected.

"Grandchild, I'd say," Matty observed aloofly.

"Matty, I'm an old man, but I'm not dead, you know. And I still appreciate a well-turned ankle as much as the next fella, but—"

"You bein' a doctor," said Matty, "I s'pose you see lots of turned ankles."

"Now, Matty—"

" 'Til this morning?"

"What?"

"You said the mother wouldn't let this picture girl of yours call you 'til this morning."

Pagitt nodded. "Apparently when her mother wouldn't get out

of bed, the daughter decided enough was enough and had Cal make the call."

"Where was Cal when all this started? Don't seem like she'd've put up with that kind've behavior for long. Seems like she'd've called you whether the woman wanted it or not. You know how stubborn she is."

"She wasn't there," said Pagitt. "Said she was up at Ragged Island between storms, making sure the summer houses she takes care of were shut up tight. Stayed up there right through it."

"She always was a hard worker," said Matty. More high praise. "Had to be, of course, after her father died. Too bad about the drink."

"Anyway," said Pagitt, draining the dregs of his cup, "I gave her some sedatives, which she didn't seem to mind taking. I guess all that, coming on the heels of what happened yesterday. I'm sure you've heard."

"Oh, yes. Down at the post office. Some awful," said Matty sincerely. "Awful. They say it was a heart attack." She attached a look that had question marks in it.

"Seems so," Pagitt replied. Gammidge had asked him to tell people that Johnny Bermann had died of a heart attack, so that's what he told them. However, because Joel Philbrook had found the body and been there when it was uncovered, he didn't give his version of the story much chance. Once it hit the hardware store and Irma Louise's House of Beauty . . ."

"Awful lot of strange rumors flying around," said Matty. The statement was also a question.

"Bound to be," said Pagitt, slapping his knees as if eager to conclude the conversation. He stood up.

Matty regarded him closely. "What was Johnny Bermann doin' up there, do you s'pose?"

"Someone else will have to figure that out. And if you ask me," he said, leaning close to Matty as she stood up to meet him halfway, "they've got their work cut out. Now, I'd best get on with what I came here for, before I forget. Has the old reprobate kept the neighborhood up with his yammering?" He started up the stairs and Matty chugged along behind, wiping her hands on her apron.

"He did worse that than, Doctor. When I come home from the mail, he was sittin' by the window—which was open, mind you—and he'd been smokin' his pipe. You give him a good talkin' to, will you?"

Pagitt smiled. As amazed as he'd been by Crisp's physical improvement, he'd been less optimistic about his emotional recovery. He had doubted whether the old man had the will to rejoin the living. That he was up and about, and smoking that disgusting pipe, was good news. "Did you talk to him?"

"You best believe I did," Matty affirmed. "I let him have it with both lips."

"Then I don't think I have much to add."

"But you're the doctor," said Matty. Pagitt hesitated on the landing and Matty bustled around him so she'd be first at Crisp's door, which she rapped with her knuckle. "Winston?" she said softly. "You awake?"

"I am," came the voice from within. "And my ears have been burning."

Outside the door Matty beckoned Pagitt toward her with her finger. "Let's don't talk about Johnny Bermann around Winston," she whispered. "After all he's been through, I don't want him to get upset."

Pagitt understood.

"If you're going to talk about me, at least do it so I can hear," said Crisp, whose one good ear strained to do the work of two.

Matty opened the door and ushered Pagitt into the room. "Doc Pagitt's come to tell you to behave yourself."

The smile with which Crisp met the news of his visitor vanished from his face when he saw Pagitt. "Good heavens, Warren," he said with a start. "What's happened to you?"

"Bad as all that, is it?" Pagitt replied, smiling in a vain attempt to turn aside the concern. "Used to be I could stay up for a few days running and nobody noticed. Must be getting old."

"I told him he won't have to worry about gettin' much older at this rate," Matty said. "I'm going down to put some more water on. You want more tea, Doctor?"

"No. No thanks, Matty. I'm fine."

"Winston, you're going to have some Postum. It'll help you sleep," she prescribed. Crisp knew better than to argue.

After Matty left, Pagitt sat on the edge of the bed, taking Crisp's wrist automatically. "What's this I hear about you hanging yourself out windows and smoking?"

"Tell me what's going on, Warren," said Crisp worriedly.

"Shhh," said Pagitt as he continued counting the pulse.

"My pulse is fine, and you know it," said Winston, retrieving his wrist from Pagitt's grasp. "What's going on? Whose body did you bring to the funeral parlor this morning?"

Pagitt looked at the window and realized what Crisp would have seen if he had been up and about. He sighed. "Matty told me not to say anything. She doesn't want you upset."

"Very well," Crisp reasoned calmly. "Someone has died, under suspicious circumstances—"

"Who said anything about suspicious circumstances?"

Crisp trained his penetrating gray eyes on Pagitt. "I hardly think Nate Gammidge would be involved if whoever it is had died in the natural flow of things. Now, what do you think upsets me more, knowing who it is or not knowing who it is?"

Pagitt relented. "But you never heard it from me," he prefaced. Carefully and methodically he laid out the particulars of his last twenty-four hours. Halfway through the description, Crisp put on his old wire-rimmed glasses. For the first time in a long time, Pagitt detected interest in the slate gray eyes. Could be just what the doctor ordered, he thought. A little mystery to occupy that once-sharp mind. Not that he wouldn't welcome a fresh perspective. Maybe he was just too exhausted to see the obvious. But as he related the details, he was

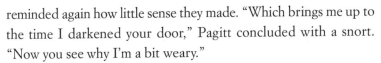

reminded again how little sense they made. "Which brings me up to the time I darkened your door," Pagitt concluded with a snort. "Now you see why I'm a bit weary."

Crisp's keen eyes stared holes in him for a moment over the tops of his glasses. Then, as if someone flipped a switch, a dreamy film seemed to close over them and he slipped miles away.

"I shouldn't have kept you up with all this," said Pagitt rising, a little disappointed. "You're tired."

"Very tired," Crisp echoed vaguely.

Pagitt was unsure what to make of the phenomena of Crisp's eyes, the abrupt change from penetrating interest to careless abstraction. Perhaps a trick of the light. At any rate, no insight would be forthcoming.

"Good night," Pagitt said, unable to dispel the notion that Crisp had somehow aged before his eyes. He didn't know what had compelled him to spend the last half hour, exhausted as he was, relating the mystifying essentials of Johnny Bermann's death to a man clearly in no condition to be of any help.

Maybe Matty was right in speculating about Crisp's mental well-being.

APRIL 2, 1917

Oscar Bermann bent over the radio set with his eyes closed, directing all his senses to his ears as the hissing in his headphones grew faint. Carefully he adjusted the crystals, at last plucking the wavering voice from the ether. "I've got it, Johann," he yelled in heavily accented English. "I've got it again. Quick, quick, come here."

His son, a dark-complected three year old with sparkling blue eyes, ran from the kitchen, his chin covered with molasses from the spoon that Elsa, the cook, had let him lick. Taking the headset in his sticky fingers, he inserted his head between the cold metal pads and listened, eyes and ears wide open. *"Ich hore nichts, Vater."*

"In English, boy. In English," Oscar chided gently with a wink at Ingrid, his son's golden-haired Swedish mother, several months pregnant, who was leaning on the door frame watching them. "Isn't that right, Mother? We are Americans, ya?" He laughed.

"With a house full of gadgets, we must be," Ingrid retorted, but she couldn't hide her smile. Elsa stood in the shadow of the kitchen door, watching and listening. If everyone spoke German, her job would be much easier. She felt that, even after seventeen months on American soil, she hadn't made much progress with English. Taking the good with the bad, however, it was better than Swedish, which is what Ingrid would have everyone speak if she had her way. There was a large Swedish community on the island, mostly stonecutters and their families, so it was possible to get along with very little English. Fortunately, Mr. Bermann—older than his wife by thirty years, if a day—prevailed.

"I don't hear anything," said the boy. "No, wait. There it is!" Johnny's eyes widened further as he was able to discern words through the hiss, actual human words, spoken by someone far away, someone they didn't know, someone not connected to them by wires. "I hear him!"

"What is he saying, Johnny?"

As the boy listened intently, his eyes wandering blindly about the room, the joy on his face suddenly froze, then melted into a look of confusion.

The smile fell from Oscar's face. "What is it, my boy?"

Johnny removed the headset and held it out to his father. Oscar took it and pressed the pods to his ears. In a few seconds his eyes fixed in a stare of disbelief.

"What is it, Oscar?" Ingrid asked, taking a hesitant step or two toward him.

Her husband seemed to age years before her eyes as, slowly and deliberately, he laid down the headset and turned off the crystal set. "President Wilson has sent a war message to the Senate and is recalling General Pershing from Mexico."

Elsa took Ingrid's place in the doorway, her hands unsettled and nervous.

"A war message?" Ingrid repeated. "What is that?"

Bermann turned his deep, sad gaze from his wife to his young son. "America is going to declare war . . . on Germany."

Ingrid regarded her husband askance. "I thought you said that wouldn't happen."

"I didn't think it would," said Bermann softly. He patted the back of his son's hand. "I was wrong." A motion in the hallway caught his attention. Casting a covert glance in that direction, he saw that Elsa was gone. As Johnny watched the old man closely, all but overcome by bewilderment, he saw a look steal into his father's eyes that he had never seen before.

"Ingrid," said the old man, rising with weary effort from the horsehair sofa. "Take the boy to bed."

"But, father . . ." Johnny began in protest. The look his father gave him did not brook argument.

"What are you going to do?" said Ingrid.

"It's getting late, my love. Take the boy to bed."

Ingrid choked down an unnameable fear and, without further argument, obeyed her husband. "Come, Johann," she said. Taking his unwilling hand, she led him out of the room. "We'll wash your face by the pump. Where is your toothbrush?"

The old man followed them as far as the hall and patted the puzzled boy on the head. "It's all right, son," he said with a distant smile. "It's all right. You go with your momma, and I'll see you in the morning. There is some work I have to do. Go now. *Schnell!* Quickly!" He stood watching them for a moment, entertaining thoughts of his own, then began the long walk through darkened halls toward the back of the house.

Opening the door to the middle house, the two-story storage ell that connected the big house to the barn, he breathed deeply. He loved the unique ambrosia of smells that assaulted his senses: coal mingled with sweet oats, apples, potatoes, and onions, of which, after the long, cold winter, only the scoria remained. The goats, chickens, and Big the Cow (so named by Johann) all contributed to the peculiar aroma. It was a good, honest smell. Oscar often came here to smoke the cigars that Ingrid wouldn't let him smoke in the house.

A motion outside caught his eye, and he looked up just in time to see the Dutch gate in the side of the barn swing closed. He stepped out into the crisp, moonlit night, stopping the door behind him before the counterbalance could slam it shut, and huffed across the dooryard. Stopping outside the Dutch gate, he listened. The sound of footsteps on the stairs echoed through the huge old barn.

He eased the gate open just enough to let him squeeze in; then, entering the cavernous darkness, he closed the gate after himself.

It took a few seconds for his eyes to become accustomed to the light, or lack of it. Meanwhile the footsteps reverberating on the floor above sifted showers of hay dust through the cracks between the boards. Anemic shafts of moonlight caught the dust, marking the footsteps toward the cupola ladder. Oscar, at nearly three hundred pounds, didn't relish climbing up two flights of stairs.

"Elsa," he called. The footsteps stopped instantly. "I know you're up there. I know what you've been doing. I have known all along. Come down, girl. Give it up."

A breathless silence followed, but it was brief. The footsteps resumed, but now she was running. "Damn," he uttered. He grabbed a fire bucket from a nearby post and made his way to the foot of the first flight of stairs. By the time he arrived on the second floor he was breathless and wheezing, and the bucket was half empty.

Echoes overhead told him that Elsa was already on the cupola ladder: Because of her size and age, she'd be in the cupola in seconds. "Elsa," he called again when he had caught his breath. It was too late. The soft, sudden lighting of a match filled the cupola with brilliance, which was visible through the hatch and the cracks between the floorboards. He heard her lift the glass of the storm lantern.

"Damn the woman," he rasped under his breath. Snatching the

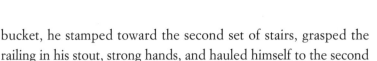

bucket, he stamped toward the second set of stairs, grasped the railing in his stout, strong hands, and hauled himself to the second floor. The ladder was about ten steps away. From where he stood he could see Elsa in the cupola. Already she was signaling. "Elsa, come down here, now!" he yelled in German, still hoping to spare himself the effort of that final, painful climb. She hurled a frightened, hate-filled glance at him before slamming shut the trapdoor of the hatch with her foot.

Anger propelled him forward now. With one hand holding the fire bucket and the other grasping the rungs, he started up the ladder sideways in an effort to keep his substantial paunch out of the way. It was a long climb to the top, but he proceeded with an agility that belied his bulk and was borne of much practice. In a few seconds he was at the top and could hear the hollow, metallic clicking of the shutter of the lantern as she worked it up and down. There was a paint hook on the handle of the bucket. He fixed it over the uppermost rung of the ladder and pounded the trapdoor sharply with his meaty fist.

"Open up, Elsa!" he barked in German.

The rhythmic clatter continued.

Bracing his feet securely on opposite sides of the same rung, he wedged himself under the trapdoor and, with his forearms, gave a mighty heave. The latch with which Elsa had locked the door held firmly, but the hinges separated at the joint, sending the little door sharply back against the wall, where it splintered. He grabbed Elsa's ankle. "Put that down, now."

Elsa, resolved to die if she had to, stared out the window toward Eastern Bay and continued sending the signal. Oscar made his way, grunting and sweating, halfway through the hatch, at which point she turned suddenly and began kicking at him. In raising his arms to defend himself, he nearly fell.

Catching himself at the last moment, and oblivious in his rage to the blows and kicks that rained upon him, he grabbed her ankle again.

"Traitor!" She spat the word at him.

"I am not the traitor," Oscar replied through the blood that trickled from his nose and eyebrow. "You are." With a flick of his wrist, he pulled her foot from under her. She crashed to the boards, impaling her temple on the pointed filigree atop the lantern cap, which she had placed on the floor. All resistance fled in an instant.

As she fell, the lantern had slipped from her fingers and shattered on the floor, sending its flames across the little room. Moving quickly, Oscar rolled Elsa's rag-doll body into the fire, smothering the worst of it. Reaching through the hatch, he grabbed the bucket from the rung and emptied it on the heaviest concentration of flames that remained. The rest he slapped out with his hands and with Elsa's greatcoat.

"Mr. Bermann, you all right?" Mr. Roberts called up to him from below.

"Everything's okay, Mr. Roberts," Bermann replied. His heart was pounding, pushing blood through his veins faster than he could breathe. His head felt light, and he thought he might pass out at any second, but it wouldn't do to have his foreman up here now.

"I saw lights," yelled Roberts from below. "Flashin'."

"Never mind, Mr. Roberts. It's all right. Everything is all right. Go home now."

It occurred to Oscar that Roberts's house, situated just across the kitchen garden from the main house, was a perfect place from which to observe any goings on in the barn, or the cupola. Odd he'd never thought of that before. Perhaps because he'd imagined that with Roberts up every day by five he must be early to bed.

How much else had he seen?

CHAPTER

5

DECEMBER 29, 1970

"YOU KNOW WHAT THEY NEED," said Leeman. He'd been leaning back in his chair and picking his knuckles while he and the other denizens of the pool hall discussed the death of Johnny Bermann.

"Why don't you tell us, Leeman?" said Olaf Ingraham, laughing as if he'd said something funny. "We can't wait."

"You gonna play, Olaf, or you gonna talk all day?" demanded Stuffy Hutchin. His tongue always pushed the ever-present Camel to the right side of his mouth when he was irritated. It did so now.

"What's the count?" said Olaf, dropping the front legs of his chair to the floor with a thud.

"If you'd spend more time playin' cards and less time jabberin' about things you don't know nothin' about, you'd know," Stuffy scolded.

Olaf was ready with a reply, but he kept it to himself. He'd never won a war of wits with Stuffy, and he didn't feel especially lucky at the moment.

"It's twelve," said Wendell, his partner, "with a three. You got another three for fifteen, that'll be four holes."

"There," Olaf snapped belligerently, slapping down an eight of clubs. "Twenty for nothin'. All I was sayin' is the Professor ain't such hot stuff as everybody thinks he is."

"You don't think so, huh?" said Stuffy, playing an eight. "Take two holes, will you, Bill? Twenty-eight."

"Damn it," said Wendell, who could feel the nickels and dimes leaving his change purse. "This is worse than gettin' your pocket picked."

Stuffy continued, "The Professor did more than you'll ever hear about."

"Oh?" Olaf retorted. "I s'pose you know all about it."

"Maybe I do, maybe I don't," said Stuffy, who had a knack of making you feel he knew a little more than anybody about everything but wasn't saying. "But I'll tell you one thing. If you don't play a card, we're gonna find someone else to take your place."

"You think there'll be a military funeral?" Bill inquired.

Leeman set his chair down on all four legs. "I didn't know he was in the military."

"Well," said Olaf contemptuously, "there's somethin' Leeman don't know. How 'bout that?"

"Was he in the war?" said Wendell, for whom there was only one war, the one over which FDR presided and Harry Truman unequivocally ended.

"He was in London," said Stuffy, letting one of his pearls loose.

"How do you know?" said Olaf, ever skeptical of Stuffy's seemingly boundless knowledge on practically everything. At the same time, he knew that if Stuffy said it, it was so. That's what riled him most.

"Ain't sayin'," Stuffy replied without malice. "But that's where he was. Worked as a translator for 'em over in the War Department, German bein' a second language to him."

"Nice safe way to pass the war," observed Wendell, whose uni-

form, worn proudly every Memorial Day and Fourth of July, identified him as Corporal W. Slocum, 17th Infantry, recipient of the
Purple Heart.

"He volunteered with the Canadians, Wen'," said Stuffy. "In '41.
That was three years before you went, wasn't it?"

Wendell took umbrage. "You're a good one to talk, Syl," he
snorted, using Stuffy's proper nickname in his agitation. "You never
even joined up."

Of course they all knew that Stuffy had tried, but his nearsight-
edness and fallen arches had made him unfit as cannon fodder in
the government's estimation. Instead he had joined the crew of a
Danish boat that had found itself in the mid-Atlantic when Germany
invaded Denmark and offered their ship and their services to the
government of the United States.

Stuffy ignored the remark, to an extent. "I remember seein'
London two days after V-E Day," he said, calmly playing a three on
his own twenty-eight because everyone else had had a "go." "Thirty-
one for two. Didn't look like a very safe place to me."

"Ever open up your mouth and have somethin' stupid come
out?" said Wendell by way of apology. "I just hate comin' in here
and losin' cribbage day after day, is all. Gets to you after a while."

"Must," said Stuffy stoically. "Maybe you'd best take a few days
off."

"Wonder if he ever finished that book he was workin' on," said
Leeman in an effort to take a little frost off the windows. "That's
what he come back here for, you know."

"He was writin' a book?" said Wendell. "What kind of book?
About the war?"

It was Bill's first count; he came two holes shy of going out. "It
was about his old man," he said.

"That's right," said Leeman. "You and him was friends, right?"

"I wouldn't say friends, really. We jammed sometimes."

Bill was an exceptional clarinet player, and it was common knowledge that he'd played with black people down in New Orleans

or Memphis back in the fifties. All his cronies on the island had heard the stories, so when he said "jammed," everyone knew what he meant.

"He played the accordion," Bill explained. "A few of us would get together up to his house and play—Goose and Doris Mavery, Brud Clayton, Hinkey Barton sometimes."

"What's Hinkey play?" said Leeman. He'd never known a lobsterman to play anything but a radio.

"Slap bass," said Bill. "Pretty good, too. He went to the Boston Conservatory of Music, you know."

"Hinkey did?" said Olaf, amazed. Here he'd moored his boat right next to Hinkey's all these years, and this is the first he'd heard of Hinkey going to college. Just goes to show. "Didn't know they taught slap bass down there," he muttered to himself.

Bill nodded as Stuffy counted them out for the win.

"So, he was writin' 'bout the old man," said Olaf. " 'Bout what happened to him on the island?"

"I s'pose so," said Bill. He shuffled the dog-eared cards and began dealing the next game. "That's our dime there, Stuff," he said, referring to a coin that had been orphaned in the most recent transfer from Wendell's purse to Stuffy's pocket. "He called the book *The Accused*," added Bill.

"Did you read any of it?" Leeman asked.

Bill shook his head. "Nope. Wasn't anything to read yet. He was just doin' research. Lot of it goes into a book like that, you know. He mentioned it one night when we were sittin' around waitin' for the others to show up, is all."

"What did he do before he come here?" said Wendell, throwing a four in the crib.

"I can tell you that," Leeman volunteered. "He was a history professor down in New Hampshire. Dartmouth."

"That's right," Bill affirmed.

"Was he retired?" Wendell asked. "He wasn't old enough for that, was he?"

"No. He was just takin' a sabbatical," said Bill.

"What's that? Like a workin' holiday, ain't it?"

"Kind've. They can take a year or two off to do research and such."

"Must be nice," said Olaf. "I wouldn't mind takin' a couple years off lobsterin'."

A thought-filled hush ensued during which the soft *thlick-thlick* of overused cards was the only sound. The adding was done in their heads and the pegging in silence.

"I think the old man really was a spy," Wendell said at last. As a boy of fifteen he and Mo Robinson, in patriotic fervor, set fire to Mr. Bermann's hayrick and sent it rolling down the hill from the barn toward the big house. Fortunately, in retrospect, it fetched up in the rough about halfway and just stood there burning in the middle of the field. They had watched from behind the little chapel when Mr. Bermann came thundering out of the barn—three hundred pounds of fury, the memory of which shook Wendell to the core even after fifty-three years—bellowing at the top of his lungs for Roberts, who came out of his house, not ten yards from where the boys were hidden, still pulling on his pants.

Mo and Wendell had seen the blinking light in the cupola, and they'd seen Bermann come out of the barn. They put two and two together. But they'd never said anything to anyone for fear of being connected to the fire. Mo Robinson had taken the secret with him to his grave on the battlefields of France not ten months later. And Wendell would take it to his own grave.

" 'Course he wasn't," said Leeman, who hadn't been born until two wars later. "What would any spy be doin' out on this rock in the middle of nowhere?"

"Oh, what do you know about it, Leeman?" Wendell retorted sharply. Surreal as it seemed now, he remembered the anti-German fervor that prevailed at the time—fueled by a constant barrage of propaganda from Washington—how everyone in town felt that, somehow, Penobscot Island was the very center of the war, the seemingly peaceful eye of a world-consuming hurricane. He remembered how patriotic he'd felt, how much a part of the war effort, with his heart beating against the back of his teeth, watching the hayrick burn.

"There was things goin' on out here you don't know nothin' about," said Wendell. "Half the town still remembers that German submarine that was sunk by the destroyer out between here and Matinicus." That battle, which many islanders watched from the shores of James Island, had become a fixture of local lore.

"Well," said Leeman, "they way I hear it, he done more good than harm and was run off the island just because he was a German."

Brenda had been in the back washing dishes, but she heard the exchange and, now that her chores were done, sat down beside Stuffy, lit a cigarette she'd taken from behind his ear, and entered the conversation with both feet. "Nobody knows," she said categorically. "Least of all you guys. I'd say the reason why Johnny come back is he was a history professor, and here was a piece of history right in his own family. He come to clear it up, I'd say."

Bill considered this likely. "That's what I figure." He didn't look up from his cards but did raise his eyebrows as far as they would go. "He said there were boxes full of family papers up in the attic. Spent a lot of time goin' through 'em. I wouldn't be surprised if he had in mind to clear the family name."

"But what if what he found don't clear the old man?" Olaf speculated. "What if it proves the town done him a favor by just runnin' him off instead've stringin' 'im up?"

"I think it was too long ago," Bill speculated. "I wouldn't be surprised if Brenda's right. He was a scholar, so I don't think he set out to find anything in particular but the truth."

"But," said Leeman, "if he don't like what he finds, he don't have to tell anybody about it."

"He'd burn the evidence," said Wendell, who had fire on the brain at the moment.

The silence performed an encore.

"I'd say whatever he found changed him somehow," said Bill after consideration.

Brenda flicked an ash into a cup of congealed coffee. "What do you mean?"

Bill studied his cards. "He was pretty sociable when he first came to the island. Seemed to make an effort to fit in. Then, a few months ago, something happened."

"Like what?" Brenda prodded.

"Can't say," said Bill. "He just stopped havin' us up there. Pretty much shut himself away. Had his phone taken out. Got his mail and groceries delivered. Finally had the electricity shut off."

Bill shrugged and continued. "I went up to see how he was last fall sometime. Doris was with me. At first he didn't come to the door. We figured maybe he was out walkin' somewhere. He used to walk a lot out on James Island. We were just about to leave when the door opened. The man looked like he'd been dragged through a keyhole. Didn't even seem to recognize us and said he'd appreciate it if everyone would just leave him alone. So, that's what we did."

"He had company up there day before yesterday," said Brenda.

"He did?" said Bill incredulously. "Who?"

"Don't know. Some fella from away. Bald guy, 'bout fifty or sixty, according to Snotty." Snotty Spofford was Brenda's nephew.

"What does Snotty know about it?" Olaf challenged.

Brenda was ready with the coup de gras. "He's the one takes groceries and mail up there. I guess he knows more about Johnny Bermann than you do, Olaf."

"Who do you s'pose that could've been?" asked Wendell.

Brenda snuffed the cigarette in the coffee cup and rose from the table. "Don't know. He left on the last boat yesterday, Snotty says."

Everyone thought this over. The winter population swelled about Christmastime with the return of college students and former islanders who had moved far away to Portland or Massachusetts, but strangers seldom visited at this time of year.

Leeman's train of thought had taken a different track. "Wonder

if what he found in them trunks is what changed him," he speculated. "Maybe somebody ought to go up there and see."

"Who's the house belong to now?" said Brenda. "He wasn't
married. Were there any brothers or sisters?"

Not that anyone recalled.

"All that property," said Brenda softly. "Must belong to someone."

It rained that afternoon—hard. By dark, at about four-thirty, a
brutal high swept down from Canada and thrust a wedge of numb-
ingly cold air under the warm front that had brought the rain. The
result was both dazzling and deadly. Ice. No exterior surface escaped.
Trees turned into brittle dowagers chained to the earth by a super-
abundance of diamonds. They leaned heavily on power lines, which
in turn sagged nearly to the ground in places. Elsewhere, wires
snapped under the pressure, writhing violently in the streets and on
sidewalks like headless electric serpents.

Sandra Billings's cocker spaniel sunk his teeth into one and was
electrocuted. He'd been appropriately named: Sparky.

By morning, most islanders were hermetically sealed in their
homes. Though the high had bullied the warm front out to sea and
the sun shown brilliantly—told and retold a billion times in inex-
pressible displays of startling beauty—it was cold as a corpse's kiss.

Among the few who ventured out were the children—to whom
a world encased in ice was not only a day off from school but one
that offered more rides than the Lobster Festival—and the line
crew, for whom the day was hell. Electricity was supplied to the
island by a temperamental underwater cable from the mainland, so
outages were not uncommon on the island. In such emergencies,
power was produced by an ancient, cantankerous generator that,
over the years, had earned its name "Beelzebub." When that failed
in the middle of winter, the outages were not merely inconvenient,
they were potentially deadly. Pipes froze and water mains burst.
People who had no fireplace or woodstove lit space heaters and gas
barbecue grills indoors in an effort to keep warm.

Carbon monoxide poisoning was a constant threat and figured in one of Doc Pagitt's recurring nightmares. A phone call summons him to one of the dilapidated old saltwater farms that dot the shore. He arrives too late. As if entering a Wyeth painting—soulless and cold—he wanders from room to room, each empty save for the gaping cadaver of a once-loved family member. At the last door, with his hand on the porcelain knob, he hesitates. One day he'll have the dream in which he opens the door. That morning his wife will find him dead.

Jennine Pagitt didn't want to wake him. He'd finally rolled into bed at two o'clock that morning, having slept no more than three hours at a stretch in the previous forty-eight, and now it was only a little past five. Still. "Paj," she said, rubbing his shoulder softly. She'd done this more times than she could count in their forty-odd years together. "Paj, you got a call."

Pagitt had had his hand on the porcelain knob. Someone was calling his name. Someone needed him. Later. Later he'd open the door.

"What time is it?" he mumbled. He rubbed his eyes and squinted at the alarm clock. He couldn't read it. "Where are my specs?"

She retrieved the thick-rimmed glasses from the bedside table and handed them to him. "Here. It's going on quarter past five."

Pagitt's head collapsed on the pillow. "In the morning?"

"Hm-hmm."

"The same morning?" he asked, almost pleadingly.

" 'Fraid so," she said softly. "I brought you some coffee."

Pagitt struggled to a semiupright position and breathed deeply, trying to inhale the caffeine. "It's cold in here. Is the fire out?"

"Nearly. I just brought in a wheelbarrow load of wood from the barn and stoked the stove enough to heat the coffee."

It was a gentle way of reminding him he'd forgotten to fill the woodbox.

"Sorry."

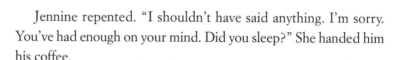

Jennine repented. "I shouldn't have said anything. I'm sorry. You've had enough on your mind. Did you sleep?" She handed him his coffee.

"Must have," he said, sipping contentedly. "I had dreams."

Neither said anything for a while. He needed time for his brain to clear.

"Who is it?" he said finally.

"It's that woman up at Captain Hall's," she said, referring to Mrs. Emerson's house by the name of its builder, whose address for the past 150 years had been Robert's cemetery. "The daughter called. Seems her mother had a bad night."

"May have," said Pagitt. They were quiet while he drank his coffee, the only breakfast he'd have today. He drained the cup and handed it to his wife. "But I bet it was longer than mine." He smiled a feeble smile, then, kicking back the covers, climbed out of bed. "I've got to take a shower."

"No hot water," Jennine reminded softly.

He hadn't made it beyond the end of the bed. The thought of a cold shower in a cold house in midwinter froze him in his tracks. He sighed from the soles of his feet to his tired shoulders, stood silently for a moment, massaging the folds of his face with an old man's hands, then lifted his trousers from the bedpost and put them on. "Have you looked outside?"

"Pretty clear, I think. It's going to be a mess underfoot, though, with all that rain turning the snow to slush like it did, and freezing over hard. You be careful out there. Your bones won't heal as fast as they used to." Jennine smiled.

Pagitt put on his spectacles and drew her into focus. She knew what he was going to say, but she let him say it. "You've had a long pull, old girl. Not exactly what you thought being a doctor's wife was going to be like, was it?"

"You know what, old thing?" she replied gently. "I'm glad you didn't turn out to be the kind of man I wanted when I was twenty. He'd've been pretty useless in the long run."

They seldom said anything original anymore. They'd said it all. Heard it all. Still, although the words themselves had become a comfortable ritual, the meaning they carried deepened with every retelling, a meaning that far outstripped the capacity of mere words to express. He held her head in his hands and kissed her forehead. "I'm off."

The lights were on at the Emerson house, punching square yellow holes in the deep predawn. The house itself was indiscernible. Pagitt parked his car at the bottom of the hill and looked out over the harbor. With the exception of pale smudges of kerosene lanterns here and there, the town was swaddled in an eerie blanket of darkness. With no familiar lights to give him his bearings, the town he'd known from childhood was suddenly unfamiliar and, in its unfamiliarity, somehow threatening. His breath draped the still, salt-laden air with a vagrant necklace of steam.

Mrs. Emerson's house would, he knew, be warm. He could hear the generator purring in the shed.

Keeping to the crusty snow at the edge of the drive to give him a workable foothold, he trudged up the hill.

"Doctor!"

The voice startled him and he nearly lost his footing, but he managed to maintain his equilibrium by jabbing his walking stick into the snow and using it for leverage.

"Miss Quindenan?"

"Sorry," said Margaret, who was standing beside the path. Only the white lace collar of her nightshirt showing above the folds of her cloak marked her presence. "I didn't mean to startle you."

"Then you picked the wrong way to go about it," said Pagitt, a tinge of alarm frosting his reply. He plodded toward her. "You shouldn't be out here. You don't look dressed for it."

"I've grown used to the cold," Margaret replied. "I wanted to talk to you before you went into the house."

Pagitt had pulled nearly abreast of her now and could make out her silhouette against a black tangle of evergreens. "About your mother?"

Margaret made a quiet sound of affirmation and, taking his arm, accompanied him the remainder of the way. "I'm frightened, Doctor. She's not getting any better," Margaret began.

"How do you mean?"

The young woman searched for words. "Well, I'm not sure exactly. It's just that I've never known mother to act like this. As I told you before, until a few days ago she was fine, the happiest I'd ever seen her. Then it was like somebody pulled some kind of emotional plug or something. She's been up all night again, pacing. She hasn't slept at all that I know of."

Pagitt knew the feeling.

"Or eaten," the young woman continued. "But she doesn't seem to be sick. No fever or chills or anything." She stopped in front of him and trapped his eyes in the depth of her gaze. "I'm scared, Doctor Pagitt. I'm afraid she's losing her mind."

"What does she say?"

"Oh, she hasn't changed her tune. She says she'll be fine, that nothing's wrong, don't bother the doctor—all that kind of foolishness. But if she's really losing her mind, she'd be the last person to know it, wouldn't she? I mean, don't people who are losing their minds think they're perfectly sane and all the rest of the world is going crazy?"

Pagitt would have been hard pressed to follow that logic in the best of times. Still groggy with sleep and rapidly numbing with cold, he let it pass.

"She's reciting nursery rhymes," Margaret volunteered.

"Nursery rhymes?"

"When she thinks I'm not listening."

"Such as?" he asked conversationally. All he wanted was to get inside where there was warmth. Real warmth. Not the imaginary warmth of a wood fire in the fireplace but real forced hot air from a fire-breathing, oil-guzzling furnace.

"Only one, actually," said Margaret. "And just part of that: 'One shoe off and one shoe on, diddle-diddle-dumplin', my poor John.' Over and over."

Had Pagitt not already stopped in his tracks, he would have done so.

Margaret, however, apparently unaware of the weight of her words, turned toward the house and gently tugged at his elbow, and they resumed their climb. "I always thought it was 'my son John,' didn't you?"

Pagitt wrestled with the noisy speculation that was ransacking his brain. "Yes, as I recall."

"She must have learned it different in England."

"I hadn't noticed an accent. Your mother's from England?"

"Oh, no. She's not. They were stationed there during the war, she and my dad. In London. He was an attaché and she was a nurse. They stayed on afterward. I was born there, but I don't remember anything about it. We came home when I was two or so. Anyway, I imagine that's where she learned 'my poor John.'"

As they arrived at the foot of the steps, their feet crunched on rock salt that had been strewn liberally from the porch to the clothesline. She held a finger to her lips.

"She doesn't know I'm coming?"

"Oh, she knows. I told her. I just wanted you to know she's going to tell you there's nothing to worry about and ask you to go home. But . . ."

"But what?"

Margaret didn't reply, although she seemed desperately trying to frame her thoughts.

"You think she might hurt herself?" Pagitt speculated.

He could see her clearly now, in the shallow luminance at the edge of the porch light's reach. She nodded as they climbed the stairs, their hollow footsteps resounding like thunder in Pagitt's ears.

"Where's Cal?"

"In bed. She's worn herself to a frazzle, poor woman. What with minding those houses up at Ragged Island during the storm and taking care of mother, she's not in much better shape herself. I thought she should sleep in, so I didn't trouble her."

"So you've been up all night with your mother?"

"I felt I should. She's on the love seat in the corner of the parlor, half asleep. But pretty soon she'll jump up again and start pacing. You'll see." She shuddered. "It's awful. I feel so helpless."

Pagitt sensed that the young woman had not said all that was on her mind. Whatever was holding her back needed to be nudged aside. "There's something else, isn't there?"

It was as if he'd thrown her a lifeline. She grabbed at it. "Yes . . . oh, yes, Doctor Pagitt. She . . . she talks to herself when she paces. It's just as if I wasn't there. Or she talks to me as if I were a child."

"And?"

The words didn't want to come, but she forced them. "She said something earlier this morning."

"Said what?" said Pagitt, forgetting the cold.

"Well, I can't be sure. I mean, she was mumbling. But it sounded like she said—"

A sudden shattering of broken glass severed the sentence.

"WHAT WAS IT?" said Crisp.

"Oh, I don't know," Pagitt responded. "Some piece of bric-a-brac. I guess she heard us talking."

"You probably startled her." Crisp resituated himself in a vain attempt to accommodate his chafed skin. "But what I meant was, what was it she said?"

"Oh," said Pagitt with a smile. "I'll come to that in a minute. First, I examined her, which she wasn't any too thrilled about but put up with for her daughter's sake. I couldn't find anything medically wrong."

"Psychologically?"

"Well, it didn't take a psychiatrist to figure out that the ballast had shifted." Pagitt picked distractedly at some woolen pills on the knees of his brown pants. "Afterward she wouldn't go to bed, so Margaret and I made her comfortable on the love seat, or as comfortable as anyone can be on one of those things. Then Margaret walked me outside. It was getting light about that time. Strange light that time of day, and I've seen too much of it lately."

Crisp was intimate with the surreal light of gunmetal gray that precedes dawn. It illumined those brief, nightmarish parts of the day when he, and people like him, did their darkest deeds.

An unvisited memory sprang from Crisp's unconscious and replayed itself in the cluttered landscape of his mind. King Farouk had just been ousted. The intentions of his successor, Gamal Abdel Nasser, weren't yet clear, though he was known to have decidedly leftist leanings. Crisp had been tasked to see that certain sensitive documents were retrieved from Montaza, Farouk's palace overlooking the Mediterranean northeast of Alexandria, before the populace could get their hands on them.

Intelligence reports indicated that the palace itself was overrun with troops but they had thus far contented themselves with abusing the finery. Soon, however, if the rumors were accurate, Nasser would announce his plans to make the place his seat of government. Then the clearing out would begin in earnest. The only chance of success would be to take advantage of the one factor that worked in Crisp's favor: The rebels, having been so long on the offensive and now swollen with victory, would be lax about security. Compounding this advantage was the knowledge, gleaned from a two-year posting in Cairo at an earlier stage in his career, that Egyptians, generally a late-night people, tended to be sluggish in the wee hours—the time of day he chose to conduct the last active mission of his career.

In the end, he had been proven wrong about the mind-set of the rebels. Nasser had sharpened them into an unexpectedly vigilant fighting force. By the conclusion of the operation, which Crisp administered from offshore in a specially outfitted Coast Guard inflatable, too many bodies, oozing blood in the two-dimensional light of dawn, littered the palace grounds. But no one was left alive to connect the theft to the thieves, not even the young navy frogman who, badly wounded in the shoulder, had swum the half mile from shore with the papers in a waterproof pouch. He had handed them to Crisp with the last of his strength before slipping quietly into the sea—another face in the waxworks of horrors that served as the backdrop for Crisp's every thought, waking or sleeping.

"And?" Crisp prodded Pagitt, shaking off the memory.

"It startled me to see her in that light. Her eyes were dim with dark circles. I can't explain it. Sounds foolish now, but I felt like she wasn't real." He laughed. "Does sound foolish right out loud like that." He tried to sell a wary smile, but there were no takers. "Probably the whole thing's colored by what she said."

"I was hoping you'd get around to that."

Pagitt ruminated a moment. "She said she caught something else her mother had said in amongst the poetry. She said—the mother this is, not Margaret . . ."

"I understand," Crisp replied patiently.

"She said, 'Poor John, he never knew.' I think that's it. Pretty close anyway. Then, as if right on cue, we heard her inside. Mrs. Quindenan. She'd gotten up and was wandering around. Margaret had left the door open a crack so she could keep an eye on her. She said the nursery rhyme 'Diddle-diddle-dumpling' . . ."

"My poor John," Crisp concluded. "You're thinking she was referring to Johnny Bermann?"

"I didn't have to think anything, any more than I'd have to wonder if it hurt if somebody hit me over the head with a heavy object. It all fits. Her nervousness all of a sudden, coming on the night after they found the body. Her inability to sleep. Repeating that rhyme over and over: 'One shoe off and one shoe on, my son John.'"

"My 'poor' John," Crisp corrected.

"'Son,' 'poor,' whichever. It all fits. Even the name. John. That's what they called Johann. And," he said, leaning close enough so Crisp could see the beginnings of a cataract in his left eye, "Joel Philbrook seems to think those footprints in the snow up at Everette's belonged to a woman."

Crisp sat up a little more, folded his pillow in half, and stuffed it behind him. "Which leads you to conclude . . . what?"

"Why, that whatever happened up there, she knows all about it, of course. Doesn't it you?" He asked eagerly. "Might've done the deed herself." Pagitt would be only too happy to be proved wrong. The image of Mrs. Quindenan wasting in prison was, for some reason, especially disturbing. Handsome woman.

"I can see why you'd entertain the notion," said Crisp, but he'd commit to no more.

"And you wouldn't?"

Crisp inclined his head somewhat, pinching between his thumb and forefinger one of the 1,298 tufts of cotton on the bedspread, and directed a thoughtful gaze at Pagitt over the top of his glasses. "No. I think the evidence you've just presented argues her innocence."

Pagitt looked incredulous. He sifted distractedly through the little brown bottles of medicine on Crisp's bedside table, concerned, for the moment, that there might be a hallucinogen among them. "Okay, let's imagine we're in a court of law. I'm the prosecution and I've just made my case. Argue me down."

Crisp assented with a smile. "Very well. Ladies and gentlemen of the jury," he began, addressing a regiment of get-well cards that Matty had arranged on the bureau. "The prosecution's witnesses have asserted under oath that, apart from being in unusually good spirits, the defendant, Mrs., ah . . . Mrs. . . . ."

"Quindenan," said Pagitt, filling in the blank.

"Thank you, Mr. Prosecutor," said Crisp. "Mrs. Quindenan exhibited none of those signs of anxiety *prior* to the day of the murder that manifested themselves thereafter.

"The evidence, however, suggests a crime that required elaborate planning. Are we to believe, as the prosecution suggests, that Mrs. Quindenan was, in her daughter's own words, 'the happiest I'd seen her in ages' in the days leading up to the crime—during which time she must have been coldheartedly devising Mr. Bermann's death—and that somehow she became nervous and anxious only *after* successfully carrying out her plan, as if she'd made no emotional preparation for the consequences of her actions and they had somehow taken her by surprise?

"Let's consider another possibility. Let us assume, for reasons that still remain obscure, that Mrs. Quindenan and Mr. Bermann arranged a meeting at the Everette cottage, and that they had done so sometime prior to the actual meeting itself. Let us further assume then that the prospect of the meeting was not unpleasant to Mrs. Quindenan, hence her high spirits in anticipation of the event.

"The day arrives. Mrs. Quindenan, despite the exigencies of the weather, makes her way to the cottage and there, in sharp contradistinction to her expectations, finds Mr. Bermann not warm, welcoming, and animated—for whatever purposes they may have covenanted—but dead. Not only dead but murdered. It is this horror, and the fact that again, for reasons unknown, she is unable to share it or seek counsel for it, that accounts for the delicacy of her emotional state since that day.

"No, ladies and gentlemen of the jury. Mrs. Quindenan did not kill Johann Bermann. She merely found him dead."

Crisp nodded respectfully at the get-well cards, loosed the tuft of cotton he'd been troubling between his fingers during the soliloquy, and folded his hands on his stomach. "The defense rests."

Pagitt shook his head slowly and huffed a note of irony through his nose. "And the prosecution goes and shoots itself," he said. "Now I know what it feels like to be Hamilton Burger."

"Pardon?"

"That fellow who's always losing to Perry Mason," Pagitt explained. "Still, I can't see why she wouldn't tell anyone. I mean, if I found a body—"

"What if theirs was a meeting of lovers?"

"She was a married woman," Pagitt said reflexively.

Crisp raised an eyebrow in reply.

Pagitt sighed. "I see what you mean."

The prosecution was startled by the mental agility of the defense. Pagitt, like most of the people in town, had, until last summer, regarded Winston Crisp as a benign, somewhat absentminded character. Of course, there were rumors that hinted at a colorful past, but even so, he didn't stand out as either particularly gifted or uncommonly eccentric among a population that teamed with gifted eccentrics.

Events, however, had proven otherwise, revealing a side of Crisp that few knew existed. If his recent performance was any indication, that aspect of the old gentleman was not only back, but back with bells on.

"How old is the daughter, would you say?" said Crisp, inspecting his cuticles.

"Hard to tell exactly," Pagitt replied thoughtfully. "Like I told Matty yesterday, I figure she's in her early to mid-twenties or thereabouts."

Crisp nodded as if he'd expected as much. "I wonder, Doctor, do you suppose it would be all right if I went down to the poolroom for an hour or so?" He held up his hand to stifle Pagitt's immediate response. "If you say yes, I'll have a little leverage to get around Matty. If not, I'll never shift her."

Pagitt considered carefully. "You've come along well, Winston. You mind my calling you Winston?"

"Please do," said Crisp, graciously admitting Pagitt to his circle of useful intimates.

"But you're awfully weak. I'd advise against your leaving the house for a while. If you were to so much as catch a cold now, in your state, well . . . I hate to think. And this ice . . ."

"I see," said Crisp. He raised his eyes to the window and watched a dance of snowflakes caught in an eddy of wind outside.

"Give it a while. Two to three weeks, say." Pagitt stood up and collected his things. "I don't imagine there's much going on down there anyway, with the power out and all."

That was probably true. Still, lying in bed for an extended period of time when one is in a coma is fine, but it holds little attraction for the noncomatose. Crisp's patience with his convalescence was wearing thin.

"It's certainly warm enough in here though," Pagitt continued.

"What does Matty use to heat the house?"

"Oil, generally. But since the blower's not working, she must be using the woodstove in the living room. That and the kerosene stove in the kitchen generate enough heat to constitute a warm front. You know Matty, she frets if it gets below seventy."

Pagitt laughed. "Doesn't seem much danger of that. Even if she runs out of wood, the storm lanterns she's got lit would heat half the town. Well," he put his hand on the doorknob, "you take care of yourself. The important thing is don't overdo it. That's what happens with people who've been sick any length of time, you know. Once they feel better, they overdo it. And at your age . . ."

"Understood," said Crisp with a smile.

"Good." Pagitt turned to leave.

"I suppose," said Crisp, preempting Pagitt's departure, "someone has notified the woman's husband."

"Mr. Quindenan?" Pagitt quizzed. "Well, I don't know, to be honest. I suppose so. The daughter must have called. I'm sure she would have."

"Then he'll be turning up soon, I expect."

"Expect so," said Pagitt, though the comment didn't carry much conviction. "I would, if I were he." Again he turned to leave. Again Crisp preempted. "Have you ever met him?"

Pagitt raised an eyebrow, but it was no defense against Crisp's expression of insipid curiosity. "Not to speak to, if that's what you mean."

"No," said Crisp. "I was just wondering . . . You'd know him if you saw him?"

"I suppose so, yes," said Pagitt. "Average-looking guy, I'd say. Why?"

"Oh," said Crisp, seeming to wake from a trace, "I just like being able to picture people. Helps me sort things out."

Pagitt glanced habitually at his watch and shrugged. "Well, like I said, average. Brown hair going gray. Balding a good bit. Fitter than most men his age—to look at, anyway. Not average in that sense."

"The daughter . . . she takes after her mother, you say?"

"I do," said Pagitt, a wry smile beginning on his face. "I also say I'm being grilled like a cheap fillet."

A slow grin spread across Crisp's face. "I must be losing my touch."

"Not if you're a prizefighter," Pagitt replied with a laugh. He shut the door. "What do you want to know?"

"I'm hoping you don't mind if I keep that to myself for the time being," Crisp said. "I have an idea, a little theory, and since certain people won't allow me out-of-doors, I have to gather information from passersby."

"Like a trap-door spider."

"Pardon?"

Pagitt folded his glasses and put them in his pocket. "Don't you get *National Geographic?*"

"Matty does," Crisp replied, a little nonplussed. "I'm afraid I don't."

"A month or two ago there was an article about one of nature's diabolical little oddities called a trap-door spider. Lives in the desert out in the Southwest somewhere. Seems it digs a hole and puts a door on it. A real door, with hinges made of webbing. When some poor unsuspecting bug comes hopping along, it hits that door and . . ." Pagitt slapped the desktop so hard that the floor shook and the crystals hanging from the lampshade on the dresser awoke with a start, filling the room with anxious tinkerbells of light. "It drills some part of its biological apparatus into the victim and feasts on its insides, all while the poor thing's still alive. Makes the meal last for days."

Crisp's look of alarm took on a quizzical patina. "And that's what I remind you of?"

Pagitt felt he had one-upped the old man. He crossed his arms and did a Cheshire cat impersonation. "Out with it. What do you want to know?"

"Just what Mr. Quindenan looks like," Crisp replied with an innocence that somehow discomfited the physician. "That's all."

Pagitt thought it best to divest himself of whatever facts he might knowingly or unknowingly possess. He was tempted to check the ceiling for a trapdoor. "Miss Quindenan—Margaret—is the image of her mother, but darker."

"Then her father's dark?"

Pagitt unknowingly adopted Crisp's quizzical expression. "Well, no, come to think of it. Quite light, as a matter of fact." A searching gaze at Crisp's flaccid face told him nothing. "Must be a bogie in the woodpile somewhere."

Crisp seemed to have stopped listening. His eyelids were at half-mast, and Pagitt figured he'd overstayed his welcome. "Well, I'll be off." He picked up his things and, once again, turned to the door.

Crisp arrested him with an unexpected request. "Could you do me a favor?"

"Sure. If I can."

"Do you happen to know if Nate Gammidge is still here on the island?"

"I guess he must be; the ferry's frozen in. I imagine he's down at the motel, though."

"Would you mind stopping by and asking him if he could come up and see me?"

There was a poignancy in Crisp's voice that made Pagitt think he must be very lonely. Of course, that was what he was supposed to think. "You wouldn't rather call?"

Crisp didn't think so. The only phone was downstairs, well within the sweep of Matty's radar. If she heard him inviting anyone over for a visit, especially someone like Gammidge, whom she associated, rightly or wrongly, with all the troubles that had befallen her star boarder, she'd put the kibosh on those plans in short order. On the other hand, if Gammidge showed up at the door, her inbred compunction to be hospitable might mitigate her more motherly sensibilities.

"Well, if you're sure you're up to it," said Pagitt. "I'm going by that way shortly. Anything else?"

"Oh, no, no. You've been good company, Doctor. Thank you."

Pagitt couldn't point to the moment when the transition had taken place, but it suddenly struck him how frail Crisp seemed. Helpless. He cast his patient a last glance before leaving the room. The image that accompanied him down the stairs was that of an old man, his head tilted almost imbecilically to one side, without a trace of the incisive intelligence so recently exhibited in the case of Pagitt v. Quindenan. Had that appearance of intelligence been an anomaly, a brief bubbling to the surface of an earlier edition of Crisp, a part whose pages were about to close forever?

"Colder than a witch's left tit in here," Kingsbury complained.

Although Gammidge might have taken issue with the terminology, he couldn't dispute the accuracy of the sentiment. There hadn't been a fire in the Franklin stove since Johnny Bermann last tended it two days ago. The frigid wind that blew steadily up the open rise from Eastern Bay had invaded the big, old house with icy tendrils. They wove together in an invisible fabric through which it took effort to move. "I don't imagine there's much insulation in these walls," said Gammidge, absentmindedly tugging at a brittle piece of loose, water-stained wallpaper, which turned to dust in his hand.

"Insulation?" said Kingsbury. "They never heard of such a thing when this place was built. Ain't been used in winter for a dog's age, so it was never winterized. No furnace. No hot water. No electricity. Can't have been very pleasant for him up here all alone."

Kingsbury blew into the bright purple mittens that Maggie had knit him for Christmas. "You know, all the houses were like this once. No insulation. I swear, I don't know how they made it through the winter in the old days."

Gammidge agreed. Johnny had apparently confined his activities to the kitchen. His bed, neatly made and piled with wool blankets that reeked of mothballs, sat in the middle of the room, close enough to the stove so he could reach the wood box and stoke the fire without much effort. That would be helpful in the middle of the night.

More wool blankets hung in the interior doorways. The parlor, which faced the ocean, was further sealed with a sheet of plastic that had been stapled on all sides. Two worn wool blankets hung loosely from the other doorway. The blankets were badly frayed on the left side, indicating frequent use. "He must have a woodpile out here," Kingsbury observed, raising the blanket enough for a peek. "Wonder where he kept his food."

Gammidge expressed surprise that the windows were boarded over. "Seems like the sunlight would've warmed up the place a good bit."

"If it comes to letting the sun in or keeping the wind out," Kingsbury observed, letting the blanket drop back into place, "you keep the wind out. 'Specially since there ain't much sun this time've year anyway." He crossed to an ancient rolltop desk tucked in the corner on the side of the stove opposite the doorway and began mindlessly thumbing through orderly stacks of papers. "I can still feel it, right through the boards and glass and all. He was a teacher, they say."

"History professor at Dartmouth."

"That's down to New Hampshire, ain't it?" At that moment something caught Kingsbury's eye. "What in hell is this s'posed to be?"

Gammidge looked up from the chest of drawers he'd been sifting through. In the dingy light, he saw the constable holding a small leather-bound book close to his eyes as he leafed through its pages with a look alternating between befuddlement and disgust. "If he was the one who wrote this gibberish," said Kingsbury, "I don't wonder half the college kids are smokin' dope."

"What is it?" said Gammidge, stepping over a pile of magazines on his way across the room.

Kingsbury tossed him the book. "Gibberish," he pronounced with contempt and resumed his investigation of the other stacks on the desk. "If you ask me, I'd say he got a little too close to the fumes in here."

Gammidge, who had never been very good at playing catch, retrieved the book from the floor and turned it over in his hands. The red leather binding was brittle with age and in places worn thin with use. "Looks old," he said.

"Hmph," Kingsbury editorialized. He had found some old newspapers he *could* decipher and was perusing them with growing interest. "The old *Spectator*. They stopped printing this years ago. He must've been using it to research that book they say he was working on."

The red leather cover had apparently spared the pages within from the ravages of time. Though worn, they seemed supple and not overly dry as Gammidge riffled through them. Inside the front cover, written in ink in the elegant hand of an earlier age, were the words: "Property of Oscar Bermann, Bermann Estate, Penobscot Island, Maine."

Below them, tilting wildly up the page, was another announcement, "Poperty of ME, Johny," written in wax crayon, each character boldly inscribed in a different color.

"Johann," Gammidge said to himself. He could almost see the young boy bending intently over his labors, carefully constructing this proclamation of ownership, his tongue wedged between his teeth and protruding from the side of his mouth in earnest concentration as he carefully shaped the letters.

Johann had left similar impressions on the next few pages, which, though lined, were otherwise blank. Then Gammidge arrived at the pages that elicited Kingsbury's indignation.

The pages, written in pencil in a very neat hand, presented nothing unusual at first glance. Words were separated, sentences ended with punctuation, and paragraphs were uniformly indented. A second look, however, revealed that the words weren't in English and, Gammidge was sure, did not represent any other spoken language.

"Code," he said aloud.

"Huh?" said Kingsbury, his attention already having strayed from the newspaper to the contents of various pigeonholes in the desk. He was poking through them in a perfunctory manner. "You say something?"

During his recent interviews with the natives, Gammidge had been brought up to date on island lore concerning the Bermanns. If it became common knowledge that a codebook had been found on the estate, he shuddered to think what the finely tuned machinery of the island gossip mill might churn out. "Oh, I was just talking to myself." He made a display of dropping the book back on the desk. "Find anything else?"

Kingsbury shrugged. "Just a bunch of junk, far's I can tell. Kinda artsy-fartsy stuff you'd expect from a fella like that."

"Guess you're right," said Gammidge, tainting the phrase with a deliberate tone of disappointment. "Well, no sense wasting any more time up here. Why don't you go warm up the truck. I'll see if I can find something to hang over the shed door to keep out the skunks and squirrels."

Kingsbury thought that was a waste of time, and said so, but went out to start the truck nonetheless.

Gammidge waited for the truck door to slam. As soon as it had, he swept the red leather book from the desk and tucked it into his inside pocket. He buttoned his coat, pulled on his gloves, and, after waiting a reasonable amount of time, left the house, carefully fastening both the inner door and the screen door behind him.

CHAPTER 7

"EVENING, MISS GILCHRIST," said Gammidge. "Matty," he ventured as he removed his hat and stomped hard on the doorstep to get the ice and snow off his boots. "Is the Professor home?" The word was not fully out of his mouth when he remembered that Matty didn't like the nickname the islanders had given Crisp. "Winston, I mean," he added meekly.

Matty was clearly of two minds. The names of two Biblical characters occurred to her as she deliberated: Jonah or Jeremiah, whichever one always brought bad news. Whoever it was, that was Gammidge. Fortunately for him, however, there were deeper instincts at work in Matty than those that compelled her to want to hover around Crisp like a hen around her chicks: those of the Yankee housekeeper, and they demanded that she be hospitable, whoever the caller. Of course, there was some consolation in the fact that this, too, was a Biblical principle.

Crisp had read his maid aright. "Come on in, Mr. Gammidge," she said after an almost imperceptible hesitation. "Can't have you standin' out there in the cold. What'll you have?"

Not without a sigh of relief, Gammidge crossed the threshold, handed Matty his coat and hat, and fell into her wake as she bustled toward the kitchen, the first stop for any visitor.

"What's that I smell?" asked Gammidge, inhaling deeply. "Something with molasses?"

"Oh, I just threw together some molasses cookies and gingerbread men." He'd noticed her baking. Must be some good in the man. "I don't suppose I could interest you in some?"

As she removed the lid from the cookie jar, the warm, welcoming smell of freshly baked cookies awoke his salivary glands in anticipation. "If you toss in a glass of milk, you've got yourself a bargain."

Just what she was going to suggest. You know, come to think of it, Gammidge wasn't such a suspicious character after all. Of course, he had his job to do, and that was one thing, but a man who knows molasses from brown sugar, well, there. "You help yourself to the cookies, Mr. Gammidge. I'll get the milk." She propelled herself to the refrigerator, watching him with quick little glances as he took two perfect cookies from the jar. "Take as many as you like. Otherwise I'll eat 'em, and Lord knows I don't need that. 'Course, Winston's only just back on solid food."

Over four cookies and two tall glasses of milk, Gammidge talked about everything he could think of that had nothing to do with why he'd come. He talked lovingly of his wife as well as his two kids, who were off at school up in Orono ("Must be awful for them, so far from the ocean," Matty sympathized); about Sagacious, his Lab retriever; about hunting and ice fishing; about life on the mainland, which he was wise enough to compare unfavorably with life on the island; and about how times had changed, "and not for the better, either."

By the time he'd finished, Matty had been nodding approval so vigorously that her neck hurt. She rubbed it with a fleshy hand. Listening to Gammidge was a lot like listening to a poet. And poets, as Winston had told her, have to love what they're writing about.

"Speaking of poetry," she said aloud, not realizing that they hadn't been, "I s'pose you'll want to pop up and see Winston for a minute or two." Despite the thrall in which she'd been cast, she wasn't so far gone that she neglected to emphasize the last few words.

Gammidge wasn't sure where the reference to poetry had come from, or what it had to do with the Professor, but he knew an open door when he saw one, and he jumped through it like a trained dog. "As a matter of fact, I would like that," he said, judiciously adding, "Of course, only if you think he's up to it."

"Well," Matty replied thoughtfully, happy that Gammidge recognized her as the final arbiter in matters regarding the patient, "I think it'll be okay. But, like I said—"

"Only a minute or two," Gammidge interrupted, underscoring the fact that he got the point. He held up three fingers in a Boy Scout salute. "Promise."

Matty's familiar one-knuckle knock on Crisp's door elicited a sleepy response from within. "Winston?" she said softly, slowly opening the door and poking her head into the dimly lit room. "You up?"

Gammidge, from his position over Matty's shoulder, heard a faint reply in the affirmative.

"Someone to see you," Matty said. "It's Mr. Gammidge. You mind?"

Crisp cleared his throat. "No, no. Please, send him in."

"You might want to sit up and get yourself together a little," Matty suggested, stepping into the room and half closing the door behind her, so Gammidge had to follow with his ears. "You look like you been folded wet and left to dry."

Gammidge chuckled silently at the gentle comedy that followed as Matty propped and straightened, fluffed, brushed, and whatever else she felt needed to be done to make Crisp presentable—all to the music of meaningless chatter—while Crisp impotently protested that he was fine and that Nate wouldn't care if his hair was combed or there wasn't a pleat in his pajama sleeves. " 'Course he would,"

Matty reposted, "he's not from Mongolia's backside, you know." She was thinking of the fact that he knew the difference between molasses and brown sugar, *and* that he'd asked for a napkin. He was a man of some breeding.

"There," Matty pronounced, opening the door widely and gesturing Gammidge in. "I can't do anything else with him." Squeezing by Gammidge in the doorway, she held up a finger of admonition and added an exclamation point—in boldface type—with her eyes, succinctly mouthing the words "one or two minutes."

The body language was not wasted on Gammidge. Before closing the door behind him, he said, loud enough for Matty to hear, "Well, Winston, so good to see you. I'm afraid I can't stay but a minute or two, but I just wanted to see how you're doing."

Then the door closed and the voices fell. Matty, feeling like a cat that had just had its belly rubbed, descended the stairs with a smile.

"You must have done some fast talking to get past her," said Crisp, holding out his hand, which Gammidge shook as if it might fall off. "I'm all right, really. The doctor gives me hours to live yet." He smiled, and Gammidge relaxed. "Pull up a chair."

"I really can only stay a bit," said Gammidge. "I promised. You know how she worries."

Crisp put on his wire-rimmed glasses and looked more like Jimmy Stewart's grandfather than ever. "Did Pagitt find you down at the motel?" he asked, inclining his good ear toward his guest.

"Pagitt? No. Was he looking for me?"

"Oh, I thought . . . He was here this morning and I asked him if he'd stop by the motel and ask if you'd mind coming up to see me."

"Nope," said Gammidge. He was studying Crisp with the open-faced scrutiny that a two year old might give a particularly lifelike wax effigy. "You made it," he said simply, managing somehow to embody both amazement and gratefulness in the words.

"So far," said Crisp. "Most of me, anyway." He held up his left hand and exhibited the well-healed stump of his missing finger with that peculiar pride that only men seem capable of at such a display.

"And two toes?"

Crisp would have showed them as well, but Gammidge forbade it. "No, that's okay. Really. Hurt much?"

"I guess I was mostly dead during the painful part," Crisp replied.

"Thank God."

"I do."

Gammidge nodded for a minute like a dashboard doll. "Good to see you. You had us mighty worried for a while there."

"Well, I hope you won't tell me how good I look. Your expression when you saw me said it all."

Gammidge was relieved. He hated to lie. "I guess you look all right, all things considered." There was no concealing his alarm at the discrepancy between the Crisp he'd known and the one who lay before him now.

Crisp had been feeling pretty spry, actually. Fortunately, from the bed, he couldn't see himself in the only mirror in the room. "I got your card. Thank you."

"Card? Oh, yes. Well, truth be told, I guess my wife must've sent it. Women, you know."

"Well, it was nice of her."

There was a manly silence during which Gammidge felt the little red book burning holes in his coat pocket. He'd expected to lay it in Crisp's hands, but from the look of things, he doubted the old man was up to it. "Town really rallied 'round you, from what I hear," he said conversationally.

"Rallied 'round" was an understatement. Since his revival, Matty had chronicled all the efforts of the islanders on his behalf, everything from prayer vigils at the Union Church to Lady's Circle suppers and a bingo night at the high school to raise money to cover his medical bills. During the summer a number of artists had even held an auction of their works for the same purpose. All this without knowing whether he was a pauper living out his last days on Social

Security or a millionaire living quietly on interest. No questions had been asked. No thanks were expected. He was in trouble, so everyone did whatever they could, same as they would for any other islander.

"They did indeed," Crisp murmured, surveying Matty's most recent display of cards, letters, and flowers that, even now, arrived on an almost daily basis. Many were from people with whom he'd never exchanged more than a word of greeting at the post office. "Very humbling."

Crisp raised his eyes, and Gammidge noticed they were a little watery. He noticed something else as well. They weren't decrepit like the rest of him. They were deep and searching and, to tell the truth, made him feel a little uncomfortable. "Well, Mr. Gammidge. I believe you're looking for some help with the murder of Johann Bermann."

Gammidge was startled. He'd just about made up his mind to write off his mission as a lost cause and had been, at that very second, trying to think of a graceful way out. "Oh, I don't . . . I'm afraid—"

"And you have something for me in the inside pocket of your coat. Left side," Crisp continued. "May I see it?"

Overawed, Gammidge undid the top buttons of his coat and produced the book. "I found it up at the Bermann place," he stammered, handing it over to Crisp. "How in hell did you know?"

"Comes from spending a lot of time abroad," Crisp said matter-of-factly. He inspected the introductory pages. "I'd always tap my pocket to make sure my passport was there. It became habitual after a while. People do the same with their wallets. That's how pick-pockets know which pocket to go for. They study their victim for a minute or two to see which pocket gets the tap. You've been tapping your pocket ever since you got here."

"Have I?" said Gammidge. "I didn't even realize—"

"And I figured it was for me because you braved Matty—the greatest of terrors—to bring it. As for the murder, that's your busi-

ness. As you were kind enough to allow me to assist you in a previous investigation, and we've got another one on our hands . . ."

Gammidge shook his head. "Seems so simple when you put it
that way," he observed, a little demystified after a peek in the con-
jurer's box. "Well, what do you make of it?" He nodded at the book.

Crisp had stopped perusing after the first page of the code and
was now fixed on it with all his mind. "A substitution code. *Chiffre
carré*," he said under his breath, his pulse quickening. "No repeats
that make any sense on the face of it. Punctuation in place. Doesn't
seem to be monoalphabetic." He glanced quickly at Gammidge,
who detected in that glance the joy of someone who had just been
given a pearl of great price. "Very unusual, that. Indicates an almost
arrogance that the code can't be deciphered." He began thumbing
hungrily through the pages, finally arriving at the end. He examined
the binding—front, back, and edge as well as the few blank pages
preceding and following the text—with special attention to Johnny's
crayon scrawl. "This is wonderful," he said, unable to mask a tone
of reverence. "A thing of beauty." Again he turned his attention to
Gammidge. "Tell me, where exactly did you find this?"

"Well, it wasn't me, exactly," Gammidge replied, a little discon-
certed by the eagerness in Crisp's eyes. "Kingsbury was poking
around in an old desk up at the Bermann place."

"Very interesting. You're familiar with the story?"

"Just what little I've picked up here and there in the last couple've days."

While recapitulating the story, Crisp was inwardly distressed to
find that a number of salient points—specifics inconsequential to
the telling—had slipped into a darkened room in his memory and
double-bolted the door from within. The only fear he hadn't outlived was that of losing his mind. Was this forgetfulness just the
trailing edge of his illness or a harbinger of things to come?

"And the house stayed pretty much empty, from what I understand, until Johnny returned—some time ago," Crisp concluded the
story. How long ago, he couldn't remember.

Gammidge had noticed that none of the telling was in the first person. "You spent summers on the island in those days, didn't you? You didn't know all this was going on?"

"I spent summers here up 'til '06 or '07. Then college. Then the army. Then government service, the war. I didn't start coming back regularly 'til well after the dust had settled."

"Hmph," Gammidge editorialized. "So, you figure that was the code Bermann used to communicate with German boats offshore?"

Crisp shrugged. "Someone was communicating with someone," he said enigmatically. The retelling of the Bermann story, bookended by events in his own life that seemed so distant as to have happened to someone else, had led the tendrils of his mind down a number of ancient rabbit trails. Odd. The more distant the memory, the clearer it was. With effort he corralled his thoughts and brought them to bear on the present.

"This book interests me because codes are—rather were—my business. But I can't imagine why it should interest you so much, especially since you didn't really know anything about the Bermanns."

Gammidge's eyes were fixed on a pattern in the wallpaper. He didn't want the memory of what he was about to relate to fix itself in his mind. It was no use. "I found a piece of paper on the body— on Johnny Bermann. In one of his pockets." He turned his gaze to Crisp.

"In code?" Crisp ventured.

Gammidge nodded slowly; reaching out, he tapped the book. "This code, near as I can tell. When I found the book, I figured there'd be a clue, and if anyone could figure it out . . ."

Crisp held out his hand. Gammidge stared at it blankly for a few seconds. The skin was wrinkled and covered with age spots. It was shiny at the knuckles and wrist and almost translucent in places, revealing the blue veins beneath. But it was perfectly steady. Slowly, but not reluctantly, he removed the piece of paper from his pocket and surrendered it to Crisp, who studied it hungrily, making approving noises in his throat as he digested the cipher with his eyes.

The only discernible words adorned the upper margin of the page. "Happy birthday," Crisp read aloud. He looked quizzically at Gammidge. "Was it?"

"Was what?"

Crisp rattled the paper for emphasis. "Was it Bermann's birthday the day he was found?"

"I don't know," said Gammidge, a little embarrassed. "I'll ask around."

Crisp resumed his perusal of the paper. "I wonder," he said at length, "could I impose upon you to go up there again? Alone?"

"What for?"

"I have reason to believe that if you look carefully—and I mean very carefully, under and behind the drawers, all through the desk, inside and out, everywhere—you'll eventually find the set of numbers that's the key to this code."

"Key?"

"You remember I said the composer of this code was arrogant? Perhaps I should have said confident. It's because this kind of code can't be broken without a key. In some cases the key is a word. In this case, I'm sure, we're looking for numbers."

"It's getting dark," Gammidge protested. "And there's no light up there."

"Matty will lend you a flashlight," said Crisp, his eyes willful and insistent in a strange, helpless way. "I'm afraid it's the only way you're going to find out the meaning of the note you found."

Gammidge cringed. Penobscot Island had proven altogether too spooky for him of late. Although he never thought of himself as having much imagination, he discovered that he had more than enough to anticipate a host of unpleasant, supernatural things that might happen to him if he embarked on Crisp's errand. Mitigating this impulse, however, was the nagging suspicion that his fears smacked of weakness. "Can't it wait 'til morning?" He let his eyes do the pleading.

"Mr. Gammidge," Matty sang from the bottom of the stairs in a wavering contralto. "Wouldn't you like a cup of tea before you go?"

Neither Crisp nor Gammidge failed to recognize that the emphasis was on "go" rather than "tea." "I'll be right down, Matty," Gammidge replied. "I'm just saying good-bye."

Matty paused for a moment, weighing the merits of this response. Then, apparently satisfied, she scooted toward the kitchen in her faux fur slippers. Crisp spoke quickly, under his breath. "I don't think anyone would see you if you went tonight," he said. "Something tells me it's very important that no one see you."

The caution in Crisp's voice did little to allay the wellspring of irrational fear that was attempting to have its way with Gammidge's soul. He was about to say that the best way to ensure not being seen was not to go when the persistent voice of duty prevailed. "It's awful cold out."

"Matty will lend you a scarf," said Crisp, settling back against his pillow, withering visibly before Gammidge's eyes like a punctured balloon. "Nothing like a good warm scarf to keep out the cold," he said, his voice rasping at the back of his throat, as befitting the old man he'd seamlessly become.

Gammidge had seen this phenomenon before, but his inability to tell whether it was just a trick of eye made it doubly unnerving. He exhaled deeply. "Oh, well. Sooner I get started, sooner it'll be over."

Crisp, his glasses hanging precipitously from the end of his nose at a comic angle, had closed his eyes. His only response was a deep, contented sigh.

As he descended the stairs, Gammidge struggled with the knowledge that he was being used. Shamelessly so. However, unlike many in his profession, he had no delusions about his own abilities. Once again he found himself in unfathomable waters, stuck on the island in the dead of winter, faced with an inexplicable crime. The Professor had delivered the goods the last time, and Gammidge had gotten a promotion and a raise, so why not let him have at it again?

Even a Crisp of diminished abilities probably had twice the deductive logic of a roomful of Gammidges. He was smart enough to know that.

Of course he had no car, so he had to walk. And of course it wouldn't make any difference if he had a car anyway. Only a four-wheel drive like Luther Kingsbury's could make headway on the corrugated moonscape of ice that the roads had become. And of course there was no electricity, so no streetlights would mark the way. The selfish sliver of moon that peeked through the scudding clouds every now and then seemed reluctant to give up more light than would allow him to see anything beyond the dullest outline in the dark. And of course not only had a blistering cold once again settled over the island, but the wind that brought it was rimmed with rows of frigid teeth, viciously nipping at every square millimeter of exposed flesh like airborne arctic piranhas.

Gammidge entertained himself with an expanding litany of complaints as he slipped and slid through the lightless night on his fool's errand. Matty had warned him that the batteries in the flashlight were weak, so he used it sparingly, flicking it on and off whenever the way was unsure, or just to assure himself that it still worked and that the leafless trees that lined the road were just trees and nothing else.

He imagined what would happen if he died of exposure, scarf or no scarf. How would he explain *that* to his wife? He'd never hear the end of it. It wasn't difficult, in his present state of mind, to imagine in the night a living creature, a huge, nocturnal malevolence poking holes in his pathetic defenses, thrusting icicles into the exposed places and letting all the warmth out.

About a mile to go.

The island seemed like a ghost town with only the pungent smell of burning wood in the air to testify to habitation. The windows in most of the houses stared blankly out at the predatory night, playing dead.

CHAPTER 8

BILLY PRINGLE COULDN'T GET BACK TO SLEEP. A big black
housefly had, for some reason, forsaken the comfort of
hibernation among the window weights in favor of banging
itself against the ceiling and walls of Billy's one-room shack on the
edge of town like a soul in torment at the gates of hell. Its buzz had
been loud enough to wake him from the dreamless void, so he gave
his Coleman lantern a few pumps and lit it, then lay back down on
his bed, watching.

The thoughts that occurred to him as he watched were not those
that would occur to the average person, and they had little to do
with the fly. He noticed that, apart from the buzzing of the fly, there
was no sound, only a thick, tangible silence. He wondered how
much silence would weigh if you could cut off a slice and put it on
the big Toledo scale down at the fish plant. Then he wondered what
it would look like, but he couldn't come up with anything. So he
took the opposite tack: What did sound look like? Depends on the
sound, of course. His favorite sound was from chickadees. That was

a light blue sound with a little green and white around the edges and it smelled of spruce and fir. His second-favorite sound was the ocean, but that was harder to define than the bird's simple song. Sometimes it played with the rocks and sand on the shore, giggling; then it was bright white sparkles spread on see-through green. Sometimes it was angry, lashing at the rocks with irrational fury, the way Missy Philbrook sometimes beat up on her husband, Joby, who, like the granite rocks that rimmed the island, just stood and took it. Then it was gray and white with flashes of violence—that would be red—to keep it stirred up even after the anger was gone.

Sound was colors then, Billy reasoned. So silence must be no colors.

Nope. That wasn't right either. The most silent thing he knew was the night sky. Not when it was dull and foggy; then it was full of sounds—the sound that mist made as it congregated on sprills and leaves, melded into drops, and splattered onto other sprills and leaves or onto the ground or into puddles. That kind of night was packed with noise: peepers and crickets, little rustles and noises, some from outside your head, some from inside. Nope. The most silent thing was the wide-open night sky when you could see right up to the sparkle in God's eye. That's what his Aunt Matty always said on really clear nights: deeply silent but busting with light. Speaking of Matty, one of these days he'd have to get around to eating that meat loaf she'd given him.

Billy couldn't see all the way to the twinkle in God's eye, but on a good night he could see to the edge of the universe with the naked eye. He was intimate with each of the individual elements that make up the Crab nebulae and its sisters, which science knew only as multi-colored smudges on thick glass plates. He'd peered deep into the abyss of black holes and been entertained for hours by what he found on the other side. He even knew when and how the world would end.

None of this was remarkable to Billy. Although he knew he was different from others, it never occurred to him that they were different from him, and had been ever since he'd fallen off a cliff as a child and landed on his head. If everyone wanted to talk about the price of haddock and what time Peggy Tilton dragged herself home the other night rather than the things he thought about, it must be because that's what they wanted. Billy was comfortable with that.

It never occurred to him to kill the fly, either, though it was fat and slow and drugged with sleep. He'd wait to go to sleep until it settled somewhere or knocked itself out.

A knock at the door startled him. No one knocked on his door at the best of times. He got up with his bedding wrapped around him and, looking more like a derelict moth emerging from its cocoon than anything else, stepped across the room. He opened the door and saw a stranger balancing himself on the sawn-off railroad tie that constituted his doorstep.

"Evening," said Gammidge, his teeth rattling in his head.

"Evening," Billy said, punctuating the reply, as he did every second or third sentence, with a soft raspberry—another eccentricity resulting from the blow to his head.

"I'm about freezing to death out here. Saw your light and thought you might have a fire going." Gammidge suddenly became aware that there had been no outrush of warm air when the door was opened to him.

"I don't keep fires much," said Billy. He stood aside and Gammidge stumped in, to what purpose Billy wasn't sure. Company would be welcome, at least. Turns out his imagination wasn't so dormant a critter as his fifth-grade teacher, Mrs. Billington, had led him to suppose. It had been having a field day.

"No fire on a night like this?" said Gammidge in disbelief. "It can't be more than two degrees outside." Or inside, he added to himself as he took in his surroundings.

One thing Billy had noticed in his study of human nature was that people loved to talk about the weather. Most often it was the first thing they talked about when meeting and the last thing when parting. It's just about all anyone ever spoke to him about. "Cold out, you say?" he remarked convivially.

"Very," said Gammidge. "If I were you, I'd have a nice roaring fire in that stove on a night like this." He nodded at the antique parlor stove in the middle of the room.

"That don't seem likely," Billy observed.

"Pardon?"

"It don't seem likely that if you was me you'd have a fire going."

"Why is that?" asked Gammidge, a little nonplussed.

" 'Cause I'm me, and I don't," Billy explained. "Then again, I ain't out on a night like this, so I wouldn't know."

Gammidge scratched his head. Twice. With a dubious glance or two he took in his surroundings. The first thing that struck him was that there were no interior walls. The two-by-four frame of the building was exposed, as was the insulation that had been stapled to it, its brown paper facing doing double duty as wallpaper. That was just as well, as it didn't seem to have much insulating to do.

The bare plywood floor was littered with debris that might have been reclaimed from the dump—a wheelless wheelbarrow, a doorless refrigerator—everything minus the thing that made it what it was. Things were outwardly recognizable but, for practical purposes, useless.

All this he took in at a glance. "Name's Gammidge," he said, holding out his hand.

Billy studied Gammidge's hand as if it had just materialized from thin air, independent of the body to which it was attached. He'd never shaken hands before, but he'd seen it done. He grabbed it solemnly with both hands and gave it a heave or two that nearly yanked Gammidge from his socks. "I'm Billy, Gammidge."

"You're a Gammidge, too!" said Gammidge, misunderstanding.

"Nope," said Billy, taking the question as if it followed naturally. "I'm a Billy."

Gammidge suddenly felt he was in the middle of a vaudeville routine without a script. He needed to get a handle on the conversation. "You were in bed, I see."

"Still am, mostly," Billy replied, shrugging his shoulders so the blankets billowed around him. "Here," he said, removing one of his layers and holding it out. "You look like you could use this."

Gammidge was too cold to stand on ceremony. He took the thick wool blanket and wrapped himself in it, then sat on an upturned crate near the stove, where it was easier to pretend he was getting warm.

Hosting company was new to Billy, but he knew the first thing that Matty always did when he was at her house was offer him food. "You want some meat loaf?" he said.

Gammidge followed his nod to a Tupperware container on a narrow pine shelf near the front door. The look of amusement he returned to Billy quickly dissolved before the sincerity evident on his face. "Ah . . . no. Thanks. I ate not . . . not long ago."

Billy nodded. He sat on the edge of his bed, wondering what he should do next.

Gammidge continued his visual inspection of the cabin and was just beginning to appreciate the collection of human flotsam—tin cans, tires, paper cups, bottles, boxes, and similar detritus of every description, all held to the stringers and studs by nails—when a peculiar tickling on his neck made him suddenly suspect he wasn't the only one of God's creatures enjoying the warmth of the blanket. He slipped it off and put it on the bed. "Well, thanks for your hospitality. Sorry I got you up and . . . and everything. I'm warmed up some, so I guess I'll be on my way." He edged toward the door.

"Where you going?"

"Oh, I've . . . just . . ." He nodded up Robert's Road.

Billy compressed his eyebrows in perplexity. "Ain't nothin' up that way. Just Robert's cemetery and the Bermann place." He considered the evidence. "You ain't dressed for a funeral, and you don't have any flowers, so you ain't goin' to the cemetery," he deduced aloud. "So you're goin' to the Bermann place."

Gammidge tried to respond, but his brain hadn't caught up with his mouth, so he just muttered.

"He's dead, you know," said Billy.

"Yes."

"That's where you're goin'?"

There was no point denying it. "Yes," said Gammidge, trying desperately to frame the response to the question he knew must inevitably follow.

It didn't.

"I'll go with you," Billy declared. He tossed off his blankets, revealing that he was fully dressed with the exception of his coat, hat, and mittens. These he retrieved from a bentwood hat stand that was propped against the wall, in concession to the fact that one of its legs was missing. Aside from the bed and the box, it was the only thing that could be described, however broadly, as furniture.

Billy opened the door and ushered his guest into the night.

"Don't you want to close your door?" Gammidge reminded him as they struck off across the ridged remains of Billy's garden.

Billy slowed his pace and thought this over. "Why?" he said finally.

As none of the pat answers seemed to apply, Gammidge fell in step behind his guide as they headed up the icy road.

Gammidge was glad for the company as the road descended through a tunnel of evergreens. He thought of the last time he'd come this way—only last year—to exhume a body. A shiver raced from the back of his neck to the base of his spine, and every instinct told him to turn and run.

Instinct. That's what the Professor had that he didn't. And it was Crisp's instinct that had Gammidge and his unlikely companion on this godforsaken stretch of road in the middle of the night. Oddly, there was some comfort in that. They walked on in silence, devoting most of their attention to staying upright on the rutted ice.

By the time they crested the final hill, the knowledge that the cemetery lay in the darkness off to their right chased all thoughts of the cold from Gammidge's mind.

"There's somebody there," said Billy.

Gammidge froze in his tracks. "Where?" he said, raking the

graveyard with the full beam of his flashlight.

"Not out there," Billy said. "That's just the cemetery."

Somewhat abashed, Gammidge turned the light on his companion's face. "Where?" he repeated.

Billy pointed toward the Bermann house. Thin slivers of light were leaking around the boards that covered the windows.

Gammidge clicked off the flashlight. "Who do you suppose would be up here this time of night?" he whispered rhetorically.

"We would," Billy replied with uncompromising logic.

Assuming an attitude of stealth—to the degree possible on glare ice—Gammidge crossed the yard to the kitchen window and pressed his face against a narrow seam between the boards. "Can't make out who it is," he said under his breath.

The words hadn't left his lips when a sudden scream impaled the moment on the night. Before Gammidge could respond, a muffled thud and the sound of footsteps in the house were punctuated by the riflelike report of the screen door as it slammed against the clapboards. A wild figure in oilskins burst onto the porch clutching something in its arms.

At that instant Gammidge found his tongue. "Hey!" He tried to turn on the flashlight, but his fingers, frozen despite the thick woolen mittens, refused to cooperate. The figure hesitated for a second, but by the time Gammidge managed to flip the switch it had fled, slipping and falling and clawing its way frantically across the treacherous ground, leaving in its wake a trail of papers that waved a gentle farewell.

Gammidge threw the weak beam of light into the darkness, but it failed to snare the figure, which by now had dragged itself to the head of the rutted road and was descending toward the graveyard.

Gammidge's next thought was of Billy. The thud he had heard just before the apparition appeared took on a sudden, sinister dimension. Bracing himself against the side of the house, he made his way to the porch, then pulled himself up the steps and across the ice-encrusted boards to where the door stood open like a wound.

"Billy?" he said, probing the darkness with the anemic shaft of light. "You in there?"

"I was, last I knew," Billy replied weakly.

Relief washed over Gammidge like a cool wave on a hot summer day, animating him from head to toe. With the light, he followed the voice to its source.

Billy lay on the floor by the desk with blood on his cheek and a look of profound bewilderment in his eyes. Gammidge rushed to his side and helped him to a sitting position. "Are you all right?"

Billy considered the question. "One and one is two. Two and two is four," he recited slowly. Satisfied that his senses had survived at the elemental level, he proceeded to higher mathematics. "Twelve times three is thirty-six. Four times nine is forty-nine."

"Thirty-six," Gammidge corrected worriedly.

"What is?"

"Four times nine is thirty-six."

"Same as twelve times three?" Raspberry.

"Same," said Gammidge.

"Then I guess I'm all right," Billy replied sincerely. "I always get that one wrong."

Gammidge would have laughed if his throat hadn't been stuffed with his heart. "What happened?"

"Good question," Billy replied slowly. "I figured the best way to find out who was in here was to ask 'em. I come through the door and she spun around like one've them Jewish things."

"She? It was a woman?"

"Most are, aren't they?" said Billy, worried that something fundamental to his understanding was about to be challenged. "Then she screamed."

Gammidge recalled the scream. He had been too shocked to notice at the time, but Billy was right. It was a woman. "Did you see who it was?"

Billy shook his head. "Not enough light, and she had that big hat on. I was just about to tell her it was only me when she hauls off and swipes at me with somethin'." He searched the floor with the negligible aid of Gammidge's rapidly weakening flashlight. "This, I bet," he said, picking up an old Underwood typewriter.

"She hit you with that?" Gammidge cried. "It's a good thing you're still alive."

"It's heavy," Billy reasoned, replacing it on the floor. "Took most of her strength just to swing it, I imagine. There wasn't much meat behind it by the time it got to my face."

Gammidge, not wishing to get too lost, retrieved a dangling thread of the conversation. "Jewish things?"

"You know," said Billy, making spinning motions with his forefinger. "Like a top."

"Oh, a dreidel."

"Dreidel," Billy repeated, his finger slowing its rotation. "I like that word. Learned it from the *Reader's Digest.* Dreidel. That's what she spun like."

"Well," said Gammidge after a thought-gathering silence. "It could've been a lot worse."

"You think so?" said Billy, massaging his cheek doubtfully.

"I mean, you could have been killed."

Billy thought about that. "Anyone could," he announced finally, "if you hit 'em hard enough."

Gammidge's boots weren't tall enough for these waters. "We'd best get you back to town and have the doctor look at you."

"I'm okay," said Billy flatly. "No sense wakin' up Doc. He ain't had a lot of sleep lately."

There wasn't much life left in the flashlight, but Gammidge applied it to a diligent search of the desk and its immediate environs.

"What're you lookin' for?" Billy asked.

"Well, it's kind of hard to explain," said Gammidge. "A set of numbers—maybe letters—written a long time ago by someone who wanted to keep them secret."

"Numbers? Like one, two, three?"

"Something like that," said Gammidge, pulling papers from the pigeonholes and probing the interior with the light. He got his face as close as possible to the opening and looked for the telltale code. "But not necessarily in order."

"Like a telephone number?" Billy asked.

Good analogy. "Just like a telephone number, Billy. That's what I'm looking for."

"There ain't no telephone up here," Billy observed. Gammidge ransacked the remaining surfaces as the light dwindled. "That's a joke," said Billy after a while.

Gammidge stopped what he was doing and held the flashlight up to his companion's face. Billy was smiling. "About no phone," Billy explained. "That was the joke part."

How much had been the joke part? Gammidge wondered. He laughed. It was too dark to do anything else. "Good joke, Billy. Well, if there's anything up here worth finding, we could be walking on it for all we know. We'd best head back."

"What do you s'pose she was after?" said Billy as they shut the door and descended the steps.

At that moment Gammidge stepped on a piece of paper. He picked it up. "She had an armload of these." A trail of similar papers stood out dimly against the icy earth. "They might tell us something. Give me a hand picking them up, will you?"

There weren't as many as he'd expected at first. Five in all between the house and the top of the hill. Gammidge held the specimens up to his eyes and pointed the flashlight at them, but it had ceased to be a tool and was now simply an accessory. He couldn't make anything out. "This feels like newspaper," he said. "Hard to tell. If you see any more along the way, pick 'em up."

There were none.

By the time they reached Billy's place, the inside of Gammidge's thighs were aching from the strain of opposing his muscles to the ice—a sensation he hadn't known since he was a kid, waking up sore after the first night of ice skating—but he wasn't cold anymore. In fact, he'd been sweating pretty profusely under the knit cap.

"Thanks, Billy," he said, groping for his companion's hand in the dark. "You go on back to bed and rest yourself. You sure you're going to be all right?"

"Not if you listen to most folks," said Billy enigmatically. He started down the narrow side trail that cut through the stand of sumac to his house. "That was another joke," he called behind him. Raspberry.

Gammidge descended into a hollow. By the time he reached the top of the next hill, a thick layer of high-altitude clouds had obliterated all the dim lights of heaven with one sweeping gesture and cast the island in a pitch of darkness more profound than any he'd ever known. Afraid he might wander off the road, he held his right hand—still armed with the sightless flashlight—in front of his face to shield himself from branches.

Somewhere up ahead, he recalled, there was a fork in the road. The left fork led back to town. He didn't know where the right fork led.

Even familiar places acquire sinister dimensions in the dark—his right shin bore permanent scars as testimony to the times he'd tried to negotiate his way to bed after the late news when his wife had turned off the reading light—and this was by no means a familiar place. His memory began sketching frantic abstracts in an unconscious effort to reconcile itself with his senses. Had the road been so rugged underfoot before? Had the trees crowded it so closely?

Was it the *right* fork that led to town?

He slapped the flashlight a couple of times, like a midwife trying to startle breath into the lungs of a stillborn babe. Nothing happened.

The darkness—abetted by unreasoning fear—assumed a malevolent personality, closing in on him from all directions with evil intent. He chided himself inwardly for the foolishness of the thoughts that churned unbidden in his brain, but he didn't rebuke them aloud, for fear that some voice in the night would reply in their behalf.

He took another step, and bashed his persecuted shin against an outcrop of granite. His leg jerked up reflexively. With an epithetical oath, he seized the offended limb with both hands, dropping the flashlight in the process.

In an instant it struck him as strange that there was no corresponding clatter of the light on the ground. It was as if, in the thick blackness that cradled him, the laws of physics had been temporarily suspended. Then came a wicked series of crashes and loud complaints as the flashlight beat itself to death on rocks far below. Twice before it expired, it flickered on, its impotent Mayday consumed by the uncaring darkness.

Carefully, as the realization of how close he'd come to grave danger bore in on him, Gammidge unbent, releasing his bruised leg and lowering it gingerly to the ground, as if it had been made of TNT. "Damn," he said. He would have said more, but his foot was no sooner planted than it slipped from under him as violently as if it had been pushed. His hands flung out instinctively. One of them seized a branch, which broke at his touch as the empty night grappled him to its frozen breast.

"Matty?" Crisp called from the top of the stairs.

Matty cascaded into the hall, drying her hands on her apron, her eyes wide with alarm. "Winston, what are you doing out of bed?" She started up the stairs. He knew she would pick him up bodily and carry him back to bed if she had to.

He stayed her advance with a raised hand. "I will, Matty. I will."

She stopped halfway up the stairs and looked at him doubtfully.

"Promise," he said, crossing his heart.

She relented. "Well, what are you hollerin' about? You okay?"

"Has Mr. Gammidge been by this morning?"

"Goodness no," Matty replied. After all, Gammidge was from the mainland. "I don't expect to see him before seven."

"No," said Crisp. "I suppose that's true."

"True as north," said Matty. "Now, you go back to bed and I'll send him up when he comes."

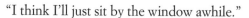

"I think I'll just sit by the window awhile."

"You'll do no such thing," Matty retorted, threatening to charge up the stairs, in which case Crisp knew he'd stand about as much chance as the Spanish on San Juan Hill. "I promise I won't open it," he said, adding under his breath "far."

"*You* promised you'd get right back to bed and *that's* the promise you're going to keep, young man," scolded Matty, flushed with glory. Winston needed taking in hand for his own good, and, by gorry, good is what he was going to get.

Crisp surrendered. "All right, all right," he said. There must be something poetic about being treated like a two year old at both ends of life, but he found great comfort in the fact that Matty really cared. Not too long ago he'd resigned himself to the likelihood that he'd have no one to care at this stage of life. Of course, he'd never expected to live this long.

Imagine, he'd outlived them all.

He wondered how maternal Matty would be, how much she would care for him, if she knew the truth about his past, all the people he'd hastened to the grave, all those faces that lined the corridors of his dreams.

"But you'll send him up as soon as he gets here?"

"I might, if you get back in bed by the time I count to ten."

Crisp defied her until six, but she stood her ground, so he turned and shuffled back to his room. "All right," he called. "I'm in bed."

"Good," said Matty, adding to herself, "see that you stay there." She wasn't going to press her luck.

An hour labored by during which Crisp stared out the open window at a world in which he no longer felt a part. The road crew excepted, there was virtually no traffic. No one afoot. Even the seagulls seemed to have found elsewhere to go. His anxiety rose with each passing minute. Gammidge should have come by now.

Hearing Matty's distinctive tread on the stairs, he hustled back to the bed and climbed in, the thick down comforter just settling into place as the door opened. "Winston?" she said, tapping softly as she entered. "You awa—" Then she saw the open window. "My good Lord, Winston," she said, flinging the door wide and marching across the room.

"Just a crack, Matty," Crisp complained. "For fresh air."

"That fresh air could freeze squid," Matty pronounced, closing the window. She wrinkled her forehead, wondering where that analogy had come from.

"Is Gammidge here?" Perhaps he'd nodded off for a minute and not heard the front door.

" 'Fraid not. I was thinking he probably slept in this morning. Could be he was up late last night. You know how they are."

By "they" Crisp knew she meant people from away, whose habits were far more nocturnal than hers and who, as far as she was concerned, represented a different branch on the tree of life than people on the island.

Not that she wasn't right.

"But Luther Kingsbury just called, looking for him. Said there was no sign of him down to the Tidewater. His bed hadn't been slept in and the mint was still on his pillow. Elaine says he was fierce for them mints."

That explained the disquiet that Crisp had felt. He'd sent Gammidge to his death.

CHAPTER

9

◆

"RACHEL CARLSON WAS HANGIN' OUT LAUNDRY when she heard this weird cry comin' over the creek," said Leeman Russell, leaning importantly against the counter and helping himself to a homemade sugar doughnut. "Thought it was a loon at first," he added. He took a bite of the doughnut and washed it down with a loud gulp or two of black coffee. The Island Grocery, where he worked, was closed because of the ice—for the second day in a row—so he'd be dividing his day between the diner and the pool hall, if it opened up. " 'Course after a second or two, she could tell it wasn't no loon. Then she figured out it was some-body callin' for help."

"That ain't the way I heard it," said Buddy Conway, managing—as with all his sentences—to make a single hurried word of the phrase. He gestured for more coffee, and his wife, Miriam, filled his cup. The name of the restaurant was Buddy's Come 'n' Get It, but anyone on the island would tell you it was Miriam who did most of the "getting" while Buddy pontificated from a well-worn stool at the end of the counter, near the cash register. He'd have responded similarly to anything said by Leeman, his second cousin on his father's side and fourth cousin once removed on his mother's.

"Well, I heard it right from Luther Kingsbury," Leeman protested. "He was the one she called to go up and check it out. I guess he ought to know."

"He don't know his ass from his uncle," Buddy replied disdainfully. He hadn't realized that Leeman's information was pretty much firsthand. The face-saving move had been reflexive. He tossed a nervous, demeaning laugh at the congregation of landlocked lobstermen, where it found no takers.

"Go on, Leeman," said Goose Mavery a tall, stoop-shouldered old man in faded denim overalls whose face reminded one less of a goose than a particularly reflective basset hound. Goose, well into his seventies, was on the road crew and had been clearing branches from the power lines for the last two days on about four hours' sleep. He and Earl would be at it again after coffee break, so they didn't have much time to catch up on the latest news. "You said Matty Gilchrist called Luther 'bout him, too. Why, do you s'pose?"

"The Professor must've put her up to it," Leeman speculated.

"How's he doing these days?" Earl asked softly. Elder Candage's voice—seldom heard outside the Latter Day Saints fellowship, where he preached gentle homilies on Sunday mornings, and the Memorial Day service at Carver's Cemetery—commanded a certain amount of attention.

Leeman had been meaning to drop in on Crisp one of these days. Now he wished he had. All he had to offer in reply was hearsay. "Gettin' better," he said abashedly. "Far's I know."

"Good," said Earl. "We've been praying for him."

Something in the delivery of the words made everyone look at the floor for a second. Goose tugged respectfully at the visor of his felt hat.

"What's that old coot got to do with anything?" said Buddy in

lieu of *amen*. "He's still mostly dead, ain't he? What would he care
if Gammidge turned up gone?"

"Half dead he's still got more sense than you do," Leeman said
sharply. It was an uncharacteristic retort, and he reretted having said
it but he was growing weary of defending Crisp to the feebleminded.
However, no one else dissented from the opinion.

"Got ya, Buddy," said Young Bennett, who was sitting next to
his grandfather, Old Bennett. His father's nickname had been Young
once, but now it was 'Tween, because the birth of his son put him
between his father and the new Young Bennett.

"You pay for that coffee yet?" Buddy demanded.

Young Bennett scrounged for a dime, but his grandfather came
to the rescue with two bits, which he slapped on the counter. "And
he'll have another. And so will everyone else while you're at it."

Miriam poured with a smile.

"Why else would she call Luther?" asked Leeman, more to himself than anyone else.

Goose caught Earl looking at his watch and knew he didn't have
much time to get the rest of the story. "He up to the medical center
now, that Gammidge fella?"

"Far's I know," said Leeman. It irked him not to have more firsthand news, but all the ice made it too hard to get around.

"I just can't figure what he was doin' way up there in the middle
of the night," said Goose. He drained the dregs from his mug and
labored to his feet. Earl was already halfway out the door. "Lucky
he didn't break his neck 'stead of just his leg."

Bergie Bergstrom had been quietly straining coffee though the
immense overgrowth of his black walrus mustache. "Could have
easy enough," he suggested, refilling his meerschaum pipe with the
Borkum Riff that he kept loose in the pocket of his plaid overcoat.
His voice was shaggy, as befitting the walrus he seemed, and when
his words finally found the air they were exhausted by the journey
around the pipe stem and through the underbrush. "Another twenty
feet that way and he'd've gone base over apex right off the cliff into

Indian Creek. Pretty lucky he just fell down that slag heap, if you ask me."

"Lucky man," echoed Goose before reluctantly departing in the closing wake of his fellow laborer. He slowed long enough to keep the door from slamming behind him.

Having informed Miriam that it was time to change the tank of gas that fueled the grill, Buddy took up Goose's theme. "What was he doin' up in that neck of the woods anyway? I thought he was s'posed to be investigatin' how Johnny Bermann died."

"Maybe he was," said Leeman.

"Well, someone ought to've given him a compass, then," Buddy retorted. "That's the wrong end've the island."

"He was prob'ly up to the Bermann place," Bergie speculated.

"What for?" said Buddy. "That ain't where he died."

Bergie shrugged his upper lip. "Seein' if he was up to anything that might get him killed."

"Killed?" said Buddy. "I thought he committed suicide."

"Had a heart attack," asserted his better half.

"Mighty strange way to die," said Bergie. "'Sides, why would Gammidge come over if it was just a suicide or a heart attack."

"Somebody killed him?" said Miriam hesitantly.

Buddy wasn't a ready convert to the notion. "Why would anybody kill him?"

"That's the whole point of what Bergie was sayin', ain't it?" said Leeman. "If Gammidge was lookin' around up to the Bermann place, maybe he was tryin' to find evidence of why someone would want to kill him."

"Like what?" said Buddy. "Just writin' a book, wasn't he?"

"'Bout his grandfather," said Leeman.

Miriam leaned over the counter, cradling her ample bosom in the crooks of her folded arms. "I seen on *Mannix* where this fella killed this fella 'cause he was writin' a biography . . . or autobiography. I always get them two confused. Which is the one you write about yourself? Auto, ain't it? Anyway, he was afraid there was goin' to be something bad about him in there . . . the second fella . . . 'cause of somethin' they did together when they was young. Robbed a bank, or somethin'. I don't remember. So anyways, he killed him." She snapped her fingers. "What if that's what happened with Johnny Bermann—somethin' like that?"

Buddy was about to find her something to do when she shot him a glance that twenty-seven years of marriage had taught him meant, just try it, bub. Having a well-developed instinct for survival, he edited on the exhale. "Why don't . . . what if that was a long time ago. Even if there was somethin' in there, who'd care anymore?"

"What was Rachel Carlson doing hangin' clothes in this weather's what I want to know," said Miriam as she turned toward the closet to check the gas. "And how'd she wash 'em in the first place, with the power down?"

Leeman wiped the powdered sugar from his mouth with his sleeve. "Depends on what it was, I'd say. No way of tellin' what he might've turned up."

Buddy shook his head. "I don't see it. Too long ago. You can't be talkin' 'bout nothin' so important that anybody'd care 'bout it after all this time."

"I don't know about that," said Bergie. "People have secrets, you know."

"That's just what I mean. Who'd care about any secrets people had a hundred years ago?"

"Ain't a hundred," said Leeman. "We're talkin' the First World War. That's only fifty or sixty years ago." He wasn't sure which.

"Might as well be a hundred for all anybody cares," said Buddy, who hated to see a good argument bogged down by facts. "No sir. Whatever got him killed, it didn't have nothin' to do with what he was writin'. Couldn't've."

"You can't say that for sure," Leeman countered. "I think there's more to this than meets the eye, and I'd just as soon not toss the baby out with the bathwater." He felt the reason that cliches became cliches was because they were heavy with meaning. Having woven two into a single sentence constituted, he felt, the equivalent of a verbal sledgehammer.

"Some sad, I'd say," said Miriam. Checking to see if the gas was flowing, she turned on a burner and held a match to it. When it caught, she blew out the match and shut off the burner. "Johnny Bermann, I mean. Him dyin' like that up there all alone. Nobody should die like that."

"Don't make no sense," said Buddy. "One shoe off and one shoe on."

"Diddle-diddle-dumplin', my son John," said Miriam. "Some queer, I call it." She took some bacon off the grill and set it in neat rows on a stack of paper towels.

Crisp's relief was soul deep. "I don't think I've been so glad to hear anything in my life, Leeman," he said. "Just a sprained leg, you say?"

"Pulled tendon, Doc Pagitt says," said Leeman, sipping the hot tea that had somehow manifested itself at his elbow not five minutes after he'd taken a seat at Crisp's bedside. A little skim milk and two heaping sugars, just the way he liked it. "Left leg. Thought it was broke at first, they did. But I just been up there and saw him myself. Talked to Doc, too. So I got it firsthand." There was a subtle note of pride in his voice. Let Buddy try to doubt him now. "Just a pulled tendon," he said, massaging the back of his leg, "here, behind his knee."

Crisp absorbed the information. "Fell down a hole, you say?"

Leeman nodded. "He was up to the Bermann place, for some reason."

"You don't say," said Crisp. He sipped his tea thoughtfully. Not much transpired on the island that Leeman Russell was not privy to. As such, he was an invaluable resource and, carefully played, could be Crisp's arms and legs, so long as he was made to feel that the initiation was his.

" 'Course it was pitch black, like it has been every night since this goshdarn ice storm. Seems his flashlight petered out on him on the way back, and he took the wrong turn up to the head of Indian Creek. You know, where the road forks there? So he ended up down by the slag heap near the quarry." Leeman used his free hand to swoosh the air. "And down he goes, right up to here." He drew a line across his upper thigh. "Couple more inches and he'd've been the last of his line."

Crisp chuckled encouragingly.

"Doc Pagitt said that," said Leeman, always ready to give credit where credit was due.

"Nothing broken, though?"

Leeman shook his head. "Nope. Bruised some bad, though."

"I'm sorry to hear it." His sorrow was genuine, though heavily mingled with relief. "On the way back, you say?"

"Yup. Oh, I almost forgot," said Leeman, removing a knot of papers from the left-hand pocket of his coat. "He give me these to give you."

Crisp's heart picked up its pace. "What are they?" he asked as he reached for them without any great show of interest.

"Don't know. Old newspapers, looks like," said Leeman, who was not interested in any information that had been lying around long enough to have been written down. It smacked of history, his worst subject in high school. "He just told me to give 'em to you."

Crisp glanced at them as he slid them onto the table. "I'll get to them eventually," he said, feigning lack of interest. "He didn't mention anything about numbers, did he?"

"Numbers? What kind of numbers?"

"Just that he'd mentioned something about numbers," Crisp replied vaguely.

Numbers suggested Leeman's second-worse subject, math. "Nope. No numbers. Not that I remember."

"Oh," said Crisp, trying to conceal his disappointment. "Well . . ." He thought a moment. "Tell me something, Leeman," he said finally. He lowered his voice, inclined his body from the waist up toward his guest, and tilted his good ear in his direction, establishing an air of confidentiality, even secrecy. "What do you know about Mr. Bermann?" It was important to know what Leeman knew, because it would soon be common knowledge.

"Johnny?" said Leeman, taking a bite of one of Matty's chewy gingersnaps and casting a sidelong glance of curiosity at Crisp's left hand, where the finger used to be. "Well, now, his family goes back a long way, you know."

Crisp leaned a little more. "Tell me their story."

Fifteen minutes later, having stopped to correct himself numerous times regarding the names of specific family members and their relationships with one another, Leeman had exhausted his general knowledge of the Bermann family, up to and including that morning's dispute with Buddy Conway.

Halfway through the monologue, Crisp had straightened up, settled back onto his pillows, and closed his eyes. Every now and then, however, he'd softly say, "Is that so?" or "Well, I didn't know that," which was sufficient to keep the story flowing—a story that, Crisp imagined, pretty closely resembled the one he could extract from anyone in town regarding Johnny's history since leaving the island with his father. The one drawback, of course, was that none of Leeman's information was firsthand. He was too young. If only he could get down to the hardware store or the pool hall, whose denizens were of sufficient antiquity to have been alive at the time. He had no doubt that, whether they were conscious of it or not, they possessed information that would fill in some very important lacuna in the narrative.

"Bermann was in the navy, you say?"

"Army, Professor," said Leeman, taking a final sip from a teacup that had been empty for some time. He leaned toward Crisp and raised his voice. "I said he was in the army."

"Oh, yes," Crisp agreed. "So you did. And in London during the war."

"London, England," Leeman added for clarity. "That's right."

Crisp's thoughts drifted to London during the war. After thirty days of continuous bombardment, St. Paul's, Westminster Abbey, and the Houses of Parliament presided miraculously over thousands of charred acres, the soulless stumps of buildings and debris that the city had become.

During the day, inhabitants wandered aimlessly through the rubble, listening for the cries of loved ones that never came, sifting the stones and concrete for anything tangible to confirm the notion—harder to imagine every day—that there had been a world before the war. Most able-bodied men and women, as well as whatever older children hadn't been shuttled off to the countryside, were employed in clearing certain streets so that official cars and emergency vehicles could thread the wounded wasteland with painful stitches of alarm.

At night, they huddled in tube stations and in makeshift tents along the promenade by the embankment, refugees among the ruins of their homeland. There they sang songs with subdued courage, allowed themselves to be subjected to patriotic sermons and propagandist speeches, and awaited the air-raid sirens.

A gray-faced man had stopped Crisp one day as he hurried through the blackened dreamscape. " 'Scuse me, sir," said the man. Ordinarily Crisp wouldn't have stopped, but the man succeeded in grabbing his sleeve when he had slowed to negotiate a small forest of reinforcing bars.

"What is it?" Crisp snapped.

"Oh, you're a Yank."

"Well?"

"Never mind, then," said the man. "I was wonderin' if this was Milk Street." He surveyed the wreckage of his neighborhood, his heart stunned beyond tears, his eyes acquiring the blank look of the utterly misplaced that Crisp had come to know so well. "I come to find my house," the man said, more to the wasteland than to Crisp. "I can't even find the road."

Crisp, stung by the almost mindless look of abandonment in the man's eyes, shook himself free and hastened on his errand. Precious time had already been lost.

Once at 19 Kettering Square, across from the entrance to the War Rooms, he clawed through the ruins of the gatekeeper's cottage on a little island on the edge of the Serpentine. "The bedroom," he said, ransacking the wreckage of the house with his eyes. "How in hell am I supposed to know where . . ."

Then he saw the wood door, still half on its hinges, with the *V* scratched on it. It splintered against the wall as he charged into the room. An old mattress lay partially buried beneath the crumbled remains of the ceiling. Almost like a madman—his heart pounding and beads of salty sweat forming on his forehead despite the frigid air of an English midwinter day—he dug away the timbers and plaster with his bare hands, stopping frequently to glance at his watch. Finally he was able to lift the edge of the mattress. He thrust his arm beneath it, his fingers searching blindly. When they touched the cold steel of a rifle barrel, he froze for a moment and took a deep breath. He was about to engage in a gamble that could change the course of the war. He'd need a steady hand.

No sooner had he settled himself behind the remains of the bedroom wall and affixed the scope to the rifle than the black Rolls, its headlights constricted to slits with black tape, and all but the driver's window covered with black paper, purred into view at the far end of Regent Street and, right on cue, turned toward the War Rooms.

Crisp brushed a few shards of glass from the windowsill and rested the rifle barrel on it. He nuzzled the gun stock between his cheek and shoulder and rested the ridge of his right eyebrow against the scope. It was the only thing that didn't condense with moisture upon coming into contact with his superheated flesh because he had brought the scope with him.

The limousine came to a stop just as he brought the crosshairs into focus. He quickly scanned the car from front to back, aligned the gun sight with the rear window of the car, took a few deep breaths, and waited.

Every day at 4:45 P.M., Winston Churchill emerged from the War Rooms and made his way to Buckingham Palace for his five o'clock conference with the king. Every day but today. Crisp raised his left wrist to his left eye and, without lowering the weapon, quickly glanced at his watch. It was 4:48. Three minutes late.

4:49 came and went. 4:50. 4:51. Crisp tried to blink the sweat from his eyes. 4:52. 4:53. The minutes dragged by like a march of one-legged men. He'd gotten his breath back and was able to hold the barrel reasonably still, but he was feeling sick to his stomach and could hardly swallow around the knot of tension that had risen to his throat. 4:54.

A loud clank shot through the silence of the neighborhood as someone inside threw the bolts on the door of six-inch-thick steel plate. This was it.

A moment later, Churchill, surrounded by an entourage of generals and bowler-hatted functionaries and ministers, emerged, squinting, into the pale dome of daylight. Crisp framed him perfectly in the crosshairs, which were now rock steady.

Customarily the small cadre of bodyguards surrounded the prime minister and shuttled him into his car in no more than three seconds. Today, however, they hung back a little, because Churchill seemed to linger. He stepped to the edge of the sidewalk, relit the cigar upon which he'd been chewing, and ran his clear, beady eyes around the environs of Green Park, as if thinking that perhaps he'd do a painting of it one day.

Churchill's line of sight was quickly drawing abreast of the gatekeeper's cottage. Just as it did, Crisp squeezed the trigger three times in rapid succession.

Churchill crumpled to the ground.

Crisp fired three more shots at the rear window of the limousine to buy an extra second or two. Then, leaving the empty rifle resting on the window ledge, he was out the back of the cottage.

There had been no time to rehearse the escape. Crisp cursed the gray-faced man as he scrambled over the remains of a wood outbuilding, but he more deeply cursed himself. Always allow time for the unexpected, always a minute or two for the gray-faced men who pop up in the midst of the best-laid plans.

Seconds later the sickening thud and ricochet of bullets could be heard all around him, followed immediately by the distant reports of the pistols that sent them. Only pistols, at least, thought Crisp. It would take a lucky shot; already he was almost out of range.

A gaggle of geese, apparently more alarmed by a gangly fugitive hurtling through their midst than by the war in general, dispersed before him squawking and scolding as he jumped into the frigid water on the far side of the island. Up to his knees, he plunged headlong across the narrow tail of the Serpentine to the small wood on the opposite side where, if God was in His heaven, a car would be waiting.

That day, God was in His heaven.

The next morning the newspapers throughout the land exclaimed news of the assassination attempt in hundred-point bold type. By day's end, Britain had been roused from its stultifying miasma of defeatism and lethargy to proclamations of solidarity that would, ultimately, give birth to almost superhuman acts of national will.

The mission had been a success. Churchill could play the British like a harp.

". . . He wasn't a soldier though," Leeman was saying. "Not a regular soldier, anyway. Had flat feet or somethin'. Far's I understand, he was a translator. He grew up speakin' German, you know."

"I see," Crisp replied, a little more sleepily than he'd intended. It was a long way from London to the present.

Funny, Leeman hadn't noticed the lines of fatigue around the old man's eyes before. Must be the light. He remembered Matty's injunction to keep the visit short, and he wasn't willing to risk her wrath. "I gotta go," he said, taking a futile sip at the empty china cup and placing it in its matching saucer. "Matty'll have my hide."

A smile tugged at the corners of Crisp's mouth. "We can't have that."

Leeman slapped his knees and stood up. "Well, you take care of yourself, Professor. Now I've seen you I can tell everyone you'll be up and around in no time." He cast a casual glance out the window. "Best you stay in bed now, though. All that ice out there. You ain't missin' nothin'." He started for the door, but something occurred to him as he reached for the knob. "Professor?"

Crisp beckoned the question with his eyes.

Leeman hesitated. He'd been told not to say anything that might get Crisp excited, but he just had to know. "What do *you* make of Johnny's dyin' up there like that?"

"Well, Leeman, I'll just have to think about that awhile," said Crisp, pushing his gold-rimmed glasses down his nose and staring over them. "But I wouldn't be surprised if we can work it out."

"We?"

"If you're willing to help me."

"You serious?"

"As a funeral," said Crisp, repeating a phrase that seemed to carry a good deal of weight at the pool hall.

Leeman would much rather bathe in the reflected glory of a firsthand account of a newsworthy event than take an active part in it, especially if participation suggested either discomfort or danger, but sometimes one had to make sacrifices for one's art. "Okay, Pr'fessor. What do you need me to do?"

"MIM AND PORTEOUS HINKLEY'S DAUGHTER BETH, who is just three years old, was rushed to the hospital on the mainland in Puppy Ledbetter's lobster boat last Tuesday evening," Crisp read from the *Spectator*. "Seems she got a peppermint candy stuck in her nose and no amount of coaxing would get it out. Mim says Beth's sworn off peppermint. Pup says he stopped to haul a few traps on the way back. The *Spectator* wonders if, given the fact it was a moonless night, Pup could be sure they were all his.

"Speaking of momentous events on the mainland, the Penobscot Sluggers proved poor houseguests for the three teams that hosted games this weekend. Friday night Camden's Screaming Eagles got their wings singed in a 19–3 rout by our 'batty' boys in blue. Saturday morning saw them off to a slow start against Rockland High School's Dockers. (The *Spectator* wonders if there might have been just a tad too much celebrating at the Thorndike the night before—you know how the city lights affect us islanders!) However, they clawed their way to a 14–12 come-from-behind win in the last of the ninth in their conquest of big game. Dan Arey brought out the big guns, putting the ball over the left-field fence three times in all. Finally, Sunday afternoon (thanks in no small part to Walt Burgess' fast ball, the *Spectator* is told) our fishermen filleted Belfast's Great White Sharks 21–0."

The dateline read Tuesday, September 10, 1935. Crisp's vague recollection of Porteous Hinkley was of a very large, pleasant-faced boy who, though eight to ten years old at the time, sucked his thumb in public with blissful insouciance.

Crisp finished scanning the brittle yellow pages of the single-sheet newspaper, one of five in the bundle that Gammidge had forwarded through Leeman. None of the composite names rang a bell; most of them came from the "interCrispian" period of island life— all those years he'd been away. Yet the family names were familiar enough.

There was no byline for the *Spectator* column. Self-preservation, thought Crisp with a smile. He wondered how long the writer had managed to keep his identity secret. It was definitely a man.

Pencil marks here and there suggested that Johnny Bermann had used the papers for part of his research. Crisp was about to put the papers in chronological order and read through the checked items when a headline caught his attention.

" 'Cailey Hall Still Missing,' " he read aloud. The words had been heavily underlined. Gently, he flattened the page against his lap table and studied the article. "Miss Cailey Hall, 17, daughter of Mr. & Mrs. Dan Hall, went missing Saturday night and has not been seen or heard from since. She was last seen leaving the Nostalgia Dance at the Memorial Hall, during the eleven o'clock intermission, by her best friend Connie Dickey. Miss Dickey, according to Constable Stu Mullins, said Miss Hall seemed nervous and excited, but hadn't taken her into her confidence as to the cause. Miss Dickey reported that this is significant, since the two had never had secrets from each other.

"Shortly after eleven, according to Miss Dickey, Miss Hall went up Main Street in the direction of Pequot, where she lives, insisting that Miss Dickey not follow. This, too, is singular, Miss Dickey asserts, as the two are customarily inseparable."

A crease ran through the next paragraph from which a network of tiny veins spread out in all directions, making the print nearly illegible. Holding the paper under the light, Crisp squinted at it for all he was worth.

"It is common knowledge," he read, "but no less noteworthy for the fact, that most of the town turned out to conduct a search for the young woman when her mother reported her missing at two o'clock Sunday morning. Almost to the exclusion of all other business, the search has continued, day and night, since then.

"This correspondent joins the family and the community in most heartfelt prayer that the headline in this paper next week will read 'Cailey Hall, Found Alive and Well!'"

The article was circled in pencil, beneath which someone, presumably Johnny Bermann, had recently scrawled hastily in pencil: "She's on James Island. Southwest."

"Winston!"

Matty's voice dragged him unceremoniously back from the past. "It's nearly noon. Have you taken your pill?"

"I will, Matty," Crisp replied, still suspended between the past and the present.

"Winston? Did you say something?"

"I'll take it now," he called to her. He unscrewed the top from one of the two bottles at his bedside.

"The white one," Matty reminded him with an operatic trill. "Not the green one."

"Not the green one," said Crisp under his breath, inspecting the green pill in his hand. "I wonder if it makes a difference." He took the green pill in protest and washed it down with a gulp of water. He waited a second. He was still alive. "Okay. It's gone."

"Good," Matty replied from the foot of the stairs. "I'll be up with lunch soon's that's had a chance to settle."

There was no doubt that Matty's motherliness could be somewhat suffocating at times, but Crisp nipped a nascent bud of resentment, reminding himself that if it weren't for her, he wouldn't be alive. Besides, she really did do all things for his own good, although, like the Lord, she worketh in mysterious ways her wonders to perform. He cast a quick, guilty glance at the bottle of white pills as he placed the bottle of green ones beside it. "I'm a crabby old fart," he said aloud.

"Toasted ham and cheese," Crisp could hear Matty sing as she toddled back to the kitchen, "and tomato soup."

Crisp smiled. He liked tomato soup. Fixing his glasses a little more firmly on his nose, he resumed reading. A number of small advertisements brought to mind businesses that had burst briefly into flower and withered in the chilly autumn of the Great Depression. Odd designation, thought Crisp of the word *great*. The Great War. Merely the prelude to a greater war. The Great Depression. Who knew? The Greater Depression? The Greatest Depression?

Rabbit trails. The landscape of his brain was littered with them. Somehow he'd always managed to bypass them. But with age came an almost insuperable compulsion to run them down, to follow that curious inclination of the head toward the imagined voices that beckoned from just a little farther that way.

What difference did it make what path he chose? Didn't they all lead to the same place? Wasn't there a cozy oblong hole at the end of each?

Johnny Bermann had known where Cailey Hall was.

The thought scurried across one of the trails, seizing his attention. He opened his eyes, which he hadn't realized were closed, and shook his head.

Pulling himself to a sitting position on the edge of the bed, he dipped a washcloth into the basin of cold water on the bedside table and swabbed his face. Icy fingers surged deep into his brain and tore away the cobwebs.

"Where was Johnny Bermann in"—he glanced at the dateline again—"September 1935?" he said aloud. Marshaling the few facts he recalled from the obituary in the *Rockland Telegraph,* he did some simple math. "He would have been twenty or twenty-one. Cailey . . . ," he consulted the *Spectator,* "seventeen. The Bermann estate is in the general direction of Pequot."

Talking aloud helped him focus his thoughts.

"Here we go," said Matty, bursting into the room with the dinner tray. Crisp, once professionally and constitutionally impervious to shock, leapt in his skin. The ensuing realization that he must have been down rabbit trails a lot longer than he'd thought was not a comforting one.

"What are you doing half out of bed, Winston?" she said, her suspicion thinly veiled. She stole a quick glance at the window and the row of pipes and sniffed the air for telltale signs of Edgeworth. Everything was satisfactory. Still, Winston had worked for the government. Like the IRS, he had ways.

"Just washing my face." His voice, despite his best efforts, was a little shaky. He swung his legs back under the covers, arranged his blankets the way Matty liked them, and replaced the lap table over his legs. "That smells good, my dear."

She set the tray on the table. "See that you eat every bit of it." She tucked a napkin down the neck of his green-and-white-striped pajamas, spread it over his chest, and was just about to straighten out his blankets when she saw the paper. "My goodness gracious— the *Spectator.* Where on earth did you get this old thing?"

He would have responded, but she was already immersed, reading bits and pieces aloud, laughing, editorializing, commiserating. "Oh, my goodness. Wasn't that some terrible," she said, lighting on the front page of the issue that Crisp had been reading. "Cailey Hall. Poor thing. You know about that?"

"I just read it. All I know is what's there."

Matty reviewed the article. "That's it in a nutshell, far's I know," she said. "Disappeared. 'Course she's dead, poor thing. Prob'ly

fell down a hole somewhere that night, just like Mr. Gammidge did.
One've these days some kid'll be climbing around the rock piles
and . . ."

She shivered.

Crisp felt there was more, so he lubricated the brief silence with
a dose of commiseration. "Sad."

Matty shook off a personal reverie and came back. "Ayuh. Some
sad. I remember that next day, the whole town turned out, like it
says there. Constable Mullins got us all together up by the flagpole
and divided us into groups.

"Our job with the lady's auxiliary was to search from the bog
down back of the church, across the head of Indian Creek, over to
the slag on the side of Armburst Hill. I remember like it was yesterday."

"And no one found anything?"

"Nope," Matty replied sadly, adding a quick "nope" on the
inhale. "It was like she vanished. 'Course, after that everyone figured she'd turn up in the tide somewheres. I tell you, more than
most of the lobstermen didn't much want to go out for a few days.
Nobody wanted to find somethin' like that in their pot warp.

"Anyway. She didn't. That's why I figure she must've fallen
down a hole somewhere that none of us could find her."

"Who searched James Island?" Crisp wondered.

"James Island? Why would anyone look way out there? Says
right here," said Matty, tapping the paper, "she was last seen headin'
uptown, to Pequot."

"*Toward* Pequot," Crisp corrected.

"That's what I said," said Matty. "To Pequot. She'd've turned by
the fountain or down Clamshell Alley if she was going to James
Island."

"So nobody searched in that direction?"

" 'Course not," said Matty. She almost added, you poor thing,
but managed to keep the addendum to herself. She fluffed his
pillow instead.

"Did you know her?"

Matty, feeling that this was the closet thing to an invitation she was likely to get, sat on the edge of the bed. "I knew who she was," she said. "Knew her to say hello to and whatnot, if that's what you mean. But I was in my thirties by that time. She was just a teenager."

"Seventeen," said Crisp.

"Seventeen," Matty echoed, making a requiem of the word. "I knew Audrey and Dan, her parents. You knew Dan, didn't you?"

"Not that I recall."

Matty sorted out the chronology. "No. I guess not. He was a couple years younger than me. That'd make you ten or eleven years older.

"Anyway, her mother, Audrey, was from over to East Haven. She was a Bennett."

"Are they still on the island?" The unspoken question was, what became of them? Crisp knew that if they were still in town he'd have heard of them. But even with an islander as free with information as Matty, it helped to approach things from a position of supposed ignorance.

"Goodness, no," Matty replied, tying off the exclamation with just the faintest trace of a titter. "They went back up to East Haven and took over her folks' place when they died or moved to Florida." In Matty's mind the distinction, if any, was slim.

"What was she like, this . . ."

"Cailey?" said Matty.

"Yes. Cailey. What was she like?"

"Pert, I'd say," Matty replied with almost nervous haste. "I was just thinkin' that's a word you hear sometimes, and I don't guess it's always complimentary, but it's not bad in her case. That's what she was. Pretty in a plain way. Turned-up nose. Blue eyes. Hard worker," she added, saving the highest encomium for last. "All them Halls work hard."

"What exactly do you mean by 'pert'?"

"Well," Matty studied the question a moment. "Light. Carefree.

I don't remember seein' her when she wasn't laughing and happy. That kind of girl."

"Pert?"

"Pert," Matty reiterated. " 'Course—"

Crisp sensed a hesitation. "Of course, what?"

"Well, it's not somethin' I like to say."

"Let me guess," Crisp ventured. "She had a reputation?"

Matty's busy hands came briefly to rest in her lap. She bowed her head slightly and allowed her reticence to reply.

"I see," said Crisp. Little doubt, then, what she was excited about that night she left the dance. "I don't suppose you'd know if she was seeing anyone in particular at the time." Matty's reaction told him at once that the question had been too direct.

Sensing that Winston's interest was too much for his own good, she stood up and, with two quick brushes at her apron front, swept up the subject and prepared to return it to the dustbin of memories.

"Not that I know of. 'Course, I wouldn't know," she declared. "That was a long time ago." She began to scoop up the newspapers. "If you want somethin' to read, I can get you—"

Crisp detained her with a touch. "No. Leave them, please. I find they tell me a lot about the island that I didn't know."

She was skeptical. "Too much, maybe," she said. Nevertheless, she relented. She folded the papers neatly and stacked them one atop another in chronological order. "You didn't tell me where you got them."

"Leeman brought them."

"Leeman?"

"From someone else who has an interest in island history."

"Someone else?"

"One of the boys," said Crisp, using the term Matty applied to anyone over sixty who spent most of his time at the hardware store.

"You'd think they'd have somethin' better to do," said Matty. She'd have said the same if they spent their time redeeming the lost in the slums of Calcutta. "Your soup's gettin' cold."

He took an appeasing spoonful or two. She was right. Cold. "Have you heard anything about the power?" He said conversationally.

"They say Beelzebub will be up and runnin' sometime tonight or tomorrow, but only half the town's gettin' power at a time. As far as anyone knows, we'll get it on this side of the bridge from six in the mornin' 'til two in the afternoon. They'll have it on the other side from then 'til midnight. That ought to hold us 'til they fix the cable from the mainland. Sometime next week they say. I was talkin' to Phyllis Clayton down at the post office, and she said . . ."

Phyllis Clayton apparently had a lot to say, which was fine with Crisp. During the retelling, he leafed casually through the papers until he found the one he was looking for. He opened the page and, with seeming indifference, ran a forefinger slowly back and forth beneath an underlined segment of text. He moved his finger to the rhythm of Matty's monologue, which in time drew Matty's unconscious attention. "Who is it wrote all over them papers, Winston?" she said at last, interrupting herself. "Wasn't you, was it?" Despite all the changes in the world lately, what with instant pudding and women setting fire to their underwear, she couldn't help but feel there was something almost sacrilegious about writing on printed pages.

"Pardon?" Crisp said, as if his mind had been elsewhere. "Oh, no. They were like this when I got them." He continued massaging the words.

"Lou Ann O'Connor," Matty read, furrowing her brow. "I know that name."

"Pardon?" said Crisp sleepily.

"This name that's underlined," said Matty, brushing his finger aside. "Lou Ann O'Connor."

Crisp looked at the paper. "I don't recall hearing it."

"It's not an island name. She was a summer girl back about that time. Used to babysit for one've the families up to the Thoroughfare. Called her a governess, but she was a babysitter. I remember you'd see her in town with the kids more often than you'd see most folks from that end of the island. Spent a lot of time with 'em up at the quarry. She was real friendly. Very polite."

"What family did she work for?" Crisp asked, with only conversational interest.

"Oh, gorry. Now isn't that funny, I don't remember," Matty said, with an authoritative pat to the pillow and another to a wayward wisp of hair on her forehead as she stood. "Comfy?"

"Perfectly," said Crisp. "Perfectly comfy."

"Anybody to home?" The voice, not readily identifiable to either Crisp or Matty—as evidenced by their exchange of puzzled glances —came from the foyer.

"Now who do you s'pose that is?" said Matty.

"Professor?" came the voice again, a little nearer this time.

Crisp knew the voice. The breath smelled of smoke and Moxie. And the esses, making their way around the four teeth that occupied the speaker's mouth, gave it away. "Sylvester Hutchin," he said.

"Gilbert Hutchin?" said Matty in disbelief, calling the visitor by his proper name, which Crisp had never heard. She made her way toward the door. "What on earth do you s'pose he's doin' here? Next thing you know we'll hear the Pope's playing eight ball down to the pool hall."

Stuffy was standing at the bottom of the stairs, his felt hat crumpled in his hands, when Matty stepped onto the landing. It struck her instantly that he looked more like a fish out of water than a fish out of water, so, natural hostess that she was, she endeavored to put him at ease. "Come on, Gilbert," she said, as if he was a frequent visitor. "Did I hear you call for Winston?"

"Hi, Matty," said Stuffy. He'd heard from Crisp that Matty didn't allow smoking in the house, so he'd stubbed his cigarette outside. He felt naked without it in the corner of his mouth. "I hear he's doin' better."

"He is," said Matty. "Thank the Lord."

For the next moment or two, neither seemed sure what to say.

"Can I see him?" he asked.

Matty was flustered. Why all the sudden interest in Winston? Where were all these people during the long months he'd been comatose? she wanted to ask, but Stuffy preempted her. "I got somethin' for him." He produced a crumpled brown paper bag, clearly containing a bottle, from beneath his hat.

"What's in there?" Matty asked with sharply rising suspicion.

Stuffy withdrew the bottle and held it aloft for her inspection. "Moxie. Brenda sent it up from Tib's."

"The pool hall's open?"

"Not exactly," Stuffy replied. "Furnace is out."

"I thought so."

"Pipes burst, apparently. She was down there, Brenda was, and saw things in the fridge was frozen solid." He held the Moxie bottle up to the hall light and, shutting one eye tight, cast the appraising squint of a connoisseur over it with the other. "It's mostly thawed now." He lowered the bottle. "I put it under the woodstove down to the shack for an hour or so."

A gift. This complicated things. Blank refusal and an invitation to come back some other time were clearly impossible. "Just a minute," Matty said. "I'll see if he's up to it."

She bustled back to Crisp's bedroom door and tapped lightly. "Winston?" she said, poking her head into the room. "You up to another visitor?"

The response her eyes pleaded for was, no more visitors today—I really think I should just do as you say and get to sleep once I've finished my lunch. Crisp knew that. But a visit from Stuffy was something out of the ordinary. Absent the pleasure of being bested at cribbage, it was the next best thing to visiting the poolroom in person. "Send him up," said Crisp.

The defeat in Matty's eyes as she stared at him almost made him relent. Almost. "I'm fine, Matty. It'll be nice to see him."

CHAPTER
11

S TUFFY'S DISCOMFITURE WAS EVIDENT. He was a stranger in a strange land, and things such as doilies and hand-painted porcelain bric-a-brac filled him with a kind of domestic panic. The displaced creature sitting rigid in the ladder-back chair at Crisp's bedside bore very little resemblance to the supremely self-confident Stuffy of pool hall legend. Here, in Matty's domain, he was manifestly Gilbert.

Commiseration made stranger bedfellows than politics, thought Crisp. "This is a surprise," he said.

"No more to you than me," said Stuffy somewhat cryptically. He produced the bottle from the bag and set it on the beside table with a modicum of ceremony. "Moxie!" exclaimed Crisp. It was a treat to which even Matty couldn't object, because she was of the opinion that anything tasting that bad had to be beneficial to one's health. Crisp liked it. He twisted the bottle so the label was facing him. "Thank you."

Stuffy shrugged. "Brenda sent it. She was cleanin' out the fridge."

He explained about the burst pipes. "She'd've chucked it."

Crisp smiled deeply. "Well, it's nice of her to think of me. Now," he said, wanting to bring as quick an end as possible to Stuffy's suffering, "what's up?"

"Hmm?" said Stuffy, arrested in the discovery of his surroundings. "What?"

"I think we know each other pretty well, don't we?"

Stuffy nodded slowly, and a smile came to the corners of his all-but-toothless mouth. "I'd say so."

"Then let's have it."

Any reticence on Stuffy's part was quickly overcome. "I was up to the medical center, gettin' my prostrate checked—you ever have prostrate problems, P'rfessor?"

Crisp shook his head. "Thankfully, no." He doubted Matty would allow it.

Stuffy nodded again. "Well, anyway, I was up there this mornin', in the room next to Gammidge's—"

"Oh? Did you speak to him?"

"Not at first. I heard him talkin' to Leeman Russell. I know he give him somethin' to give you."

Crisp drew back the bedspread that he'd let fall casually over the newspapers. "These."

Stuffy took a pair of reading glasses from the pocket of his plaid flannel shirt, rested them on the end of his nose, and leaned toward the papers, squinting. "*Spectator*?" he said. He raised his eyes to meet Crisp's gaze with mild interrogation. "Ain't seen that in ages." He sat back in his seat, then folded the glasses carefully and returned them to his pocket. "Interestin' readin'?"

"Very."

Stuffy nodded, satisfied for the moment with the give-and-take. It was his turn to give. "When I was on my way out, I seen him in there. Thought I should find out how he was doin'. I 'spect Leeman told you?"

"Yes. He was here not long ago."

"I figured," said Stuffy, crumpling his hat in his lap. "Anyway, we talked a little. Nice enough fella."

This was high praise indeed, thought Crisp, from one so economical with it.

"Guess you've told him some about me, so he knew who I was."

"I'm sure I mentioned you," said Crisp. "He gave you a message for me?"

Stuffy abruptly sat up even straighter but quickly recovered from his demonstration of surprise, and stretched. "He did, as a matter of fact," he said with all the lack of interest he could muster. "Said you might want to know that Johnny's birthday was May 23."

"Did he mention a year?"

"Nineteen fourteen."

"Oh-five-two-three-one-four," Crisp abbreviated. His pulse quickened as he stole a covert glance at Old Man Bermann's codebook. "Would you write that down for me?"

"Already did," said Stuffy with a grin. He nodded at the brown paper bag. Crisp retrieved it from the bedside table and found 1914 scratched in pencil among the creases. It was his turn to nod. "There's somethin' else," Stuffy added.

Crisp queried him with a look.

"He says there was someone up there when he got there."

"At the Bermann place?" said Crisp with undisguised amazement. "Last night?"

Stuffy nodded.

"Who?"

"He don't know who she was."

"She?" Crisp echoed, his alarm growing. It would be a desperate woman indeed whose errand drove her out on such a night. That there were such women on the island, however, he knew firsthand. One of them had sent one of his fingers and two toes into the afterlife. He shuddered imperceptibly.

"According to Billy Pringle."

"Billy Pringle?" Crisp quickly realized that his every sentence lately had been a question. He held up a hand. "How about giving me the whole story."

"Thought I was," said Stuffy.

"Well . . . maybe it's my age, but I need a little more detail."

Stuffy decided this made sense. He rerelated the story with as much detail as he could recall. "So they chased her up toward the cemetery," he concluded. "But there wasn't no sign of her. Just them," he nodded at the papers on Crisp's lap, "far's I can tell."

"Poor Billy," said Crisp. "Is he all right?"

"Hard to tell with Billy," said Stuffy. "I seen him down to the shore catchin' tide crabs this mornin'. Seemed good as ever. I don't guess that one or two blows to the head make much difference to him, one way or the other."

"Well, I'm sorry to hear he was injured."

Stuffy, resting his elbow on his knee and cradling his chin in his hand, scrutinized Matty's invalid carefully. His was the only gaze, aside from Matty's, under which Crisp had ever felt any discomfort. "What do you make of it?"

"Of what?" Crisp replied vaguely. "Billy Pringle?"

"Nope," said Stuffy, letting his silence beg the remainder of the question. It was a technique that Crisp had used often over the years.

"Frankly, I'm not sure," Crisp relented, having lost the brief battle of wits that followed. His long convalescence had cost him his edge. "I get only bits and pieces up here."

"Like a dog on a leash," Stuffy philosophized.

Crisp felt it an apt, if not particularly poetic, analogy.

"What's Doc say?"

"I think he's as much intimidated by Matty's tyranny of mercy as I am," said Crisp. "I've talked to him about this business. He told me what he knew. What he says about my condition once he's out of the room . . ." Crisp shrugged. "He seems amazed I'm alive."

"I hear ya," said Stuffy, who shared the amazement. "So, what do you need?"

"How do you mean?"

"I mean," said Stuffy, rising slowly and walking to the window, "Johnny Bermann was murdered. Don't try denyin' it," he admonished as Crisp inhaled to do so, "and the trail's probably frozen solid, like everything else around here. Or soon will be." He turned from his perusal of the neighborhood. "Luther Kingsbury's a nice enough fella, but he ain't no Sherlock Holmes, if you get my drift." He was going to add that he ain't even Nancy Drew but thought better of it. "As for Nate Gammidge," he continued, "well, I got a lot of respect for a man who knows his limits. And since nobody up to Augusta cares about this case, I don't see much chance of it gettin' solved . . . without you."

Crisp felt curiously humbled by the compliment. "What do you suggest?"

Stuffy shuffled thoughtfully across the room, stopping at the foot of the bed. "You do the suggestin'," he said. "Then we'll go from there."

"Well," Crisp deliberated. "There are two things I'd like to look into."

"The body?" Stuffy hazarded.

"That's one," said Crisp, holding up one finger. "And the place it happened." He held up a second finger.

"Everette's."

It occurred to Crisp that it was a good thing there were only two points, because his third finger was missing. "Do you know anyone with one of those instant cameras?"

"A Polaroid? Luther has one."

"Luther Kingsbury?" Crisp couldn't keep the surprise from his voice. He hadn't imagined that the island police force was so technologically advanced. "Do you think he could take some pictures for me?"

"I said he had one," Stuffy replied, allowing a suggestion of his poolroom persona to surface. "I didn't say he knew how to use it." He cast a sly glance at Crisp. "I guess between the two of us we can make sense of it. You want pictures of the Everette place?"

"No," Crisp said. "The body."

A visible shiver coursed through Stuffy, but once committed he wasn't about to balk at an unpleasant task. "I'll talk to Charlie Williams."

"Has a funeral been scheduled?"

"Not so far as I know," said Stuffy. "Charlie wants to get the body over to the mainland for a proper autopsy, but that could be days with the ferry not runnin'. Airfield's layered with ice, too. Could be next week 'fore a plane can land unless we get a good thaw. Besides, I hear he's havin' a hell of a time tryin' to come up with family to tell him what to do."

"Has he checked with the school? Johnny was a professor at Dartmouth, I understand. Surely they'd have records of family."

Stuffy shrugged. "Dunno. I'll mention it." He turned to the task at hand. "I guess ol' Johnny's gonna stay put long enough for some pictures. What of?"

"Everything," Crisp replied solemnly. "Especially the feet and knees."

"You don't seem to have much trouble comin' by information up here," Stuffy remarked. "Why not pictures of Everette's, too?"

"I want to go there myself," said Crisp.

"You?" said Stuffy with alarm. Rumors he'd heard that Crisp was only inches from death didn't seem, upon presentation of the corpus delicti, much exaggerated. "It wouldn't be easy gettin' up there in the best of times for someone in your, well . . ."

"You don't think I'm up to it?"

Stuffy thought that was putting it kindly but didn't say so.

"I can't deny that," Crisp continued. "But if we're going to get to the bottom of this, I've got to see the place firsthand. There's too much a camera might miss." The doubt in Stuffy's eyes made him hesitate. "Don't you think we can come up with a way to get me there?"

As Stuffy stared at him in deliberation, Crisp realized what was odd about him—no cigarette. He'd never seen Stuffy without a

Camel, lit or unlit, dangling from the left-hand corner of his mouth.

"I reckon there's a way," Stuffy said at last. "Coke-Cola sign."

Crisp turned his good ear a little more toward the speaker. "Pardon?"

"Coke-Cola sign," came the confident reply. "My nephew got Ed White to give him the old Coke-Cola sign that used to hang outside the drugstore. It's metal, 'bout six feet long, three feet wide. Curled up at the ends like a flyin' carpet. Kids use it for a sled."

The light was beginning to dawn.

"I figure we can get most of the way in there in a good truck. Luther's got four-wheel drive. Then we can set you on that Coke-Cola sign and pull you up to the house. We'd have to bundle you up pretty good." He considered the patient doubtfully. "You sure you wanna do it?"

He was sure.

"When?"

Crisp looked out the window. It was already getting dark. "Tomorrow morning," he said. "By nine-fifteen?"

"What's she gonna say?" asked Stuffy, with a nod downstairs.

"She does her shopping every day at nine."

Stuffy grimaced. "Oh, by the way, did you know there was someone visitin' Johnny day 'fore yesterday?"

"Visiting? Who?"

"Don't know," said Stuffy. "Brenda says it was some fella from away. Fifty-five or so. Bald. He left on the last boat same day, just 'fore the ice set in."

Crisp worked on the code a long time. He eyes drifted perpetually back and forth between the numbers written in pencil on the brown paper bag and the handwritten note. It should have been easy, much easier than he was making it. Once, not long ago, he'd have been able to break it in minutes. Of course, he'd been mostly dead for the better part of a year, if that was any excuse.

He was having trouble staying focused. The harder he tried to concentrate, the less control he seemed able to exercise over his thoughts. Like mental shovels, they seemed prone to dig around in the past. Everytime he'd call them back to the present, they'd come dragging cartloads of memories behind them. Succumbing to an ineluctable weakness of age, his mind got on its knees and sifted through them—like a child under the tree on Christmas morning— turning over odd little nuggets he thought were long buried and gone.

He'd lived a very long time.

Back and forth went the little cart, deep into the dark recesses of his mind. Back and forth with odds and ends of his life. Little shreds of smells, tattered rags of sounds, broken bits of colored quartz that spun in the light of day, each facet presenting the briefest glimpse of a memory—only long enough to seem familiar—begging to be remembered before spinning away into the abyss forever. These were farewells. His memory was being erased.

Back and forth went the little carts. Back and forth.

Suddenly, as if struck by lightning, Crisp was shocked back to the present. As he came to consciousness, he realized that the back of his neck and shoulders still tingled, and he wondered if he'd fallen and hit himself.

He hadn't. He was still in bed, firmly propped by a buttress of pillows that Matty had constructed to defend him from a fall. It was dark outside. The only light came from the lamp on the bedside table. Something had awakened him. What was it? Had someone called? He listened. No call was forthcoming. No noise. It was so still that he wondered for a moment if he'd gone deaf. He cleared his throat and was relieved to discover that at least he could still hear and make noises.

What had awakened him?

Back and forth.

Back and forth! It was a thought! What did it mean? Back and forth. Back and forth. Almost senselessly his eyes fell on the little set of numbers that Stuffy had scratched on the bag. "Back and forth," said Crisp aloud as he pulled them into focus. "Back and . . ."

So simple. He began to laugh, or as near a laugh as his sleep-filled throat would allow.

"Winston, did you call?" said Matty from the bottom of the stairs. "No, Matty," he answered, drawing the handwritten note into the circle of light on the edge of his bed. He fixed his glasses on the bridge of his nose. "No, my dear. I'm perfectly fine."

Matty waited a moment or two, unsure whether or not to take his word for it, until she heard him humming, which he never did, and decided he was at least happy. She went back to the kitchen to work on supper.

For the next few minutes Crisp functioned with a clarity of mind of which he'd begun to doubt himself capable. Working in his head, he counted alternately backward and forward from each successive letter in the note by the increment prescribed by each of the numbers in the birthdate in sequence. It wasn't long before he had a full and satisfactory translation of the code. He repeated it under his breath.

"Dear Yo, Meet me at Everette's, 10 A.M. Tuesday. There's something you should know. Always, L."

"Yo," Crisp echoed to himself. Obviously a nickname for Johann. L., then, in support of the evidence, had known him intimately. "But who is L?" he said aloud. "Louise? Lois? Mary Lou?" There was no doubt that a woman's hand had written the message.

He studied the note for another minute or so, as if to glean something from it by osmosis. All the letters were capitalized and collected on two evenly spaced lines. The margins were exact on either side. An orderly, methodical woman, then. Johann had no family. Therefore, given the intimate terms of the salutation, it could be assumed that they were contemporaries. "Woman in her mid-fifties," he intoned in summation. A woman who didn't want their meeting to be discovered. Married? More than likely. They had probably shared an experience at Everette's at some time in the past. Possibly romantic. Would have been in summer, because the house, like all those on the Thoroughfare, was closed after Labor Day. A summer fling?

"He was from the other end of the island," Crisp thought aloud. "So it must have been she who was connected with the Everette's somehow." He ruled out family: She wouldn't have said "Everette's"; she'd have said "the house" or "the old place." Houseguest, then? Domestic help?

Of course, the code itself was a clue. Johann had spent enough time with this mystery woman, at sometime in the past, to teach her his father's code. Not a likely pursuit for two adults. No. It was an adolescent act—innocent and secretive.

Thus far everything pointed to a friendship that had begun years before, probably when they were in their teens. Crisp did the math. That would have put them together sometime in the 1930s.

Johnny had been on the island then.

The paper suggested one final possibility. What if the code had been developed for reasons more practical than recreational? The inference? An unsanctioned relationship.

To Crisp—who, though a non-native, had become sensitized over the years to certain unspoken realities of the island's social structure—there was one jarring implausibility that gave a hollow ring to his deductions, assuming they were correct. These two people didn't, for all intents and purposes, inhabit the same planet. Even today, the year-round fishing village at the south end of the island and the wealthy summer resort community on the northwest coast were poles apart. In those days, it would have been highly unlikely that the two would even have met, much less struck up a relationship.

Highly unlikely, he concluded. " 'There's something you should know,' " he read aloud. He remembered Pagitt's speculations about Anne Quindenan. But the person who wrote the note was L. Not a permutation of Anne.

"Oh? What's that?" said Matty, who, having bumped the door open with an ample hip, was bearing down on him with a dinner tray.

He had been so lost in concentration that he hadn't heard her coming. It was a troubling realization that he'd lost so much of his defensive reflex. "Oh, I was . . . I was . . . You should know that I really enjoyed the sandwich you gave me for lunch. I think my taste is coming back."

"Not if you're going to drink that and like it," Matty said, tossing a contemptuous tilt of the head at the bottle of Moxie. "Only thing that stuff's good for is a doorstop. Here's dinner. Let's clear all this mess away."

Before he could protest, she had set the tray on the bedside table and swept up the documents that had surrounded him and whisked them to the bureau, by which time they had been neatly folded and straightened in her awesomely domestic hands. "Now, you tuck into this," she said, setting before him a steaming plate of baked chicken, roasted potatoes ("little ones from the can, just like you like"), baby carrots in a brown-sugar-and-honey glaze, and buttered Brussels sprouts. The chicken had already been cut into bite-sized chunks. "The sprouts aren't very fresh, I'm afraid. But that was the greenest thing I could find down to the store."

No one knew better than he how important Matty believed the green component of any dinner to be. It was a notion she had adopted early in life and the years had amplified to a principal dogma of her household religion, nearly equal to that of the Second Coming.

She tucked a napkin into his pajama front. "Now, don't let it get cold."

Just then the telephone rang.

"Who do you s'pose that could be?" said Matty as she waddled out the door and down the stairs.

Crisp's mind immediately returned to consideration of the note. "'Something you should know,'" he whispered between obedient mouthfuls. At the remote periphery of his awareness, Matty chatted animatedly to a person or persons unknown.

In her absence, he made a mental resume of the facts he'd thus far acquired or assumed and tossed them into his deductive apparatus to ferment.

"It's for you," said Matty, forcing her way to the center of his consciousness with this most unlikely pronouncement. No one ever called for Crisp. She was carrying a telephone, which she set on the bed while she took the cord in search of a receptacle. "It's long distance," she said, adding under her breath, "I know there's a telephone plug around here somewhere."

"It's called a jack," said Crisp.

"No," said Matty busily. "He'd be a Mike."

"Pardon?"

"Not Jack, Mike. . . . Ah, here it is. I knew there was one up here. I guess it still works." She plugged the cord into the jack. "There." She returned to the bed, picked up the phone, and held it to her ear. "Hello? Hello? Are you there? Ah, good. Good. All right. Here's Winston." She held out the phone.

"Who is it?" Crisp mouthed.

"It's Michael, like I said. Michael Jessup," she replied in a loud whisper. "He's the attorney general."

"Michael?" said Crisp into the phone, still unsure as to who might respond.

"Mr. Crisp," said an instantly familiar voice at the other end of the line. "How're you doing these days? Much better, from what I hear."

The state's attorney general had proved only modestly helpful in their previous experience, only as it was convenient to him. Nevertheless, as the son of an old associate—now deceased, like so many old associates—Crisp extended him the courtesy of a hearing.

"Better than I have a right to," he replied, making an effort to keep the frost out of his voice. "What can I do for you, Mr. Jessup?"

"Michael, please," said Jessup. Crisp didn't acknowledge the comment. "Yes . . . well . . . I've just been on the phone with Gammidge. Nasty fall he had."

"Very unfortunate," Crisp replied. "I'm sorry for him. Of

course, it could have been worse. If he'd taken a step or two . . ."

"Yes, yes," said Jessup, as if the possibility hadn't occurred to him. "That's true. Anyway, seems he's under doctor's orders to stay in bed for a few days."

"I'm not surprised, given the ice we have out here. He wouldn't make it far on crutches."

"No. I'm sure it's best he stays put. However, that sets his investigation back a good bit."

"The Bermann investigation? You're familiar with the case?"

"Familiar? More than familiar. The chancellor of the University of Maine is a close friend of Bermann's and, incidentally, mine. They went to graduate school together, I gather. Anyway, he's been breathing down my neck ever since it happened. I'm not going to say it has anything to do with his plans to run for governor next year. . . . Anyway, the details, as I heard them, were so extraordinary that I was sure Gammidge would have it wrapped up in a day or two."

Crisp bent a brow. "I'm not sure I follow."

"What?"

"Well, if you considered the details extraordinary . . ."

"Oh, I see what you mean. No. I meant I thought the facts would be obvious once the dust had cleared. They often are with sensational cases."

This was true. "Not in this case, I'm afraid," Crisp replied. Also true.

"No. Which is why I called you. To be perfectly honest, Gammidge asked me to call you."

Crisp didn't reply.

"The reason I'd called him, apart from wanting to find out how he was doing, was to tell him they found a match on the fingerprints he sent up."

"And?"

"They belong to a woman named Anne Quindenan."

Some essence of his deeper self had been calling a long time, trying to force the obvious into the waning circle of light that was his consciousness. Now, suddenly, mention of the name triggered a rare moment of deductive kismet and the connection was made. "Lou Ann O'Connor," he whispered spontaneously.

An indescribable rush quickened his pulse as the piece clicked almost audibly into place.

CHAPTER

12

❦

"**P**ARDON?" SAID THE VOICE on the other end of the line.
"What? Oh, nothing." Crisp had forgotten that someone
was listening. "I was just thinking out loud. What were
you saying?"

"Mrs. Quindenan," Michael reminded him.

"Oh, yes. Mrs. Quindenan."

Matty had been fluttering around in the background, struggling
not to eavesdrop, but her limit of resolve had been breached. "Mrs.
Quindenan?" she said, alighting on the end of the bed. "What about
her?"

"This is a confidential conversation, Matty."

Matty didn't budge.

"Pardon?" said Michael in the earpiece.

"It's . . . I'm talking to my . . . to"—what was Matty to him?—
"my landlady," he stammered finally. The word left an unsatisfactory taste in his mouth. "Matty," he amended. "Hold a second,
please." He muffled the phone against his shoulder. "Matty?"

"That's the one staying up at Emerson's over the holidays with her family," she said, ignoring the admonition in his eyes.

"Yes, Matty, I know. Mr. and Mrs. Quindenan."

"Paul Quindenan?" Jessup's voice crackled over the wire.

"Yes," said Crisp. "Why?"

There was a heavy sigh on the other end of the line. "Wonderful," said Jessup with a tone that was wearily facetious.

"You know him?"

"You do, too. Undersecretary of Defense Paul Quindenan."

Crisp, personal agent of various administrations of both parties in years past, had put politics behind him when he'd moved to the island. He was sure he'd never heard of Paul Quindenan. "Matty," he said softly, shielding the mouthpiece with his palm, "would you mind fixing me a cup of Ovaltine?"

Matty, lest she be considered in the least interested in someone else's telephone conversation, was on her feet in the same second, but her will was battling a powerful native curiosity. The contest projected itself on her face in a rapid succession of expressions, none fully formed. "Of course, Winston," she said and left the room. When he heard her footsteps on the stairs he called after her, "And please hang up the extension."

Doubly thwarted, Matty resumed her descent in a blue mood. She toyed with the thought of not bringing cookies with the Ovaltine, but she instantly dismissed the notion as having been given her by the Evil One, whom she rebuked in no uncertain terms.

Crisp pressed the receiver to his good ear. "Sorry, Michael."

"That's all right. I heard."

"Word travels fast enough out here as it is."

"I understand."

"Now, why did you call? You think Mrs. Quindenan murdered Johnny Bermann?"

"I've got a set of fingerprints, Winston. That's all."

"Not much of a case."

"No. Circumstantial at best."

"And?" said Crisp, sensing hesitation on Jessup's part.

"Well, if you want it in black and white, I'm not about to lay any charges against the wife of the undersecretary of defense unless I can make them stick. Political realities."

Crisp understood. "What would you like me to do?"

"Find out how long she's going to be on the island. If she's going to be there a while, we don't necessarily have to take any steps right away. I mean, where can she go?"

"House arrest," said Crisp, "without her knowing it."

"That's the idea," said Jessup. "We need time to get evidence. Something solid."

Jessup's use of the word "we" was not lost on Crisp. "You realize, I'm not in the best position to—"

"I know, Winston," said Jessup, with a presumptuous familiarity that would have been right at home on Penobscot Island. "But I don't have anywhere else to turn. I can't send my people out there. You know how those islanders are with strangers. But you're in. They've accepted you."

Crisp felt an unexpected flush of pride at the observation.

"If anyone can build a case, you can. I'll tell Gammidge and the constable . . . what's his name?"

"Kingsbury."

"Right," said Jessup, not bothering to repeat the name of someone so low on the totem pole. "I'll tell the county sheriff to let you take the lead. I don't think anyone will mind. They know you can do more from your bed than they can do on the spot."

It was a clumsy compliment, and Crisp bridled somewhat. Manipulation was an art; to hear it so artlessly done was insulting. Nevertheless, he felt so close to solving the case already that he put his feelings aside. "I'll do what I can."

The sigh that squeezed through the receiver embodied Jessup's relief. "Great. Good. Good. If you'll just make a report every now and then, let me know what's up and how things are proceeding."

"When you talk to Luther Kingsbury," said Crisp, who had

never been one to file reports, "tell him to come see me." He hung up without saying good-bye.

"That's fine by me," said Gammidge. He arched his back again, trying to stretch his weakened muscles. "I wanted him in charge all along. But what can he do from his bed?"

Kingsbury took a banana from the tray at Gammidge's bedside. "You gonna eat this?" he said, peeling it.

Any protest would be tardy. "Help yourself," said Gammidge. He'd saved the banana from breakfast and was going to have it when he watched *The Andy Griffith Show.*

Half the banana was consigned to the abyss before Luther responded to Nate's question. "He can take the load off me, that's what he can do," Luther said. "I'll be like that soldier in the sermon last Sunday; he can telleth me where to go and I'll goeth, and what to do and I'll doeth it. Suits me fine. 'Cause, 'tween you and me, right now I'm 'bout as useful as Jell-O without a mold, as Maggie says." He tossed the banana peel into the trash can.

Gammidge could empathize. He had no illusions about his own deductive powers and would be more than happy to serve as Crisp's hands and feet. Well, hands, anyway. However, he didn't like feeling useless and helpless. "Doc says I can get up day after tomorrow," he reminded himself aloud.

"Did you know who she was?" asked Kingsbury after a brief pause. He thoughtlessly tried on one of a pair of rubber surgical gloves he'd removed from a box behind the door.

"Who? Mrs. Quindenan?"

Kingsbury nodded.

"No. 'Course not. You?"

"No, I didn't," he said emphatically. "How could I?" There was another hiatus in the conversation. Luther had managed to get a glove on but was having a hard time getting it off. He began rolling it at the wrist. "You think she did it?"

Gammidge shot a quick glance out at the hall. "Shh," he said sharply, then lowered his voice to a whisper. "We don't need this getting out."

"Nobody heard," said Kingsbury, who had given up rolling the glove off and was tugging at the fingers, which expanded like rubber bands, then snapped back, eliciting epithets of pain. "What the heck kind of stupid inventions are these?" He eyed a pair of scissors and lowered his voice. "You think she did it?" he asked again.

Gammidge had been watching the comedy at an unconscious level and couldn't help but wonder if Kingsbury had a single bullet in his left shirt pocket, like Barney Fife. "Not for me to decide," he said, shaking off a mild hypnosis.

"That was her," said Evelyn Swears. Her arthritis was giving her a hard time. She had to stop often and massage her hands as she picked the tinsel from the tree.

The needles were dry and fell to the floor at a touch. "But the smell," Evelyn would say, and allow the smell to answer for itself. There comes a time, of course, when a Christmas tree crosses that subjective line between festive ornament and fire hazard, a line that Evelyn's tree had crossed some week to ten days ago. But she'd always had a hard time throwing out the tree and took some inde-finable pride in the fact that she'd once held off until February. In 1951, it was.

"I still can't place her."

Becky Gable and Evelyn, both widows, both childless since Becky's son, Pokey, was killed in Korea, had been best friends since Armburst Hill was more granite than trees. One seldom heard either of them mentioned without the other. Like Laurel and Hardy. Spic and Span. Lately Becky's memory had developed a lot of foggy patches: "The old gears are slippin'," Evelyn's nephew Morris had said, tapping the side of his head, but that was all right. Evelyn and Becky had practically lived in the same skin for the better part of seventy years, so Evelyn kept the memories for both of them, even reminding Becky, when requested to do so, of her husband, Buddy, who had died of a heart attack some fifteen years ago. "Tell me about that man," she would say, sitting back in the Queen Anne chair by the window with a cup of hot tea cradled in her hands.

As far as Evelyn was concerned, Buddy had had a lot in common with the plagues of Egypt: mean-spirited, tight with his money, and contentious and unyielding in the demands for domestic perfection that he had placed upon his wife. He had made her miserable for forty years. But at this stage in life, Evelyn figured, Becky didn't need to know that. So, in these periodic retellings, she supplanted Buddy with the man Becky had always wanted and gave them a wonderful life together.

There was no one to tell her otherwise.

At the end of the recitation, Becky's gaze would drift out the window and over the harbor. "It was a wonderful life, wasn't it, Ev?" Evelyn would think of her own marriage to Harry, and a lump would rise to her throat and a tear to her eye. "Yes, it was. Some wonderful." She'd wonder if they had blueberry muffins in heaven. They were Harry's favorite.

"Well, you know the Emerson woman," said Evelyn, patiently repeating the story as she resumed divesting the tree of its finery. "She lives out on James Island in Cap'n Hall's house."

"Oh, oh, yes," Becky replied. She knew the place, though it didn't bring to mind anyone named Emerson, and her expression said so. Evelyn plodded on.

"She was an Everette growin' up. Summer people. They had one've them big houses up this side of the Thoroughfare."

"Oh, yes," said Becky, knitting her eyebrows over a reluctant orna-ment hook. "Up to the Thoroughfare. And now she's an Emerson, lives up to Captain Hall's house." It helped to repeat the facts more or less in order every now and then. "Married another 'E.'"

Evelyn hadn't thought about that. "Yes, I guess she did."

"Save her having to get new monograms on the linens," Becky

observed practically. "I guess that's how rich people keep their money."

"I s'pose that's so. Well, they had this girl up there to help with the children. Her name was Lou Ann O'Connor. 'Course, she's all grown up now. That's that woman who's stayin' up to Captain Hall's now. Name's Anne Quindenan these days."

"Not Lou Ann?"

"Nope. I guess she got rid of the Lou part and added an 'e.'"

"I can understand that," said Becky with a series of nods. The only Lou she knew was Lou Barton. He used to dip her pigtails in the inkwell in third grade. He'd bear some getting rid of, unless fifty years as a Mason had straightened him out. She doubted it. "She's the one with the daughter?"

"That's right, dear," said Evelyn. It was going to take half an hour to vacuum the sprills. They were everywhere. "Her name's Margaret."

"Margaret," Becky echoed. She was remembering shreds of this conversation from its previous telling some ten minutes ago. "She's the one who young Johnny Bermann put in his will?"

"So I hear."

"Left her the old place and everything?"

Evelyn nodded. This was the third telling, all told, and the newness had worn off.

"Why, do you s'pose?"

"Well, that's just it, isn't it? That's what everyone wants to know. You want more tea, dear?"

It was more than Luther Kingsbury could make sense of. Why would anyone trash Billy Pringle's place? Yet there was no denying it as he stood in the open doorway, surveying the scene. The place was a mess, even by Billy's standards.

"I guess this is pooched," said Billy, retrieving Matty's meat loaf from the floor and sniffing it. He put it back in the Tupperware, which he returned to the narrow shelf set into the wall. "Maybe not."

"Anything missing, Billy?"

Billy looked around. "Kinda hard to tell," he said. "I don't think so. If he took something, I guess he's welcome to it."

"Still, it ain't right that someone should bust into your place and . . ." And what? Make a mess? The charge would never stick. "And push your stuff around," said Luther. He'd just come to deliver a loaf of bread that Maggie had made, as he did once a week, and found the door open and Billy standing in the middle of the room looking around like someone who'd awakened to find himself in a strange, new world.

"It happened this morning?"

Billy nodded. "I was down to the shore, crabbin'." The statement reminded Billy of something. He rummaged gently through the pocket of his flannel shirt and produced a small crab, its tiny claws opening and closing in a futile display of self-defense. "*Brachyrhyncha,*" he said, displaying the creature in his open palm for Kingsbury's inspection.

"Oh, yeah." Kingsbury nodded in consideration of the exhibition. "What time did you leave?"

"Just after light when the tide's right. Like always," said Billy. He carefully stroked the back of the crab, which, seeming to sense the complete absence of hostility, folded its legs and blew bubbles. " 'Cept Sundays, 'course." He returned the crab to his pocket. "Got back just a minute or two before you come. What kind is it?" he added, flicking an index finger at the tinfoil package. He sniffed the air once or twice. "Oatmeal?"

"Oh, sorry." Luther handed the fresh bread, still warm through its wrappings, to Billy. "Yup. I guess so."

Billy, nodding appreciatively, took the loaf and cradled it to his chest in both arms. He inhaled deeply—his eyes closed and his head back—and smiled deeply. "Maggie done a good thing," he said. Raspberry. He studied the look of concern on Kingsbury's face. "I wouldn't worry 'bout it, Luther."

Kingsbury was worried. Who would have done such a thing to

Billy? "Whoever done this was looking for something," he deduced aloud.

"What, d'you s'pose?" said Billy, petting the loaf of oatmeal bread, now in the crook of one arm, as if it were a kitten.

That's what doubly confounded Kingsbury. If someone was going to break in anywhere to steal anything, it wouldn't be Billy's. Everyone knew there was nothing here worth anything. Even someone from away wouldn't have to dig far to figure that out. "You haven't come by anything lately, have you? I mean, anything worth anything?"

Billy cupped a protective hand over his pocket. "What d'you mean?"

Luther didn't know what he meant. "I don't know. Have you found anything?"

Billy made an effort to look as though he was thinking hard. People liked it when he did that. "Nope," he said at last. Then he thought of the papers that he and Gammidge had picked up off the ground at the Bermann place. Of course, they hadn't really been lost exactly, which seemed a necessary prerequisite to being found. But they had looked for them; that seemed to satisfy the requirement. "Papers," he said in response to the thought.

"Papers?"

"Up to Bermann's. Me and Gammidge was up there last night, you know."

"Yeah, I know."

"You know there was someone up there already?"

Kingsbury knew that, too. Gammidge had told him the whole story. Another brow bender. "Yes."

"A woman."

"Yes."

"Well, she dropped some papers when she was runnin' away and we found 'em, me an' Gammidge."

Kingsbury assessed the information. "She saw you, didn't she? That woman up there?"

"I don't know," Billy responded slowly, his free hand going to his head. "She saw me enough to hit me with a typewriter. Would you say that means she knew who I was or didn't know who I was?"

Luther considered the question only long enough to decide to ignore it. "If she saw you, maybe she figures you picked up them papers."

"I did," said Billy truthfully.

"Maybe she figures you kept 'em."

"I didn't. I give 'em to Gammidge."

"I know that," said Luther. "And you know that."

"And Gammidge knows that," said Billy, falling into the rhythm of the exchange.

"But that don't mean she knows it. If she figures you have 'em, she could've come to get 'em."

Billy's face twisted into a knot of perplexity. "A woman done this?" he said, taking in his surroundings at a glance. In his experience women were pretty exact in their domestic habits. They made meat loaf and bread, washed laundry, generally folding and creasing the world wherever they came in contact with it.

"Makes sense, don't it?" said Luther. "Everyone knows you don't hang around here after daybreak if the tide's out. Wouldn't be much to come up here 'fore light, then wait in the woods out back 'til you're gone."

"Makes sense?" Billy echoed feebly. Not to him, it didn't. "A woman done this?"

Usually when women came to the shack, they straightened things up, often to the extent that he couldn't find anything. Aunt Matty came up once a year, like the monsoons in India, and turned the whole place inside out to clean things he never thought to look into. She'd chuck most of the leftovers that people had given him, and more than half the stuff he'd so painstakingly collected from the roadsides and the town dump. The process took two days, during which time he stayed out of the way, sleeping in a tree house he'd

built out in the woods, where he'd hidden his most sacred possessions, until Hurricane Matty blew itself out.

"Gammidge don't have 'em," Kingsbury thought out loud.

"Who does?"

Putting two and two together, Kingsbury figured that the last
thing the Professor needed was a visit from the kind of woman who
could make such a mess of Billy Pringle's. "Never mind," he said.
"Don't let that bread get stale."

APRIL 2, 1917

The ground was still too hard to dig a grave. Old Man Bermann
traipsed the familiar path through the woods along the western shore
with Elsa's lifeless body, limp and doll-like and hastily bound with
canvas, draped over one of his massive shoulders. His breathing was
labored and his nose ran with the cold, so he sniffed constantly, each
sniff bearing with it the thick smell of smoke that clung to his black
wool coat, a pungent reminder of the hayrick that, even now, smol-
dered in the dooryard. How on God's green earth had that happened? His mind entertained a blur of unsatisfactory possibilities as
he plodded, ducking and weaving, through the thicket, unable to
shake the feeling that someone was following, watching.

Less than an hour ago, he had learned that his adoptive nation
was about to declare war on his homeland, something he had bent
all his efforts toward preventing. In the subsequent minutes he had
uncovered the treachery of his maid and committed what amounted
to cold-blooded murder. To have these events punctuated by the
spontaneous combustion of a hayrick, driven across the dooryard
by some unseen banshee, superimposed a layer of the surreal that
begged a Wagnerian score.

Had he been a superstitious man, it would not have been difficult to mistake the sound of the tattered remnants of wind wandering through the thick trees as an accusing whisper from the

throat of the dead woman. Her head, from his constant ducking, now rested on his shoulder like a slumbering child, and from time to time her cold blue lips brushed his ear.

There was a deep fissure in the rock, well above high water, in a white granite bluff at the far end of the point. The body would keep there for a few weeks until the earth softened.

He'd grabbed an old horse blanket from the barn before striking out and, wrapping it tightly around Elsa's body, used the handholds created by its folds to lower her gently into the cleft. Then he buried her with hundreds of fist-sized rocks, gathered painstakingly from the beach, to keep her safe from the gulls and coons.

It'd be hell digging her out again, come time, but there wasn't any choice.

With the last rock he scratched a modest cross in the ledge.

It was nearly dawn by the time he finished. His back ached from picking up the rocks, his legs ached from carrying armloads of them up from the beach, his brow was blanketed with sweat despite the cold, and his heart was leaden in his chest. He mourned for Elsa. She was a good German girl who had probably, in her estimation, sacrificed a good deal to serve her country at the remotest edges of a foreign land. It took little imagination to picture her parents, probably simple country folk, forever awaiting her return, raising hopeful eyes from their work to the door at every uncustomary sound, every stranger's footfall on the dirt lane, every windy creak of the garden gate, never knowing that she had paid the ultimate price in service to the homeland. A hero, now quietly decomposing in an unmarked grave on a distant shore.

What would he tell Ingrid and Johnny?

He bowed his head and folded his hands. "Father," he said, "witness of hearts, you know what sins this young woman carries to the grave and which would condemn her before you on Judgment Day. But you know she died an untimely death, without the chance to make her peace, so I beg you, in your mercy, cover her transgressions with Christ's blood, and keep her soul safe against His return."

Tears stood in his eyes as he raised his head to heaven. "And cover me, Lord, that my sin not separate you from me forever. Forgive me in Christ for what I have done."

He picked up the rock he had used to scratch the cross and tossed it into the grave.

"Amen."

He never returned to retrieve the body.

CHAPTER
13

"SOMETHING STICKY?" said Crisp. "What do you mean?" Kingsbury had come to see if Crisp could make any sense of his latest discovery—the break-in at Billy Pringle's. Crisp's response, a moderate sideways tilt of the head and an "is that so?" failed to satisfy. Subsequently, as they addressed the logistics for tomorrow's ride to the Everette place, Kingsbury had recited a litany of the many pieces of evidence that puzzled him. His right shoulder raised and lowered almost imperceptibly. "Sticky," he said. "And it smelled of Ivory soap."

Mention of the adhesive residue on Johnny Bermann's wrists had been omitted from Pagitt's report. This was the first that Crisp had heard of it.

Intermittent gusts of wind hurled angry fistfuls of ice at the window, which brought to Crisp's mind images of petulant partisans venting their fury against the gates of the Bastille.

"Describe it to me."

Kingsbury looked as if he'd been asked to explain the theory of relativity. "His wrists was sticky," he said after a moment's hesitation. "And smelled like Ivory soap."

It was a pagan's prayer—more words, no more meaning. Crisp would have to be more specific in his questioning.

"How far up and down the arms were they sticky?"

"Oh, 'bout this far up," Kingsbury replied, pointing at a place two to three inches toward his elbow from his wrist. "To here," he added, indicating the base of his thumb.

"Two to three inches wide?"

" 'Bout."

"Was there any discoloration?"

"Not that I noticed."

"Was the stickiness all around the wrist or just on one side?"

Funny he should ask that. Charlie Williams had mentioned that the stickiness seemed confined to the outside of the wrists. "Why'd you ask that?"

Crisp ignored the question. "The chair he was sitting in had arms, didn't it? Open arms?"

Kingsbury reflected. "Matter of fact, it did. Wood chair from the dining room, I'd say. Same color. Blue. The end chairs had arms. That was one of 'em."

Crisp nodded in a way that Kingsbury found disconcerting. How did he know about the chair?

"The bruises on his knees, tell me about that."

Once again Kingsbury felt inadequate. "Well, they was bruised black-and-blue."

"Where exactly? Here?" Crisp asked, tossing the blankets aside and slapping his legs just above the knee.

Kingsbury would have been startled by the unexpected revelation of Crisp's extremities at the best of times. The prospect was doubly unsettling because the old man's legs seemed little more than brittle sticks of chalk, laced with a delicate network of light blue veins. " 'Bout there," Kingsbury agreed, looking away quickly.

Crisp replaced the blankets.

"Tell me about his feet."

Kingsbury marshaled his memory. "Well, one foot had a shoe and sock on, the other had nothing."

"And they were both shriveled?"

Kingsbury nodded. "Both."

"Was there anything else unusual?"

" 'Bout everything, I guess," said Kingsbury.

"In particular?" Crisp insisted.

"Like what?"

"Well," Crisp said patiently, "smells, for instance."

Kingsbury thought back. "Smells? What kind of smells?"

"The house had been closed up for a long time, hadn't it?" Crisp asked, the calmness of his voice belying his rising frustration.

"Yup."

"You've been in those houses when they've been closed up?"

"Sure, everytime there's a break-in."

"What did they smell like?"

"Mothballs and mildew," Kingsbury quietly responded without hesitation.

"Is that what Everette's place smelled like?"

"No, come to think of it," he said, surprising himself with this hidden piece of information.

"What did it smell like?"

"Bug spray," Kingsbury replied, again without any hesitation. "That's what it was. That and a touch of sulfur from the match someone used to light the candle in the dining room. Smells hang a long time in still air. Places like them's awful still."

"Bug spray?" Crisp hadn't expected such an unequivocal response. "You're sure?"

"Bug spray," Kingsbury replied definitively. "Not too strong, but no doubt that's what it was."

"Did you happen to notice if the smell was stronger in one place than another—say, stronger nearer the body than elsewhere in the house?"

Kingsbury sniffed to activate his olfactory senses. "Not that I recall. What's all this about?"

Crisp deflected the question. "I want you to do something for me, Luther."

"Sure, if I can."

"This may sound a little strange, but I want you to go over to Charlie Williams's and smell Johnny Bermann's feet."

Kingsbury considered this a moment, then, contrary to Crisp's expectations, nodded with no outward display of bemusement. "Then what?"

"Don't you wonder why I want you to do that?"

"Nope," Kingsbury deduced. "I figure you got your reasons. Mine ain't to reason why, like the fella says."

Crisp was amused, and it was only with difficulty that he sorted out the smile on his face before Kingsbury saw it. "Well, that would be most helpful."

"Like I said, though," Kingsbury continued, "the smell was pretty much the same everywhere, not just around the body."

"Still . . . ," said Crisp.

"Whatever you say." Kingsbury accepted the instructions without further comment. "That all?"

"Yes," Crisp replied. "For now. Just let me know what you find."

"Sure. I can do that in ten minutes. I don't guess you're goin' anywhere 'til I get back." He laughed.

"That seems a safe bet," Crisp replied noncommittally.

"Oh, by the way, here's them Polaroids you asked for." Kingsbury removed a small packet of photographs, wrapped in rubber bands, from one of his inner pockets and tossed it on the bed. "I ain't much of a photographer, I'm afraid, but them's better than a poke in the eye, I guess." He opened the door and looked down the stairs. "Uh-oh, I hope you wasn't plannin' to take a nap."

"Why?"

"Got company." He craned his neck around the door and leveled a meaningful gaze at Crisp. "Quindenan woman."

"Anne?" said Crisp. He sat up instinctively, tucked the photos under his pillow, and began sorting himself out.

"The daughter," said Kingsbury. "I'll tell you somethin', bub, she ain't too hard to look at. Pretty as a . . ." He plundered his memory for an adequate analogy but found those available wanting. "Damned if I know. Wonder what brung her out on a night like this, d'you s'pose? Well, I'll be back in five minutes."

"Leave the door open."

"Sure thing."

As the constable's footsteps thumped loudly down the carpeted stairs, Crisp inclined his good ear toward the door and heard Matty complaining to the newcomer that he'd had too many visitors for his own good and would she please come back some other time.

"It's all right, Matty," said Kingsbury as he left. "He knows she's here."

Matty leveled an inquisitional stare at the constable.

"I just told him. He's expectin' her. Miss Quindenan," he said with a nod as he passed the young woman in the hall.

"Mr. Kingsbury," Margaret responded politely.

He retrieved his hat from the stand beside the door, then was gone.

"You'd think this was Grand Central Station," Matty said under her breath after only a moment's hesitation. She took Margaret's cloak and hung it on the coat stand. "Well, dear, you may as well go on up. How do you take your tea?"

"Tea?" Margaret said. It was a question for which she hadn't rehearsed an answer. "I . . . I . . ."

"Sugar?"

"No. No. Plain, please."

"Water's hot," Matty said briskly. "I'll bring it up in three minutes." In her estimation, tea that hadn't steeped three minutes wasn't much more than dishwater.

"Thank you, Miss Gilchrist," said Margaret from the bottom step.

"Matty," said Matty, already on her way to the kitchen. "Everyone calls me Matty."

"Thank you, Matty," said Margaret. "I know that Mr. Crisp isn't well. Honestly, I wouldn't have come, but Mr. Gammidge told me I should talk to him. I won't keep him long. I promise."

It sounded just like the kind of thing that Mr. Gammidge would do. "First door at the top of the stairs," Matty directed. "Polite young woman," she said to herself. Then, having conferred that blessing, she went to fulfill her commission.

"Mr. Crisp?" Margaret called softly as she reached the landing.

"Come in, Miss Quindenan," said Crisp, having sorted himself out as much as possible on short notice.

The young woman entered the room face first, peeking around the door. "I'm so sorry to bother you," she said, settling her eyes upon him.

Crisp had prepared a benign smile, but it was transformed to a gape as he returned her gaze. Although both Pagitt and Kingsbury had said she was uncommonly beautiful, they'd neglected to mention that her eyes could stop the heart. The poet residing at Crisp's core bobbed to the surface, unprepared and sputtering, completely at a loss for words.

The woman that followed the eyes into the room compounded the effect exponentially. Crisp was breathless, a condition with possibly fatal consequences to a man his age.

"Are you all right?" she asked with gentle concern, reaching a tentative hand in his direction.

Over the course of the years, Crisp had developed a professional aplomb that had served him well in the most extreme circumstances. However, it had never rendered him immune to female beauty, which now stood before him in the extreme. His reaction, however, wasn't what it might have been in his youth, but one of simple, almost childlike awe. He hadn't subscribed to the popular notion that angels possessed female characteristics. Perhaps he'd been wrong.

"Miss . . . ," he said. It was all he could manage.

"Quindenan," she reminded him. Doctor Pagitt had told her that the old man was feeble, but she wasn't prepared for the invalid confronting her. How could he possibly be of any use? She hesitated halfway from the door. "I . . . I shouldn't have come."

"No," Crisp said, a little too quickly. "No, please. Sit. Sit." He reached toward the chair recently vacated by Kingsbury. "Please," he assured in response to the doubt in her eyes. Magnificent eyes.

She sat, her posture perfect, her every motion sending the struggling poet vainly to his thesaurus. Crisp was aware that he was staring, but he couldn't help it. "How may I help you, Miss Quindenan," he said. Ask what you will, said the poet within. Shall I fall on my sword? Shall I stop the sun and planets in their eternal dance? It was the best he could do on short notice.

"I . . . I'm so confused," she began. She had turned her eyes to her hands in her lap. Her fingers massaged one another distractedly. "I just . . . I went up to the medical center to talk to Mr. Gammidge, and he said that I should come see you."

Thou art a man of rare discernment, thought the poet, lapsing into King James English. We are forever beholden. "I hope I can help," said Crisp. "What's it about?"

Margaret faltered in indecision. "Are you sure?"

"Please," Crisp said.

Having quickly collected himself, Crisp had relaxed, and something in his demeanor exerted a calming influence. "Very well," she hazarded. "It's about . . . you know Mr. Bermann, the man whose body they found at Everette's?"

"Yes."

"Well, I got a call from his lawyer, a man in Rockland named Brennan, and—"

"And he told you that Mr. Bermann had left everything to you in his will," Crisp concluded.

The young woman's eyes widened. "How did you know?"

Crisp smiled. "I guess everyone in town knows by this time.

Gossip has no natural enemies on the island."

Margaret conceded this with a slight shake of the head. "I don't
. . . didn't even know the man, Mr. Crisp. I swear. Why on earth
would he have left everything to me?"

"Did you tell your mother?"

"Of course I did. First thing."

"And what did she say?"

She sat up straighter and looked directly at him. "She said, 'He
knew.' That's all. It was like she was talking to herself, though, not
to me. She's been in this weird fog for the last few days anyway. She
walks around—"

"I know," said Crisp. "Doc Pagitt told me."

Who are you? Margaret wanted to ask. And why does everyone
tell you everything. And why am I here? "Really?" She made no
attempt to conceal her perplexity.

"What did Mr. Gammidge tell you about me?" said Crisp,
sensing her discomfiture.

"Nothing, really. He just said you could help, if anyone could. I
don't know why he thinks so. I realize this is terribly unfair of me to
come barging in like this, but—"

"I've had some experience with this type of thing," Crisp
explained.

"You're a detective?"

"If you like," he said with a slight nod. "Mr. Gammidge and I
have worked together in the past. I realize that my being bedridden
doesn't exactly engender confidence, but I assure you, my mental
faculties are relatively intact." He wasn't sure if that was a lie or not,
but as she relaxed visibly it seemed to be justified.

"A detective? Oh, I'm so glad to hear it," she sighed. Her hands
ceased their anxious knitting and settled in her lap. "I wish he'd
said."

The task ahead of Crisp was not a pleasant one, and the
domestic fallout would change her life forever, but, perhaps due to
his long confinement, his legendary, catlike patience had worn thin.

Unsettling images were beginning to take place in the fog of facts and speculation, and he wanted to give them names before they wove themselves into his dreams. "Miss Quindenan," he said, seizing her with his serious eyes, "what kind of detective are you?"

"Me? None at all."

"You think not?" Crisp replied gently. He held out his hand.

Unsure of his intentions at first, she faltered. His hand was steady and sure, and the look in his eyes begged her to take it. She relented. His fingers were as warm and soft as old leather as they held her hand with just enough pressure so she knew she could retrieve it at any time. "You're cold," he said.

She smiled awkwardly. "This is Maine. It's winter."

He smiled back. "I remember my father telling me there was no Santa Claus," he said, the smile lines at the corners of his eyes deepening slightly. "He hated to tell me, and I hated to hear it. I don't know who took it hardest. But it was time."

"You're going to tell me something I don't want to hear?" she asked tentatively.

"I'm just going to ask you some questions, and we'll see if you're not a better detective than you think you are." Her hand trembled in his. "If you're ready."

She took a deep breath, fixed her bottomless eyes on his, and nodded. "I'm ready," she said, a little hesitantly.

"Where was your mother during the war?"

"In England. My father was stationed there."

"He was with the diplomatic corps?"

"That's right."

"Probably spent a lot of time traveling," Crisp surmised.

"Yes. I suppose, but—"

"Johnny Bermann was in London at the same time," Crisp interjected. "He was seconded to the War Cabinet as a translator."

"You think they met? He and my parents?"

"I have no doubt he met your mother, at least." He tried to let his expression deliver the next line.

"What are you implying?" said Margaret. She tried to take her hand back, but he wouldn't let her.

"They'd met before, here on the island," Crisp said evenly. "When they were teenagers. They fell in love."

"No!" she said, snapping her hand away as she stood up sharply. "She's never said anything about that to me. She doesn't know him. She'd have told me!"

"Even if she was still in love with him?"

Margaret looked frantically around the room, as if searching for a way to escape, but her feet were rooted to the spot. "You don't know what you're saying. My mother loves my father!"

"I don't doubt it," said Crisp. "But she loved Johnny, too. Please, sit."

For an uncomfortably long time she stood unmoving, indecision evident in every gesture. Then, slowly, as if her legs couldn't support her anymore, she descended to the chair. He held out his hand again, but she ignored it. He let it lie on top of the blanket beside him. Then he proceeded to ask her questions to which he already knew the answer.

"Tell me, how did your mother seem before the discovery of Johnny's body?"

"Happy," said Margaret without thinking. "She was the happiest I'd ever seen her."

"And afterward?"

She realized what he was getting at, and it was too late to parry. "She changed."

"Doc Pagitt says she began reciting nursery rhymes."

"'Diddle-diddle-dumplin', my poor John,'" Margaret recited, her voice barely audible.

"One shoe off and one shoe on," said Crisp. "Margaret?"

She raised her chin and looked at him, her eyes thick with tears.

"Johnny Bermann was found with one shoe off and one shoe on."

Margaret's lip began to quiver and the tears cascaded down her face. "I don't understand," she said helplessly.

"I think you do. Your mother went out that day, didn't she?"
Margaret nodded.

"When she left, was she happy?"

"Yes."

"And when she returned, everything had changed?"

Margaret mouthed the affirmative, but nothing came out. Her mind was racing ahead. "What are you saying?"

Crisp stared blankly at his arm. What was he saying? "Your mother and Johnny Bermann had arranged a rendezvous at Everette's. It was a place familiar to them both. Far from town. Discreet. No doubt Kitty Emerson has keys lying around the house where you're staying. She's an Everette, you know."

Margaret didn't reply. She knew.

"I think that when your mother got there—to Everette's—she found him dead," he said bluntly, not wishing to prolong the agony.

Intuitively she lay her hand on his, tears spilling from her eyes as she raised them to the ceiling. She breathed deeply. It made too much sense to deny. "Go on," she said.

"How old are you, exactly?"

"Twenty-six."

"When would you have been conceived?"

She flashed a challenging, heartbreaking glance at him. Confronted with Crisp's steadfast confidence, she looked quickly away. "1944."

"You're a beautiful woman," Crisp said, so softly he could barely hear himself. "So is your mother. Where do you think your black hair comes from?"

Once again she looked at the ceiling and sighed.

"You never suspected?"

She shook her head.

"Do you think your father knows?"

"If he does, he's never shown it. He's always been the kindest, most wonderful . . ." The deluge that had been threatening broke forth in full-throated sobs of anguish as she threw herself onto his chest. He folded her in his arms and tenderly stroked her hair. She stayed that way until the tears were gone, absorbed by the bedspread. "I'm sorry," she said, sitting up. Her left hand smoothed the bedclothes insensibly. She showed no signs of embarrassment, as she might have had he been a younger man. He handed her a tissue and she blew her nose.

"It must have been horrible for her," she said softly. Then her voice rose sharply, her words revealing the conflict raging within her. "I can't believe she'd have done this to Daddy!" She took another tissue from the container on the bedside table and wiped her eyes.

"Here we go," Matty said brightly as she entered the room, preceded by a heavily laden tea tray. Margaret turned away so Matty wouldn't see that she'd been crying. "Just half a cup for you, Winston," she said. "Or you'll be up all night."

Matty cleared a place on the table and poured out two fragrant, steaming cups. She handed one to Winston and held the other for his guest. "Here you go, dear. You'll want something warm inside before you go out on a night like this."

Margaret turned to take the cup, tossing a feeble smile at Matty. "Thanks."

"Why, you've been crying," said Matty, abruptly setting the teapot on the tray. "Winston, she's been crying. What's the trouble, dear?" She put her hands on Margaret's shoulders and began patting her earnestly. "Winston? What's the matter?"

Margaret dabbed her eyes hastily and, fixing a more convincing smile, turned to Matty. "I'm all right, Miss Gilchrist . . . Matty," she said. "Really. It's just that . . . just that—"

"She's worried about her mother," Crisp offered.

"Oh, there, there," said Matty, patting a little harder. "There, now. She's going to be fine. Just nerves, is all. Lord knows, there's enough to make anybody nervous these days, what with the power out and all this ice and people fallin' in holes and havin' heart attacks in empty houses." The speech summarized Matty's frustration. "Now, just you let Doc Pagitt worry about your mother. Between him and Cal, why she'll be on her feet in no time. There, now."

"I'm sure you're right," Margaret responded, mastering herself with admirable effort. "I haven't had much sleep lately. Everything is magnified when you're tired."

"Why, of course it is. Don't you drink this tea," said Matty, taking the cup from her and putting it on the tray. "You don't want that. You want Postum. That'll help you sleep. Winston, you have Postum, too. She held out the tray to receive his cup, which he relinquished. The reluctant yielding to the inevitable. "I'll be back in two shakes," Matty announced and bustled from the room. In her wake the air knit together a brief canopy of silence.

"He knew I was his daughter," Margaret said at last. "That's what my mother meant when she said he knew."

"His only child, as far as anyone knows," Crisp added in conclusion. "He never married."

"So he left me all he had."

"So it seems."

A brief thunder of footsteps erupted on the stairs, heralding the arrival of Kingsbury. "Well, Professor," he said without prelude as he entered the room. He cast a quick glance at Margaret. " 'Scuse me, Miss. This'll just take a minute." He turned to Crisp. "Them items you sent me to check out?"

"Yes?"

"Seems they've been cleaned up"—he was searching for a collection of words with which to skirt the issue in Margaret's presence—"in the normal course of things, you know."

Crisp nodded. "I see. Too bad."

"It was bug spray, though," Kingsbury continued. "Charlie says he noticed the smell. It reminded him of somethin', but he couldn't remember what it was 'til I asked if that's what it was."

"I wondered," said Crisp softly.

Margaret looked from Crisp, whose expression was Sphinx-like, to Kingsbury, whose expression told her nothing whatever.

"Thank you, Luther," said Crisp, attempting to embody dismissal in the words.

Kingsbury, whose wife had often scolded him for his tendency to ogle, was busy trying not to seem to be absorbing Margaret in his peripheral vision.

"Is there anything else, Luther?" Crisp prodded.

"Hmm? Oh! No. Nope." Had he forgotten something? "There wasn't anything else, was there?"

"I don't think so."

Something in Crisp's tone reminded Kingsbury that his presence at that particular time, though anticipated, hadn't been invited. "Well," he said, "I guess I better get . . ." He was about to say get home to supper, but it was too early for that. "Goin'," he amended on the fly.

"THIS COULD ALL JUST BE SPECULATION," said Margaret when she and Crisp were alone. Only a thin veil of Aqua Velva attested to Kingsbury's having been with them. "What if it was something else that upset Mother? You don't have any proof, do you?"

"I just got a call from the attorney general," Crisp replied. "Her fingerprints were found there. Fresh fingerprints."

The words ignited fires of doubt in Margaret's soul. Crisp let them burn for a while.

"What other fingerprints did they find?" she said at last, staring at her hands.

"Johnny Bermann's."

"And?" she said, raising her eyes to his.

He shook his head.

"Then just the two of them were there."

"As far as the evidence is concerned," said Crisp. "Of course, others may turn up. Even if they don't, it doesn't mean there was no one else there. They could have been wearing gloves, which is to be expected in this weather, actually."

"So you think they had this . . . this rendezvous, and when she got there she found him . . . like that?"

"That's what I think," said Crisp.

"That's what must have happened, isn't it? I mean, it's obvious; he had a heart attack while he was waiting and she . . ." It was impossible not to put herself in her mother's place. "How horrible," she said, not attempting to check the tears that spilled to her cheeks.

"He was murdered," said Crisp bluntly.

Margaret was arrested midsob. "What?"

"Premeditated, as far as I can tell," Crisp continued. He had committed to a course and was determined to see it through, whatever the consequences.

"Murdered?" Margaret whispered. Even her tears were perfect. "Someone killed him?"

"Someone," he said, letting the word hang in the air, where it mingled with Kingsbury's Aqua Velva.

"But I thought he had a heard attack."

"That's the official line, for now. Heart attack or suicide. It would help the investigation if no one knew too much."

"How?"

"In the course of interrogation, a suspect might let some piece of information slip that hasn't been released to the public. That indicates prior knowledge. However, I don't expect the story to hold long, given the way news gets around, as you've seen. In fact, I'd be surprised if most of the island didn't already suspect as much."

"But who would have done such a thing?"

Crisp heard Matty's tread on the stairs and knew it was pointless to pursue the conversation until they had disposed of the Postum.

"That wasn't so bad," said Margaret, putting her cup on the tray. The molasses cookies, shortbread, and apple spice cupcakes remained untouched.

186 THE DEAD OF WINTER

"Matty swears by it."

Margaret wasn't sitting straight anymore. Her elbows were on her knees and her hands massaged her forehead. Crisp waited.

"I know what you're trying to tell me," she said.

"You do?"

"Everything you've said—the old love affair, the rendezvous, a murder, fingerprints, and the dead man leaving me everything—people are going to think my mother . . . that my mother killed . . ." Unable to finish the sentence, she buried her face in her hands and sobbed silently.

He handed her a tissue. Lifting her face from her hands, she grabbed it like a lifeline. "She didn't kill him, Mr. Crisp. She didn't do it. She couldn't. You said she loved him."

Crisp held out his hand and she clasped it fervently between her own, wet with tears. "You don't think she would do such a thing, do you?"

The desperation in her voice was exceeded by the look of utter abandonment in her eyes. "No," he said simply. "I don't think your mother killed Johnny Bermann."

She sniffed once or twice and dabbed at her eyes and nose with the tissue, not removing her gaze from him for an instant. "But other people do? The police?"

"You have to understand," Crisp explained, "in cases like this, the authorities are guided by evidence. They have to be. They don't have a lifetime's knowledge of your mother, like you do. All they have are the facts available to them."

Margaret sighed deeply. "And they don't look good, do they?"

Crisp tried to put a hopeful face on it. "All they have are the fingerprints, and the will. The emotional change could be explained in a number of ways in a court of law."

"What about everything else—the affair, their being in London, the possibility of his being my . . . my . . ."

"That's all surmise on my part." Crisp didn't feel it advisable to mention the coded note at the moment.

"Have you told anyone?" she asked suddenly.

In light of the recent events in his life, her eagerness—though perfectly natural—put him on the defensive. "No one who'll repeat it," he said cryptically.

"But you'll have to tell, won't you?" she said. She stood up slowly and began to pace back and forth between the bed and the window.

He watched her carefully, his pulse quickening for either of two reasons that came immediately to mind. First, she was, to his way of thinking, beautiful beyond description—the most perfectly symmetrical human being he had ever encountered.

Second, she might be planning to kill him. Not likely, but certainly a consideration. As far as he was concerned, given the fact that he had been in a coma for much of the last year, it had been only weeks since another young woman tried to hasten the inevitable, in this same room. The memory was warm.

Finally she stopped beside the bed. She had reached a resolution of some kind, and it showed. "What can I do?"

"How do you mean?" said Crisp, working to not seem relieved.

"My mother did not murder that man, Professor Crisp. You were right when you said the police don't know her like I do. A leopard doesn't change its spots, and my mother didn't all of a sudden become a calculating murderess. I know it. And I'll do whatever I can to help prove it."

"She hasn't been charged with anything yet," said Crisp encouragingly. "It may never come to that. As I said, new evidence might turn up at any moment."

Having expended her nervous energy, Margaret settled at the end of the bed. "I'm still frightened, Mr. Crisp. It looks bad."

"Circumstantial, for the time being," Crisp replied.

"If Mr. Bermann was murdered . . . Now I feel silly calling him that if he was my father."

"There are tests—"

"Not now," she protested. "Mother's the important one now. As

I was saying," she sniffed back a tear with resolve and sat up straight again, "if Mr. Bermann was murdered, it had to be by someone who knew they were going to meet at Everette's. That can't have been many people, especially if it was supposed to be a secret."

Inwardly, Crisp stood bolt upright. From the mouths of babes.

"Of course," he said, with a calmness belying the almost cataclysmic grinding to life of the gears in his mind. The universe was suddenly much smaller. Who could possibly have known of Anne's secret liaison with Johnny Bermann? He proposed the question casually.

Margaret thought carefully. "I can't imagine," she said.

"Does she have any friends on the island? Close friends?"

"Not apart from Kitty Emerson. They've known each other for years."

"She'd been Mrs. Emerson's governess, I understand."

"Yes."

"How long?"

"I don't know, really. Several years at least. By the time Kitty was too old for a governess, they'd become friends. Have been ever since. You should hear them on the phone. They talk for hours. In fact, it was Kitty who introduced Mom and Dad . . . Paul."

She lowered her head. "Everything's changing, isn't it?" she said, just above a whisper.

"I'm sorry. Did you say something?"

The look she directed at him was full of questions.

"I'm a little hard of hearing," Crisp explained, cupping his good ear. "I'm sorry."

Margaret shook her head slightly. "It's not important," she said, a little louder than necessary. "I was just talking to myself."

"Did your mother and Kitty talk often?" Crisp said, trying to get the conversation back on track.

"Once a week or so, at least. The day after Christmas, most recently."

"What did they talk about?" Crisp was buying time, trying to occupy her until he could think of a question worth asking. His face portrayed nothing but calm confidence.

"I don't know. Everything. Anything. I tuned them out," she said with a laugh. "And that's not easy." Something occurred to her. "Funny, come to think of it, that last call . . . after Christmas? It wasn't as loud—"

"Animated?"

"Animated, right. It wasn't as animated as usual. At least not on this end. Mom was awfully quiet, whispering almost."

Suddenly Crisp was interested. "Really? How did your mother seem at the time, do you remember?"

The young woman thought a moment. "She was giggling. I remember sitting in the living room, laughing to myself. I thought she sounded just like a schoolgirl."

"And that didn't change after she hung up?"

Margaret shook her head. "No. It got worse, if anything. She was like a kid with—" She stopped short.

"I beg your pardon?"

"I don't think I want to say anything else," Margaret said softly. "I've said too much already."

"Like a kid with a secret, you were going to say?" Crisp hazarded.

She hung her head in response.

"Is there anyone else she might have confided in?"

Margaret shook her head.

"Your father . . . Mr. Quindenan?"

"No." She hesitated. "They don't have that kind of relationship. They . . . ," she forced out the words, "weren't close. In the last few years, they—"

"The housekeeper?" Crisp interrupted to alleviate her embarrassment.

"Cal? Goodness, no. Mother's a . . . well . . . a snob, to put it bluntly. Very class conscious, you know? Gets it from Daddy." She smiled at a mild irony. "Not that Cal exactly invites intimacy. She does her work without complaining but doesn't go far out of her way to make us feel at home." She looked up apologetically. "I mean, she's not rude or anything. It's just . . ."

Crisp was familiar with the customary attitude of islanders toward folks "from away," especially among members of the fishing community. "I understand," he said. "I wouldn't take it personally."

"Oh, I don't. She's civil and very helpful. An excellent cook, as well. It's just that it's not hard to imagine she's got a calendar hung behind a door in the pantry where she's marking off the days 'til we're gone." She laughed lightly. "Sad, in a way. I'd really like to get to know her. She's a remarkable woman. The hardest worker, man or woman, I've ever seen." She hadn't seen Matty in action, Crisp conceded. "Of course, I suppose you know she has a drinking problem?"

Crisp nodded. Margaret seemed relieved. "I hate to say that. She seems to have mastered it, for the most part. There was only one morning she slept in. She's caretaker for two or three houses on Ragged Island. You know where that is?"

"Yes," Crisp replied.

"She was up there when the storm hit, 'battening down the hatches,' as Dr. Pagitt says." She smiled. "He says those places are at the ends of the earth, down little dirt roads. She probably has to walk miles in to them in some cases, in all kinds of weather." She shivered. "Remarkable, I think. She has other jobs, too."

Crisp had made an informal study of island women over the years, and Margaret's observations thus far described most of them. A very different breed from members of the sex he'd known in Washington: angular, predatory women who laughed too loudly and had, like most of the men of his acquaintance, abandoned themselves to themselves. They would have been uncomfortable among island women, who were mostly round and soft—except their tongues—and whose perfume was a bracing nectar of sea salt, juniper, sun-dried bedspreads, and something warm in the oven. "Remarkable," Crisp agreed.

"I'm afraid her dedication is telling on her."

"How so?"

"She looks exhausted. Having to tend mother on top of all her other responsibilities, I should imagine. Up all hours. I doubt she's slept any more than mother. She's frazzled." The image of Cal's haunted, hollow eyes reminded her of another's. "And poor Dr. Pagitt doesn't look as though he can keep up much longer, either."

"I think that job would wear out men half his age," Crisp agreed.

"Speaking of which," said the young woman, rising suddenly, "I told Miss Gilchrist I wouldn't keep you long. I'm afraid she's not going to be very happy with me."

Crisp thought about the upcoming truancy. Although he looked forward to the trip to Everette's for more than purely professional reasons—it would be wonderful to get outside—he realized that any hope that Matty wouldn't find out about it was futile, as was any form of rationale he might concoct to appease her.

"Thank you for coming by," he said kindly. "I'm sorry that—"

"You've given me a lot to think about, Mr. Crisp," she said quickly. "I'm not the same person I was twenty minutes ago." She paused and smiled awkwardly. "In more ways than one."

There was nothing left to say. She reached tentatively in his direction. He reciprocated, bitterly conscious that there were only four fingers on the hand he offered her. They touched briefly, and she left.

It had been a tiring day. He fell asleep examining the Polaroids that Kingsbury had given him.

Crisp had been waiting to hear Matty close the front door. He glanced at his watch as he wound it. Ten past nine. All morning, it seemed, she'd been in and out, up and down, back and forth, hovering over him like a neurotic mother hen. Had he had enough to eat? Was he warm enough? Did he promise not to open the window or smoke his filthy pipe? As each minute crawled by on sloth's feet, his anxiety grew. If Stuffy and Kingsbury showed up before she left, the plan would dissolve in dust and ashes.

Finally, after one last admonition to "stay away from that window," she pulled the front door shut behind her, its distinctive rattle echoing through the empty house.

The echo hadn't died before his feet were on the floor. Minutes later, having extracted his warmest clothes from the closet, he was sitting on the edge of the bed, fully dressed—and exhausted.

He imagined what Matty would say when, assuming he survived the day, she had him on the carpet for his foolhardiness. She would, of course, be right in every particular.

The front door opened and his heart lumped in his throat. "Stuffy?" he called.

"Not particularly," came the unexpected reply. It was Doc Pagitt.

For an instant Crisp considered diving under the covers, but it was too late; the demon was at the bedroom door. Crisp girded himself against the assault.

"Well, look at you," said Pagitt, making no effort to conceal the arching of a suspicious eyebrow. "Matty just hailed me down and asked me to come keep an eye on you 'til she gets back." He put his bag heavily on the bed beside Crisp. "Good thing I hopped right over, I guess, or I'd've missed you."

Crisp was half wishing Pagitt would scold him back into bed. Having already pretty much overwhelmed the limits of his physical resources, he realized that the impending journey had lost much of its appeal. "I'm having a very vivid memory of a time I was caught with my fingers in the cookie jar," he said.

"I'm not surprised," Pagitt replied, settling himself in the chair. "What's so important that you're willing to put us all through the inconvenience of a midwinter funeral?"

"Johnny Bermann," said Crisp, letting the name suffice as an explanation.

"Oh, you planning on joining him?"

Crisp laughed weakly. "Not if I can help it."

"The best way you can help it is to stay put."

There was no argument.

"Where were you going?"

Crisp picked up on the past tense. "Everette's. To have a look around."

"For what, exactly?"

"Evidence," said Crisp. "I've got some ideas about how Johnny died. But I don't want to say anything until I've had a chance to confirm them."

"Why don't you just send Luther up there?" Pagitt read a world of meaning in the look that Crisp lobbed over his glasses. "Well, I'm sure you could find someone to go up there and look things over."

"You?"

"Hardly," Pagitt replied flatly.

"Gammidge?"

They both knew that the county coroner was out of the picture. "How about Leeman?"

"He's . . . busy," said Crisp, without further explanation.

"How about—"

"Tell me something, Doc," Crisp interjected. "Who do you send to a sick patient when you're under the weather?"

"I don't get under the weather," Pagitt replied reflexively. "No one else is qualified to . . ." He absorbed the meaning of his words, and nodded. He extracted a thermometer from his bag, shook it down, and stuck it in Crisp's mouth, at the same time pinching the patient's wrist between his fingers. "I get your point," he said. He counted the pulse for a few seconds in silence. "May as well stay out and freeze to death, you know, as face Matty later on."

Crisp conceded that that was an option.

"I gather you've got some help?"

"Yes. Stuffy Hutchin and Luther Kingsbury."

"Oh, it's suicide, then," Pagitt quipped. "Just so I'll know what to write on the toe tags." He rose from the bed and snapped his bag shut. "Well, that's not in my line, and I don't want to know about it. Meanwhile, least I can do is head on up to the medical center and make sure there are three beds free."

Crisp smiled. "I appreciate that."

Pagitt leveled an austere gaze at his patient. "No talking you out of it, I suppose."

"I wish you could," Crisp said truthfully. "But the information I'm able to get secondhand is just enough to let me know I'm not getting the whole picture. I need to see some things myself."

Pagitt thought for a moment. "I'll tell Matty I've taken you up to the medical center for some tests."

"She'll worry."

"Don't fret about that. You just get back safely, hear?"

"I hear and obey," said Crisp with a weak salute. "Has the autopsy been completed?"

Pagitt deadpanned. "Shouldn't we wait 'til you're deceased?"

"Johnny Bermann's autopsy," Crisp parried good-naturedly.

"I know, I know," said Pagitt, dabbing his eyes. "Yes. Massive heart failure."

Crisp was surprised. "That's it?"

"Officially."

"Unofficially?"

"I probably shouldn't say. Doctor-patient confidentiality."

"Even though the patient is dead?"

Pagitt shrugged. "Johnny had a preexisting condition."

"Being?"

"He had a congenital heart defect."

"How bad?"

"Bad enough to keep him out of the army during the war."

"I see," said Crisp. "Was it common knowledge?"

"Not as far as I know. He was on medication, and since the medical center is the only dispensary out here, that's where he got his prescription filled."

"So anyone who works up there would have had access to that information?"

"I suppose," Pagitt conceded. "But I've got to tell you, the people up there are mighty discreet. Any one of 'em knows things about their fellow islanders that could prove embarrassing if it was common knowledge. I'm not saying no one's been tempted. You know how it is in a small place like this. But to the best of my knowledge there's never been a whisper outside those walls. I'd vouch for every one of them."

Crisp's back was hurting from sitting up without a backrest. He propped himself up with a pillow. "For the sake of argument, let's assume someone came by this private piece of information. Let's assume further that this person had a reason for wanting our Mr. Bermann dead. How could the person best use the information to accomplish that end?"

Pagitt, in the pattern established by Margaret Quindenan before him, began pacing as he thought. "A number of ways, I guess. Shock comes to mind as the least problematic. The resulting heart failure would be written off as a simple heart attack, no questions asked."

Crisp shook his head. "Too risky. You'd have to really be able to get inside his head to figure out what would terrify him that much."

Pagitt stopped his perambulations. "I know what you're getting at. Makes sense that whoever killed him knew about the condition and used it against him. But who knew him that well?" he asked rhetorically. "Other than Anne Quindenan, and we've been over that."

Only one person that Crisp could think of.

"Besides," Pagitt continued thoughtfully, "the whole point of shock is catching someone off guard. Seems pretty clear that Bermann knew whoever it was who was up there with him. Knew them pretty well, I'd say."

"How about poison?"

"No sign of it in his system," said Pagitt.

"How many did you test for?"

"Specifically? None. I'm just saying none turned up in the course of the autopsy."

"What's the principal chemical in household insecticide? The lethal ingredient?"

"I wouldn't know," said Pagitt.

"Nor do I."

"Why do you ask?"

Crisp ignored the question. "Find out, would you?"

"Charlie said he smelled bug spray on Johnny Bermann."

"Find out if there's any in the body," said Crisp.

Pagitt picked up his bag and walked to the door. He stood for a moment with his hand on the doorknob. "Frankly, I hope you get to the bottom of it, Winston. You can't have this kind of thing happening in a small town without ripping holes in the social fabric. Folks are family out here, whether they like one another or not. Even the ones who move here from off island eventually earn a grudging bastard-child brand of acceptance."

"A death in the family," said Crisp knowingly.

"Exactly." At that moment there was a disturbance in the hall. Pagitt opened the door. "The Keystone Kops have arrived," he said, with just the slightest hint of acerbity.

CHAPTER 15

THE COCA-COLA SIGN, a sheet-metal flying carpet, performed as advertised, although an unexpected moment of suspense presented itself when Kingsbury and Stuffy Hutchin were wading through the first ranks of snowdrifts between the driveway and Everette's house, each of them confident that the other had the rope. Had Kingsbury not responded with a good deal more alacrity than one would have thought him capable, Crisp would have had the sled ride of a lifetime down the long, undulating slope to the deep, ice-encrusted waters of the bay.

Nevertheless, Crisp was savoring every delicious moment of the outing, and his poet's soul was a seething cauldron of hyperbole, although he couldn't extract a single worthy phrase to describe his exhilaration at being outside. He'd scarcely dared hope he'd ever see the open sky again or feel the brittle nip of winter wind, much less enjoy the pleasure of a sled ride.

Little more than flesh and bones, Crisp was weak as a newborn kitten. As for the color of his skin, if not for the many layers of clothes that cocooned him, he would have blended against the snowy background without much difficulty.

The old house loomed ahead, seeming to eye their approach with suspicion in every vacant window. Crisp surveyed the dooryard with misgiving. The snow had been trampled flat by crowds of the curious—professional and amateur alike—squashing any hope he had of learning something from footprints.

"Been a lot of gawkers up here," said Stuffy, rolling the Camel stub to the left side of his mouth as he strained with his physical effort.

"Hard to keep 'em away," said Kingsbury. "You know how folks are."

"They know it was murder, then?" said Crisp, worried that any evidence inside the house might have been destroyed as well.

"Not officially," said Kingsbury. "But it'd be a Christmas miracle if it wasn't all over town by noon of the day Joel found the body. He ain't about to keep somethin' like that from his cronies down to the hardware store. Might as well take out an ad in the *New York Times*. It'd be an awful strange way to commit suicide. And he ain't likely to've had a heart attack and tossed a sheet over himself, is he?"

"You hold on, Professor," said Stuffy. "I'll get up on the porch with the rope, and pull. Luther, you get behind and push. No, don't push the Professor. Get right down and push on the sign. Ready, Professor?"

Crisp braced himself with his arms. "I think so," he said doubtfully.

Fortunately the steps weren't steep, or the passenger would have tumbled into Kingsbury's lap on Stuffy's first heave. As it happened, Crisp managed to right himself at the critical moment. Balance was preserved until Kingsbury could throw his weight behind the makeshift sled and propel it the remaining three or four feet onto the porch.

Crisp was stunned by how exhausted he was. Though he hadn't been the one doing the work, the demands placed upon his body by

the reactions of his natural gyroscope during the rolling ride had
sapped his strength entirely. His breath was coming in gasps, the
frigid air biting at his lungs as he drew it in.

"You okay, Professor?" said Stuffy, himself out of breath.

"I think . . . I," Crisp panted between breaths, but the remaining
words of assurance wouldn't come. He nodded weakly, and held up
his hand.

"What does he want?" Kingsbury asked.

"I think he wants to rest a minute," Stuffy hazarded. "That right,
Professor? You want to rest a minute?"

Crisp nodded.

"He up to it, you think?" said Kingsbury. "You up to it, Professor?" he added, a little louder.

Crisp held up an index finger. "Rest," he said. Even as he tried
to catch his breath, he was becoming painfully aware of how poor
his circulation was. Cold was creeping into his bones despite the
layers of clothing, and it embraced him with a deadly chill as thoroughly pervasive as seawater. His missing digits proclaimed their
absence loudly.

Pagitt had been right in warning him. Matty would be right
when she scolded him. He hoped he lived to hear it. "Cold," he
said, embracing himself. In the thick wreaths of steam that issued
from his mouth and nostrils, he imagined warmth taking flight from
the core of his being.

"I've got just the thing," said Luther. He hurried back to the
truck and returned a minute later with a scarred metal Thermos.
"Hot soup." He unscrewed the white plastic cap of the Thermos,
which would serve as a cup, then the red plastic stopper, releasing
a fragrant cloud of steam. He filled the cup. "Maggie wouldn't let
me out in this weather without somethin' hot," he said, handing the
cup to Crisp. "Drink slow. It's right off the stove."

The warmth penetrated Crisp's thick woolen mittens as he cradled the cup in his hands. He felt lightheaded and knew it was
because his brain wasn't getting enough oxygen. His heart was gath-

ering heat from his extremities in a last-ditch effort to save itself. The steam was warm on his face. He breathed it deep into his lungs. It felt moist and soothing. He took a sip of the hot liquid and held it in his mouth for a second. Chicken soup. He loved chicken soup. When at last he swallowed, it was as if the faint promise of spring had whispered through the bowels of his being. He took another sip, a little larger this time. Then another, larger still, imbibing life with every draught.

Kingsbury and Stuffy exchanged doubtful glances, and Stuffy shook his head, mouthing the words, let's get him home.

Kingsbury took the lead. "We'd better get you home, Professor. It ain't doin' you no good bein' here in this kind of weather. Too damn cold. I'm half froze to death myself," he lied. Actually, he never much noticed the cold.

"No," Crisp replied breathlessly. They waited while he took another couple of sips. Finally, he handed the cup back to Kingsbury. "Thank you, Luther," he said with a heartfelt nod at Maggie's sagacity. "I'm all right."

"I seen healthier fish on a plate," Stuffy remarked pointedly. "This wasn't such a good idea. Luther's right. We've got to get you back to town while there's somethin' left to put in bed."

Crisp inhaled slowly. "Get my walker, Stuffy. Please."

Stuffy was heartened by the sense of command in Crisp's voice, however faint. "You sure?"

"I'm sure," said Crisp. It was his turn to lie. The only thing he was sure of at the moment was that he'd just knocked pretty loudly on death's door, and no one had answered. Must be a reason, Matty would say.

Five minutes later they were inside the house, where, if possible, it was even colder. "I'll keep this handy," said Kingsbury, tapping the Thermos. "You holler if you need it."

"Thank you, Luther. I will."

The air was completely still. Crisp sniffed. Mothballs. Musty linen.

Kingsbury sniffed. "I don't smell that bug spray anymore. Wasn't very strong to begin with."

They had guided Crisp to the piano stool. He leaned forward on the old grand piano, burying his mouth in the crook of his arm, where he could warm the air before breathing it in. He studied the room.

"That's where the body was," said Kingsbury, pointing through the large arch that divided the sitting room from the living room. "There's the chair, see? Has arms, like I said. Everything's been left just the way it was. Me an' Doc and Gammidge is the only ones that've been in here since."

"And Joel Philbrook," Stuffy reminded them.

" 'Since,' I said." Kingsbury turned to Crisp. "Nothin' else's been touched."

"What's that?" said Crisp, releasing an index finger from the warmth of his fist just long enough to point at a frozen puddle on the floor behind the chair.

"Don't know," said Kingsbury, going to investigate. He took off his glove and bent down to run his finger over the spot. "Ice," he pronounced. He looked up at the ceiling. "Must be some kind of leak. I better tell Joel."

"Stuffy, would you mind going upstairs?" Crisp asked from the crook of his arm. "See if there's anything overhead that might leak. Maybe a bathroom."

"Sure thing."

Kingsbury sniffed his finger. "There's that smell again, Professor," he said. "Bug spray."

"May I?" said Crisp, raising his head.

Kingsbury returned to the piano and held his finger under Crisp's nose. Crisp inhaled. The smell was faint but discernible. Definitely chemical. "I see what you mean." His eyes wandered carefully around the room until he saw something that made him sit up. "There's tape around the windows. Why would that be?"

Kingsbury followed his gaze to the bay windows overlooking the

Thoroughfare. "Tape, around the windows?"

So there was. The trim on each of the windows was carefully framed with a wide ribbon of masking tape.

"Nothing up there," said Stuffy, returning. "No plumbing anywhere on that side, from what I can tell. It'd be turned off anyway."

"Thanks, Stuf," said Crisp.

"What do you make of this, Syl?" said Kingsbury from the front room.

"What?"

"Pr'fessor noticed the windows are taped."

Stuffy quickly inspected the rest of the windows. "They all are."

"Why, do you s'pose? Insulation?"

"If that stuff could keep out the cold, I'd have my house wrapped in it," said Stuffy.

"Might keep out the wind a little," Kingsbury figured.

"These places get awful warm in the summer," said Stuffy. "They want all the breeze they can get. I seen a whole closet full of screens upstairs. They use 'em, too."

Crisp listened carefully to the speculation.

"Windows taped up there?" asked Kingsbury.

"Not that I noticed."

"How 'bout the doors?"

Stuffy inspected the porch door. "Nothing here now," he said, running his fingers along the uprights. "But there was. Still sticky. Little bit of paint missin' here and there."

"Hermetically sealed," Crisp observed. "Do me a favor, Luther. Look in that room off to the right. See if you can find something that might have been used to carry water."

Kingsbury had no sooner entered the room than he returned carrying a much-used dishpan. "Somethin' like this?"

Crisp smiled inside. "Anything in it?"

"Yup." He brought the pan to Crisp. "Two or three inches, froze solid."

"What was it hidden under?"

Kingsbury looked askance at Crisp. "A couple of life jackets," he said. "How'd you know?"

Crisp had lowered his nose to the pan. "Same smell."

"Darnedest thing," said Kingsbury.

"That's what Johnny Bermann's feet were soaked in," said Crisp.

"What good would that do?" Kingsbury asked.

"Many kinds of poison are absorbed through the skin. The feet are especially susceptible."

"Where'd they get water, Pr'fessor? Like Syl said, the plumbin's all been shut down and winterized."

"Well, let me see the pan."

Kingsbury held the pan in front of Crisp. He ran his finger over the surface of the frozen liquid and put it to his tongue. "Seawater."

"Makes sense," said Stuffy. He took a Camel from the pack in his inside coat pocket and stuck it between his lips.

A thought occurred to Kingsbury. "Then someone took it to the closet to hide it and spilled some on the floor."

"The puddle," said Stuffy.

"Someone in a hurry," Crisp thought aloud. "Otherwise they'd have disposed of it properly."

"Why would they be in a hurry?" Kingsbury asked.

"What are the possibilities?" said Crisp.

"Somethin' went wrong?"

"Like what?"

As Kingsbury considered the question, the answer hit him like an electric shock. "Somebody showed up unexpected."

"Sooner than expected anyway," said Crisp noncommittally.

"Makes sense to me," said Stuffy, somewhat grudgingly. "Somebody shows up right in the middle of whatever was goin' on . . . this foot-soakin' business . . . and the murderer seen 'em comin'—"

"That's it," Crisp interrupted. "Let's assume you're the murderer," he said, turning to Stuffy. "You've planned this whole business carefully. Why here?"

"It's out of the way," said Kingsbury.

"Nobody but Joel comes up here all winter," said Stuffy. "And he don't come none too often, if I know Joel."

"Not someone who'd be likely to drop in during a storm, would you say?"

"So? What're you gettin' at?"

"I know," said Stuffy. "Whoever done this knew they wouldn't get interrupted by anyone showin' up enexpected, so they wouldn't've kept gettin' up to go to the front of the house to see if the way was clear."

"So?" Crisp prompted.

"But you just said they probably *was* interrupted," Kingsbury protested.

"But not by someone unexpected," said Stuffy, sorting out the puzzle pieces in his mind. "If they kept an eye on the dooryard, it's because they *was* expectin' someone."

"I believe you've got the tail of the beast," said Crisp.

"All right," Kingsbury allowed. "If they was expectin' somebody, why the rush to clean up when that somebody showed up?"

"Two reasons come to mind," said Crisp. "First, whoever was coming expected to find Johnny Bermann alone."

"Fair enough," said Kingsbury. "Second?"

"Timing," Crisp replied. "I think the killer intended whoever it was—the one they did expect—to show up when the deed had been done and everything was cleaned up." The thought, spoken aloud like that, presented another possible dimension to the crime: What if the murderer wasn't trying to make Johnny Bermann's death appear a suicide? What if the murderer had intended evidence to point to the third party—Anne Quindenan? He decided to keep the notion to himself for the time being.

"But things didn't happen like they were s'posed to," Stuffy said knowingly.

"Namely?" Crisp prodded again.

"Johnny Bermann didn't die like he was s'posed to."

"I agree," said Crisp.

"Then why not just shoot him, or stab him?" Kingsbury wondered. "There's prob'ly some good knives in the kitchen."

"Because it was supposed to look like a heart attack," Crisp explained patiently. He held up a hand in response to the question forming behind Kingsbury's perplexed frown "Here's what I think happened. The killer, or killers, knew that Johnny Bermann was going to meet someone here."

"What in hell for?" asked Kingsbury, unable to contain the question as it occurred to him.

"Obvious," said Stuffy. "Romance."

"Take a hell of a lot more heat than that thing could put out 'fore Maggie'd get romantic in this old icebox," said Kingsbury, nodding at the Franklin stove.

"Be that as it may," said Crisp. "Let's assume that's the case. The killer knew about it—"

"How?" asked Kingsbury impatiently.

"Let him get a word in edgewise, will you, Luther?" Stuffy demanded. "Go on ahead, Professor."

"Thank you," said Crisp. "Frankly, Luther, I don't know. For now, let's just say that somehow the killer found out they were going to meet up here. The killer also knew that Johnny would be here well before the rendezvous, probably to make things ready. Heat the place up, and so on. There being no electricity, of course, Johnny lit a candle or two."

"That's the light Alby seen when he was comin' 'cross the Thoroughfare," Kingsbury surmised.

"Very likely," Crisp agreed. "Even a dim light would have been visible on a gray day like that was. I'm surprised no smoke was seen."

"Depends on the wood they was burnin'," said Stuffy. "Dry old maple wouldn't make enough smoke to amount to anything."

"Really?" said Crisp. "I didn't know that."

"Okay," Luther intervened. "How're you sayin' Johnny was killed?"

"Poison."

"The bug spray?"

"Something like it."

"You'd have to spray that stuff down someone's throat to kill 'em."

Crisp raised a knowing eyebrow. "Perhaps not, if the victim had a heart condition that made him particularly susceptible."

"Johnny had a heart condition?" asked Stuffy.

"According to Doc Pagitt, yes," said Crisp. "And what you said about spraying it down his throat," he added, tilting his head toward Kingsbury, "might not be far off the mark."

"Really?"

"What does the evidence tell us? Why were the windows taped up? Not to keep out the cold or the wind. You've both given good reasons for that. What then? I'd say to keep something in."

"Bug spray fumes?" Kingsbury ventured.

Crisp nodded. "The murderer was aware of Johnny Bermann's condition."

Kingsbury drew a breath to ask how, but Crisp stilled him with an upraised hand. "Just for the sake of argument, let's say that's how it was."

Kingsbury relented.

"Learning of the rendezvous, the murderer decided to arrange Johnny Bermann's death in a way that would make it appear either natural—a result of his heart condition—or a suicide." He kept the final alternative to himself for the moment.

"He taped the windows up and sprayed the place with insecticide."

"Must've worn some kind of face mask," Stuffy suggested.

"They sell them at the hardware store," said Crisp. "Yes, something like that, no doubt.

"I use 'em myself when I'm sandin' boat bottoms," said Stuffy.

"I expect the killer's idea was just to hide upstairs, or in a closet, after Johnny arrived. By that time the cloud would have settled but the chemical would still be in the air, perhaps not heavily enough—given the powerful smell of mothballs—to raise suspicion but still strong enough to do the job, providing he inhaled enough of it.

"The killer waited and watched. When he saw Johnny coming, he removed the tape from the door, then went and hid somewhere. Meanwhile, Johnny comes in and, suspecting nothing amiss, goes about the business of making things ready for his visitor.

"After a few minutes, he starts to feel sick—headache and nausea, I suspect. He probably sat somewhere, or laid down to see if it would pass. It didn't. It got worse. As the poison worked its way into his lungs, his system reacted violently in an effort to get rid of it."

"Which explains the mess we found in the toilet," said Kingsbury. "Both ends."

"The plan was working, to an extent. But something was wrong. Maybe enough fresh air had come in when he entered the house or was coming in under the untaped door. Whatever the case, he wasn't ingesting enough poison to do the job in time."

"Spray more bug spray?" Stuffy offered.

Crisp shook his head. "No. It hadn't worked as expected. The killer was under pressure. The second party was going to show up any minute. The killer panicked and abandoned the original plan in favor of something more direct.

"Johnny Bermann would have been considerably weakened by the loss of fluid. He may have been delirious, even unconscious. The murderer puts him in a chair and tapes his arms to the armrests."

"Which explains the stickiness on his forearms," said Kingsbury, impressed by how easily unfathomable mysteries could be explained. "What about the Ivory?"

Crisp held up a hand. "The pesticide was probably soluble, a powder of some kind. I expect that when the spray didn't do the job, the killer mixed the remainder with water in some kind of portable container."

"Then takes off Johnny's shoes and socks and puts his feet in it," said Stuffy.

"Exactly," said Crisp. "But Johnny Bermann is having convulsions by this time. His body is contracting, balling up in a knot, raising his feet out of the water."

"So the murderer pushes down on his knees," Kingsbury speculated. "Them bruises."

"Why the one shoe off, one shoe on, business?" Stuffy asked directly, a rare occurrence.

"When Mr. Bermann finally died, the killer immediately fell back on his first plan," explained Crisp. " If things were cleaned up, there would be no reason to suppose that Johnny hadn't died of natural causes, at best. Suicide at worst." He reserved the third option. "But when the tape was removed from his wrists, the residue of the adhesive remained."

"So the killer tries to get it off with Ivory soap," Kingsbury deduced enthusiastically.

Crisp nodded and continued. "Probably using water from the dishpan. But he wasn't as careful as he might have been had his plans not gone awry. As he was carrying the pan to the closet, probably intending to come back and do a more thorough cleaning later, a little spilled. He'd get that later, too. The first thing was to put Johnny's shoes and socks back on.

"He dressed one foot, then he must have heard something outside—a car door perhaps? He went to look out the front window."

"And saw someone comin'," Stuffy concluded, working his cigarette butt to the assertive side of his mouth.

"The woman," said Kingsbury.

"So it would seem," said Crisp. "He ran and hid, probably in the same place he'd hidden earlier."

"He could've killed the woman, too," Kingsbury added excitedly.

"Possibly," said Crisp. "But I don't think there was much real danger to her. This person had planned carefully for fear of being caught, and so much had already gone wrong. I don't think he'd have much faith in his ability to pull off another convincing 'accident.' Obviously, the killer expected that the woman would run back to town and sound the alarm, so it was too late to change anything. My bet is that he was out the door as soon as the woman left and was out of sight."

"What about the footprints?" said Kingsbury. "They was mostly filled with snow by the time I saw 'em, but there's no reason to doubt that Joel was right when he figured there was only two sets—one a man going to the house, and another a woman comin' and goin'. That accounts for Johnny Bermann and the woman who visited him. Nobody else."

"Did anyone think to check the other side of the house?"

" 'Course not." Kingsbury said incredulously. He almost laughed. "That goes straight down to the ocean!"

Crisp simply looked at him.

"All right, dammit. I'll go look."

When the door slammed behind Kingsbury, Stuffy propped his foot on the piano stool and lit his soggy cigarette. "Seems to me, if everything happened the way you say, there should be lots of evidence around here."

"I agree. There should be some trace of adhesive under the arms of that chair," Crisp said, nodding at the next room. "There should be a bag of powdered insecticide somewhere, pretty substantial wads of tape, and a closet from which the murderer could get a clear look at his handiwork."

"Easy enough to check out," said Stuffy pragmatically, and he set off to do so.

Crisp felt himself weakening again. He twisted the top off Kingsbury's Thermos and poured himself another cup of Maggie's chicken soup, the elixir of life.

"Why?" he whispered through the steam.

Outside the window, the icicles began to melt.

"I S'POSE YOU FOUND IT ALL," said Olaf Ingraham—ever the skeptic—as he dealt the cards. Tib's Pool Hall, traditionally the last place on the island to close at night, had adopted early hours since Beelzebub had come on-line from 6 A.M. 'til 2 P.M. south of the Main Street bridge, 2 P.M. 'til midnight to the north, as Matty had predicted via Phyllis Clayton.

It was here, through a perpetual pall of tobacco smoke, that Stuffy had delivered the update, with Crisp's blessing. "There was adhesive under the arms of the chair, just like the Professor said there would be. And footprints in a layer of dust on the floor in the only closet that had a lookout on both rooms. None of the other closets in the whole house had footprints in 'em."

"What about the insecticide?" Olaf pressed.

"No sign of that," Stuffy conceded. "But it'll turn up."

"And the footprints?"

"Two sets," said Stuffy. "One comin' and one goin'." He played an eight on Harry Young's seven. "Fifteen for two."

"Goin' where?" Harry complained. "Ain't nothing but ledge and ocean on that side."

"There was tracks down to the boathouse," Stuffy explained patiently. "You playin', Bill?"

Bill played a four for nineteen.

"So that's how the killer got there, in a boat," said Harry, taking a swig on his empty Coke bottle. He called toward the counter. "Brenda! Coke, and don't forget my nickel deposit on the bottle."

Harry turned back to Stuffy. "You think they'd've looked there first time around."

"Didn't seem necessary at the time, I don't s'pose," Stuffy replied. "Three for thirty."

"Go," said Bill when reminded that it was his turn again. He'd been listening carefully. "There's something that doesn't make sense, though, if you think about it."

"What's that?" said Stuffy.

"How did this killer know about Johnny Bermann's heart condition? Seems he kept it pretty much to himself, 'cept for Doc Pagitt."

"There's a good point," said Harry. "Doc wouldn't've told nobody. Brenda!"

"Hold your horses," Brenda called from behind the counter.

"And how did he know they were meeting up there in the first place?" Bill concluded. "Seems they went to a lot of trouble to keep it secret. It doesn't seem likely they would have told anyone else, much less someone who wanted to see Johnny dead."

"That's what gets me," said Brenda, dropping the bottle on top of Harry's crib with some authority. "Why'd anyone want to see Johnny dead in the first place? Pretty harmless fella, I'd say."

"Professor reckons the woman he was meetin' was married," said Stuffy, without looking up from his cards.

"Oh," said Brenda, to whom things suddenly appeared in a whole new light. "That'd be one who'd want Johnny dead ... the husband."

Stuffy counted out his points. "Fifteen two, four, six, three is nine and right jack is ten."

"Margaret Quindenan's not married," Brenda observed.

"Margaret's her name, you say?" asked Althea Billings, ducking out from the dryer, the better to hear the conversation.

"That's right," said Irma Louise, proprietress of the House of Beauty, as she prepared a noxious mix of chemicals with which to turn her customer's hair unnatural colors. "She comes in to the whole property."

"What do you make of that?" said Dot Thompson, her voice echoing from the sink.

"You don't s'pose she was the woman he was meeting with, do you?" said Althea, her singsong voice rising nearly an octave between her first and last "you."

"Had to be someone," Irma observed pragmatically.

"That's true," said Dot from the sink. "Had to be someone."

Althea thought this over. "But she's awful young. She'd be half his age."

"Less," said Irma disdainfully. "But you know how men are."

" 'Course it's all right for men to see younger women," said Dot, not without some bitterness. "But just you turn it the other way around and you'll have the whole town talkin' 'fore you know it."

The conversation digressed for a while into various particulars of sexual inequity, resolving, as it always did, on the fact that ladies' rooms should be twice the size of men's rooms or the ratio should be two to one. "You never see a line outside a men's room," said Althea.

"That's 'cause they go outside in the bushes," Irma said with a laugh, and the others joined in.

When things settled down, Althea mopped a trickle of blue dye from her forehead. "He didn't seem the type, though," she said.

"Oh, you can never tell with men," Dot perceived. "It's the quiet ones you have to watch out for. The loud ones are all talk and no action."

Althea broke the brief silence that followed that declaration. "I heard talk it might be a married woman. That would've been her footprints in the dooryard. But whose were those down to the shore?"

"Sounds like one've them love triangles to me," said Irma.

"How do you mean?" asked Althea.

"Remember what Norm Philbrook did when he found his wife, Missy, steppin' out with Cray Lawson?"

"Sunk his boat," Dot remembered. " 'Bout the worst thing a man could do."

"Not quite," said Irma, drawing a finger meaningfully across her throat.

Althea's eyes widened like saucers. "You think that's what happened? Someone come in on Johnny and the woman, and killed him?"

"That makes no sense," said Dot. "Elsewise they'd've found 'em both dead."

"Not necessarily," Irma replied calmly. "Supposin' after doin' away with Johnny Bermann, the murderer took the woman home with him. Said if she ever talked, same thing could happen to her. Somethin' like that."

"Then they left in different directions?" said Dot incredulously.

"Have to, wouldn't they?" Irma countered. "He couldn't leave the boat he come in, and she'd've had a car or truck."

"Who do you s'pose it could've been?" said Althea, with child-like wonder.

"That's the question, isn't it?" said Irma.

"You know," said Althea breathlessly, "this sounds just like somethin' off *The Guidin' Light*."

"Nope," said Dot. "From what I heard, it wasn't no crime of passion. It was all thought out."

Irma considered this and warmed to the idea. "What if the murderer found out that Johnny was meetin' his wife up at Everette's, and he planned everything out?"

This scenario struck Dot as plausible. "Now, you may have something there, Irm'."

"Well then," said Althea, "that leaves Margaret Quindenan out, don't it?"

"That's why he looked like he was cryin'," said Jerry Oakes, slipping a hook through a herring's eye and spooling the line into the trawl tub. When business was slow, as it generally was after Christmas, he baited trawl for extra cash. "It was them chemicals."

"Professor figured all this out, you say?" said Mont Billings. This news would be worth fifteen or twenty minutes in Pharty's chair once the hardware store opened this afternoon. Mont would be first in line when the power came on.

"Stuffy and Luther took him up there," said Jerry. "Dragged him up on some kind of sled they rigged up. Luther says he was too weak to even stand up, so they set him down by this piano they got up there, and he just looks around and starts sayin' this happened here and that happened there, and Luther and Stuffy start pokin' around like he tells 'em to, and they find everything just the way he said they would. Put ol' Sherlock Holmes right in the shade, Luther says."

Woodrow Martin, whose voice seldom rose above a whisper, was sitting by the stove, whittling twigs off a stack of spruce bows in preparation for bending. "Ain't that somethin'," he said. "Last I heard he was two-thirds dead himself. I guess his brain ain't much worse for wear."

"I wouldn't say so," Jerry agreed, pulling another six feet of line through his fingers. "I hear he told Doc Pagitt and Charlie Williams to open Johnny up again and look for that poison—bug spray or whatever it was—and they found it."

"Missed it the first time around, did they?" said Mont.

Jerry didn't know. "Once they figured out he died of heart failure, I guess they didn't look no further."

"So, they know it was poison done the job."

"Seems so," said Jerry.

"Next question is, who done it, and why."

"Professor's workin' on that now, I bet. I tell you," said Jerry, "I wouldn't want to be the killer once that old fella starts firin' on all cylinders." He tapped his temple meaningfully.

The men entertained their own thoughts for a few minutes. Jerry finished one line of trawl, rolled the tub out of the way, and started a new one. Woodrow laced a bow through the bending frame with practiced hands, and Mont poured himself another cup of coffee.

"Awful thing," sighed Woodrow at last, "to think there's a murderer on the island. Someone we wave at on the road, sit next to at the church supper. Makes you think twice about takin' a walk at night, don't it?"

Secret was a relative term in this isolated world and generally implied something that everyone knew but no one spoke about. In a few words, Woodrow had framed the real horror underlying all the island's conversation that morning: Someone had slipped the net. One of them held a secret indeed. And that one was a murderer.

Crisp scanned one last time through the document Leeman had tossed on his bed. He'd done a good job of research. It had taken him the better part of three days, but between the Island Historical Society, the library, town records, and interviews with two or three people still alive who had worked at the Bermann estate in its heyday, he'd compiled a list of birthdays, anniversaries, and other important dates pertaining to the immediate family. Unfortunately, none of them turned out to be a key to the code used in Oscar's diary.

Crisp was bitterly disappointed. He had no doubt that the documents at his fingertips held the answers to a number of critical questions, but without the key they would hold those answers forever.

"All that work for nothin'," said Leeman. He was disappointed, too. "I thought sure it was in there somewhere. Makes me almost mad enough to swear."

"The numbers may not have had any personal significance at all." Crisp opened Bermann's coded notebook and held it under the light, as if he hoped that the now-familiar characters would somehow tell him something new. "It could just as easily have been an arbitrary set, or one determined by his employers."

"Whoever they were," said Leeman.

Crisp ran his fingers absentmindedly across the page. Leeman watched the old fingers trace the old words on the old paper. Suddenly he noticed something. "What's that?" Leeman said. He grabbed the book from Crisp's hands and held the page at a sharp angle to the storm lantern.

"You see something?"

Leeman leaned close to the page, tilting the book back and forth, trying to make out something. "Writing. 'P'? No. 'R.E.' I can't make out if that's a 'W' or a 'U.' It's that old, fancy kind of writing."

"Let me see." Crisp adjusted the glasses on his nose and leaned into the light. "Where are you looking?"

"Here."

Crisp followed Leeman's finger, then raised worried eyes. "There's nothing there, Leeman."

"Not in ink," said Leeman. "It's just pressed in, like somebody was writing on a piece of paper over this one."

Crisp squinted at the page and silently cursed his eyes. It had been there all along.

"Try to make it out."

"I am. A 'V.' That's what it is—a 'V' and a period. I thought it was a 'W.'"

"Anything else?" Crisp asked eagerly.

"Numbers, looks like. Two ones separated by a dash, then one of these things." He punched a colon in the air with his finger.

"A colon?"

"Right."

Instantly Crisp understood the significance of the letters. "There's more? Another number?"

"Yup. Twenty-three."

"Twenty-three? Are you sure?"

"Right there," said Leeman, pointing at the significant character as he tipped the page in Crisp's direction. Crisp still couldn't see it.

From momentary elation, Crisp was suddenly perplexed. If memory served, the number didn't apply. "Excuse me, Leeman," he said, reaching for the drawer of his bedside table. Leeman hitched his chair out of the way as Crisp opened the drawer and took out the Bible that Matty had put there. Leaning toward the light, he flipped quickly to the eleventh chapter of Revelation. "I didn't think so. There are only nineteen verses in chapter eleven."

"That's what this is?" Leeman tapped the book in his hand.

"Must be. Rev. is the abbreviation for Revelation. Eleven is the chapter, followed by a colon, then the number. You're sure it says twenty-three?"

Leeman pressed himself as close to the book as the strength of his eyes would permit, then read aloud, "Twenty-three." He sat up and shook his head. "That's all I see. It's pretty clear."

A vague smile crept to the corners of Crisp's mouth. "Is there any chance that the two and three are separated by a hyphen?"

"A dash, you mean?" asked Leeman for clarification. He looked closely. "Darned if they ain't." The eyes he turned to Crisp were full of admiration. "I wouldn't've noticed if I hadn't looked for it."

"Revelation eleven, verses two and three." Crisp traced the page to the indicated verses and read aloud: " 'But exclude the outer court; do not measure it, because it has been given to the Gentiles. They will trample on the holy city for forty-two months. And I will give power to my two witnesses; and they will prophesy for twelve hundred and sixty days, clothed in sackcloth.' "

Once again Leeman's hopes were dashed. "Them Bible people was crazy."

"Enigmatic, at any rate," said Crisp. In the dim reaches of the past, he'd had to play a cardinal of the Catholic Church. In the process, he'd memorized a section of Paul's first letter to the Corinthians that had bothered him ever since; chapter 1: verses 20–25. It returned to him now, in response to Leeman's evaluation, but he decided to keep it to himself.

"Be that as it may," said Crisp, "Old Man Bermann wasn't crazy, at any rate." He shut the Bible and thumped it loudly. "We've just had a revelation, my friend."

"We have?"

Crisp placed the Bible in the drawer and closed it. "There are two sets of numbers in the verses I just read—forty-two and twelve hundred and sixty."

"They're the key?"

"There's one way to find out." Crisp held out his hand and Leeman gave him Bermann's codebook, which he opened to the first page. "The code is both deceptively simple and flawlessly complex," he said with one craftsman's admiration for the work of another. "He was so confident of the code that he included punctuation." Leeman saw a sparkle in Crisp's eyes. "Beautiful arrogance."

"Beautiful?"

"Read the first word."

Contorting himself so as to be as close to parallel to the page as possible, Leeman spelled the word aloud. 'X-q-o-k-m-h-p.' He sat up. "Gobbledygook."

"Here." Crisp handed Leeman the pad of paper and a pencil from the bedside table. "Write down the word." Leeman did so. "Now, write the code number."

"Revelation Eleven?"

"No, no. The numbers in the verse: four-two-one-two-six-oh. Just write it up in the corner there, somewhere out of the way."

Leeman scratched out the number. "What now?"

Crisp leaned back against his pillow. "We have to find out if he was working backward or forward. Increase the number of the first letter by the first number."

"Huh?"

"The first letter is 'X,' right?"

Leeman consulted the page. "Yup."

"The first number in the code is four. What letter comes fourth after 'X' in the alphabet?" Crisp queried patiently.

Leeman ran through the latter part of the alphabet aloud, counting four after 'X' on his fingers. "I run out of alphabet."

"Start back at the beginning."

"With 'A'?"

Crisp nodded.

Leeman worked out the puzzle. " 'B.' "

"Good. Now do the rest of the word the same way."

"Increase the second letter by the second number?"

"Yes."

Crisp closed his eyes and listened with a profound sense of contentment as Leeman labored over the cipher. "Add two to 'Q' and you get . . . 'S.'"

"He was working backward," said Crisp without opening his eyes. "Go back from the letters rather than forward."

"I haven't finished the word yet."

"You did enough," said Crisp. "I can't think of any word that begins with 'BS,' can you?"

Leeman was tempted to say he could think of something that 'BS' signified, but he refrained. "So, I go backward four from 'X' for the first one?"

"See what happens."

In the long silence that followed, Crisp made a conscious effort not to work the word out mentally, preferring to share in Leeman's exultation when it appeared on the page.

"Nope," Leeman pronounced finally. "I thought I had 'er there for a second. But it fell apart."

Crisp opened his eyes and turned toward his fellow code breaker with renewed interest. "What do you mean?"

"See for yourself." Leeman handed him the paper. "I thought it was going to say 'tonight.'"

"T-O-N-I-G-M," said Crisp, reading what Leeman had written. "Zero is a reverser," he said with admiration.

"Pardon?"

"It's an old trick. Cryptologists often put in what's called a 'reverser,' an element that turns the code around. It seems that Mr. Bermann used the zero."

"What's that mean in English?"

"It means that you count in the opposite direction every time you reach a zero."

"What if there's no zero in the code?"

"Then you pick any one of the numbers in the code."

Leeman considered this for a moment, and Crisp let him. "So the T-O-N-I-G is right. Then the 'H' stays an 'H,' cause it's zero— no change?" He tossed a questioning glance at Crisp, who nodded. "Then I start countin' forward from the next letter after that?"

"Try it."

Leeman counted again. " 'T!' " he exclaimed. "The word's 'tonight'!"

"By George, I think he's got it," Crisp said with a chuckle.

"Can I do the rest of it?"

"By all means."

The following half hour was filled with the sounds of intense concentration as Leeman wrestled with each letter. "This is givin' me a goshdarn headache," he said at one point, but he didn't stop until the sentence was decoded. "There!" he said, handing Crisp the paper, now heavily marked and smudged with erasures, but the sentence was clear.

Crisp read it aloud. " 'Tonight. Two signals, at eight and eleven. No reply.' "

He held out his hand. "Well done, Leeman. You're an official code breaker."

Leeman pumped the offered hand with unabashed pride. "We did it!" After a few seconds his eyes fell to the codebook. "That's hard work. It'll take forever to go through the whole thing."

"Not necessarily," said Crisp. "There are a lot of similar entries. I think we can take it for granted that they're pretty much the same thing, a record of when Mr. Bermann was sending his signals."

"Who to, do you s'pose?"

"I think that may be revealed in these other entries," said Crisp, pointing at the irregular items scattered throughout the book. "It will be interesting to see what Oscar has to say for himself."

17

CRISP WAS ALONE IN HIS ROOM, with a silence so profound it seemed to gather 'round him, and peek over his shoulders as he read:

The Accused
Introduction

"My father, Oscar Bermann, arrived on Penobscot Island in the spring of 1914 aboard the coasting steamship *Hurricane*. With him, in addition to all his earthly possessions, were my mother, Ingrid, a native of Oslo, Norway, and Elsa, our cook and housekeeper from Germany, a woman in her mid-twenties who had joined the family the week immediately prior to our departure for the United States.

"Within two years my mother had died during childbirth. She and the child are buried on the property at Robert's cemetery, and I have seen their graves. Elsa had disappeared under mysterious circumstances, and father had been labeled a spy and run off the island, taking me with him.

"I undertook the writing of this book in the faithful expectation that I would find, among the family archives, which still exist in boxes in the attic at the island estate, evidence with which to dispel the cloud of suspicion surrounding his memory and prove conclusively—to my own satisfaction, if no one else's (for there are always those who prefer scandal and hearsay to truth)—that he was not a traitor to his adopted country, as he himself maintained until his dying day, but an innocent man, unjustly maligned.

"However, my responsibilities as a scholar supersede those of the dutiful son. I am bound, therefore, to state the truth as it accords with the evidence. Namely, that the islanders were right: My father was both a traitor and a spy. Yet treason and espionage may have been among the least of his crimes, as counted in the courts of heaven. He may have been a murderer as well. Rumors and innuendo aside, it is his own words that stand as the most damning witness against him. In this book, I will present as evidence the translation of a codebook written in his own hand, a book in the margins of which, as a child, I had innocently scribbled my name in crayon.

"In writing this book, I will be rewriting the father of my memory, transforming the gentle giant—whose ready smile is, even now, the center of gravity around which my most vivid childhood recollections orbit—into a startlingly treacherous, duplicitous, and evil malignancy, the personification of that moral aberration in the Teutonic spirit that has so pitifully and poignantly manifested itself in our recent history.

"From the ashes of the man I loved with all my trusting heart, who was to me—in word and deed—the father I would wish for every child, I must create a hateful man in order that you, the reader, will find both his nature and his memory repugnant, as his actions deserve."

Crisp was shaken. He smoothed the handwritten pages on his lap and set them beside him on the bed. These three pathetic pieces of paper—written, rewritten, erased, evidently discarded and retrieved to be edited yet again and again until they were nearly transparent in places, and ultimately crumpled a final time and cast into a neglected corner—represented the sum total of Johnny Bermann's book about his father. Five years of work. A work that might have continued endlessly had not his death intervened.

Johnny had set himself a task he couldn't do—rewrite the man he loved. Every stroke of the pen would have been a repudiation of his own existence. If, by the end, he wasn't mad, he must have been separated from madness by the very narrowest of threads.

There were several other pages, also discarded, on which notes had been made—confused, fragmentary thoughts apparently written at whatever angle the paper happened to come to hand when a thought occurred to him. On one page in particular, one sentence had been written several times, almost like an exercise in penmanship: "Cailey Hall is six feet deep, Sweet William's lost at sea."

"Sweet William?" Crisp quizzed the shadows aloud. Who was he, and what did he have to do with Cailey Hall? Maybe Matty would know, assuming she ever condescended to speak to him again. The tongue-lashing he'd anticipated wasn't half as bad as the silent treatment he'd gotten ever since Stuffy and Luther Kingsbury dragged him home, half dead with exhaustion, after their expedition to the north end of the island. In nearly twenty-four hours she hadn't said a word directly to him, although he didn't fail to catch meaningful snippets from the running monologue that accompanied her customary ministrations.

While the domestic cold front intensified, a thaw had set in over the island in general, however briefly. One could almost imagine the ice was melting. It was time to test one of Johnny's cryptic hypotheses: to see just how mad he was.

Seventeen men, mostly members of the volunteer fire department, showed up just after first light the next morning in the little dirt parking lot on James Island in response to Luther Kingsbury's enigmatic request for manpower. Most had brought shovels, in keeping with his brief instructions. Goose Arey and Olaf Ingraham had brought their hunting dogs, a rarity on the moors of the nature preserve, where dogs were generally forbidden.

"All right, Luther," said Hal Davis sleepily. He was fire chief that year. "We're here. Now, what's this all about?"

"Seems like the least you could do is have some coffee and doughnuts for us if you're gonna drag us out this time've day," Olaf complained.

Others joined in a murmur of discontent.

Luther held up his hand and, with a few simple words, stilled the crowd. "We're lookin' for a grave."

"You want us to dig up the cemetery?" said Nick Pendleton, referring to the small family plot in the center of the island, a cluster of white marble tombstones covered with orange lichen. The stones had inclined toward one another at odd angles over a hundred years or so, forming cliques of two or three that seemed to be keeping secrets from their neighbors.

"No," said Luther with all the authority he could muster. He was pointedly aware that he didn't enjoy the unqualified confidence of his congregation. "We're lookin' for an unmarked grave, down on the southwest point near Daddy James."

Some traveler with an active imagination had fancied the outline of a face in the shape of the rocks on a bluff and dubbed it Daddy James in antiquity, and the name had stuck, although the particular outcropping to which it referred had long since been obscured by overgrowth. Its general location, however, was fixed at the south-western end of the island.

"Whose grave?" said someone, a question that was immediately echoed by several others.

"Can't say," said Luther, bracing for the tirade that this response would inevitably elicit. He wasn't disappointed. He waited stoically for the comments, some of which called his parentage into question, to die down. Knowing that it was coming helped. He'd have known it even if Crisp hadn't told him to expect it. "All I can tell you is, the Professor said he suspects there's a body buried out there in an unmarked grave."

"That old fart," said Olaf with disgust. He'd developed a dislike for the off-islander based primarily on the fact that everyone else seemed to like and respect him. If that wasn't suspicious, he didn't know what was, and he wasn't about to be taken in. "If you'd said that when you called last night, you'd've saved me the trip down here. I'm headin' home for some hot breakfast. Anyone else comin'?"

The rest of the men milled about a little more aggressively but made no move toward their trucks.

"Oh, to hell with you. You want to waste your time, that's your business. Come on, Buck," he said, tugging his dog's lead.

His departure, from the slam of the truck door to the torrent of rocks thrown up by spinning wheels as he peeled down the rutted road, was comically theatrical. Especially for a fisherman.

"Ol' Olaf ain't much use 'til he gets his coffee, is he?" said Nick slyly. "Not much after," said someone else. There was a muffled ripple of laughter.

"Well, Luther, I guess if the Professor thinks there's a grave out here, it's worth a look," said Hal Davis. "Anyplace in particular?"

Luther shrugged. "Ground's all pretty rocky down there, far's I know. Can't be that many places to dig a hole deep enough to bury somebody. I'd look where there's somethin' growing. Trees. Bushes. Anything bigger'n grass."

"Okay, men," Hal called. "You heard him. Fan out. Tiny, you take these guys 'round the shore way." He divided the men with a sweep of his arm. "The rest of you follow me over the crown."

As the men departed, dark two-dimensional silhouettes against a daguerrotype of moor and sky, they spread out down the blueberry paths that covered the breast of the island like a network of veins. Soon the dull thud and echo of spades on frosty topsoil could be heard across the bluff.

Goose Arey's dog, Renfro, confronted with so much virgin territory, engaged in a campaign of conquest that would have done a conquistador proud, marking every rock and bush until he ran dry. Apparently realizing the futility of further effort, he joined his master, who was digging around the base of a thick, stunted spruce tree that bent inland, away from the prevailing wind. He was sniffing excitedly at the edges of the hole in a way that indicated nothing more than affable willingness and canine curiosity when he suddenly jumped into the hole and began digging furiously. "Luther!" Goose called. "Hal! Renfro's found somethin'." He stood back and let the dog, a much more effective digger than he was, have at it.

Within a minute everyone within hearing had gathered around Goose, careful to stay clear of the dirt, rocks, and roots that flew between Renfro's legs as he continued to dig with increasing eagerness.

"He's onto somethin'," observed someone at the edge of the group.

"Probably come up with an old boot," said someone else, at which the rest chuckled uncomfortably. None of them took his eyes from the front paws, now little more than a blur as they dug deeper and deeper. Something was down there. None of them wanted it to be a body, yet they couldn't tear their eyes away.

"Look!" cried someone close enough to see down the hole. "He's got somethin'. Drag 'im off, Goose. Drag 'im off."

It took two men to detach the dog from its single-minded chore. When they finally dragged him from the hole, he held a skeletal forearm and hand in his jaws. He settled on his haunches to enjoy the fruit of his labor and did not relinquish it freely, even to Goose. Finally, however, his growling, vicelike jaws were pried open and the relics retrieved.

"You hold him tight, Goose," said Luther. He produced a Polaroid from his shoulder pack and took a picture of the hole, the bright flash engraving the scene on the mind of everyone there.

"Luther, can you tell us who's down there?" asked Hal Davis.

"Cailey Hall," said Luther. "It's Cailey Hall, after all these years."

"Then, she didn't fall overboard," said one of the men.

"No," said Hal. "And she didn't fall in there and bury herself."

The momentary silence that folded itself over the scene was suddenly fractured by a cry of alarm from the other side of the knoll. "Luther! Hey, guys!" All eyes turned toward Mo Osgood as he crested the hill, waving frantically. "We found it! Down under the bluff. Come on."

After another restless night during which Anne Quindenan had wandered the halls mumbling to herself, Cal Jackens, exhausted with listening, had been asleep less than an hour when the trucks drove by. Vehicular traffic of any kind on James Island was rare. That there should be such a parade at this time of day drew her to the window.

The parking lot where the trucks came to a stop was less than an eighth of a mile away. The vehicles disgorged seventeen men, the better part of the volunteer fire department, with shovels, picks, and dogs. A feeble hope had fluttered across Cal's soul when Olaf Ingraham took off in a cloud of dust. But then it fell to earth with echoes of helpless desperation as the rest of the men—damn their souls—spread out across the island. She especially watched Goose Arey—a heavyset man whose lumbering gait would have made him easily identifiable at twice the distance—who seemed drawn to the lonely spruce at the top of the knoll as if it had called to him. For a long time he dug with a mechanical mindlessness, and for a moment he seemed about to give up—a moment upon which all her hopes and plans, all her hard work, hinged.

Then the dog took an interest.

Things were falling apart faster than she could put them together in her mind. She needed time. Time to make a plan. Time to think. But there was none. It was as if all these years there had been some invisible entity watching over her shoulder, and now it had turned on her, revealing all her carefully hidden secrets.

Time was running out. Willy had retired from the merchant marines and was coming home soon. He had nowhere else to go.

"Look what you done, Willy," Cal whispered, her words condensing on the windowpane. She turned away as the men tumbled toward the grave site.

Why? Why after all this time had they turned up to start poking around? Who put them up to it? She couldn't shake the growing feeling that someone was inside her head, reading her most secret thoughts.

"WINSTON!" Matty's cry, to the drumbeat of her hurried footsteps on the stairs, woke him from a dreamless sleep.

"Matty?" he replied weakly. Perhaps he'd been dreaming. But the footsteps continued. He pulled himself up on his elbows and squinted at the old wind-up alarm clock. Nine o'clock. She'd never let him sleep this late.

She arrived breathlessly, flinging his door open without the customary tap. "Winston! They say Mrs. Quindenan killed Johnny Bermann!"

"Mrs. Quindenan?" Crisp repeated. He felt for his glasses on the bedside table and slipped them on. "What are you talking about, Matty? Slow down and pull yourself together."

She sat on the edge of the bed, resting a hand on her breast to steady her breathing. "I had the radio on after breakfast—listening to Paul Harvey, like I always do. Then right after it was over, the news come on. You know I usually shut that off, 'cause I can't stand to hear them body counts from Vietnam every day. Terrible thing to do to them boys' mothers and fathers, I think, isn't it, Winston? Anyway, I didn't have time to shut it off, 'cause I had my hands in dishwater.

"The announcer come on and said someone told the press that Mrs. Quindenan's fingerprints was found up at Everette's, and that she and Johnny Bermann were . . . well . . . *involved* with each other." She turned worried eyes to him. "Is that true, Winston? Were they? Did you see Mrs. Quindenan's fingerprints when you were up there?"

Crisp's head was spinning. Who would have leaked that information to the press? Michael Jessup? If so, why? What did he have to gain by it?

Further speculation was abbreviated by the ringing of the phone. Matty answered it. "Hello? Yes. Yes, I'll see if he's in. Hold on a second." She cupped her hand over the receiver. "It's the attorney general. Do you want to speak to him?"

Crisp took the phone. "Michael?"

"Winston. What happened?" Jessup said without preamble. "I thought we agreed to keep the fingerprint business under our hats. That was the idea, wasn't it?"

"My hat has been firmly on my head," said Crisp. "I was just wondering about yours."

"What are you saying? You haven't been talking to the press?"

"No."

"You're sure?"

Crisp let the question pass.

"It's just . . . I thought maybe you were trying to smoke somebody out," said Jessup in lieu of an apology. "What about the other two, Gammidge and the constable . . . ," he consulted his notes, "Kingsbury, is it? Either of them the talkative type?"

It was a valid question from Jessup's perspective. He didn't know them the way Crisp did. They'd leaked only what he'd told them to leak. The same was true of Stuffy Hutchin. "Neither of them have said anything."

"You're sure?"

"I'm sure."

"Then who could have done it? Have there been any reporters poking around out there?"

"We've been frozen in," Crisp reminded him. "The ferry wasn't able to get through the ice until yesterday evening."

"Mmm. I'd forgotten. Well, I know the cast of characters. None of them has been around here either."

"Then someone at your office dropped a dime."

Jessup didn't raise an immediate protest.

"You think so, too. Don't you?" said Crisp.

"Hold on a second," said Jessup. Crisp listened as the receiver was placed on the desk. In the background he heard Jessup tell his secretary he wasn't to be disturbed, then a door closed and Jessup picked up the phone. "Winston?"

"Here."

"I trust the people who work in the office. They're competent professionals who've kept their mouths shut in cases more sensational than this."

"But?"

"I had a visitor night before last."

Crisp let his silence beg the question.

"Augustus Knight."

"Chancellor of the university?"

Jessup nodded reluctantly on his end of the line. "The lab report about the fingerprints was on my desk when he came in. It was on top of a pile of papers. I'd been looking at it earlier."

"And you let him read it?"

"Let him? Of course not. But during the course of the conversation, he said he'd like a cup of coffee. My secretary had gone home, so I went to get us some."

"And you left the paper on the desk, where he could see it," Crisp stated.

"I'd forgotten all about it," Jessup explained. "It was an accident."

"So you called me, hoping I'd been the one to leak the story."

"It'd sure be a lot easier if you had."

"No doubt."

"It must have been Knight."

"Why would he have done it?"

"That's the thing," said Jessup, clearly frustrated. "I don't know. Seems like he's been at my elbow every time I've turned around lately. Always on the pretext that he and Bermann were roommates during their postgrad years and that he wants me to get to the bottom of this thing. You know how that is. But hell, I've gone two years at a time without hearing boo out of him, and now he's always tripping over my shadow. He also seems pretty anxious to get his hands on the book that Bermann was writing. He says it could be valuable to history and he'd hate it to get lost in probate if anyone should contest the will."

Crisp thought of the three worry-worn pages. "Then he knows that everything was left to Margaret Quindenan?"

"He's the one who told me," said Jessup. "He just happened to be in Rockland that day and dropped by for the reading of the will. Apparently Bermann's attorney is an old friend of his."

"What do you know about his relationship with Bermann?" Crisp asked.

"Whose? Knight's? Nothing. Should I?"

"If Knight released that information to the press, it was for a reason," said Crisp. "My guess is it had something to do with Johnny's book."

"I'll look into it."

"Be discreet," Crisp cautioned. "In my experience, there's nothing as dangerous as a political animal whose career is threatened."

To Jessup, a political animal, the warning was doubly weighty. "Point taken."

"Meanwhile," said Crisp, "I'd like a photo of Knight. Can you arrange that?"

"You have a library on the island?"

The Carnegie-funded library, just down the street from Matty's, had been named Best Small Library in the State for six of the last nine years. "Yes."

"His picture's on the front page of the education supplement in last weekend's *Bangor Daily News*."

"Good," said Crisp. "Let me know what you find out."

"Same for you," said Jessup, and hung up.

"Well, what was that all about?" said Matty, apparently forgetting she had made up her mind not to speak to him. During the conversation, she had cleaned the room within an inch of its life.

"More of the same," Crisp replied. "Young Mr. Jessup thought I might have been the one who leaked the story to the press."

"You?" said Matty in disbelief. "How could you? You didn't even know about it." Apparently there was something sheepish in the look with which Crisp responded to the statement. "What are you looking sheepish about? You didn't know, did you?"

"I'm working on the case, Matty," he said, suddenly feeling every inch the sheep.

"Officially?"

Crisp nodded.

"In your condition?"

Crisp continued nodding.

Matty propped her hands on her hips and shook her head. "You knew that Mrs. Quindenan's fingerprints were found up to Everette's?"

"Yes."

It occurred to Crisp that, now that the post office was open again, Matty would be getting an earful about recent events. He decided to give her as much of the official version as he thought prudent, with emphasis on what he had discovered on the ill-advised jaunt to Everette's. "You know, Matty," he concluded, in an effort to mend the rift, "if not for you, I'd never have known that Lou Ann O'Connor was Anne Quindenan."

"You don't say," said Matty modestly. "Well, it's nice to know I

I serve a purpose. Sometimes I wonder, you know."

"Some purpose," he said with a smile.

She laughed. "I s'pose I'm being selfish, wanting you to stay alive as long as possible," she said. "You pay regular."

Crisp joined in the laugh at his expense. "How would you like to take me out on a date?" he said at last.

"A date?" said Matty, unconsciously patting at her hair. "Where to?"

"The library."

"Well look who's here!" said Alice Gould from behind the desk as Crisp entered the library on Matty's arm. "How're you doing, Professor?"

"Much better, thank you, Alice," said Crisp, deeply self-conscious that all eyes in the room were on him.

"Better? Pliable would be better than what you were, from what I hear. You had us worried, you know."

There was a soft murmur of assent from various aisles and tables around the room, which Crisp acknowledged with a nod. "Sorry. Believe me, I'll go out of my way to see it doesn't happen again."

"Well, see that it doesn't." Alice directed a meaningful glance at Matty through glasses as thick as Coke bottles. "You do as she tells you, and you'll be all right."

"That's what I try to tell him," said Matty.

"I think I'd like to sit down," Crisp said. Unfortunately, he meant it. He was feeling his age and then some. Matty guided him to a nearby table, pulled out a round-backed chair, and saw him comfortably settled.

"What's your pleasure, Professor?" said Alice. "I've gotten some wonderful poetry in since you were here last. As a matter of fact, I thought of you when I read the new anthology from the University of—"

"Not right now, thank you, Alice." He told her what he was looking for.

" 'Course I've got it," said Alice, retrieving the newspaper from a stack at the end of one of the shelves and slapping it on the table in front of him. "I thought you hated newspapers."

"As a rule," Crisp admitted. He began leafing through the sections. "I'm looking for something specific this time."

"Well, I'll leave you to it," said Alice, retreating. "Let me know when you're ready for some good poetry. Maybe we can start our reading group again."

That was Crisp's most fervent hope. Of all his pastimes, prior to the extraordinary events of the last year, his favorite by far had been the Tuesday night poetry group: four or five "word birds," as Alice called them, for whom she unlocked the library door after hours. Always there were muffins, coffee, and camaraderie—and these were pleasant—but it was the passion that Crisp loved. Each of the people in the group—a retired lawyer, the high-school English teacher, Alice, and, unless otherwise occupied, the pastor of the Union Church—were truly gifted readers, able to bring the words to life, translate them from the page to the heart and mind.

For some time Crisp had entertained the notion of surreptitiously inserting one of his own poems in the cycle of those to be read on a given night. Even now, though, his heart trembled at the thought, and his palms began to sweat. These people knew good poetry. They also knew bad poetry and were unstinting with the scorn and contempt they heaped upon it.

"That would be nice, Alice. Perhaps in a month or two."

"Just let me know," Alice replied. "I'll get the old gang together."

Meanwhile, Matty had been sorting through the newspaper. "Here's the section you're looking for, Winston." She pushed aside the rest of the paper and straightened out the education section. "Is this him?"

The only picture above the fold was that of a balding man in his mid-fifties. His eyes were small and sharp, and the smile was a little too wide and seemed uncomfortable on his face.

Matty read the headline: "U of M Chancellor to Test Political Waters?"

Crisp, who had been raised in the old school of library etiquette—which held that "thou shalt not speak aloud in a library" was the eleventh commandment—rose from the table and carried the paper to the front desk. "Alice, may I borrow this?" he whispered. "I need this picture."

"How about I save you the trouble of lugging the whole thing around," said Alice, sweeping the newspaper from the desk. "Most of it's just advertising anyway." She went into her office and emerged seconds later with a copy of the photo. "That'll be ten cents please," she said, holding out her hand.

"Oh, ah . . ." Crisp patted his pockets, then turned to Matty. "Mat? Do you have a dime?"

"A dime? I'm sure I do." She lifted her purse to the table and began rummaging through its deep, dark interior.

"Reminds me of Kathleen Kenyan at the ruins of Jericho," said Alice, tapping Crisp on the shoulder and handing him the copy. "I was just teasing. Here, no charge."

Crisp received the gift with suitable grace. "Thank you, Alice."

Alice rested her elbows on the counter. "Do you believe in miracles, Professor?"

"Miracles? Well, do you mean . . . ah, supernatural—"

"I mean miracles, plain and simple," said Alice. " 'Cause from what I understand, you're responsible for one."

"I am?"

"You are if Leeman Russell was telling me the truth last week. I looked up from what I was doing and saw him over in the corner of the town history section. I practically had to pinch myself."

"Why is that?"

"Professor, the only time Leeman Russell darkens that door is during the annual bake sale. I couldn't resist going over and asking him if he wanted any help with the big words, and he said he was doing research for you."

Crisp laughed softly behind his hand, in keeping with library etiquette. "So he was."

"Well, that explains it. For a while I thought I must be doing something right—suddenly seeing folks in here who probably haven't seen the inside of a book since school days."

"There were others?" said Crisp.

"Just one. Cal Jackens. I don't suppose you sent her over as well?"

Matty had collected her things and joined them at the counter. "Bandy? In here?" she said with a laugh. "They must be handin' out mittens in hell, if you'll excuse the expression."

"Bandy?" said Crisp. The name was unfamiliar.

"Cal Jackens," said Matty. "They used to call her Bandy when she was in school because her legs were bowed somethin' awful when she was little. Looking back, it was probably malnutrition. 'Course, kids don't know, do they? Wicked cruel they can be sometimes."

"Did you have a nickname, Mat?" Crisp asked. It occurred to him that, Bandy aside, women on the island, as a rule, didn't have nicknames.

"Not really," said Matty. " 'Course Matty is short for Matilda, but I don't guess that's a proper nickname." She turned to Alice. "What was she reading?"

"Well, it wasn't poetry, I can guarantee that," said Alice. "Even miracles have their limits. What was it? Something practical, as I recall. . . . Oh, I know! The medical encyclopedia. I remember asking her if she was planning to take up brain surgery. 'Course I should've known better than to expect a laugh out of old Cal."

"I'm afraid there hasn't been much laughter in her life," said Matty.

"How so?" said Crisp, only politely curious.

Matty chronicled Bandy's formative years, her drinking problem, and her lonely life, concluding with, "She's a good worker, though."

"That she is," Alice agreed heartily.

"This brother of hers you mentioned, Willy. I don't know of any Willy Wiley," said Crisp, who, during the recitation, had taken a seat on a stool at the counter.

"He's been off with the merchant marines since Methuselah was a boy," said Matty.

"You know," said Alice, "I confess, I'd clean forgotten about Willy 'til you mentioned him just now. 'Course, he'd be some years older than me, so there's not much to remember."

Matty turned her head slightly. "Not for some," she said under her breath.

Crisp and Alice exchanged glances. "What does that mean?" Alice said.

Matty weighed her words carefully. "Willy was . . . a trouble-maker."

"What kind of trouble?" asked Alice.

"He had twice the strength of everyone else," said Matty. "And half the brains. I remember I was chaperoning the junior prom down at the Memorial Hall one year and some kids came to tell me he was beatin' up Patchy Knowlton. I ran outside and got between 'em." She shuddered. "For half a second I thought Willy was going to . . . well, I don't know what he would've done. Cal come tearin' out of nowhere and dragged him off by his ears. 'Sweetie' they called him. I hate to think what he would've done if she hadn't been there."

" 'Sweet William's lost at sea,' " said Crisp to himself.

"What'd you say, Winston?"

Crisp ignored the interrogative. "You say he's been gone a long time. How long, exactly?"

"Oh, I don't know," said Matty. "It's so long . . . what would you say, Alice?"

Alice had already made her way to a tall glass-paneled bookcase that stood off in the corner with its back against the wall. Block letters in Magic Marker on a piece of yellowed poster board cryptically identified the contents as LOCAL. "It isn't knowledge that makes a great librarian," she said as she opened the doors and began riffling through a bundle of papers, "it's knowing where to find it. Ah! Here we go."

The librarian had extracted a ream of newsprint from the middle of the bundle, and as she returned to the table she removed the rubber band that held the pages together. Crisp recognized at once what they were. "The *Spectator*."

"You remember that?" said Alice.

"He's got some copies up to the house," said Matty, surveying the documents over Crisp's shoulder. "Someone gave 'em to him. You remember that, Winston. You was readin' the one 'bout Cailey Hall."

"Oh, poor Cailey," Alice eulogized. "That was September of '35."

"You remember the date?" said Matty, impressed.

"And will like it was carved on my forehead," said Alice. "The Nostalgia Dance. That was the night Herbie proposed to me, halfway through *Begin the Beguine*. I fainted. When I come around, he'd dragged me over to the folding chairs and was waving the program in my face to bring me to. Told me I'd made him the happiest man alive. I asked him why, and he said it was because I said 'yes.'"

"Well, you must have," Matty reasoned. "You married him."

Alice's expression was thoroughly inscrutable. "That's what he said."

"Everybody liked Herbie," said Matty after a moment. "He was a good man."

"That he was, Matilda. That he was," Alice agreed. "Gone over seven years now. Seems like yesterday."

"Time goes awful fast, don't it?"

"It does." The librarian's eyes misted noticeably on the other side of her Coke-bottle glasses. As she sifted efficiently through the past issues of the old island weekly, the edges of the pages turned to ash and drifted to the floor. "Here." She removed the pertinent issue and smoothed it carefully on the table in front of Crisp.

"'Cailey Hall Still Missing,'" she read. "Biggest headline they ever had."

"Funny how this talk of Willy and Cailey brings somethin' to mind," said Matty.

Crisp was curious. "What's that?"

"Well, you know how we were sayin' how folks can be cruel. Cailey was cruel to Sweetie, in a way."

"How do you mean?" Alice wanted to know.

"Oh, you remember how she was," said Matty, selecting her words carefully so as not to defame the dead. "She liked attention."

"She was a flirt," Alice interpreted for Crisp's benefit. "That's what she was."

"That night I chaperoned the dance, I remember she was flirtin' with Willy. Tellin' him he was so strong and—"

"That sounds like Cailey, all right," Alice confirmed. "I don't think there was anything mean in it, though. I don't think she wanted to hurt anybody."

"That's the thing about teasin'," said Matty. "It ain't what the teaser means by teasin', it's how the other fella takes it."

"That's true," said Alice. "Very true. Willy, being the way he was, probably thought she was playing up to him."

"That's just what he would've thought," Matty agreed. "He started showin' off to her, pickin' up bystanders and tossin' 'em around like he did."

"Guess he figured he wasn't going to win her over with wits," Alice observed dryly.

Crisp was struggling to get his bearings. "This was the night of the Nostalgia Dance?"

"Oh, no," said Matty. "I wasn't there that night. This was sometime during the summer. Probably the Fourth of July or Labor Day dance. I really don't remember."

"Then they weren't together the night of the Nostalgia Dance?" Crisp asked, turning to Alice.

The librarian cast a net across her memory but came up empty.

She shook her head. "Not that I recall," she said, then smiled. "Of course, I had stars in my eyes that night. Far as I can remember, Herbie and I were the only ones there."

The women shared a warm chuckle.

Crisp took a pen from his pocket and scratched out the caption below the photo of the chancellor. "Do me a favor, Alice."

"Sure thing, if I can."

"Make one or two more copies of this for me."

"No problem." The librarian embarked on her errand.

"What is it, Winston?" Matty asked. "Why do you want all the pictures of that fella?"

Crisp leaned conspiratorially close to Matty and lowered his voice to a whisper. "This gentleman," he said, tapping the newspaper photo with his forefinger, "has a secret. And I want to know what it is."

"HE WAS THE ONE!" said Leeman, slapping the kitchen table with the flat of his hand. It had taken him no more than a quick stop at Buddy's Come 'n' Get It to ascertain, on the testimony of no less than three witnesses, that the man in the photo and the stranger who visited Johnny Bermann the day before his death were one and the same. "Who is he?"

"I know how you take your tea, Leeman," said Matty as she hung his coat in the hall. "But I can never remember if you take milk in your coffee."

"Evaporated milk, if you got it," said Leeman through a mouthful of chocolate doughnut. "Good doughnuts, Mat."

Matty liked Leeman. "'Course I've got evaporated milk. And now that the power's back on, I don't have to go out on the porch to get it."

"Kept stuff out on the porch, did you?" asked Leeman conversationally.

"In the wood box," said Matty, "to keep animals out of it. Worked pretty good. 'Course, it took time to thaw everything out."

"Better froze than moldy, my mother says. I don't think we're out of the woods yet, though. Did you hear the weather this mornin'?"

"Yes, another storm on the way."

"Snow inland, freezin' rain on the coast. Winds up to forty-five knots, they say. And that power line's just jury-rigged, you know. If it holds, it'll be a miracle."

"Well, at least they've got Beelzebub up and runnin'," said Matty hopefully.

"Half a day's electricity is better than none."

"That's true. But if that old thing will run three days straight, it'll be a second miracle. Anyway," Leeman said, taking another bite of doughnut before turning to Crisp, "who is he?"

"An unknown quantity at the moment," Crisp prevaricated. He fidgeted in the old wicker wheelchair that Matty had found for him as he deliberated how best to follow up on this intriguing piece of information.

Matty placed a coffee cup on a coaster in front of Leeman. "What business do you suppose he could've had with Johnny Bermann?"

"He couldn't have had nothin' to do with Johnny's murder," Leeman asserted, "if that's what you're thinkin'. He left on the last boat the night 'fore they found Johnny."

"Indeed," said Crisp pensively. "But that doesn't leave him out of the picture."

"As the murderer?" said Leeman, nearly choking on the last bite of doughnut. " 'Course it does, if he wasn't even on the island when Johnny was killed."

"Leeman, what if I placed a bomb in your car, set it to go off tomorrow, then left on the boat?"

The rationale struck Leeman hard. "Shoot, you could be in Timbuktu when it went off."

Crisp inclined his head meaningfully.

"You think that's what happened?" asked Leeman. "You think this fella set things up somehow so Johnny would die later on, just in the course of things? Don't that beat all."

"It's a possibility," said Crisp. "I don't think it's a good idea to discard a notion just because it doesn't seem likely."

"Speakin' of unknown quantities, fella come over this mornin' on the boat," said Leeman after a brief lapse. "Stranger."

"One man?"

"Yup."

"Did you see him?"

"Nope. They did down to Buddy's. Couple of 'em seen him get off. He was walkin'."

"No car?"

"Nope."

"How was he dressed?"

"Like Leo Dosty," said Leeman, referring to the insurance representative from Rockland who visited the island once a month to service accounts. Although he had made a great deal of headway in gaining acceptance among the islanders after twenty-odd years of patient effort, Leo had gotten as close as he ever would, because he wore a necktie. The company required him to wear it. Islanders had an instinctive mistrust of anyone who wore a necktie during the week.

" 'Cept he was wearin' this long tan raincoatlike thing," continued Leeman. "You know, like Columbo wears."

"A trenchcoat?" said Matty.

"Trenchcoat, that's it," said Leeman.

"David Niven wore a trenchcoat in a movie I saw once," said Matty dreamily. "I always thought he was very good looking."

"Not practical outerwear in this kind of weather," Crisp observed. "Does anybody know where he went?"

"Straight up to Charlie Williams's, from what I hear."

"Next stop, Mrs. Emerson's," Crisp said under his breath.

"You say somethin', Professor?"

Crisp was silent for a moment. "I've got another job for you, Leeman. If you're up to it."

• • •

The town hadn't seen so much excitement since Garry Moore was grand marshal of the Fourth of July parade in 1966. A television news crew had come over on the last boat the day before and taken up residence at the Tidewater Motel. Curious islanders, eager to appear anything but curious islanders, were walking slower than usual along Main Street to see if they could glimpse a familiar face.

"It ain't Walter Cronkite," said Pharty MacPherson from the hardware store window.

"How about that Garrick Utley?" suggested Petey Lamont. "They always send him places no one's ever heard of."

Pharty peered keenly through the window. "Wouldn't know him if he hit me with a stick. You don't s'pose it's that blond woman, do you?"

"I think we'd've heard if there was a woman with 'em," said Drew from his seat by the stove.

"I s'pose," Pharty acquiesced. "You know who I'd like to see is them Huntley-Brinkley fellas. Them's the ones I watch."

"Those fellas are anchors," Drew said. "They stay at the station there in New York. What you're goin' to get out here is correspondents. Like Garrick Utley and that blond woman . . . what's 'er name?"

"Walter Cronkite sails his boat up to East Haven all the time," said Petey.

"Not when he's anchorin' the news, he don't," Drew countered.

"They'll get to the bottom of this Johnny Bermann business," said Pharty. "You just see if they don't."

"My money's on the Professor," said Stump, who had been drifting in and out of the conversation for the last hour or so. He had an empty paper towel roll in his hand and was tapping it lightly against his knee. "I tell you, the way he put 'em on to Cailey Hall . . ."

"And that other one," Petey joined in, returning to the theme that had dominated the conversation that morning. "Two bodies. There he is up there, flat on his back and half dead, and he tells Luther to go out there and dig around. How do you s'pose he done that?"

"I'd say witchcraft if I didn't know better," said Pharty semi-seriously.

"Mathematics," said Drew knowingly.

Petey bent a skeptical eyebrow. "What do you mean, 'mathematics'?"

Drew brushed some wood chips from his wool pants with the back of his hand. "He puts two and two together."

"Well, I'd like to know where he come up with the twos to put together," said Petey. "After all these years."

"Who do you s'pose she is . . . the other one?" asked Stump.

Things had settled down on Main Street, so Pharty left the window and took a seat near the stove. "Luther got Esther Poole to look at her at Charlie's."

"Esther Poole? What in hell for?" said Petey.

"Makes sense, if you think about it." Having stoked his corncob pipe with tobacco, Drew touched a safety match to the surface of the hot woodstove and the tip burst into flame. "Esther's curator of the historical society. She might be able to turn up someone who went missin', or at least she'll be able to identify the clothes the woman was wearin'."

"What time they're from, you mean?" said Stump.

"Yup."

"Wasn't much left of 'em, from what I hear," said Petey.

"Her neither," Pharty added. He took a butterscotch wrapper from the ashtray and ran it under his prodigious nose, inhaling deeply.

"Wouldn't take much," said Drew, sucking loudly at the stem of the pipe and drawing the flame deep into the bole.

"You think he expected 'em to find two bodies out there?" Petey wondered.

Drew shook out the match, then opened the stove door and tossed it in. "Who knows?" he said. "Wouldn't put it past him, though."

"Can't help get the feelin' you could start diggin' most anywhere an' come up with a body these days," said Pharty.

"I thought I was going to be sick," said Esther Poole. She closed her eyes and surrendered to a vigorous shampoo at the hands of Irma Louise.

"I can't imagine," said Irma Louise, a little off her rhythm after three days of being closed because of the power outage. "Tilt your head back a little farther, Esther." Esther submitted. "There."

Sophie Bergstrom had been leafing through a copy of *Good Housekeeping* ever since Esther started talking but hadn't laid eyes on it since. She studied Irma in the mirror. "Me neither. Just bones, though, you say?"

"Skin, bones, and a few rags," said Esther.

Esther's shudder vibrated through Irma's fingers. "So you didn't recognize her?"

"Hardly," said Esther. "She died long before my time."

"A settler, you think?" Sophie asked.

"Oh, no. Not so long ago as that. I'd say her clothes—what was left of 'em—put her back about 1900 or so."

"I swear your hair gets thicker every month, Esther," said Irma. "I'm usin' up all my hot water. . . . Well, 1900 isn't so long ago, really."

"Not for some of us," said Esther dryly.

"And you don't know of anyone who went missin' about that time?" Sophie asked.

"That's the thing," said Esther. "I don't. I even went over the tax rolls. Everyone's present and accounted for s'far's I can tell. Nobody went missing except some granite workers, who probably just packed up and left when the quarries started closing."

" 'Course, they were all men," said Irma.

"Of course they were," Esther agreed.

"She must've floated over from another island," Sophie speculated, gracefully shifting her abundant posterior on the parson's bench that served as Irma Louise's waiting room. "Even from the mainland."

"And buried herself?" Esther replied with just the slightest tartness.

"Well, someone could've found her in the surf, couldn't they, and buried her?" Sophie reasoned.

Esther doubted that. "I'll tell you something, missy," she said with authority. "If there's somebody from this island who could find a body on the shore and not have the news all over town within two hours, I've never met 'em."

"Besides," Irma said, removing a warm towel from the radiator and wrapping it snugly around Esther's head. "No one would just stick her in the ground like that. They'd give her a Christian funeral, like they've always done for sailors that wash ashore now and then."

Just then the door opened. "Well, if it isn't Matty Gilchrist," said Irma Louise, looking up. "I was expectin' you last week, wasn't I?"

"Well, yes," said Matty. She took off her coat and hung it on the rack near the door. "But things have been a little busy lately."

"I should say. And your Professor's right in the middle of it, from what I hear," said Irma Louise.

"Her Professor." Matty liked that. It was a public acknowledgment of her proprietary interest in Winston. She took her place beside Sophie on the parson's bench. "He shouldn't be troubling himself about such things as far as I'm concerned," Matty said. "After all he's been through, and at his age."

"He's had a year or two, hasn't he?" said Esther, rising from the sink.

"Not much of a retirement, if you ask me," Matty agreed.

"Lost toes and fingers in that freezer, didn't he?" said Sophie.

Matty pressed a pleat of her skirt between her thumb and forefinger. "One finger and two toes."

"Horrible," Sophie commiserated. "How'd he ever come to know Cailey Hall was buried on James Island, Matty? Do you know?"

"No idea." Matty shook her head. "All I know is, he was lookin' through some old issues of *The Spectator*—"

"*The Spectator?* Where on earth did he come by that?" Esther wanted to know.

"Leeman Russell brought 'em to him, he says," Matty replied. "I'd water this wandering Jew if I were you, Irma. Do you think it should be so close to the window?"

"You couldn't kill that old thing with a gun," said Irma. "I'll water it one've these days."

"Winston read about Cailey in the *Spectator*?" Sophie asked.

"Yes. I come in on him readin' it. He asked me some questions and the next thing you know . . ." She allowed the sentence to finish itself in the minds of her hearers.

"Up she turns on James Island," said Irma.

"Up she turns," said Sophie.

Esther and Sophie exchanged places. Esther took up the *Good Housekeeping* and began leafing through it from the beginning. "I remember that day, don't you, girls? How they got us all together up by the flagpole and divided us up?"

They all remembered.

"Funny thing," said Matty. "Winston asked me if we'd searched James Island, and I told him no. 'Course we hadn't, had we? Everybody figured she went up Pequot way, didn't they? Or maybe 'round the mountain. Why on earth would she've gone out to James Island?"

"To meet someone," Esther and Irma hypothesized in unison.

"No better place for that kind of thing," Irma observed.

Matty cleared her throat meaningfully.

"What does the Professor make of all these strangers—these television people and that FBI man?" Sophie asked.

It hadn't taken the island grapevine long to determine who the stranger was. His name was Robert Rowan and he had come from the FBI's northeastern bureau in Boston in an "unofficial capacity, to assist authorities in the investigation."

"I'm sure he doesn't confide in me," said Matty ruefully.

"Keeps things close, does he?" Irma suggested.

"That's the way they are, them detectives," said Sophie reverently.

Olaf Ingraham was smarting with acute embarrassment. He'd spent most of the day at his fish house, out of sight and out of mind. Normally, he'd have gone to Tib's at about ten o'clock, but it didn't take much to imagine what he'd be put through there. To think they found two bodies. And where was he? At Buddy's Come 'n' Get It telling everyone who'd listen what a useless piece of flotsam Winston Crisp was.

Damn that old man. Why did he ever have to come to the island in the first place?

About four in the afternoon, when Olaf could take his self-imposed confinement no longer, he stepped outside the shack. The temperature had plummeted, as the forecast had predicted, and a thick, high bank of clouds to the northwest was approaching rapidly on an angry wind. He turned up his collar and climbed into his truck. Buck, his dog, was waiting, and they went for a ride.

He really hadn't consciously planned to go to James Island, but he found himself crossing the bridge five minutes later.

Just over the bridge the woods were thick, and the road made a sharp turn to the right through the evergreens. An eighth of a mile farther on, it made a more gentle turn to the left, and the woods ended abruptly. The ragged blacktop straightened out, rising to the undulating crest of a hill where the Ledges Inn and a couple of elegant old houses—the Emerson home among them—overlooked the harbor, the southern bay, and the moors. It was as he made the last turn out of the trees that he saw a woman rushing toward him. He slammed on the brakes, nearly sending Buck through the windshield. The dog recovered quickly and cast a reproving glance at his master.

"Sorry, Buck," said Olaf, especially sensitive to reproof at the moment. "But it looks like we got us a damsel in distress. You stay here." Leaving the engine running, Olaf got out of the cab just as the woman was hurtling past the passenger side of the truck. He quickly recognized her as one of Mrs. Emerson's houseguests—the young Quindenan woman. He ran around the back of the truck. "Whoa," he said, grabbing her by the elbows as she tried to run past him. "Miss Quindenan? You okay?"

Clearly she was not. Her eyes were wide with shock or panic. She had dressed in a hurry, without a hat or gloves, and her coat was unbuttoned. "It's Cal," Margaret blurted out. "She's gone."

"Gone? Gone where?" Olaf asked, his voice a little husky with a fear he seemed to absorb from her.

"I don't know," Margaret cried, her breast heaving as she tried to catch her breath. "I think she's lost her mind."

"Here," said Olaf, pulling her beside the passenger door of the truck, which he opened. "Hitch over, Buck. There, you get in where it's warm, and we'll see what we can do. Hitch over, Buck!"

Buck grudgingly yielded his place.

"Now," said Olaf when they were safe in the warmth of the cab. "Take it slow and tell me what happened."

Margaret sniffed back her frightened tears and collected herself with admirable effort. "I'd been for a walk down the harborside path."

"A walk?" Olaf interjected incredulously. "In this weather?"

"I enjoy the cold," Margaret replied.

"You must. So, what happened?"

"When I got back to the house, mother seemed at her wit's end. She said Cal had locked herself in her room and taken up a terrible wailing kind of noise. Mother couldn't describe it. She tried to call the doctor, but the phone is out, and Mother's in no condition to go outdoors herself."

"So I hear." Olaf eased the truck into gear and let it drift up the road.

"After half an hour or so of this crying or wailing or whatever it was, Cal burst out of her room and tore down the stairs and out of the house, with nothing on but her pajamas and a housecoat." Despite the warmth in the truck, Margaret gathered the collar of her coat close to her throat.

"How long ago was this?"

"Ten minutes. Fifteen, maybe," Margaret answered. "Shouldn't we go get the constable?"

"Time for that later," said Olaf. "There's only three places she could be, far's I can see. If she went across the bridge, somebody'll find her and take her in. If she went overboard, that's all she wrote. The only other place she could be—"

"The moors," Margaret concluded.

"And if she's out there," said Olaf as he turned the truck down the rutted dirt road that cut across the marsh to the parking area, "there's no time to go get help. Dig around under the seat. There's some gloves down there. You put 'em on and button up that coat. We'll have to hurry."

Margaret did as she was told. By the time they arrived at the parking lot, she had buttoned the coat up to her neck and pulled on the thick orange insulated rubber gloves.

"Come on, Buck," said Olaf, getting out of the truck. He left the motor running and the heater on. "Go find 'er, boy. Go find Cal."

The dog, a massive mixed breed, was off across the darkening moors in an instant.

"Can he find her?" Margaret asked as they fell into his wake. "Doesn't he need her scent?"

"What for?" said Olaf seriously. "I just told him who he was lookin' for."

Margaret cast a quizzical glance at her unlikely companion, but his expression was deadly earnest.

Minutes later, above the rising wind, they heard Buck's muffled though unmistakable deep-chested bark coming from near the lone tree at the top of the knoll. Simultaneously a bloodcurdling scream clawed its way through the gathering darkness, seizing their souls in its grip. The barking continued as the would-be rescuers tumbled toward the knoll through blackberry bushes that grabbed at their clothing like the desperate hands of the damned.

Hurtling headlong, faster than he'd run since school days, Olaf nearly fell into the hole, and would have had he not collided with Buck. "Good boy," he said breathlessly, massaging the dog's massive cranium. "What'd you find, boy?" As he looked into the hole, there rose from it another terrifying scream, unlike anything Olaf had heard before. His hair stood on end and his blood seemed to freeze in his veins. There lay Cal, at the bottom of the hole, loosely wrapped in her housecoat, white as death, staring up at him with eyes that bespoke a nameless horror.

"Cal?" said Olaf, shaking the fright from his consciousness with tremendous effort. "You're gonna be all right, old girl. Help's here." He started down into the hole just as Margaret arrived, puffing billows of steam. They were torn from her lips by the wind, which also whipped her hair in furious waves.

"You!" Cal screamed at the sight of Margaret. Her cry froze Olaf in his tracks. With what seemed the last reserve of her strength, Cal dragged herself up on an elbow at the bottom of the grave and pointed an accusing finger at the young woman. "You're killing me!"

B ERGIE SETTLED HIMSELF INTO HIS EASY CHAIR in front of
the TV and waited for Ruby to bring him his supper. He'd
smelled the little onions the moment he walked through the
door. That meant ham, sweet potatoes, and peas. Life was good.

The television was on, but the sound was off and would stay that
way until the local news at six o'clock. Whatever had happened that
day in the wider world, it couldn't hold a candle to the events that
were unfolding on Penobscot Island.

"So that FBI fella took the Quindenan girl into custody?" Ruby
asked from the kitchen, her pleasant, musical voice laced with an
undercurrent of amazement.

"House arrest, he called it," said Bergie. He selected his easy-
chair pipe from among others in the magazine rack beside his chair
and began to clean it, putting it to his lips now and then to check
the draw. "She can go outdoors but she has to stay on James Island."

Ruby brought in Bergie's predinner coffee, shaking the TV tray
to a standing position with an expert hand and putting the cup

within easy reach. "And Cal's up to the medical center, you say?"

Bergie nodded. "She had hypothermia."

"I shouldn't wonder," said Ruby, returning to the kitchen. "Poor thing."

They entertained their own thoughts for the next few minutes, then Ruby returned with the main course. "It don't make sense to me," she said, leaning against the doorway at the conclusion of her chore.

"What's that?" said Bergie. His eyes were on the silent TV screen as he ate.

"None of it," Ruby replied after brief consideration. "One minute the news is that Mrs. Quindenan's a suspect in Johnny Bermann's murder. Now Margaret's under arrest for tryin' to kill Cal." She found the echo of her own words unsatisfactory. "That especially don't make sense. Margaret's half Cal's weight. How's she s'posed to have lugged her out to the moors and heaved 'er in that grave? Not to mention the fact that Cal could pretty much mop the floor with any man on the island."

Bergie nodded. As a girl, Cal had been the first female on a lobster boat, serving as her father's sternman from the time she was eight. At first she had been subjected to a fair amount of friendly ridicule, but all that changed the day she bested Benny Howell in arm wrestling two out of three. It happened right at the lobster pound. Everybody saw it. She was sixteen by that time and had been hauling with Benny summers since her father died. The memory was still clear in Bergie's memory. Benny had never been beaten. The stigma of being bested by a girl remained with him until the day his body was pulled up in a tangle of pot warp some years later.

"Good point," said Bergie between mouthfuls.

"No sense," Ruby repeated with a shake of the head. Her eyes, too, were on the mesmerizing pictures on the screen, but her thoughts were elsewhere. "Mrs. Quindenan just come to the island three or four weeks ago. How's she s'posed to have fallen in love with Johnny Bermann in that time? That's what they're sayin' downtown—they was havin' an affair. He's been mostly a hermit for months now. How do you fall in love with a hermit?"

"He took a walk out to James Island every day," Bergie replied. "Went the back way 'round Armburst Hill and over the bridge, so he never come into town. But I know lots of people seen him out there."

"I've seen him myself a hundred times," said Ruby. "Him and ten or fifteen other people who take regular walks out there. If he'd been poppin' up to see her at Mrs. Emerson's, everyone and his brother would've know it. Same as if he'd been meetin' her out on the moors. Nossir. I don't see no chance they had time to fall in love."

Bergie took a forkful of peas and sweet potatoes. "Why would he leave his property to the girl?"

It was a rhetorical question, one that had been voiced many times in the last few days, and Ruby let it lie. "What are they doin' with Cailey and that other one, do you know?"

"They're over to Charlie's, just like Johnny," said Bergie.

"Must be gettin' awfully crowded over there. He only has one table, don't he?"

Bergie shrugged as he leaned forward to turn up the sound. "He's shut the heat off to keep things cool. 'Course, it wouldn't make much difference with Cailey and the other one. But Johnny'd be gettin' pretty ripe. . . . Quiet, now. The news is on."

Crisp had been informed of the impending arrival of his guest and was waiting by the door in his wheelchair when he arrived.

"Nate," he said warmly as the coroner entered the foyer, a cane in one hand and Luther Kingsbury and Dr. Pagitt alternately affixed to the other. "Good to see you up and around."

"Good to be out of that damned bed," said Nate sincerely. No one could appreciate being out of bed more than Crisp. "Pardon my French, Matty. That coffee I smell?"

"Just finished perkin'," said Matty from the kitchen. "You boys come on in and make yourselves to home."

When they were seated at the table and the small talk had been dispensed with, the conversation revolved to the issues at hand. It took less than ten minutes for Crisp and Gammidge to bring each other up to date. Kingsbury listened, but his attention was divided. Matty had outdone herself with the chocolate chip cookies.

"I have to say, with all this business about Johnny and Mrs. Quindenan in London and Margaret being Johnny's daughter, it doesn't look good for Margaret," Gammidge summarized, once his initial incredulity had worn off. He held up a hand and numbered the facts on his fingers. "She comes into all Johnny's property—one. Two, she doesn't have an alibi for the time of the murder. Three, the FBI fella found a bag of insecticide up at the Emerson place."

Crisp nodded. "What was the active ingredient?"

"Ah, something I've never heard of," said Pagitt. He conducted a search of his pockets and produced a slip of paper. "Here it is . . . chlorpyrifos, an organophosphate, apparently. The lab thinks that's what we found in the body."

"Chlorpyrifos," Crisp repeated, fixing the word in his brain. "Symptoms?"

"Exactly what you'd expect," Pagitt said meaningfully.

"Evacuation of the bowels?"

"That's first," said Pagitt. "Followed by sweating, drooling—"

"Tearing?" Crisp guessed confidently.

"Under certain conditions. Then paralysis. The poison degrades the acetylcholine at the nerve endings. Of course, the symptoms would be intensified if it were administered in higher levels."

"And if the victim had a preexisting heart condition," Crisp hypothesized. He folded the information into his thoughts. "Luther, the library is open this evening, isn't it?"

"What's tonight?" said Kingsbury. "Thursday? Yup, I think so."

"I'd like to double-check something. Would you mind looking up *chlorpyrifos* in the medical dictionary?"

"Here," said Pagitt, handing Kingsbury his note. "That's how you spell it."

"If it happens to be in there, write down the entry, would you? I'd like to see it."

Kingsbury looked skeptically at the word on the paper. "Hmm. Could take a while." He fortified himself against the task with two more cookies, which he stuffed into his pocket. "Those cookies are some good," he called to Matty, who had removed herself to the pantry. Out of sight but not out of hearing. He made his way to the foyer and gathered his things. "That wind's come up somethin' fierce," he observed to no one in particular.

"We found another wrinkle," said Pagitt when the door had closed behind the constable.

"What's that?"

Pagitt hesitated, so Gammidge took up the narrative. "Seems Johnny was dying . . . of brain cancer."

Crisp absorbed the information thoughtfully. "Do you think he knew it?"

"Must have," said Pagitt.

"Makes you wonder if his coming here had more to do with finding a home place to die than writing a book," Gammidge suggested.

"Well," said Pagitt, "I bet he had no intention of dying the way he did."

The three fell into momentary reflection, each wondering how he would react to the diagnosis of brain cancer.

"We also found a residue of Ivory soap in that pan of frozen water, Winston, like you thought," said Gammidge. "Anyway, as I was saying, what if Margaret had somehow found out that she was Johnny's daughter before you told her your suspicions?"

Crisp thought back to the young woman's reaction when he suggested the possibility. "She'd have to have been an awfully good actress."

"Seems we had another one've them in recent memory," Gammidge observed.

The statement was chillingly true.

"Let's follow that and see where it goes. Let's say she's furious about having been deceived all these years, or maybe she found out about the will and was just reacting from plain old greed."

"So she murders Johnny Bermann?" Pagitt concluded incredulously. "That doesn't seem likely, does it?"

"Perhaps not," said Gammidge. "But people have killed for less. You said yourself she's a little queer."

"Unusual, I said."

"Same thing. I'm not saying she did it, and I haven't talked to her like you fellas have. I'm just looking at the evidence, the same way that FBI man is." Once more he held up his fingers as witnesses. "Motive." He straightened out one finger. "Means." Another finger. "Opportunity." The third finger. "That's what you look for, isn't it? Any two of those would qualify someone as a good suspect. All three? . . ."

"You going to take that one to court, Winston?" asked Pagitt, recalling Crisp's defense of Mrs. Quindenan when he had voiced his suspicions.

Crisp smiled benignly. "Not at present."

"Well, in light of your comments at one of our previous meetings," said Pagitt, a little disappointed, "we'd have to assume that Mrs. Quindenan and Johnny made a date to meet at Everette's, for whatever reason."

"Continue," said Crisp.

"Then Margaret found out about it."

"How?" said Gammidge.

"I might be able to supply that," said Crisp. "Margaret mentioned that her mother often spoke to Mrs. Emerson, from whom she apparently had no secrets, on the phone. It wouldn't be hard to imagine her eavesdropping on one of these conversations. As a matter of fact, she said her mother was particularly excited on one of these occasions, a call that took place last Sunday. According to Margaret, her mother was giggling like a schoolgirl."

"You think she told Mrs. Emerson she was going to meet Johnny up at Everette's?" said Gammidge, his brow arching in query.

"Of that I have no doubt," said Crisp.

"Okay," said Pagitt. "Margaret overhears that conversation, or at least her mother's side of it. She sees her chance to get retribution, or set things right, or come into property—whatever she wants to do."

"Of course, she'd have to know about Johnny Bermann's heart condition," Crisp interjected.

"Yes, there is that."

"And she'd have to understand the possible effect that insecticide would have on him."

"Well, she could—"

"And she'd have to have made her way to Everette's sometime between Monday and early Tuesday to make arrangements. Of course, the first storm hit Monday. Does she have an alibi for Tuesday morning?"

Pagitt felt the foundation shifting under him. "I thought we weren't going to court," he said weakly.

"I'm just following your lead," said Crisp. "And there's also the problem of the boat."

"Boat?"

"It seems likely that the murderer came and went from Everette's in a boat. And that in pretty stormy seas."

"Anywhere from three to five feet at that end of the Thoroughfare," Gammidge offered. "I checked."

"Does Miss Quindenan strike you as a particularly able seaman?" Crisp asked with an appearance of innocence. "Or someone who could restrain a man—actually keep his feet in that basin—during what you have indicated must have been violent convulsions?"

Pagitt looked sidelong at Gammidge. "You're not being much help here."

Gammidge looked at Crisp. "*Somebody* killed Johnny Bermann," he stated flatly.

Crisp conceded the point with a nod.

"Who do you think it was?"

Crisp considered the question carefully. "Someone desperate," he said at last. "Someone who had mistakenly thought it would be easy to make the whole thing look like a perfectly innocent heart attack. And it might have worked, with a better knowledge of the poison, and with more time. But something unexpected happened, and as soon as the killer had to start improvising, things began falling apart."

"You don't suppose it could have been the chancellor, do you?" said Gammidge. "That deserves some looking into. He'd have been strong enough. Might be able to get around in a boat."

"I don't know enough about him to hypothesize," said Crisp.

"Hypothesis," Pagitt repeated. "That's all it is, isn't it? None of us knows anything for sure."

"Oh, we know some things," said Crisp. Just then a knock sounded on the front door. All eyes turned toward the foyer as Matty bustled down the hall from the living room, to which she had repaired to "leave the men to their talk."

"Hello, ma'am," said an unfamiliar voice. "Is there a Winston Crisp here?"

"May I say who's calling?" said Matty.

"Bob Rowan, ma'am. I'm with the FBI."

Matty was so flustered that she forgot to take his coat and offer him coffee. He was behind her when she appeared at the kitchen door. "This man's with the FBI, Winston." Her worried expression asked, what's he doing in my kitchen?

Winston nodded in welcome. "Good evening, Mr. Rowan. I've been expecting you."

Rowan smiled. "That doesn't surprise me."

"Please, come in and take a seat. Make yourself comfortable."

Pagitt and Gammidge slid aside to make room at the table and Rowan sat down.

"Matty?" said Crisp, observing the landlady fluttering indecisively in the background. "Perhaps Mr. Rowan would like some coffee."

"What? Oh. Oh, yes. I'm so sorry Mr. . . . Mr. . . ."

"Rowan," the FBI agent offered. "Coffee would be nice. It's a little raw out there."

"It certainly is. How do you take it?"

"Just a little milk, if that's all right."

"No sugar?"

"No, thank you."

Matty repaired to her tasks.

"Does it always blow like this out here?" Rowan asked conversationally.

"Actually, we don't get much wind this time of year as a rule," said Gammidge, offering his hand. "I'm Nate Gammidge."

"Ah, the county coroner. Pleased to meet you."

"And this is Doc Pagitt."

"Pleased to meet you, Doctor," Rowan said politely, shaking his hand. "I feel like I know you gentlemen already."

"Here we go," said Matty, returning to the table. "Can I get you anything else? I've got some chocolate chip cookies I made not long ago."

"That's what I smell," said Rowan. "As a matter of fact, I can't think of anything I'd like more, if it wouldn't be too much trouble."

"No trouble at all," said Matty, thinking to herself that Mr. Hoover certainly was raising some fine young boys. She went to warm some cookies in the oven.

"Had a busy day, have you?" Gammidge inquired.

"Oh, just asking around, you know. Seems everyone has a theory on Mr. Bermann's death. I must say, I've heard a few that hadn't occurred to me." He smiled ingenuously. "I take it that's what this conference is about?"

"You caught us red-handed," said Pagitt. "The Professor . . . , Mr. Crisp, was just about to tell us—"

"I understand Miss Quindenan is confined to James Island," Crisp interjected quickly. "Having to do with Cal Jackens's accusation?"

"I don't have any authority over that situation," Rowan replied softly, "as you know. Apparently Mr. Ingraham couldn't track down your constable, so he grabbed me on the street and stated the case. I went out to see Miss Quindenan. We talked a few minutes, and she said she didn't know why the woman had made the accusation. I simply suggested she confine herself to that part of the island until things were cleared up."

"Very reasonable," said Crisp. "Did you talk to Cal?"

"You mean you don't know already?" Rowan replied. "It's not easy to keep secrets out here."

It was Crisp's turn to smile. "You've learned the first rule of island life."

"I went up to see her, yes. Talk to her? No. The nurse said she'd been sedated."

"I gave it to her," Pagitt explained. "She was both mildly hypothermic and hysterical." He turned to Crisp. "You've heard the expression 'she looked like she saw a ghost'? Well, she'd been subjected to some kind of horror. Scared me just to look at her. I gave her a pretty strong dose in hopes she'll sleep through the night."

"The best thing for her now, I'm sure," said Rowan.

"You may as well know," Pagitt began, "just between us . . ."
Everyone nodded.

"She was plowed. Worse than I've seen her in years. Had to be awful careful what I gave her."

"Oh dear me," sighed Matty, who had caught the tail end of the conversation as she returned with the cookies. "Poor thing."

"Tell me," Crisp said, after a brief silence during which he was the only one comfortable. "What's brings the FBI into our little mystery?"

Rowan looked from Gammidge to Pagitt. "I'm sorry," he said. "But would you gentlemen mind letting Mr. Crisp and me have a word in private?"

"No problem," said the others, almost in unison.

"We'll be in the parlor," said Pagitt. "Matty, why don't you join us?"

"Oh," Matty began in protest, "I think I should stay here and—"

Crisp seized one of her hands as it bothered her apron. "Matty, go on in the other room for a few minutes. We'll be fine."

When superfluous personnel had left the room, Rowan pulled his chair close to Crisp and directed his conversation to his good ear. He'd done his homework, Crisp thought.

"Like I said, and you no doubt know," Rowan began, "I'm not here in an official capacity. I mean, I have no real jurisdiction in this case, since no federal laws seem to have been broken."

"But?" Crisp prodded.

"Undersecretary Quindenan is a very important man. At this moment, he's in Paris, trying to lay the groundwork for peace talks with the North Vietnamese. He's been there since Monday."

"Prior to that?"

"Washington, attending a raft of meetings at the highest level."

"I see. Does he know about any of this?"

"Not yet. And, frankly, the powers that be would like to keep it that way for the time being. As I've been told, Mr. Quindenan is kind of a linchpin at this particular point in the talks, which are being conducted with the utmost secrecy, as you may imagine. Even his family doesn't suspect where he is or what he's doing."

"So you've been sent to keep a lid on things?"

Rowan inclined his head in acquiescence. "That was the idea. Unfortunately, someone leaked information to the press."

"Do you know who it was?"

"No. Do you?"

"I believe so."

"Who?"

"The chancellor of the University of Maine."

Taken completely unawares, Rowan was unable to keep a tone of skepticism from his voice. "What does the chancellor have to do with anything?"

"That I don't know," said Crisp. "I take it you haven't spoken to the state's attorney general."

"Jessup? No. Why, should I?"

Crisp removed his glasses from his nose, folded them, and put them in his pocket. "I'm sure he'd like to know that the FBI is involved."

"That's just it," said Rowan. "We're not. The fewer people know I'm here, the better."

Crisp laughed briefly. "Olaf Ingraham came to you when he couldn't find Kingsbury."

Rowan parried good-naturedly. "And the chief topic of conversation on the island, apart from the weather, is the murder of Johnny Bermann."

"Touché," said Crisp with professional good humor. "How did you find out about me?"

"We have a mutual friend in Washington—Alfred Hanson, at Justice. He filled me in on your background. Thought you might have been brought in. In fact, he warned me to be prepared for some kind of wounded-puppy routine."

Crisp ignored the comment. "How is Mr. Hanson doing?"

"He seems fine."

"I'm glad to hear it."

"Can we get down to business now?" Rowan suggested patiently.

"Sure."

"What can you tell me?"

"What would you like to know?"

"Everything."

"That could take a while."

Rowan looked at the coffeepot. Steam from the spout had condensed in big drops on the underside of the cabinet. "There's plenty of coffee left."

"As you wish," said Crisp, and he began a detailed recital of the facts as he knew them. Rowan began writing furiously.

• • •

"Any questions?" Crisp said in conclusion.

Rowan referred to his notes. "I don't know where to start."

Further comment was cut short by a rap at the front door—soft, but not so much so that Crisp couldn't hear it. "We're a busy place tonight."

"Should I get it?" Rowan volunteered.

"Please. I doubt Matty heard."

Rowan's chair squealed loudly on the highly polished linoleum as he slid back from the table and went to the door.

Rowan was gone for what seemed an unnaturally long time. Crisp thought he heard the sound of muffled conversation, but it was hard to tell with the wind. He was just about to call Matty when Rowan returned with a strikingly beautiful woman. Crisp knew from her resemblance to Margaret that she was Anne Quindenan.

She was, aside from her shading and the color of her hair, an earlier version of her daughter. Her movements, as she removed the hood of her parka and brushed the windblown hair from her face, were deliberate. Somehow she seemed more ill at ease in the environs of Matty's kitchen than even Stuffy was.

Rowan introduced Crisp.

"Pleased to meet you, finally, Mr. Crisp," said Mrs. Quindenan as she took the seat Rowan offered her.

Crisp merely nodded and briefly shook her hand.

The woman looked uncertainly at Rowan. He offered her coffee, which she declined.

"Let me take your coat," Rowan offered. He helped her out of it and draped it over the back of another chair. When she was settled, he sat across the table from her. "Now, would you please repeat what you just told me?"

Mrs. Quindenan shifted uncomfortably in her seat. Her eyes fell to the table and, with an elegant, perfectly manicured fingernail, she began tracing one of the big blue flowers on the tablecloth. "I did it," she said softly. "I killed Johnny Bermann."

CHAPTER 21

CRISP EITHER LAUGHED OR CLEARED HIS THROAT, Rowan wasn't sure which, and after casting a quick, searching glance at Mrs. Quindenan he turned and stared out the window, not acknowledging her questioning look.

"Why are you coming forward now, Mrs. Quindenan?" Rowan asked. Despite the fact that he was a good fifteen years her junior, her tear-filled eyes had an unexpected impact on him.

"I'll be perfectly frank, Mr. Rowan," she said, her voice unhalting but barely audible. "It's because my daughter has become a suspect. If not for that, wild horses couldn't have dragged a confession from me."

"Some might wonder if you're doing it to protect her," he suggested.

"I can't help that."

"And why did you do it? Why did you kill Mr. Bermann?"

"That's my business."

"The authorities will want to know," Rowan warned.

"They'll be disappointed."

Rowan looked at Crisp, who continued to peer through spotless panes of glass at nothing in particular outside, where an angry wind was trying its best to uproot the skeletal trees.

"How?" said Crisp, without changing his expression.

"How what?" the woman responded. "How did I—"

"How did you kill him," said Rowan, taking Crisp's cue.

"You don't believe me, do you?"

Rowan said nothing.

"I did it," Mrs. Quindenan reasserted. She began tracing the flower pattern again.

"How?" Crisp repeated.

"Please," Rowan invited wearily. "I'd be interested to hear." The statement was punctuated by the rapid opening and closing of the front door.

"Holy cow," said Kingsbury as he rearranged himself in the front hall. "I ain't seen wind like that since the governor come to town." He was still speaking as he entered the kitchen. "I found it . . ." He held Pagitt's slip of paper aloft, where his arm froze briefly as he focused on Anne Quindenan. "Oh," he said, scanning the new cast of characters. "Sorry. I thought—"

"You must be Officer Kingsbury," said Rowan, rising with his hand outstretched. "I'm Bob Rowan, with the FBI."

Kingsbury, somewhat bemused, shook the offered hand as he trained an inquiring eye on Crisp.

"You're just in time," said Crisp wryly. "We're about to hear a confession."

"We are?"

"Apparently. Would you mind—"

"I heard the door . . . ," Matty huffed as she trundled in from the parlor. "Goodness gracious, I didn't hear *you* come in. Winston, why didn't you call me?"

"I'm afraid I'm not a very good host," Crisp apologized weakly.

"That's you to a T," Matty agreed. "You must be Mrs. Quindenan."

"Anne, please."

"The image of your daughter. I've seen you from a distance, of course. What can I get you? Coffee? Tea?"

"I think I will take a cup now. Tea, please."

As Matty lead her through the choices, Crisp caught Kingsbury's attention. "You say you found it?"

"I did," said Kingsbury, surrendering the piece of paper. "I wrote it down there."

"What are we looking at?" said Rowan.

"A medical definition," said Crisp.

"Bug spray," Kingsbury volunteered before Crisp could stop him.

"Bug spray?"

"Just an ingredient," said Crisp casually, reading what the constable had copied. "Luther, would you mind going into the parlor and getting Nate and Doctor Pagitt? I think they should be here."

"Oh, no, you don't!" Matty protested. "There ain't enough room in here for all of you. You go into the parlor. Luther, you tell Mr. Gammidge to put more wood on the fire."

The congregation was soon disposed in accordance with Matty's comfort. Everyone had a fresh cup of something warm and soothing at their elbow, and a hillock of cake and cookies had arisen on the coffee table. Matty reluctantly repaired to the pantry.

"Now, what's this all about?" asked Pagitt, stirring an extra half teaspoon of sugar into his tea.

With a look, Crisp directed Rowan to dispense with the preliminaries. This done, all the other men, having gasped in the right places, arranged themselves on the edge of their seats and gazed solicitously at the handsome woman.

"Whenever you're ready," said Rowan.

Anne Quindenan folded her hands and looked briefly from Crisp to Rowan before allowing her gaze to fall to the tea cup held firmly in her hands.

"Johnny and I arranged to meet at Everette's—"

"Arranged how?" Crisp asked abruptly.

"How?" she said, glancing up nervously. "What do you mean?"

The ancient eyes finally met hers again. She was taken aback by the total lack of emotion they betrayed. "How did you and Johnny Bermann plan to meet?"

"An arrangement of stones," she proceeded nervously. "At a certain place beside the path on James Island."

"Arrangement of stones?" Rowan asked. It wasn't the answer he'd expected.

"Johnny and I were . . . friends years ago, when I was working as governess for the Everettes. At first we saw each other openly. I'd often come down to the quarry with Kitty Everette and the younger ones, and he'd meet us there. We thought nothing of it."

"At first?" Rowan asked.

"Yes. But when Kitty's parents, Mr. and Mrs. Everette, found out about it, they forbade me to see him again."

"What did they have against him?" said Rowan.

"I'm not sure," was the reply. "They never said in so many words. Something to do with his family. Something that happened on the island a long time ago. Johnny wouldn't talk about it."

The natives among those present exchanged meaningful looks. "Go on."

"I was allowed to meet him one more time, to tell him good-bye. We met at the quarry. He was shocked, I think. He couldn't believe what I'd told him. For a long time we complained and felt sorry for ourselves. Romeo and Juliet."

She flashed a feeble smile at her hearers. "After a while, he said he had an idea. He had this codebook he'd found among his father's things. He said that's how we could communicate. It was an ingenious code, really, I thought." She glanced surreptitiously at Crisp. "But very simple."

"And how did you get these messages to each other?" Crisp asked pointedly.

"We both took frequent walks on James Island. Johnny figured out a way that we could pass messages without raising suspicion. You see, there's a little graveyard out there, a kind of family plot."

"Hall's," said Kingsbury. Dr. Pagitt nodded.

"I saw it this afternoon," said Rowan. Olaf Ingraham had taken him to James Island to show him where he'd found Cal.

"There's a kind of monument there," Mrs. Quindenan continued, "in white marble. The top part is a miniature obelisk that rests on a large, flat base. It's tilted a little over the years. As a result, there's a narrow aperture between the base and the needle. We'd tuck our notes in there. If anyone ever found them, which wasn't likely, they'd never make any sense of them."

"Steganography," Crisp said."

"Pardon?"

"The hiding of coded notes or ciphers," he explained. "Steganography. It's an art in some circles. Mr. Bermann was in the wrong business."

"What does this have to do with these stones you were talking about?" asked Rowan.

"The messages were love notes. It could take a long time to translate them. If we just wanted to see each other or talk about something we felt was urgent . . ." A wistful smile crept to the corners of her mouth. "Everything seemed so important and urgent to us in those days."

A frigid gust of wind pelted the side of the house with debris. The smile departed. "Johnny came up with another code, a kind of shorthand. The circle of stones."

"This has something to do with your confession, I trust," Rowan prompted.

"You wanted to know how we arranged to meet at Everette's," she reminded him. "Shall I continue?"

Rowan tossed the question to Crisp with his eyes. Crisp nodded slightly.

"Go ahead," said Rowan. He got up to pour himself another cup of coffee from the carafe that Matty had left on the tea tray.

"We collected sixteen stones from the beach. Twelve of these we arranged in a small circle, no bigger than that," she held her hands about a foot apart, "on a granite ledge just off the path as you enter the moor.

"A clock," said Crisp.

"Yes." Mrs. Quindenan seemed a little surprised. She wasn't sure he'd been listening. "The twelve o'clock stone was offset inside the circle, so we could tell what numbers the other stones represented. Two of the other stones, pieces of colored beach glass, actually, we'd place just outside the circle to indicate what time we'd be meeting. If it was to be nine o'clock, one bit of glass was placed beside the nine stone, and another by the twelve."

"Which leaves two more stones," Rowan observed.

"Yes," said Mrs. Quindenan. "One we'd place a little farther outside the circle, between the one and seven stones, to indicate which day of the week. The other, a little farther away, aligned with either the two, four, six, eight, ten, or twelve to indicate which of six prearranged places we'd meet."

"How did you know if it was supposed to be A.M. or P.M.?" Rowan asked.

"The twelve o'clock stone had two distinct sides. A.M. or P.M. would be determined by which side was up."

"Some clever," said Kingsbury unabashedly.

Crisp raised an appreciative eyebrow. Rowan leaned back in his chair and studied the woman closely over the rim of his cup. Though clearly nervous, she was nothing of the basket case he'd been led to expect. Her memory seemed clear. Her words were concise. "Very effective," he said, in response to what, exactly, it was hard to tell.

"Which brings us to this final meeting," said Crisp,

"Yes," said Mrs. Quindenan quietly.

Rowan saw her cast a worried look at Crisp, who did not respond. She looked quickly back at her hands.

"Johnny and I had an affair in London, during the war," she said flatly, rushing the words as if to exorcise herself of their meaning. "Margaret, my daughter, is Johnny's."

"We understand," said Pagitt, wishing to relieve her of her embarrassment.

"Johnny didn't know. He was shipped back to the States not long after. Margaret was born in England, and I never gave my husband any reason to believe she wasn't his daughter."

Her head had been bowed in almost palpable shame. "I should have," she whispered. Suddenly, she pulled herself together and sat upright. "Johnny and I had nothing to do with each other after that. By the time we returned to the States, I'd lost all track of him. The only thing we had in common was the island, but Kitty said he never came back. The old Bermann place was closed and becoming derelict. It was as if the earth had opened up and swallowed him."

"Kitty . . . Emerson?" said Rowan, trying to keep things clear.

"Yes. It's her house we're staying in."

"I'm assuming she knew about Margaret," said Crisp from his little cul-de-sac at the periphery of the conversation. "About Johnny's relationship to her."

Mrs. Quindenan nodded.

Rowan leaned forward. "Did anyone else?"

"No."

"You're sure?"

"Not unless she told them. I certainly didn't."

"Not directly," Crisp observed.

"I beg your pardon?" said Mrs. Quindenan.

"Nothing," said Crisp. "When you came back to the island this time, you found out he was here?"

Color rose to Mrs. Quindenan's cheeks. "I was walking on the moors one day, with Margaret, and my eyes quite naturally went to the old granite ledge as we passed it. It had been overgrown a lot. I really can't express the shock that went through me when I saw a circle of stones. It seemed as if I'd suddenly been tossed back in time.

"I left the path for a closer look. I remember Margaret coming after me, asking me what on earth I was doing. I pointed out the formation to her and we stood there looking at it. She saw no significance in it, of course. It was Johnny's way of telling me he was on the island . . . and knew I was."

"What day was this?" Rowan asked.

"Sunday."

"Then what?"

"I had a feeling that if I went to the graveyard, I'd find a note. I asked Margaret to run back to the house and get my scarf. While she was gone, I went there."

"And found a note?" said Rowan.

"Yes."

"What did it say?"

Mrs. Quindenan shook her head.

Rowan emitted a sigh of exasperation. "You're not making this easy, Mrs. Quindenan."

"I'm sorry for that," she replied sincerely. "What was in the note is nobody's business."

Rowan looked pleadingly at Crisp, whose attention seemed monopolized by a pill on his sweater that he was twisting with rapt concentration. Rowan pursued his questioning. "May I assume that whatever was in the note was what led you to . . . to do what you said you did?"

Mrs. Quindenan nodded two or three times, then applied her napkin to her eyes.

"May I also assume," Rowan added carefully, "that Johnny Bermann threatened to tell your husband about your affair?"

"You may assume that the note informed me that he had found out Margaret was his daughter. Beyond that, I can't be responsible for what you assume."

"How did he find out?" said Crisp.

"He met her one morning out on the moors. They talked. She told him who she was. Johnny was the brightest man I'd ever known. It wouldn't have taken him long to put two and two together, especially given the resemblance."

For a moment it seemed that her emotions were going to get the better of her.

"Do you want to continue?" asked Rowan.

"Yes," said Mrs. Quindenan. She drew a deep breath, sniffed back a tear, and, fixing her eyes on one of the few blank spaces of wall in Matty's parlor, provided a detailed, unemotional account of her attempt on the life of Johnny Bermann. She had known of his heart condition and had conceived the notion of using a common household poison—insecticide—to first disable, then kill him.

She wrote a coded reply inviting Johnny Bermann to a meeting and put it under the stone.

"I took Kitty's key to the house and drove up to the Reynolds place, just across the cove from Everette's, early Tuesday morning. It was still quite dark."

"Why'd you drive there?" Kingsbury interrupted. "Why not just go to Everette's?"

"I didn't want to leave any tire tracks. I knew they could be traced. I didn't know what kind of tires were on Kitty's Wagoneer, but they could have been the only of their kind on the island, for all I knew.

"From there I walked along the beach, knowing there wouldn't be any footprints when the tide came in."

She furrowed her brow, as if trying to remember something, and cast an anxious glance at Crisp. "It was still quite dark."

"So you said," Rowan observed.

"So I did," she replied nervously. "In the house I put tape along the insides of the windows and sprayed insecticide until I nearly became nauseated."

"Weren't you wearing a mask?" Crisp asked.

"Yes, of course. Like a surgical mask. Still, I felt ill. I went outside on the porch for some fresh air." Again she cast an unreciprocated glance at Crisp, and hastily looked away. "It was snowing. The tide had come in, and I couldn't walk back to the Reynolds place without leaving footprints. I was wondering what to do when I saw the boathouse, and it occurred to me that I could get a rowboat from the boathouse and row across the cove. Then I'd hide in a closet and wait for Johnny to show up. Once I'd made sure he was ... dead ..." The word seemed to choke her. She was having a hard time concentrating. Trembling visibly, she appealed to Crisp. "I can't to this, Mr. Crisp. I can't—"

"I'm sure you can," Crisp replied calmly, "if you think about what it means."

"I'm forgetting too much."

"Concentrate, Mrs. Quindenan," Gammidge said encouragingly. "It'll come back to you. No rush."

"Things don't seem to have gone as planned," Crisp prompted.

"No," she replied, hanging her head. "They didn't."

Outside, the storm had begun to unleash its full fury, lashing the window with angry tendrils of complaint, but for ten minutes there wasn't a sound in the room except the ticking of the grandmother clock in the hall and the woman's murmured monologue. With increasing difficulty she related the details exactly as Crisp had imagined them. It was nearly all there. The tape. The Ivory soap. The footprints.

"Did you make any kind of mess?" Crisp asked, almost after the fact.

"Oh, yes. Yes . . . a little water spilled from the dishpan when I took it to the closet."

"Just like we found it," Kingsbury chimed in affirmation.

"I had intended to clean up, but I was . . . with his body there, and the tears in his eyes, I thought I was going to go mad. I threw the sheet over his head, but I could feel him staring at me.

"I tried to . . . to put things right, but there was too much. I forgot my plans and panicked. I didn't know what to do next." She began to sob. "I got one shoe on, but—"

"You were frightened," said Pagitt sympathetically.

For the first time she raised her wounded eyes. "I thought I felt him move," she whispered, as if forcing the words from her lungs. "I ran." She broke into a torrent of tears, to which Matty, her maternal antennae fully extended in the next room, responded without hesitation.

"Now, now, what's going on here?" she demanded as she ran into the room. She took Anne by the arm and all but lifted her from the chair. "You come in the kitchen with me. I don't know what's been goin' on in here," she added, glaring accusingly at Crisp, "but enough is enough. You come sit by the stove, dear, and I'll pour you some fresh tea. And I've got plenty of Kleenex."

It was evident that Matty would brook no dispute, nor was any offered.

"Well, what d'you know," said Kingsbury. "Beats anything I ever heard."

"And the motive?" said Rowan, his expression ambiguous. "I'm still not clear on that."

"Whatever was in that note, I'd say," Kingsbury hypothesized. "Don't guess we'll ever know what it was. She's probably burned it."

"It explains her state of mind that night," said Pagitt, after a pregnant pause. He explained more fully for Rowan's benefit, concluding with an observation for Crisp. "Looks like Hamilton Burger wasn't so far off the mark this time, after all."

Crisp gave a magnanimous twitch of consent, at which Rowan smiled. Whatever Crisp's thoughts, he was keeping them to himself.

"We'll need a statement," said Gammidge. "Wish I'd had a stenographer."

Crisp's hands traced the cracked hard rubber of the wheels on his chair. "No doubt the press will be interested."

Luther laughed. " 'Bout time to throw 'em a bone, I guess," he said. "They ain't had much hard to chew on, from what I hear. They been camped out on James Island bridge since they ran through all the town gossips, tryin' to figure out how to get past Olaf and Buck."

"What are you talking about?" said Pagitt impatiently. Despite the fact that his theory had been vindicated, the confession had left him exhausted, with a bad taste in his mouth to boot—Matty's baked goods notwithstanding.

"Well, you know that Margaret's been holed up out there," Kingsbury replied. "Seems Olaf decided he'd protect 'er from 'em. So he parked his truck across the road on the far side with Buck— that's his dog," he added for Rowan's edification—"and his thirty-aught-six to kinda discourage anybody tryin' to get to her."

"Olaf, of all people," said Pagitt. "Sounds like he's doing penance."

At some point during the confession, Rowan had sat back comfortably in his chair and, forming a tent of his fingers and resting them on his upper lip, listened carefully while watching the frequent covert glances the suspect directed at Crisp. Luther's comment about Olaf tugged him to the present. "He wouldn't shoot anyone, would he?" asked Rowan.

Luther grinned. "I bet that's what they're wonderin'. I'll go have a talk with 'em."

"Why don't you go with him, Nate," Crisp suggested. "You, too, Warren. It's a lot to remember."

"I was hopin' someone would say that," said Luther. "Meg says I got a memory like a spaghetti strainer."

"You have something on your mind," Crisp said to Rowan after the others had departed.

Rowan drained the lukewarm dregs from his coffee cup. "That was very interesting. You know, it's strange, but while I was listening to her and watching you, an old memory came back to me."

"Is that so."

Rowan relayed it good-naturedly. "I was in a school play once, as a kid. Not being much of an actor, I got a nonspeaking part. I don't remember what, exactly—a tree or rock, some relatively inanimate object. But I got to watch everything from where I was, way over at the side of the stage. What I remember most is Mrs. Tillson, my fifth-grade teacher, standing in the wings and coaching the actors so they wouldn't blow their lines."

"Odd you should think of that," said Crisp.

"I thought so, too, coach." Rowan looked hard at Crisp. "I assume you have some reason for making my job a hell of a lot harder."

Crisp's eyes glazed over and his head sank into his shoulders. "I'm very tired, Mr. . . . . ah, Mr. Rowan," he said. "Very tired. Matty will show you out."

Rowan didn't budge. "Odd that Mrs. Quindenan didn't explain about the footprints in the front yard."

Crisp's head shook slightly. "I expect she'd have said she repented of her deed when she was on her way out to the main road. That when she passed Everette's drive, she couldn't fight the compulsion, against her better judgment, to go in and make sure he was dead."

Rowan laughed abruptly. "Yes. I have no doubt that's exactly what she would have said."

22

As Crisp struggled up from the abyss of sleep, he found it hard to tell what had awakened him. At first he thought the wind must have thrown something at the window. But the sound had echoed as a series of gunshots in his dream. Rhythmic. Staccato.

He put on his glasses and squinted at the clock. According to the fluorescent hands, it was just after three in the morning. He propped himself up on his elbows and turned his best ear toward the dark. There was no rhythm to the wind. It plundered the night in a blind frenzy, seizing all of creation with both hands, shaking it furiously, and slamming it aside as if in search of something irredeemably lost.

Had the sound spilled into his sleep to sponsor the dream, or had he dreamed the sound so vividly it woke him?

Then it came again. Someone was knocking at the front door.

The landing light came on. Matty was afoot, already scolding of any and all miscreants—the wind included—who were awake at such an ungodly hour.

She tapped lightly at his door. "Winston?" she said. "Are you awake?" Alarm was evident in her voice.

"Yes, Matty. Is someone at the door?"

The knocking came again, a little louder.

"Who do you s'pose it could be?" she said, not moving.

"Would you like me to see?" said Winston, praying she'd say no.

"Would you?"

"Just a minute." Crisp dragged himself from bed, stepped into his slippers, fetched his bathrobe from the bedpost, and hurriedly wrapped it around him. The knocking had sounded again by the time he joined her on the landing.

"Persistent," he said. "Whoever it is."

Matty saw that he was unsteady on his feet, and regretted having dragged him out of bed. But fear overwhelmed her professional pride. "We'll go down together," she said, taking his arm. "Just a minute," she called. "We're coming."

Some unemployed synapse in Crisp's imagination painted a Rockwellian parody of the situation on his mind's eye: two ancient people, clinging to each other for physical and emotional support, creeping gingerly down the stairs toward the unknown with their hearts beating a deafening tattoo in their ears. It would have been humorous had he not been one of them.

"Grammie Osgood always used to say that the only ones out after midnight were hoodlums," said Matty. "Either them or the dead."

Crisp hesitated. The unemployed synapse painted the picture of a young woman waiting on the doorstep, her translucent white body draped in grave clothes, her wild tangle of fire red hair flailing the night in mute alarm.

"You all right, Winston?"

Crisp opened his mouth to speak, but the word caught in his throat. He coughed. "Yes. I . . . I'm just a little out of breath."

At the bottom of the stairs Matty clicked on the foyer light and shuffled toward the door, Crisp's elbow firmly in her grasp. "Who is it?" she said, placing her mouth near the glass and a hand on the lock, just in case she didn't like the answer.

"It's me."

"Billy!" cried Matty. She flung the door open and the winter storm blew him in. "What on earth are you doin' out at this time of night, young man?"

Billy shut the door and, remembering his manners, scraped his feet across the rug. "Evenin', Pr'fessor. You're the one I wanted to see."

"At this time of night?" Matty exclaimed, expanding on the theme.

"Sorry," Billy apologized. "I didn't know that was what time of night it was."

"Well, it is," Matty assured him.

"Sorry. I don't s'pose you have a molasses cookie or anything, do you?"

"Look at you," Matty scolded as she led the way to the kitchen, where she flicked on a light and went straight to the cookie jar. "You're not dressed for this weather."

Billy shrugged. "I never dress for wind."

"Sit down there," said Matty, placing a plate of cookies on the table. "You'll want somethin' hot to drink. I'll get you some cocoa. What on earth? . . ." she added to herself as she scuffed her slippers toward the refrigerator. "Look at him," she said to Crisp. "Nothin' but a T-shirt and a summer jacket."

Crisp sat down beside him. "What's up, Billy?" he asked evenly.

Billy had his mouth full. His chewing slowed perceptibly as he considered the question. "You askin' what I come about?"

"Yes."

Billy was relieved. "I know that." He rummaged through the pockets of his coat, eventually producing a wad of newsprint. "I found this in the bushes up to Robert's cemetery."

"When were you up there?" Matty demanded.

"What time is it now?"

Matty glanced at the clock. "Just after three . . . in the morning." She emphasized the second half of the sentence for Billy's edification.

"Well, that would put it just a while ago."

Matty was aghast. "What were you doin' up there at this time of night?"

One of the reasons that Billy didn't often visit Matty, or anyone else for that matter, was that she seemed to come up with too many questions. And, in his experience, the more he answered, the more got asked. "Visitin' Henry Hopkins."

"Henry Hopkins," said Matty, flashing a knotted eyebrow at Crisp. "He's been dead forty years or more. You never even knew him."

"No," Billy reasoned. "Not when he was alive."

Crisp perceived that things were threatening to get metaphysical. "Anyway," he said, preempting Matty's reply, "you found this newspaper in the bushes." He unfolded the paper, spread it on the table, and ironed it with his hand. Much to his surprise, it was the page of Sunday's *Bangor Daily News* with Chancellor Knight's picture. "That's odd."

"It's got pencil writin' on it," said Billy seriously, indicating notes scribbled in the margin. "I know most of the letters. There's some little 'b's in there. Or 'd's. I get 'em mixed up sometimes. I know big 'B's. There's one at the front of 'Billy.' But them little ones . . . If it's pointin' one way it's a 'b' and if it's headed the other way she's a 'd.' Like a weathervane."

Crisp was concentrating on the handwriting. It looked familiar. "Johnny Bermann wrote this," he said finally.

"That's right," Billy agreed confidently.

"How would you know?" asked Matty more sharply than she'd intended. She was distraught with worry over the boy. If he'd only move in and let her take care of him, but she knew better than to ask . . . again.

"Figured," Billy replied. "That's why I brung . . . brang," he amended quickly, before Matty could correct him, "brang it to you,

Pr'fessor. I know you're in all this. Luther told me. And I remembered Mr. Gammidge seemed awful anxious about papers. So when I found that, I figured it might have got away the other night. I thought it must be important. 'Specially with all them 'b's."

Crisp studied the page. "I'm glad you brought it, Billy."

"I didn't know it was that time of the night," Billy repeated, by way of apology to Matty, whose posture seemed to require it. "Was it that time for you, too, Pr'fessor?"

Crisp smiled over the top of his glasses. "I think you'd find three o'clock is 'that time of night' for most people, Billy."

Billy nodded. This was useful information. "Oh."

Crisp concentrated again on the paper. It was overwritten and erased many times, much like the three pages of Johnny's manuscript. All that was legible, at least in the present light, was what seemed to be a poem written around the margins of Knight's photograph: "Knight would be Governor / The Governor would be Knight / Unless the fool / Told all he knew. / And Shakespeare said / Julius Caesar's dead."

Two lines of code followed: "Wijc cgmz lyw ij trpbdxwhe / Mmp bnyqsubq xeqho."

"Good heavens, what kind of nonsense is that?" Matty asked, reading over his shoulder. "Find a monkey, and you find the one who wrote that mess."

"It's nothing?" asked Billy, making no attempt to conceal his disappointment.

Crisp held a cautioning finger to his lips.

"Oh," said Billy, brightening. "I know what that means."

"What *what* means?" Matty called from the closet between the kitchen and the foyer to which she had repaired to find Billy a good, stout winter coat.

"Oh, you don't have to worry, Pr'fessor. Matty don't listen to me. Do you, Aunt Matty?"

"Don't I what?" said Matty, returning with a thick wool jacket, which she held before her with one hand, beating it with the other like a wayward child. "Here, you wear this, Billy. And no argument."

Billy stood up and slipped his arms into it as she held it for him. "She loves me," he said with a wide grin. "But she don't listen to me." He turned to Matty. "The Pr'fessor hushed me, Matty. We got a secret."

"Secret," Matty echoed. "I'm sure . . . Hold your arms out." Billy obeyed with a grin. "Now, are those sleeves long enough? What do you think, Winston? I got this at Milly Carver's yard sale last fall. Thought it would be good to wear for hangin' out the wash. What do you think?"

"I'll hang out the wash in it, Matty," said Billy, laughing and winking at Crisp over the shoulder of his ministering angel. "I'll even hang it with me right in it!"

"That's good, dear," she said, giving the coat front a few more authoritative brushes with her hand. "I can let the sleeves out some other time. Now, don't you go out without it, you hear?"

"Yes, ma'am," said Billy.

Crisp studied the exchange with amusement. Billy was an idiot savant. The difficulty was knowing where the idiot left off and the savant took over.

"I'm goin' to get you some boot socks, too," said Matty. "There's some in a trunk in the attic. You stay right here."

A moment later she was a pleasant memory.

Billy, much too warmly dressed for the tropical climate of Matty's kitchen, sat complacently at the table, chewing his cookie and looking earnestly at the note. "You think that's what they was tryin' to find up to my place the other night, Pr'fessor?"

"That's possible, Billy."

"Luther says he thinks it was a woman who done it. The same woman me and Gammidge bothered up to Bermann's. You think a female could've done that, Pr'fessor?"

"It makes sense, I guess."

"You think so?" said Billy, unconvinced. Female was the sex Matty belonged to, as did most of the other women on the island, as far as he knew. Not one of them would carry crabs in their pockets or eat moldy meat loaf. And they didn't make messes. They were odd that way.

Billy leaned forward and lowered his voice. "What's it say?"

Crisp had made the mistake of being ambiguous with Billy once before and in no time found himself in a morass of alternate logic from which he thought he would never escape. "I'm not sure, Billy. I'll have to study it first thing in the morning. But I'll tell you this much," he leaned toward Billy, who leaned a little more toward him, "I'm sure it's important."

"It is?"

"It is."

"I thought it might be." Billy sat back and took a satisfied bite of cookie. "All them 'b's.'"

Crisp was exhausted, unable to resist the siren call of sleep. Nevertheless, for a long time after Billy had been released on his own recognizance—more warmly dressed than he had been since the womb—and Matty had returned to her room, he lay awake in bed, unable even to close his eyes. Instead, he stared at the familiar oblong of light that the window had quartered and projected on the ceiling. The long, bare fingers of the pussy willow tree outside made shadow puppets there, but the story they told was beyond his understanding, like many things having to do with Johnny Bermann's murder.

Anne Quindenan had done well, all things considered. The little piece of theater they had arranged on the phone had been swallowed whole by everyone but Rowan. A very perceptive young man.

But what next? The questions were almost audible. The what, where, and how he had a grasp of, but why? It was clear, based on the autopsy, that Johnny had been entering his last days; Pagitt had estimated he had another month or two to live. At most. That must have been apparent to anyone who knew him, and surely the killer knew him.

Why the rush? If Johnny's death was needful for some reason, why not just let nature take its course?

All the evidence pointed in two directions, one of which he was confident was false. But there was a big, blank hole in the middle of the alternate puzzle, and without that piece it just didn't make sense. Why would anyone, including the one to whom the evidence seemed to point, kill someone so close to death?

The traditional motives didn't seem to apply. Not robbery. Not greed. Not passion. Not even hatred; the killer hadn't intended him to linger so long. Johnny posed no threat to anyone; he was living alone, shut off from the world, writing and rewriting his pitiable three-page saga while he waited for death to embrace him. Blackmail?

Crisp didn't think so.

Still, as Gammidge had observed, *somebody* killed Johnny Bermann. What if Crisp's suspicions were wrong? He'd been misdirected before.

Could the murder have been a conspiracy by two or more people? The footprints mitigated against it, but there might have been a lone perpetrator and one or more instigators staying safely in the background.

That Johnny had been the intended victim there was no doubt. But why? Crisp had the feeling that the answer was right in front of him, and that he'd have seen it long before this if only he was younger.

Who gained by Johnny's death? Margaret Quindenan. But she had been as shocked as anyone upon learning of the bequest— hadn't she? Besides, she didn't seem nearly as curious about what she'd been left as why it had been left her. And was there more to Augustus Knight's visit than evidence suggested?

Who else? Only Charlie Williams, and he'd had more business than he wanted lately.

Too many questions were still begging answers. Without them, all the evidence was circumstantial, a flimsy network of speculation held tenuously in place by conjecture that could fall apart at the discovery of new facts—or the presentation of a new perspective. And, despite the fact that everything had seemingly gone wrong for the murderer, there was still nothing *but* conjecture connecting him or her to the crime. Perhaps the note on the paper that Billy found would reveal some of the answers.

Crisp propped himself up, turned on the light, and remembered he'd left the note on the kitchen table. Too tired to fetch it but too restless to sleep, he took Oscar Bermann's notebook from the drawer in the bedside table. A challenging but not unpleasant two hours went spiraling into eternity as he deciphered a few pages at random, using the key of Johnny's birth date. Nothing presented itself that would be of riveting interest to anyone but a historian. Just as he was about to nod off, he stumbled upon three simple words followed by a colon. A salutation?

Crisp sat up, massaged his face vigorously, and resituated the glasses on his nose and the paper and pencil in his lap. An hour and a half later, it was finished.

> My Dear Johann:
>
> You always asked me what had happened to Elsa. Well, by the time you're interested enough to decode this message, you'll be old enough to know.
>
> You remember the night we were listening to the crystal set . . .

Oscar Bermann was nothing if not candid.

From Bermann's account, Crisp learned that the second body on James Island was that of a young German country girl who had been enlisted by her government to spy on Oscar, himself a suspected double agent for the United States. Aware of how things stood, Oscar had used her in turn, at the behest of the American government, to feed information—just enough of which was true to maintain her usefulness—to German ships offshore, which she did by means of a light in the cupola of the barn on the estate.

Crisp discovered that, as in most cases, there was an element of truth to the island legend.

In the end, when all sides had used the girl for their own purposes, she had proved expendable, and her remains had been discarded. An unknown soldier in a cold, distant land.

As for himself, Oscar made no excuses. The remorse that echoed from the pages was deep and genuine. Ultimately, his had been a desperate act of patriotism, but one for which he made no effort to exonerate himself.

He told where Elsa was buried—the place was marked with a cross—and asked Johann to find her and give her bones a proper Christian burial at Robert's cemetery.

Her full name was Elsa Bonhoffer.

It wasn't difficult to imagine how the body, having been buried on the shore, got to James Island, only three hundred yards across Indian Creek, especially given the fact that two hurricanes had made landfall last season. But how had it gotten reburied? Why hadn't whoever discovered it told the authorities rather than bury it?

Crisp's head was swimming with fatigue. He closed the book and let it fall to his lap as his mind, unfettered by an alert consciousness, contemplated an almost Shakespearean litany of tragedies, not the least of which was that Johnny had died believing a lie about his father. It may have been his belief in that lie, rather than the cancer eating away at his brain, that had slowly severed the delicate strands of reason that bound him to the empirical world.

Madness. Crisp had traveled the borders of that strange, dark country himself in the recent past, perhaps was yet under the influence of its pull in a way he had yet to appreciate. It was a well-populated place, the borders of which expanded to include the orbit of anyone conversant with its peculiar language, and the words of which often betrayed a brittle, unbending logic tethered to clouds of steam and demons' tails. It was that language that echoed in the very sinews of this whole affair. A reckless, calculating madness like that of a trapped animal protecting its young. A madness from which Anne and Margaret Quindenan must be protected, at all costs.

Hopefully that much had been accomplished.

By morning the wind, having heaped cresting waves of snow in some places and swept others clean with the zeal of an island housewife, had expended its fury. Only tiny circles of sky were visible through the frosted windowpanes, but it was robin's egg blue, and the hard cast of the shadows testified to a bright midwinter sun.

It was late—past nine—by the time Crisp forced himself out of bed and through the simple regimen of exercises that Doc Pagitt had given him.

Odd that Matty hadn't been up with his breakfast. Perhaps, as a result of the midnight caller, the unthinkable had happened and she'd overslept.

For the first time in nearly six months, he made his way downstairs unassisted except by his own firm grip on the banister. He was becoming used to balancing himself on eight toes. His old dogs had learned a new trick.

Granted, he could have been easily outpaced by the average snail, but he made it down the stairs, and from there down the hall to the kitchen with only the wall for support. At this rate he'd be playing basketball with the kids in the church parking lot come spring.

"Matty?" he said, rounding the kitchen door. There was no one there. The teakettle cackled self-contentedly on the iron stove, and all the ingredients for his oatmeal were laid out on the counter, but there was no Matty.

Well, he wouldn't have the satisfaction of being the first awake. But where was she?

"Matty?" he called a little louder. The kettle continued cackling and the grandmother clock continued ticking, but there was no reply.

His efforts to get to the kitchen had left him weak in the knees. He pulled himself to the table and sat down. In front of him was the newspaper that Billy had brought him. With growing interest, his eyes wandered over its handwritten message.

"KNIGHT WOULD BE GOVERNOR, / The Governor would be Knight / Unless the fool / Told all he knew." "Augustus Knight, obviously," said Crisp to the grandmother clock and the teakettle. "Augustus Knight would be governor. The Governor would be Augustus Knight, unless the fool . . . The fool? Must have been himself—the man who knew he was going mad. Unless Johnny Bermann told what he knew."

What Johnny Bermann knew was no doubt locked in the code. The key? "And Shakespeare said / Julius Caesar's dead."

"The date Caesar died, according to Shakespeare," Crisp surmised aloud. He'd memorized much of *Julius Caesar* in grade school, but he remembered only two things: the first two or three lines of Marc Antony's eulogy and the prophet's warning, "Beware the Ides of March."

Crisp tried to work it out aloud. "March 15. Three-fifteen. But what was the year?" He quickly scanned the kitchen in the faint hope there might be a dictionary or an encyclopedia tucked among the cookbooks. There wasn't. That meant a trip to the sitting room. In his present condition, that would be a feat on par with Lewis and Clark's trek through the rugged Northwest.

"Matty!" he called once more, pitifully. The answer was the same. Where is the woman? he wondered. Then it occurred to him: mail time. She might not be back for an hour or more, especially given the burden of gossip from which she'd have to free herself.

Crisp looked at the expanse of linoleum kitchen floor much as Columbus must have surveyed the ocean blue. He sighed. "A man's got to do what a man's got to do," he said to no one. He got to his feet, clutching Johnny's paper, and charted a course for the sweater rack.

Minutes later, fatigued but not wasted, he was sitting in the easy chair with Matty's afghan across his knees, tracing a crooked finger down the page of entries under *C* in the encyclopedia.

" 'Cadiz. Caedmon.' Here it is. 'Caesar, Julius. 100 to 44 B.C.' Forty-four," he repeated. "Three–fifteen–forty-four." Thus armed, he translated the code at the end of Johnny's doggerel: "They find that he purchased, / His Doctoral Thesis."

Crisp folded the paper neatly into the encyclopedia, which he closed in his lap, and lifted his gaze to the window. Not very satisfying as poetry, but certainly illuminating. According to Michael Jessup, Augustus Knight and Johnny Bermann had been roommates during their postgraduate years. What if Knight had taken a shortcut to academic achievement? No doubt Johnny would have known or at least suspected. Perhaps it was even he from whom Knight had "purchased" his doctoral thesis. That made him a threat to Knight's political ambitions. So he came out to confer with his old classmate, to find out what he had to fear from that quarter, to get the lowdown on the book Johnny was writing, which, if it were an autobiography of any kind, might include an incriminating detail in passing.

Motive.

It must have been he who brought the paper to Bermann's, perhaps as evidence that his quest for the governorship was substantive, not the ephemeral dream of an ivory tower academic.

Motive, then. But opportunity? As Leeman had pointed out, Knight left on the last boat the night before Johnny Bermann was murdered. If one thing was clear, it was that Johnny's killer had taken an active part in his death.

Besides, it wouldn't have taken Knight long to determine his advanced state of mental abstraction, if not deterioration. Knight would have turned around and gone back on the next boat, leaving only the newspaper to witness his having visited Johnny at all.

Johnny wasn't so divorced from reality, however, that he failed to discern the purpose of Knight's visit, as he so noted in the margins. Probably the last thing he ever wrote. All of which made Knight a liar and a cheat but not a murderer.

"Ah, there you are, Pr'fessor."

Crisp jumped in his skin at Leeman's entrance but quickly regained his composure. "Leeman, I didn't hear you come in." Not surprising, given the fact he'd been so engrossed in his thoughts, and that he didn't hear well anyway.

"I knocked, but nobody come to the door. How'd it go? Did she come over?"

"Yes."

"What happened?"

"She confessed."

Leeman grabbed the cane-bottomed chair from the writing desk, spun it around, and sat in it backward. "She did it, then."

"That's what she said," Crisp allowed equivocally.

"It must've been that letter you give me to take to her," Leeman said, lowering his voice and raising his eyebrows in lieu of a wink and a nod. "What'd you say in there?"

"I just asked her to give me a call."

"Did she?"

"We spoke, yes. She seemed to see that it would be best all around if she confessed."

"What'd the FBI fella say?"

Crisp smiled benignly. "His job was to keep it out of the papers, because of Mrs. Quindenan's husband."

"He's with the government, that's why," Leeman deduced.

"I expect so."

"Well," said Leeman, "it's too late now." He reached for his back pocket and produced a newspaper. "Today's *Portland Press Herald*. Take a look at that."

A fuzzy photo of Anne Quindenan, a blowup of a family snap-shot taken in warmer climes, occupied the upper-left-hand quarter of the page beneath the headline: "Wife of Government Official Confesses to Island Murder."

Crisp folded the paper and handed it back to Leeman.

"Ain't you goin' to read it?"

"I'm pretty sure I know what it says," said Crisp with a weak smile.

Leeman made another fold in the paper and stuck it back in his pocket. "I think I'll keep it. Kind've a souvenir."

"You know," said Crisp, resting his head against the back of the chair and closing his eyes, "I thought life was going to be quiet and peaceful when I moved back here."

"Looks like it might be from now on," said Leeman, unable to conceal a trace of disappointment. A minute or two passed in silence. "I guess that's it, then," he said at last. He stood up and put the chair back where it belonged. For some reason he had an over-whelming compulsion to do that kind of thing in Matty's house.

Crisp didn't respond directly. "I should imagine that's what everyone's thinking about now."

"Yup," said Leeman. "Awful sad. Awful sad." There wasn't any-thing else to say on the subject. "Oh, by the way, you told me to find out when Willy Wiley'd be comin' back," Leeman remembered after another conversational hiatus. "Looks like any day now. The ship he was on left Portland two or three days ago. If he's anything like Cal, he's prob'ly on a binge down there somewhere."

Crisp's eyes opened, and a distant spark of interest ebbed to the surface. "Is that so."

"Yup."

"Let me know when he arrives, will you?"

"Sure," said Leeman. "Why?"

"Just curiosity. Johnny wrote something interesting about him."

History again. Leeman doubted there could be much interest in that. "He ain't been back to the island in a long time. I wouldn't know him if he hit me with a pole. I wonder if anyone will recognize him after so long. Even Cal.

"Speakin' of her, Pr'fessor, that's the one thing don't fit—Olaf findin' her out in that grave like he did. Her sayin' Margaret tried to kill her."

"I understand she's changed her story somewhat," said Crisp, who had many conduits to the latest gossip in all its manifestations.

"Well, yes, she said she thought Margaret was Anne. They look a lot alike, you got to admit, and she said the glare was in her eyes, but that's who she thought it was with Olaf."

"You have a problem with that?" Crisp prodded gently.

"I do," said Leeman, retrieving his former seat and sitting determinedly. "Cal, you know, she's some rugged. I don't just mean rugged for a woman, neither. I've seen her arm-wrestle men down to the fish factory, and beat 'em. And they was tryin'!" Leeman fell into some mental wrestling of his own.

"And?"

"Well, I don't see either one of them Quindenan women—or both of 'em for that matter—haulin' her out across the island and tossin' her in a hole. Not even if she was dead. But she wasn't. She'd've put up some fight. You see any sign of a fight on Margaret or Mrs. Quindenan?"

Crisp regarded Leeman with a deepening sense of respect. "No."

"Me neither. You know what that means?"

"What?"

"They didn't no more try to kill her than you or I did, neither one of 'em," Leeman averred. "Which makes me wonder why Cal said so. Don't it you?"

The grandmother clock counted off a few more seconds of life. Crisp's eyes drifted from Leeman to the window to the afghan in his lap. "That's a good question, Leeman," he said.

"Well, I'd never've thought of her." Esther Poole bent a little lower to make sure she hadn't missed anything in her mailbox. "You say her name was Elsa?"

"She come over with 'em from Germany," Sadie Mitchell said as she sorted through her mail, tossing the junk into the large green receptacle beside the counter.

Esther stood up and tucked a few wayward hairs back under her white knit hat. "That explains why I didn't come across her in the town rolls. Domestics wouldn't've been entered. I was right about the clothes, though. Said they were from about that time."

Sadie adjusted the net shopping bag on her shoulder. "Just imagine, her turnin' up after all these years."

"And a spy," said Esther. "Imagine that. Out here of all places."

"Awful way to die. Hit on the head with somethin', Doc Pagitt says."

"Awful. . . ." Esther turned to a young woman, great with child, who had been mailing a package. "Hello, Hildy. Everything on schedule?"

Hildy patted her stomach affectionately. "Seems to be."

"Looks like you're ready whenever the call comes," Esther said good-naturedly.

"Please," said Hildy. "Can't be too soon for me. You wouldn't believe how he's been kickin'. I haven't had a night's sleep in months, it seems."

Sadie laughed. "Don't look now, but you're not likely to get much more for a while afterwards, either."

"Well, at least he won't be kickin' me," Hildy said with a chuckle.

"You think it's a boy, then?"

"Well, if it's a girl, she's no lady."

The three joined in a brief chorus of familiar laughter, then Hildy fell serious. "You were talkin' 'bout that other body they found, weren't you?"

"Yes," said Esther. "They know who it is now."

"I heard," Hildy replied. "Aunt Kate was talkin' to Matty Gilchrist at the paper store this morning."

"She was a spy, they say," said Sadie. "Seems there was some truth to the old story."

"Except we had it all turned around," said Esther, who had repeated the legend a hundred times in its accepted form. "Old Man Bermann wasn't the culprit they say he was, after all."

"No," Sadie agreed. "But he's the one who killed her."

"By accident," Esther offered in his defense. "Besides, it was war, wasn't it? You know how it is."

"Awful, though," said Hildy, rubbing her prodigious belly thoughtfully. "She wasn't even my age."

The women made noises of agreement.

"Not much more than a child, poor thing," said Sadie.

There followed a brief interval of awkward silence of the kind that can pass even among intimate friends. "Poor Mr. Bermann," said Sadie in summation. "All they put him through."

"Poor man," the others amened.

"But who buried her? That's what I'd like to know," said Sadie. "I tell you, if I found a body washed ashore, I sure wouldn't pick it up and bury it. I'd have the whole fire department out there before you could shake a stick." As she spoke, Sadie's distinctive voice rose in disbelief that someone actually had retrieved the body from the surf, buried it, and kept the news to themselves. "And she was reburied not that long ago. That's what Charlie Williams says. They could tell from the soil. A few months, maybe."

"Looks like Charlie'll have his hands full, once the ground thaws a bit," Hildy observed.

Sadie agreed. "He'll make sure everybody stays put. You can count on that."

"Three bodies," said Esther with a delicious shudder of disgust. "Imagine."

The cowbell ringing on the door of the pool hall heralded Olaf's arrival.

"There's the TV star," said Bill.

"Oh, shut up," Olaf snapped, but he was having a hard time not smiling.

"You looked a little heavier to me," said Stuffy, who was leaning well back in his chair with his feet up on the cribbage table and his hands folded behind his head. "I wouldn't've thought that was possible."

Olaf repeated his injunction.

Brenda brought him a cup of coffee without his asking. He'd been forgiven. "I thought it was some funny the way they showed you guardin' that bridge," she said admiringly.

"Guess that thirty-aught-six made 'em think twice," Bill concluded.

"No. Was Buck made 'em think twice," Olaf explained. "Every time one of 'em took a step onto the bridge, I'd send Buck out to make faces at him."

"They went cryin' to Kingsbury from what I hear," said Stuffy.

Olaf settled a little further into his seat. "Oh, he come down to talk to me, find out what was goin' on. Said them reporters was squawkin' 'bout freedom of the press and all that crap. I says to him, I says, 'You tell 'em 'bout the right to bear arms and 'bout somebody bein' innocent 'til proved guilty. You tell 'em 'bout a person's right to privacy and 'bout tresspassin'. Way I figure, that's four rights to one."

Bergie detected a minor flaw in the argument. "That's public land over there, Olaf."

Olaf grinned. "You don't tell 'em, I won't. Anyway, Luther done the right thing. He looks at me and says, 'Four rights to one. That's pretty mathematical, ain't it, Olaf?' he says. Then he turns 'round, walks back across the bridge, hops in his Jeep, and takes off without sayin' a word to them reporters. They all just stood there, gapin' like dogfish on a hook."

It took only a second for the picture to form clearly in everyone's mind. When it did, they all broke into laughter, even Stuffy.

"D'you see the picture in the *Courier* last night?" said Fossie Bergstrom, who had been enjoying the give-and-take from the periphery.

"Got it right here," said Brenda, retrieving a newspaper from the top of an empty display case and slapping it on the counter. " 'Standoff on Penobscot Island,' " she read. Stuffy took the paper, scanned it briefly, and started passing it around.

"From the distance they had to take that picture, it's hard to make out much more than the truck."

"Good thing," Olaf guffawed. "I was prob'ly givin' 'em the finger!"

"Them TV people must've had zoom lenses," said Fossie. "You turned out pretty good on the news."

"Listen to this," said Bill, the only one who'd taken the time to read beyond the caption. " 'Like a modern-day knight in shining armor, Olaf Ingraham and his massive black Labrador, Duke—' "

"That what it says?" asked Olaf, jumping to his feet and positioning himself behind Bill to read over his shoulder.

"Right there," said Bill, tracing his finger under the sentence he'd just read.

Olaf took the paper and read further. "Typical, ain't it. His name's Buck, not Duke, and he's half golden, and he's brown, not black. Three things wrong in one friggin' sentence." He chucked the paper back in Bill's lap with disdain. "That's 'bout par for the course. Makes you wonder, don't it?"

Bill found his place. "At least they spelled your name right," he said dryly. "Where was I? Let's see . . . knight in shining armor and his dog . . . Here it is: 'kept a legion of local and national reporters and film crews at bay during an eighteen-hour standoff on Penobscot Island.

" 'The reporters were attempting to gain access to Margaret Quindenan, daughter of Undersecretary of State Paul Quindenan and at the time the lead suspect in a murder investigation on this normally quiet island.

" 'The standoff is the latest in a series of bizarre events that have rocked the insular community in the last few days. . . .' "

Apart from getting a few more names wrong, the article faithfully followed the official story up to and including the arrest of Anne Quindenan, who, the article said, "after arraignment was released to the custody of County Coroner Nate Gammidge, in Rockland, pending the investigation of certain specifics of her testimony."

At the conclusion of the narrative, there was a thoughtful lapse during which everyone but Stuffy tried to frame the question they were all thinking. Brenda was first to come up with the perfect selection of words. "Why'd you do it, Olaf?"

Olaf didn't answer right away. He stared as his coffee cup and ran his finger around the lip. "That girl, Margaret, was some shook up when we found Cal out there. I mean, she was shakin' wicked. Cal was screechin' and screamin' and sayin' over and over that Margaret tried to kill 'er, and I could tell lookin' at Margaret that she didn't know what the hell was goin' on, so I told her to run on home while I saw to Cal.

"I got Cal in the truck and warmed up, and she settled down some. Then I drove 'er up to the medical center. She was quiet as a mouse by then. Didn't say nothin', just walked in with me. Afterwards I tried to find Luther, but I come across that FBI fella first, so I took him out and showed him where we found 'er and told him all about it and left it with him.

"I didn't know what to do about Margaret, so I went home."

Olaf took a minute to order his thoughts. "Next day I went down to the shore and worked in the shop most of the day, and when I got home Maggie says, 'Did you hear the FBI fella arrested Margaret Quindenan for murderin' Johnny Bermann and told her she can't leave James Island?'

"Well, I thought how shook up she was. Person in that shape might do anything, you know?" He cast an appeal to his hearers, who responded with noises or gestures of agreement. "So I says, 'Maggie,' I says, 'we should go out there and see if she's all right.' I figured she was pretty much alone out there, what with Cal gone and her mother not worth the powder to blow her to hell with, and I figured Maggie'd know what to do. So she grabbed a pie or a loaf of bread or somethin' she'd been bakin' and we hopped in the truck with Buck and drove on out there.

"It was a while after boat time. We was just about to cross the bridge when that crowd of reporters showed up, just like vultures. I knew what they was up to and figured that was about the last thing Margaret needed. So I told Maggie to go on ahead and walk up to the house, and I parked across the far end of the bridge, took my rifle off the rack, and let Buck out." He nodded at the newspaper. "I let one or two shots off in the air. Get their attention, you know? The rest is pretty much in there, I guess," he finished, gesturing toward the newspaper.

Brenda looked at Olaf with new eyes. "Well, I guess we've had enough excitement to last the winter," she said, refilling his coffee cup. "I'm glad it's over."

"Ain't over," Stuffy pronounced. All eyes turned to him.

"What do you mean?" asked Fossie, on behalf of the assembly.

"Well," said Stuffy, tossing a soggy, unsmoked cigarette into the trash and getting a fresh one from the pocket of his thick plaid shirt. "We know who killed Elsa Bonhoffer, and why they done it, but who killed Cailey Hall? Findin' the body ain't solvin' the crime, you know."

It dawned on the others that this was true.

"Don't make much difference after all this time, does it?" Fossie wondered aloud.

"Does to me," said Brenda quickly. "If somebody on this island's been a murderer all these years, I sure as hell want to know who it is. I got children."

"Me, too," said Bill.

"Could be anyone. Could be one of you, for all I know," Brenda said with mock suspicion.

The laughter that met the remark was tinged with uneasiness.

"Well?" Brenda challenged.

"She's right," said Stuffy pragmatically. "The only one I know for sure it ain't is me."

"We could all say that," said Bill.

"That's what's scary, ain't it?" said Brenda.

"That's not all," Stuffy resumed. "What was all that business of Cal sayin' the Quindenans tried to kill her? I don't think that's very likely, do you?"

Upon reflection, no one thought it likely.

"Then why'd she say that when you found her, Olaf?"

"I can't make sense of that myself," said Olaf. "Sure had her heart set on the notion, hollerin' like she did all the way to the truck. 'Course, it wouldn't've been safe to light a match 'round 'er. She was pretty far gone."

"Well," said Stuffy, "if no one put 'er in that grave, then what was she doin' there?"

"She wasn't just drunk," said Olaf. "She was out've her mind crazy. Didn't take no brain surgeon to see that."

Stuffy followed the comment along its natural course. "Then what made 'er that way?" he demanded. "No sir," he said when no answer was forthcoming. He lit his cigarette to underscore the obvious and took a long, deep drag. "It ain't over yet."

CHAPTER

24

"YOU GONNA TELL ME WHAT YOU WANTED to come up here for?" said Kingsbury as he unlocked the front door of the Emerson house.

"I just need to get something clear in my mind," said Crisp. "I can manage from here on my own, thanks." Leeman let go of his elbow and followed him and Kingsbury into the house.

"Heat's still on," Leeman observed. "Margaret's not here, is she?"

"No, she's at Gammidge's over in Rockland with her mother," Kingsbury explained. "Kitty cut short her vacation. She'll be comin' home right off."

When they had closed the door behind them, Crisp stood in the middle of the room, supported by his walker, and studied his surroundings. It amazed him how little the interior resembled the mental picture he'd formed from various descriptions he'd heard. Differences in perception. His attention rested briefly on the horsehair love seat.

Kingsbury stood and waited while Crisp completed his visual inventory of the room. "What do you want to see first?"

"Do you know which was Cal's bedroom?"

"Yup," said Kingsbury, moving to the foot of the stairs. "Right up here. Can you make it okay?"

"I think I can if you give me a hand. Leeman, would you run this up for me?"

Leeman took the walker and jogged up the stairs, his footfalls echoing through the empty house. Kingsbury took Crisp's elbow.

"Down this way," said Kingsbury when they had reached the landing a minute or so later. Leeman surrendered the walker.

"You okay, Professor?" he said. "Want to rest?"

"No, no," said Crisp, who wanted nothing more. "It'll be dark soon. Go on ahead."

Kingsbury led the way down the hall and came to a stop in front of a door at the far end. He opened it. "Here it is."

Crisp arrived a few seconds later and went in.

The room was small and sparsely furnished but not spartan. The walls were tastefully decorated, and a rich-looking rug of Oriental design warmed the polished wood floor. All the comforts a woman might wish for seemed to be provided. In fact, the femininity of the decor contrasted sharply with Crisp's perception of Cal Jackens, whom he'd never met. He wondered who chose the furnishings.

After a few seconds of cursory appraisal, Crisp moved to a window that afforded an unbroken view of the moors to the east. He smiled to himself. "Cal is doing much better today, I expect."

Kingsbury looked curiously at the back of the old man's head. "You been talkin' to Pagitt?"

Crisp didn't turn from the window. "No. I haven't spoken to him since yesterday."

"Well, as a matter of fact, she's her old self. I was up there not an hour ago. Doc says he never seen nothin' like it. Last night she was kind've in an' out of it, moanin' and whatnot, then, 'bout noon today she come 'round like someone threw a switch."

"Amazing," said Crisp without stirring. "I don't suppose they have televisions or radios in the rooms up at the medical center, do they?"

Kingsbury and Leeman exchanged puzzled glances behind Crisp's back. "Nope. They don't."

"Patients have to rely on the papers for most of their news, then," said Crisp. It was a statement, not a question, so Kingsbury left it alone. "Of course, it's a little old by then." Turning away from the window, Crisp maneuvered the walker around until he was facing them. "You wouldn't happen to know how many telephones are in the house, would you?"

Kingsbury took a mental inventory; he'd become fairly familiar with the house during Margaret's brief internment. "Three. One in the library, one in the master bedroom, and one in the living room."

"How about the pantry?" Crisp asked innocently.

"Oh, yes," Kingsbury corrected. "Now that you mention it, there's one in there, too."

"I'm glad Cal's doing so much better," said Crisp, stretching his back to exercise the muscles. "I guess I've seen all I have to, gentlemen. Let's try to get home before Matty finds me gone."

"I wonder what she's gonna do now," said Leeman as he and Kingsbury assisted Crisp back to the truck.

"Who, Margaret?" asked Kingsbury.

"No, Cal. You think she's gonna come back and work out here after everything that's happened?"

"Don't see why not," said Kingsbury. "It don't have anything to do with Mrs. Emerson, right?"

"No," said Leeman. "But things are gonna be different now that her brother's comin' home."

"Brother?" Kingsbury echoed, stunned. "Cal has a brother? I didn't know that."

"Yup," said Leeman, helping Crisp into the cab. "Willy. Sweetie, they called him. Been gone since 'fore you or me was born. Merchant marines. Ain't that right, Pr'fessor?"

"So it would seem," Crisp replied. "I expect he'll feel quite a stranger for a while."

"Well, don't that beat all," said Kingsbury. "No end of surprises out here, is there? I've lived here all my life . . ."

"They might move back into the old place at the head of the creek."

"That ain't been lived in for a hell of a long time," said Kingsbury. "Don't even have power, does it?"

Leeman didn't know.

Crisp doubted they'd end up there, but he didn't say anything. He savored the brief ride home, the familiar places, the sharp chill in the air. He took a deep, unnameable comfort in the fact that he knew the people in every house along the way, everyone they were related to, what they did for a living, what their hobbies were, what their opinions were on politics, religion, and society in general, and that everyone they passed on the road waved to them. They were family, in way.

Quite a few of them would attend his funeral one day.

Kitty Emerson was perplexed. To have been met at the ferry by Kingsbury—in his official capacity—was unexpected enough, but not nearly as startling as his request that she accompany him to Matty Gilchrist's to speak with Winston Crisp. Yet so profound was her amazement, not untouched by curiosity, that she complied without comment.

"Here she is, Pr'fessor," said Kingsbury, removing his hat at the sight of Matty. "Matty," he acknowledged with a nod.

"Hello, Luther," she said. "Hello, Mrs. Emerson. Come in, come on in. Here, let me take your coats." She disposed of the garments quickly in the closet as they passed through to the kitchen. "Now, what can I get you? Coffee? Tea?"

It had been a cold ride over on the ferry because the heaters in the cabin had failed. "I'd love some tea, Mrs. Gilchrist. If it wouldn't be too much trouble."

"Call me Matty. No bother a'tall. Sugar? Milk?"

"Just sugar, please. One teaspoon."

"Them turnovers I see, Matty?" said Kingsbury, master of the obvious.

"Help yourself, Luther."

He already had.

"Would you like one, Mrs. Emerson?" Matty invited. "They're not more than a half hour old. Still warm."

"No, thank you. I understand that Professor Crisp wanted to see me?"

Matty cringed inwardly. She didn't approve of the nickname the island had given her Winston, and it was obvious that this woman thought it was his title. "He's in the parlor. Through there. Show her the way, will you, Luther? I'll be in once the tea's made."

Crisp stood, somewhat shakily, and extended his hand as they entered. "Mrs. Emerson," he said. "Good of you to come."

"Professor Crisp," she said, taking his hand limply. "What's this all about? I really have a great deal to attend to at home. I'm sure you know—"

"I'll be brief," said Crisp, subsiding to his seat. "Please, sit."

Kitty Emerson was unbalanced by the unexpected command in his voice. With a questioning glance at Kingsbury, whose returning gaze said nothing, she did as directed.

"Well?" she said, regaining her composure.

Crisp said nothing for a moment but studied her in the narrow aperture between the tops of his glasses and his eyebrows. His arms were propped on the arms of his chair and his fingers formed a steeple against his lips.

"Professor?" she said, her artificial aplomb unraveling at the edges.

"How much do you know of what's been happening, Mrs. Emerson?" he said, so softly she had to strain to hear.

"Only what I've read in the papers and seen on television," she said. "I've spoken to Margaret, of course. But she's much too distraught to provide any details beyond those that are generally available. Why? Is there something I should know?"

"May I speak frankly?" said Crisp, still quietly.

Mrs. Emerson straightened in her seat. "Please. I'd like nothing more."

"How long has Cal been with you?"

"Cal?" she repeated, obviously surprised. "Why . . . years. I don't know. I've known her since we were children. My father used to buy lobsters from her . . . What's this all about, Professor?"

Crisp turned the question gently aside. "She's a friend, then?"

"Friend?" Mrs. Emerson was too conscious of her social position to acquiesce to the suggestion. "She works for me, Professor. Everyone knows that. She has for years. I trust her and respect her. Now," she added, a little impatiently, "may I be frank?"

"Surely."

"Why are you asking me these things?"

Crisp raised his eyes to Kingsbury. "Luther, would you mind keeping Matty company for a little while? And close the door, if you don't mind."

Kingsbury didn't mind. The closer he was to Matty's kitchen the better, as far as he was concerned. Matty, on the other hand, was not pleased. While waiting for the kettle to sing, she had sequestered herself in the closet, within earshot of the proceedings. She quickly began taking inventory of the preserves as Kingsbury shut the door. "There you are, Matty. The Pr'fessor says we should go to the kitchen." He lowered his voice. "They want a little privacy."

So did Matty, but she bit her lip. "Perhaps you wouldn't mind helpin' me get the tea things together."

"Sure thing."

"You're not going to like what I have to say," Crisp began.

"I can't imagine what that might be," said Mrs. Emerson. "Please, just say what you have to say. What's all this about Cal?"

"She murdered Johnny Bermann," Crisp said bluntly.

Mrs. Emerson leapt to her feet, staring at Crisp in manifest disbelief. "What on earth are you talking about?" She hesitated for a
moment on the verge of flight, as if suddenly finding herself shut in
a room with a madman. At the last instant, she turned to confront
him. "Professor," she said, mastering herself with great effort, "I am
scarcely able to reconcile myself to the fact that Lou Ann . . . that
Anne Quindenan confessed to the crime. And, quite honestly, if not
for the detail of her confession, which I understand completely satisfied the authorities, with things that no one but the murderer
could have known . . ." Crisp watched her closely. She was troubled
by the words as they left her lips, yet she spoke them as if unable to
do otherwise. "Quite honestly, if not for that, I wouldn't have
believed her capable of such a terrible thing.

"Now you're telling me it was Cal. What are you saying? They
did it together?"

"No. Mrs. Quindenan had nothing to do with it."

Mrs. Emerson sank to her seat, confused at a number of levels.
"But Anne . . . the authorities have—"

"I *am* the authorities for the moment," said Crisp calmly. "I
arranged for Anne's arrest, to keep her out of harm's way."

"But the confession. The details—"

"All based upon things I learned in the course of my investigation," Crisp said reassuringly. "Probably pretty close to the mark in
most particulars."

Mrs. Emerson's heavily lipsticked mouth formed a word, but no
sound came out. "Why?"

"To put Cal off her guard. Get her to tip her hand somehow.
Make a mistake." Crisp explained: "You see, there's no proof of the
kind that would hold up in court. Cal has managed to botch almost
everything. Yet, miraculously, there's simply nothing to connect her
directly to the crime."

"I can't believe this," Mrs. Emerson said dubiously when she
regained her breath. "It's not possible."

"More than possible, I'm afraid."

"It can't be," the distraught woman protested meekly. "What reason would Cal have for murdering Johnny Bermann? She didn't even know him."

"True. She didn't."

"Then why?"

"It's a long story," said Crisp. "But I'll see if I can abbreviate it. You know Cal has a brother?"

"Willy, yes. He's in the merchant marines. What of it?"

"When he was about twenty years old, he killed a girl named Cailey Hall."

"Cailey?" said Mrs. Emerson, stunned. "The girl who worked for my parents? She disappeared. She . . . She . . ."

Crisp allowed her words to sink in.

"He killed her? How? Why?"

Crisp shrugged. "Probably by accident. He was a rough young fellow who liked to impress girls with his strength. I expect he got carried away. Perhaps she led him on. In any event, it seems he went crying to Cal, whose nickname was Bandy, I understand."

"Bandy? I . . . I don't know."

"Rather than notify the authorities, as you or I would have done, they took the girl's body out to James Island and buried it. Blind fear and ignorance, I imagine."

Mrs. Emerson looked up at him from eyes that seemed unable to focus. "You can't mean it."

"The body was found earlier this week."

"Cailey?" she whispered.

"The story would have ended there, I suppose," said Crisp, his words flowing in a gentle, almost hypnotic cadence. "But they encountered two young lovers on their way back across the moor. Johnny Bermann and Lou Ann O'Connor. Johnny saw Willy."

"How could you possibly know all this?" said Mrs. Emerson, her heart racing.

Crisp inferred something from her response. "You knew about Anne and Johnny, then?"

"Well, of course. But that was a long time ago."

"I don't suppose Johnny would have thought anything of it, had it not been for the shovel," Crisp continued, leaning back a little.

"Shovel?"

"Willy was carrying a shovel at the time. Be that as it may, events took over from there. Johnny Bermann left the island within twenty-four hours to return to school—probably without even hearing of Cailey's disappearance—and no doubt dismissed the business from his mind. Lou Ann O'Connor—Anne Quindenan—as one of Cailey's coworkers, was no doubt too stunned to make any connection.

"She returned to college within a week. On those occasions when her thoughts would turn to that night on the moors, it's likely that something other than the appearance of Willy Wiley came to mind.

"Things couldn't have been better for Cal and Willy. He went to off to sea. Apparently he hasn't returned to the island since?"

"No," said Mrs. Emerson, her eyes trained on the floor. "Cal has seldom ever spoken of him."

"To mention the dead is to bring them to mind, isn't it?" he said without explanation. "Better still," he continued, "a little investigation would have identified the young couple on the moor. Cal must have been greatly relieved to learn that they both had left the island."

"Of course, Lou Ann returned regularly for a few years, but she kept to the north end of the island for the most part and, apparently, never put two and two together. So she ceased to be a threat.

"Thereafter, everything was fine until Johnny Bermann showed up again. Not as a visitor, but as a resident. Cal probably could have lived with that, because she was sure he hadn't seen her that night on James Island, but her brother was due to retire from the merchant marines within a year. Of course he'd come home. He had no other family. Nowhere else to go. What if he and Johnny met? What if Johnny, despite the years, recognized him and remembered that night and Cailey Hall's disappearance?

"The shovel, you see," said Crisp. "The shovel would tell it all.

"I expect that Johnny Bermann died a thousand ways in the months that followed as Cal considered her options. Then you left the island for the holiday, and Anne Quindenan and her daughter showed up as houseguests. Of course, Cal recognized in Margaret the young girl she'd seen on the moor, aged hardly a day. She knew in an instant that Anne Quindenan was Lou Ann O'Connor. From that realization, it was just a small step to the next—that eventually Anne and Johnny Bermann would meet. And when they did, of course they would talk about the night they last met. Perhaps about Cailey Hall. Perhaps about that man and woman they saw on the moors with the shovel. By this time, Willy's return was just weeks away. Cal became desperate."

Crisp directed a question at Mrs. Emerson. "Margaret says that you and Anne spoke often on the telephone."

Still too perplexed to speak, Mrs. Emerson nodded.

"Very candid conversations, I gather."

Hesitation. Another nod.

"In fact, she told you all about her plans to meet Johnny and about her communication with him—everything, didn't she?"

Mrs. Emerson's eyebrows contorted in an effort to recall some specifics from those long conversations, but she didn't reply.

"What you didn't know," Crisp continued, "is there was a third party to all these intimate details."

Mrs. Emerson raised her eyes briefly. All fire had gone out of them. "Cal?" she said, weakly.

"She was listening on the extension in the pantry."

There was no need to respond.

"Something you said during one of the calls must have sparked the thought that lead to the plot that eventually unfolded. In her capacity as cleaning woman at the medical center, all alone up there at night, it wouldn't have been hard for her to look up Johnny's medical records. She knew he'd been in to see Doctor Pagitt a number of times. That's how she found out about his heart condition.

"This presented the possibility that she could make his death seem like a suicide. Maybe a number of options occurred to her, but the one she settled on, after a little research at the library, was poison. Common insecticide. And what better place than Everette's to carry out the plan.

"Under the pretext of checking on the houses up at Ragged Island after the storm, she made her way to Everette's, which is only a mile or so away by water. She rowed, I expect. According to Constable Kingsbury, a boat at one of the houses on Ragged Island that was kept under the deck for the winter had been used recently.

"Beyond that," said Crisp, "I wouldn't be surprised if you could take the account as it appears in the newspaper—changing the names, of course—and hit reasonably close to the mark.

"If the poison had done its job, things would have gone without a hitch. But it didn't. I expect Cal became horrified by Johnny's reaction to the insecticide he ingested as he went about preparing for his reunion with the person who he knew, by that time, was the mother of his only child."

Mrs. Emerson's eyes flashed briefly in surprise. Not at the statement—it was evident that Anne Quindenan had kept nothing from her—but to the fact that it was no longer a secret. She allowed Crisp to continue, uninterrupted.

"One thing became crystal clear to me as I studied this case. What we were looking at were the results of desperate improvisation. Cal knew just enough to be dangerous, but she didn't know about the preliminary effects of the poisoning, at least the violence of them. She'd made no provisions, you see?

"Frankly, the whole plan was more complex than I'd have given her credit for," said Crisp, wearying visibly. "From what little I know of her.

"The final blow came the other morning, when she watched from her bedroom window as a group of men dug up a body she had recently buried."

"Whose?" said Mrs. Emerson in alarm.

"Put yourself in her place," said Crisp.

"Cailey? But that wasn't recent," she snapped from the dregs of her emotions. "That was years ago."

Crisp inclined his head. "I should have said 'reburied.'"

"The way I imagine it, she and Willy—foolish, frightened kids—had initially buried the body in the easiest place they could find, somewhere near the shore.

"I expect it didn't occur to Cal until much later, probably after a bad storm, that the body might not be beyond reach of the elements. She must have lived in constant fear that the waves would rip it from its resting place and toss it up on the beach. If there was something on the corpse to connect her death to Willy . . . Of course, there wouldn't have been by that time, but she had no way of knowing that. The demon that motivated her all along was blind ignorance and fear.

"That's the main reason she got the job working for you on James Island, so she could get down to the shore immediately after a storm, before anyone else.

"She must have been out of her mind when those two hurricanes hit last fall, one after the other. After the second one, she went along the shore path, searching the surf, and found what she feared most of all. A body. So she retrieved it."

Mrs. Emerson shuddered noticeably.

"I suppose she hid the body somewhere that day and went back to dig the grave at night, in the soft soil under the spruce tree at the top of the knoll. She reburied the body there. . . . But it wasn't Cailey Hall."

"What?" the captive audience cried, her every muscle tense.

"It was another young woman, Elsa Bonhoffer, who had died in 1917. Oddly enough, thanks to Johnny Bermann, Cailey's body was found by another group of men at almost the same time, in its original grave."

For several minutes the burden of the soliloquy rattled around the room. The indistinct murmur of Matty and Kingsbury could be heard coming from the kitchen. The grandmother clock poked holes in the silence at regular intervals while Mrs. Emerson's brain whirred through the implications of the narrative.

"This is too fantastic," she said at last. "Why wouldn't Cal simply have gone to the grave in the first place? Why would she have had to search the shore?"

Crisp had already wrestled with the question. "I expect the grave was lost. The burial had taken place in haste, at night, and she and Willy were frightened. The way things grow out there, it would have taken no time for the vegetation to remove all traces of the grave. That's in keeping with the testimony of the men who found it."

"Why 'thanks to Johnny Bermann'?" asked Mrs. Emerson.

"I beg your pardon?"

"You said Cailey Hall's grave was found thanks to Johnny Bermann. How?"

"Oh, yes. He left behind some . . . notes. As it turns out, Cal's fears were well founded. He did remember that night and, after the fact, recognized Willy Wiley. I expect that was just the type of evidence that Cal was hoping to find and destroy when she broke into Johnny's house, as well as Billy Pringle's."

He responded to the question in her eyes with an abbreviated description of those events. "Again, just the stupid acts of a desperate woman. Panic."

Mrs. Emerson had a lot to think about. "Why are you telling me this?" she asked finally.

"As I said," explained Crisp, "we have no evidence that would stand up in court. But I have a plan that might force Cal to incriminate herself." He leaned forward, piercing her with the intensity of his gaze. "And I want your help."

Mrs. Emerson realized she was not being given a choice. Inwardly she bridled. "What would I have to do?"

"Doctor Pagitt has taken Cal back to your house for the time being. I don't know what her plans are once Willy returns. I want you to insist she continue in your employ. Tell her you can't get by without her . . . that kind of thing.

"Let it fall, casually, that the police are not completely satisfied with Anne Quindenan's confession because she has no idea where certain articles were disposed of."

"What articles?"

"Several things. An insecticide atomizer and several wads of used tape. I'm sure she didn't throw them overboard, given her experience with evidence washing up on shore. They have to be somewhere."

"You suspect she'll lead you to them?"

"I hope so." He allowed her a little time to think. "Will you help us?"

"You don't think it's a bit presumptuous, asking me to keep a woman you think is some kind of . . . of murdering tigress . . . in my employ?"

Crisp smiled innocuously. "I think you'll find she's docile as a kitten by this time. And she'll never need to know you're helping us."

25

S
UDDEN SHAFTS OF HEADLIGHTS stabbed erratically through the forest. "Someone's coming," said Kingsbury. "Get back behind them trees."

Leeman stumbled over Stuffy in his haste to comply. He hadn't felt such a rush of excitement since they used to play Ghost in the Graveyard when they were kids. "Down. Get down!" Kingsbury commanded. Leading by example, he dropped to his knees behind a tangle of pungent evergreen boughs.

Stuffy look a final drag on his cigarette and ground it out in a thick sponge of moss on the forest floor. "I was beginnin' to wonder if we was on a wild goose chase."

Unseasonably warm weather was thawing the island, wreathing the monochrome twilight with clammy tendrils of mist that hovered twenty to thirty feet above the ground and were held in place by barbed harpoons of spruce and fir. A Jeep entered the clearing at the end of Everette's drive.

"It's stopped," said Leeman.

"Shh," Kingsbury snapped. "Watch."

A lone figure, darkly dressed but obviously female, emerged slowly from the truck and made a long, deliberate survey of the area. She seemed to be listening for something. The watchers in the woods held their collective breath. Apparently satisfied that the coast was clear, she stepped away from the vehicle, was silhouetted briefly in the headlights, then plunged down the slope toward the boathouse, heedless of the depth of the snow. As she walked, she removed an empty bag from the pocket of her greatcoat.

Leeman whispered, "It's her, ain't it?"

Kingsbury was watching through binoculars. "Sure looks that way to me. You two have a look." He passed the glasses to Stuffy, who required just a glance to arrive at the same conclusion before handing them to Leeman.

The woman disappeared behind the boathouse and remained there several minutes. When she reappeared, the bag was no longer empty.

Leeman held his breath to steady the binoculars as he followed her back up the slope. The uphill going was harder, as her steamy breath testified. He was reminded of a train laboring up a steep incline. Twice she stopped abruptly, once when a loon cried and again when a branch snapped like a rifle shot somewhere in the forest. Each time, her reaction was to look not in the direction from which the sound had come but at the hulking silhouette of the Everette house. Each time, as she resumed her upward progress, her steps quickened until she was running as fast as the sodden snow allowed.

The door hinges of the old Jeep creaked loudly when she opened it, and the report as it slammed shut echoed a hundred times throughout the woods and across the Thoroughfare.

Suddenly Leeman jabbed Kingsbury sharply in the ribs with his elbow. "Look."

The others looked where he was pointing.

Barely discernible in the gathering gloom was a figure dressed in white. A woman, standing just off the road.

The Jeep engine roared to life. The gears ground loudly, and the twin beacons of the headlights swept across the Thoroughfare and through the forest as the vehicle headed out the driveway. As it drew abreast of the woman in white, she stepped from behind a tree into plain sight.

Startled, Cal swung the wheel hard to the right, briefly plowing a trail through virgin snow. In the intervening instant before she was able to steer back into the established tracks and come to a stop, all her greatest horrors came vividly to life. With a nauseating thrill of fear, her eyes flashed to the rearview mirror.

There was someone there, in the dark.

She stepped on the brake, and the Jeep's taillights bathed the ghostly figure in a blood red glow.

For an instant it was Margaret Quindenan. But no, it was Lou Ann O'Connor—the girl on the moor whose eyes, together with those of poor, dead Cailey Hall, had haunted her all these years. Somehow Lou Ann had wrangled herself free of the constraints of time and was here now, walking toward the Jeep.

The living and the dead, the past and the present, were getting all jumbled up in Cal's fevered brain as the flimsy tether of reality was yanked from her grasp. Terrified, she stepped on the gas. The wheels, spinning too fast for traction, melted through the snow, finally gaining a purchase on solid ground just as she was about to collapse with fright. The Jeep leapt forward, and Cal didn't look back.

"Shut up, you stupid woman. Get a hold of yourself. You're drunk."

Kitty Emerson had been waiting on the porch when Cal returned, out of her wits and raving incoherently about having seen a ghost.

"I'm not. I haven't touched a drop," Cal cried as they entered the house, slamming the door behind them.

"Then you were imagining things," Kitty assured her. "You're overexcited. Did you get everything?"

Breathlessly, Cal held out the bag. "I think so. It was dark under the boathouse. I couldn't see."

"Never mind," said Kitty, trying her best to be calm. She opened the bag and studied the contents. "This will be enough. If there's anything left, there'll be plenty of time to clean it up later. It's almost over. Tomorrow morning the investigators will find this in Anne's room, and we'll be out of the woods."

"I tell you, I seen her plain as I'm seein' you," said Cal. "Standin' right there in the road, lookin' at me."

"You saw nothing," Kitty yelled, as much to shout down the fear rising in her own mind as to silence Cal. "Nothing." She grabbed her frantic housekeeper by the shoulders. "Look at me, Cal. Anne is dead."

"Dead?" Cal repeated. "What do you mean?"

"While you were gone, I got a telephone call from our dear Mr. Crisp. He said he wanted to talk to me in person about something important. So I went up there, and he told me Anne committed suicide at Mr. Gammidge's house in Rockland."

Cal stared at her blankly.

"Apparently the Professor, the precious old goat, overestimated her emotional stability. No one's going to doubt she's guilty now. Do you understand? That's it. It's over. And this," she lifted the bag, "will put the final piece in place. We're as good as out of it. Do you hear me?"

Cal hesitated, overwhelmed by a nameless dread. "Then it was her I saw. Back from the dead."

"It was nothing of the kind," Kitty scolded bitterly, her patience at an end. "The dead don't come back from the grave."

It was a poor choice of words. The look in Cal's eyes was of someone staring into the maw of hell itself. "They do out here," she said flatly. There was a resignation in her voice that Kitty didn't like. "It ain't gonna work, you know. None of it."

"It is," Kitty said, shaking the housekeeper roughly from her grasp. "We're almost in the clear already."

"No we ain't," said Cal, letting her desperate gaze fall to the floor. "It's the Professor."

"What of him?"

"He's right inside my head," said Cal, briefly becoming more animated. "How did he know all them things?"

"He's guessing. He said so himself. I told you that."

Cal shook her head. "You can't guess about all that." She began to massage her temples. "I heard about him. He ain't natural. He's right inside my head." She dug the heels of her hands into her eyes, as if to erase the memory of what she'd seen.

"Don't be foolish." Kitty set the bag on the bottom step of the staircase, went to the liquor cabinet, and poured a jigger of scotch, which she handed to the housekeeper. "Here. This will steady your nerves."

Cal took the glass and drank greedily. It set her throat on fire, and the warmth spread throughout her body. "Another?" she said, holding out the glass.

"Afterwards," said Kitty, putting the cap back on the bottle. "All you want. But we can't go falling apart now. We've come too far. You want Willy in the clear, don't you?" she said, shoring up her argument.

Mention of her brother gave Cal a momentary focus. It was all for him, after all. "Yes."

"Then pull yourself together. Take a deep breath and stop sniveling about ghosts and that pathetic old man. Believe me, he's got nothing."

Mrs. Emerson answered the door in her dressing gown. Her face was ashen and pale, and she hadn't slept well. Doctor Pagitt was on the doorstep, with Luther Kingsbury and another man she didn't know.

"Morning, Mrs. Emerson," said Pagitt a little stiffly. "You all right?"

"I'm fine, Doctor. Thank you." She made a halfhearted effort to straighten her hair. "It's just . . . everything. You know about Anne?"

Pagitt nodded. "Terrible."

"You think you know a person," she replied, her voice lowering. "I'm sorry. . . ." She recalled herself to the present. "Please, come in. Come in."

Pagitt and the others scuffed their shoes on the mat and entered the house. "This is Robert Rowan. He's with the authorities."

"Ma'am," said Rowan cordially. "Sorry for the inconvenience."

"I'm sure it can't be helped," said Mrs. Emerson coolly.

"You know Luther, of course," Pagitt continued.

"Of course. How do you do, Constable."

"Oh, I'm okay," said Luther, removing his hat.

"The Professor told you we were coming, didn't he?" Pagitt asked.

"Yes. He said you wanted to look in Anne's room."

"If it wouldn't be too much trouble."

"No, of course not. Turn right at the top of the stairs. Hers is the suite at the end of the hall."

"Would you mind coming with us?" Rowan asked matter-of-factly. "Just a formality," he added in response to the question in her eyes. "Have to keep everything legal, you know." He smiled. "Speaking of which, I have to give you this." He produced a neatly folded paper from his shirt pocket and handed it to her. "It's a search warrant."

Mrs. Emerson took the paper and looked at it blankly. "Warrant? Why? I thought I made it clear to the Professor that I had no objection."

"We want to wrap this all up as much as you do, Mrs. Emerson," Rowan explained solicitously. "If we don't find anything in her room, we may want to look elsewhere. Just to be sure."

"Yes. I . . . I suppose." Kitty was too exhausted to think clearly. "Well, I was going to make some breakfast . . ."

"Isn't Cal up and around?" Pagitt asked, looking surprised.

"Well, no. She . . . she had a very bad night."

"The old problem?" Pagitt guessed knowingly.

Mrs. Emerson lowered her head. "I'm afraid so. It's all been too much."

"I'm here, Doctor," said a husky voice from the top of the stairs. Cal had awakened from a fitful alcohol-induced sleep when she heard the knocking at the door. Her robe was draped around her haphazardly, and deep blue semicircles underscored eyes in which there seemed no spark of life.

"Cal," said Pagitt, instinctively starting up the stairs. "You don't look well. I shouldn't have let you out of the medical center so soon."

"I'm all right," she said, without any feeling. "Mrs. Emerson said you'd want to look at Mrs. Quindenan's room."

"We won't trouble you long," said Rowan. "As I was telling Mrs. Emerson, the whole thing's just a formality, really. Tying up loose ends, you know."

As Rowan started for the stairs, Kitty placed her hand on his shoulder. "Could I speak with you a minute?"

"Of course."

"Cal, I think everyone could use some coffee. Would you mind?"

Cal hesitated for a moment, a brief shadow of doubt crossing her face. A moment later, though, she descended the stairs and went to the kitchen. Mrs. Emerson watched until the door closed behind her.

"What is it, Mrs. Emerson?" said Rowan.

She drew him aside. Kingsbury and Pagitt arranged themselves at the bottom of the stairs and engaged in muted conversation.

"It's about Professor Crisp," she began, her voice just above a whisper. "Are you aware what he . . . he had this plan . . . ?"

"Yes, ma'am. I know all about it."

"But he said Cal did it . . . that she killed Johnny Bermann, and that Anne just confessed because he told her to. He seemed to have some crazy idea that that would make Cal give herself away, somehow."

"I know," said Rowan with a sigh.

"He said he told Anne what to say."

Rowan nodded, as if he knew what was coming. "If you ask me," he said, "it wasn't anything she didn't already know. In my opinion, that's why she committed suicide. With all the evidence out in the open, she knew it wouldn't be long 'til people put two and two together.

"I don't want to say anything against the Professor," he continued. "I'm sure he was top of the game in his day. But," he tapped his temple meaningfully, "he got it all backwards.

"I think he was a little smitten, myself. He just got it in his head that such a pretty woman couldn't do such a thing, so . . . You know how it is. I think we'll just thank him very much and let him slip into a well-deserved retirement." He winked. "There's nothing to connect Cal with any of the things he thinks she's guilty of. Don't you worry. Once we've had a little look around, we'll be out of your hair and you can get on with your life."

Kitty placed her hand on her chest. "I'm so relieved. I can't tell you . . ."

"I can imagine," Rowan commiserated.

Cal scuffed into the room in her slippers. "The coffee's on. It'll be ready in five minutes or so."

"That's about all the time it should take," said Rowan, rejoining his cohorts at the bottom of the stairs. He fixed the women with a disarming gaze and gestured theatrically up the stairs. "Ladies, shall we?"

Anne Quindenan's suite was rustic but well appointed. The door of the mahogany wardrobe stood open, revealing neatly hung clothing. Her nightdress was spread on the bed, and her slippers were arranged so she could step into them easily in the middle of the night. "Where do we start?" said Kingsbury.

"Why don't you check the wardrobe, Luther," Rowan directed.

"Doctor Pagitt, if you wouldn't mind looking under the bed, or any-where else in here that seems likely. I'll pop in and check the bath-room."

The women, who had stationed themselves by the door, traded a sharp glance and squeezed each other's hand. Mrs. Emerson, sensing Cal's heightened nervousness, mouthed words of comfort. Relax. It's almost over.

Cal squeezed Mrs. Emerson's hand a little harder and watched unblinking as Rowan disappeared into the bathroom.

Flinging open both doors of the wardrobe, Kingsbury made a thorough search of all its compartments and the pockets of the hanging clothes. Pagitt looked under the bed and thumbed gingerly through intimate articles of clothing and sweaters in a chest of drawers.

"Nothing here," he said, carefully pushing in the last drawer with his knee.

Kingsbury emerged from the closet. "Here neither. Anything in there, Rowan?" he called.

Cal began running her fingers distractedly through her tangled nest of salt-and-pepper hair. Her nervousness was growing despite Kitty's covert attempts to calm her. The attention of both women was fastened on the bathroom door.

For several seconds the sounds of cabinet doors opening and closing emanated from the private bath. When at last Rowan came back into the bedroom, he was empty-handed.

Cal shot Kitty a look of unabashed alarm. "How can that . . ."

Kitty tugged sharply at her arm. "You looked everywhere? All of you?"

"Ain't far to look in there," said Kingsbury, nodding at the wardrobe.

"Not many hiding places," Pagitt added.

Rowan seemed a little embarrassed. "I'm awful sorry, ladies. But I think we'd better look around a little more." His smile was warm, even compassionate. "We have to fill out reports, you know. Once we leave, we don't want to have our bosses sending us back because we didn't do our job."

Mrs. Emerson was dazed. "What? Oh . . . oh, yes. If you must." She gestured abstractly.

As the men filed into the hall, Mrs. Emerson tossed Cal a command with her eyes. "Why don't you straighten up in here, Cal. I'm sure Margaret will be coming to get her mother's things. We don't want her to find a mess." She waited in the doorway with one eye on Cal and the other on the men. "Where next, gentlemen?"

Kingsbury rapped his knuckles on the next door down the hall. "What's in here?"

"That's Margaret's room."

"I'll check this out," said the constable. "Why don't you fellas take that one." He pointed at the room across the hall, the door of which stood wide open.

"That's my room," said Mrs. Emerson, darting another bewildered glance at the bathroom, where she could hear Cal rifling through the vanity cabinet. "Please don't track mud on the carpet."

The men disappeared from the hallway at the same time that Cal appeared in the bathroom door, her face ashen, her eyes filled with a mingling of confusion and terror. "It ain't there," she croaked in a harsh whisper.

In an instant Mrs. Emerson had crossed the room and shoved Cal aside. "Of course it is. You've missed it. Did you look behind the toilet paper?" She didn't wait for a reply but was on her hands and knees in front of the open cabinet, rummaging frantically through its contents.

Her search was fruitless. The look in her eyes as she raised them betrayed utter dismay. "Did you move it?"

" 'Course I didn't move it," Cal snapped defensively.

"Then where is it?"

"Ladies?" Rowan called from the hall. He poked his head through the bedroom door. "Ladies, you in there?"

Mrs. Emerson sprang to her feet and made an abortive attempt to regain what remained of her composure. She squeezed Cal's arm once, hard, as she passed her in the doorway.

"We're here," she said, her voice choking with emotion. "Cal needed some help with poor . . . with poor Anne's . . ." She burst into a fit of sobs and, turning, threw her arms around Cal's neck, where she buried her head and cried. She needed time to think. What had gone wrong? She could feel Cal quaking and knew she was near the breaking point.

"I'm really very sorry, Mrs. Emerson," said Rowan compassionately. "I know it's awful to put both of you through all this, but just one more room up here. Then we'll make a quick sweep downstairs and be gone for good."

The words came like the voice of a loved one calling encouragement from the world of light beyond the grave. The women released each other. Mrs. Emerson took a wad of Kleenex from the pocket of her a gown and dabbed at her eyes. "I'm so sorry, Mr. . . . Mr. Rowan?"

Rowan nodded.

"I'm afraid I . . . I'm afraid neither Cal nor I have much emotional reserve after all . . . after . . ."

"I understand," said Rowan. "Just one more room. This would be yours, Cal?"

Cal tried to reply in the affirmative, but the word refused to come. She nodded vigorously.

"Come on, then," Rowan directed gently. "Shouldn't take a second."

The women rejoined Pagitt and Kingsbury on the landing. Rowan inhaled deeply. "Smells like the coffee's ready, Doc. The only room left is Cal's. I think she'd like to be with us while we give it a quick look. Why don't you take Mrs. Emerson down and see if you can get her to eat a little breakfast."

"That's a good idea," said Pagitt, taking Kitty firmly by the arm. "Come on with me. Let's see if I can't come up with something to help settle your nerves while I'm at it."

Mrs. Emerson was afraid what would happen if she left Cal alone, but she was already halfway down the stairs. It was too late to improvise. One more room and they'd be gone. With a quick glance over her shoulder at the housekeeper, she yielded herself to Pagitt's ministrations.

Cal watched, wide eyed as an abandoned child, as they disappeared from view. "After you," said Rowan with a sweeping gesture toward the closed door at the end of the hall.

Compelled by forces beyond her control, her brain a foggy morass of unformed thoughts, she led the way to her room.

Kingsbury held the door open when they went in and remained standing in the doorway.

"Looks like a comfy little room," Rowan said conversationally as he sifted through Cal's belongings. "You've got a great view. I think I'll bring my wife out here some day this summer. I bet she'd love it."

He made a perfunctory search of the shallow closet.

"How long have you been working for Mrs. Emerson?"

He opened and closed the dresser drawers.

"I don't know . . . ," said Cal, unable to calculate the time. "A long time. Years."

Rowan looked under the bed. "You know," he said from his hands and knees, "I've never found anything under a bed. Evidence, I mean. Have you, Kingsbury?"

"Can't say's I have."

"Never. I think anyone who tried to hide something under a bed would be about as stupid as . . . Now, what's this?" He had turned his investigation to the bottom shelf of a small bookcase that stood opposite the bed. Reaching behind a row of tall books, he removed a tightly folded brown paper shopping bag.

Cal recognized it at once. Her knees collapsed and she fell to the floor as if struck, her eyes wide, roving their sockets until the room spun madly in her head. Instantly her hands began tearing at her hair. "He's in my head," she wailed.

Kingsbury quietly closed the door.

Rowan pulled himself to the side of the fallen woman and grabbed her wrists, which were like bands of iron. "Give me a hand!" he snapped at Kingsbury. She had torn a fistful of hair from her scalp by the time they managed to get control of her arms. She was moaning like a soul in torment. "She done this," she cried at last, pointing a trembling finger at the door. "She put that here so you'd think I done it."

"Did what?" said Rowan, his voice ragged with the effort of restraining her.

She flashed wide, stricken eyes at him. "She wants you to think I done it alone. Well, I didn't. It was her. She planned it all. It was her give me the idea—"

"Before you say anything else," said Rowan, "I should tell you that anything you say . . ." He finished reading her her rights.

A confessional faucet had been turned on that nothing could contain, and neither man tried. They let it flow. By the time it had run its course, leaving Cal drowning in its wake, totally spent and exhausted, they knew all there was to know.

Mrs. Emerson looked up from her coffee cup when Rowan entered the kitchen. "You've been a long time. Where's Cal?"

"I left her upstairs with Constable Kingsbury. She's in pretty bad shape."

"Are you surprised?" said Mrs. Emerson. "After all we've been through. I think—"

"Mrs. Emerson," said Rowan, without emotion, "I arrest you for the murder of Johnny Bermann."

"TURNS OUT MRS. EMERSON PLANNED THE WHOLE THING," said Leeman, resting his root beer on his belly as he sat back in the chair and wrapped his feet around its legs. He knew that no one would interrupt him or doubt his word—he'd been in on it personally and everyone knew it—so he was darn well going to take his time. "She and Mr. Quindenan was havin' an affair. He was over to Paris, you know, workin' on somethin' top secret. *Top* secret. Anyway, he made trips back and forth over the holidays, and it wasn't his wife and daughter he come to see, if you get my drift. He was down to Washington with Mrs. Emerson. That's what was behind it all.

"Anyway, seems she made up her mind to get Mrs. Quindenan out've the way for good. But she was too smart to do it herself. Thought she was, anyway. She put Cal up to it. Set everything up.

"She knew all about Anne and Johnny," he continued slowly, "that they was lovers once or whatever. So she says to Anne, she says, 'Why don't you and Johnny go up to the old place.' That's

Everette's," he explained parenthetically. 'And no one'll be the wiser.' 'Course, she had the key and everything. So there was no problem there.

"So Anne writes a note in this secret code they'd worked up, and give it to Snotty to take up there to Johnny's with the groceries. Well, 'course since Mrs. Emerson's the one who set it up, she tells Cal to listen in on the phone when she an' Mrs. Quindenan's talkin', to get the particulars. So when she overhears Mrs. Quindenan say that Johnny wanted to get there an hour or so early so he could make things special—"

"Went up there to light the fire and set up the wine and all that," Wendell speculated, and for his efforts received a look from Leeman that made it clear that, although the information was accurate, the interruption was not appreciated.

"That's right," Leeman continued. "Anyway, when Cal hears that, she figures that's her chance.

"She and Mrs. Emerson talked it over on the phone. Planned it all out. 'Course, they knew about Johnny's heart condition. So Mrs. Emerson tells Cal to go up to the libr'ry and look up information on some kind've common poison that would kick him over the edge, and she come up with . . . well, it's in bug spray."

Leeman held his audience in the pool hall spellbound for a full twenty minutes. By now the story had all the wrinkles worked out; it was the third telling that morning. When it was over, the only sound was the bubbles popping in Leeman's soft drink, of which he took a lengthy draught.

Brenda, whose throat was dry from having forgotten to swallow during Leeman's recounting, was the first to speak. "Ain't that somethin'," she said. After a few seconds, during which no one else could think of anything appropriate to say, she followed the observation with a question. "What I don't understand is, why did Cal do it? Was Mrs. Emerson payin' 'er?"

"Nope," said Leeman, feigning weariness with the question. "You know how they found Cailey Hall?"

" 'Course we do," said Wendell, hating that Leeman was in possession of facts he was not privy to. "What's that got to do with anything?"

"Well, guess who killed her?"

Deliberately, Leeman unfolded the dark secrets that the earth had kept so long. He thought the very syllables, as they rolled over his tongue, seemed like fine wine. Not that he'd ever had any fine wine, but he imagined that must be pretty much what it was like, else why drink it?

Saint John had not had a more deeply affected audience at his first reading of Revelation.

"Cal talks when she's drunk, I guess. Mrs. Emerson listened, and figured out the whole story. After that, she just played 'er like a cheap fiddle."

Crisp chimed in as he warmed his hands over the potbellied stove. "Mrs. Emerson probably realized that, although Cal and Willy may have been guilty of stupidity, they weren't legally culpable for Cailey's death but simply of covering it up. But she knew she could turn Cal's blind ignorance and fear to her own ends. The idea was to make it look like he died a natural death."

Crisp liked being back among his cronies in the hardware store. The closeness of the place and the smell of turpentine, wood smoke, gun oil, and tobacco formed a manly ambrosia that Matty could never understand. "At least, that was the case as far as Cal was concerned," Crisp continued. "She figured that with Johnny out of the way, it was safe for Willy to come home.

"Of course, Johnny's death was of no use to Mrs. Emerson. She had to think of a way to make it look like murder, with evidence pointing at Anne Quindenan. So she concocted a scheme, one that was simple in concept but nearly impossible in execution, and sold it to Cal.

"Then came the ingenious part. Knowing Cal as she did—a fairly simple, superstitious woman given to drink and plagued by ghosts of the past—she worked subtly on her nerves during the phone calls they had in the time leading up to the murder.

"By the time Cal arrived at Everette's, her wits were so frayed that she made one blunder after the other, just as Mrs. Emerson suspected she would." Crisp neglected to mention that he had played up on the same irrational fear when he'd had Margaret make her ghostly appearance at Everette's. He nudged aside some peppermints in the candy skillet until he uncovered a bite-sized Tootsie Roll. He hadn't had one in a long time but now it was all he wanted. After so long in Matty's care, he'd built up a severe junk food deficit. No one spoke for the next minute or so as he savored the pseudo-chocolate morsel. He finally swallowed the sticky wad of candy with a look of profound satisfaction, then continued the story.

"Cal called Mrs. Emerson that night, probably from the pay phone outside the Sea Breeze, almost delirious with fright."

"Same night Margaret called Doc Pagitt to come up there to see Mrs. Quindenan," Bergie interpolated from the middle of a wreath of pipe smoke. "Said she was a basket case."

"That's right," said Crisp patiently, considering another Tootsie Roll but thinking better of it. Too much of a good thing. "But Mrs. Emerson had a plan all ready."

"Make it look like Mrs. Quindenan done it," Pharty volunteered from the bench by the window.

"Exactly."

"But how'd she know that Cal wouldn't leave evidence pointin' to herself?" said Stump, who had been scratching his head for some time.

"She didn't know," said Crisp. "But if it didn't work, all she had to lose was a housekeeper."

"Yeah," Harry interjected, "a housekeeper who could squeal on her."

Crisp had anticipated the observation. "And who would be believed? A confused, frantic drunkard or the wealthy, dignified widow of a respected surgeon?"

Harry aggravated the stubble on his chin with his leathery hand.

"Of course," Crisp continued, "they were in a perfect position to keep on planting incriminating evidence as long as it took. Which is what they tried to do last night."

Drew added another log to the fire. "Who leaked the story to the media?"

"Chancellor Knight," said Crisp. "He wanted to come to the island without attracting any attention, intending to make sure Johnny Bermann wouldn't spring any unpleasant surprises if he should run for governor, but his picture had been in the paper. I suppose he felt the best way to avoid suspicion was to direct attention elsewhere."

The display of hunting knives communed quietly with assorted items of kitchenware with whom they'd grown old. Together, they listened without comment.

"Well, tell me somethin'," Harry demanded irascibly. "Why did Cal say that girl tried to kill her when Olaf found her in that grave?"

"I think I can answer that," said Rowan. He had returned to the island on the last boat and accompanied Crisp to the hardware store. Until that time, deeply conscious of the honor conferred upon him of being allowed to join the inner circle, however briefly, he had remained quiet. "Kingsbury asked her the same question this morning, after she finished her confession.

"As the Professor suspected, she saw the men dig up the bodies the other morning from her bedroom window. You can imagine the effect it had on her."

"Not too hard," said Drew. "And I bet she turned to old Johnnie Walker for comfort."

"Just so," said Rowan. "I can't say what was in her mind when she went stumbling out on the moor and either fell or threw herself into that hole—she couldn't tell me herself—but she said when she looked up and saw Margaret standing there, she thought it was Anne. The Anne of thirty-five years ago. Like a ghost."

"First I heard've bein' haunted by the ghost of someone who's alive," said Harry.

Rowan shrugged. "The mind does strange things. Anyway, she apparently felt that those ghosts that had been haunting her all these years had come back to take their revenge, to drive her to the grave."

"The Professor told Mrs. Emerson that some inspectors was comin' over from the mainland this morning to see if they couldn't find some hard evidence connectin' Anne to the murder," said Sadie Mitchell. "Well, that was a trick to force her to do somethin'. And that's where she made her mistake."

"He lied?" said Emily, recalling some pretty stern pronouncements against the practice from Sunday's sermon.

"He worked with the government for years," Sadie reminded her.

This was significant to Emily. "Oh, yes."

"But why'd he do all that business with havin' Anne confess?" Ginger wanted to know.

"Stuffy says he just done that to keep 'em off balance," said Sadie, who had spoken to Doctor Pagitt that morning. "She wasn't never really arrested. The Professor figured as long as he threw wrenches in the works, they wouldn't have no time to plan. They'd just have to improvise. Sooner or later they'd make a mistake. He knew they might try anything, though, either one of 'em or both of 'em, if they got pushed hard enough, so that was a way to get Anne and Margaret safe off the island without tippin' his hand, like they say in the movies."

"Well, the whole business is just too much to imagine," said Emily.

"The Professor done all that," Ginger concluded. "You wouldn't think it to look at him, would you?"

Jerry Oakes was the center of attention at Buddy's Come 'n' Get It. "She was right out of her mind when they finally got 'er in the car and on the boat. Talkin' 'bout seein' ghosts and bodies comin' out've the grave and who knows what."

Jerry had come to the aid of Kingsbury and Rowan that morning at the ferry terminal when Cal, despite the handcuffs, threatened to turn violent. Once they'd secured the prisoner and were waiting for the ferry, he'd gotten the whole story from the constable, who was more than happy to relate it without stinting on details.

"How 'bout Mrs. Emerson?" asked Miriam, mechanically flipping a row of perfect pancakes on the grill. "She give 'em any trouble?"

"Not a peep. Got in the car and just set there the whole time like a statue. Luther had her cuffed to the emergency brake."

"I didn't know the town owned two set've cuffs," Mont Billings observed philosophically.

"I heard it was Kingsbury and that FBI fella switched that bag from Mrs. Quindenan's room to Cal's," said Goose. "Is that so?"

Jerry shook his head. "Nope. It was Olaf."

"Olaf?" said two or three voices in unison. "Yup," Jerry replied, pleased with the reaction. "They had to sneak him in the house, so yes'd'y evening, when Cal was up to Everette's—Luther and Stuffy and Leeman was up there watchin' her—the Professor calls up Mrs. Emerson and says he's got somethin' important to tell her. Somethin' he couldn't tell 'er on the phone.

"Well, 'course she was curious, so she went. And while she was gone, Olaf got in the house and hid, so he could switch the bag around after them women put it in Mrs. Quindenan's room . . . which is just what they did, Luther says.

"After he was sure they was asleep, he made the switch. Wasn't as hard as he thought it would be, I guess, since Cal was pretty much snookered by that time. Then he just skulked out, went home, and called Kingsbury and told 'im it was a done deal."

Brenda stacked the pancakes on a plate and set it, steaming, on the counter. A glorious crown of bright yellow butter melted atop the pile like the wicked witch of the West, and there was a brief fusillade of cutlery as all the customers helped themselves. "What did the Professor tell Mrs. Emerson?"

Jerry didn't know. "Whatever it was, it worked."

A long stillness embraced the diners, interrupted only by the sounds of thoughtful mastication. It was Goose who finally broke the silence. "Three bodies," he said. "Makes you wonder, don't it?"

Crisp had been staring out the hardware store window for a long time, but nobody interrupted him. "Johnny naming Margaret his heir was something they couldn't have planned for," he said at last. His attention returned to the men around the fire. "I don't think anyone realized that he knew she was his daughter. Anne certainly didn't. That was why she had set up the meeting with him. She felt he should know.

"It wasn't necessarily a bad thing, from Mrs. Emerson's perspective, since it might ultimately add weight to a case against Mrs. Quindenan. But it was something else they had to take into account."

"Another monkey in the works," Drew paraphrased. "Well, young man," he said, addressing Crisp, "you done one helluva job. The whole island's talkin' 'bout it."

Crisp turned away and regarded the cracks around the door of the woodstove through which the dancing flames were visible. "The ironic thing is, I didn't do anything."

He looked up at his friends. "When all is said and done, it was Johnny who pointed the finger at his own murderer." He allowed his audience to consider the fact. "It was Johnny who made me wonder if there might be another body on James Island, thanks to the suspicions he had about his father. Ultimately, it was he who led us to Cal. From her to Mrs. Emerson was a fairly short step."

"Seems more like a leap to me," said Stump.

"Not really," Crisp replied, turning his attention again to the stove. "I had suspicions about Cal before Luther and Stuffy took me up to Everette's, but when I looked at the way the murder had been planned, it just didn't mesh with the picture everyone gave me of Cal. Someone else had to be behind it, at least giving her ideas. The question was, who?

"I made a call to an old friend of mine, a private detective in New York, and asked him to do a little poking around. It didn't take him long to find out that Mrs. Emerson had been having an affair with Paul Quindenan. That gave me something to work with."

The weathered wheels of conversation ground to a creaky halt when Olaf Ingraham entered the hardware store. There was no reading the look in his eyes as he made a quick study of the occupants. With the exception of Crisp, he'd known every man in the room all his life. So had his father and grandfather.

Crisp felt curiously uneasy as the big man approached and stopped directly in front of him.

Slowly the hulking Swede held out a work-worn hand. Crisp, flushed with a deep sense of relief, took it in his and clasped it firmly. Olaf might have smiled, it was hard to tell in the light, then he turned and left the store.

The door was open, and Billy was halfway through when he saw Margaret, on her hands and knees in the corner behind Johnny Bermann's bed, going through some papers. She was so deeply engrossed that she hadn't heard his footsteps on the porch. He stopped and knocked.

She wasn't startled. She raised her eyes like someone waking from a trance, trying to pull a strange world into focus. "Yes?"

"You're Margaret, ain't you?" said Billy.

She rested her hands, still clutching a bundle of papers, on her knees. "Yes. And who are you?"

"I'm Billy."

"Billy Pringle?" she ventured. She'd heard about him.

"Billy Pringle," he said. There were few things he could assert with such conviction. "Yes."

"What can I do for you, Billy?" she asked.

He liked her eyes. They were kind, and she didn't seem nervous. He remembered why he'd come. "I brung you some meat loaf," he said, retrieving a Tupperware container from the folds of his coat and extending it to her graciously.

Margaret stood up and rounded the bed. "Why, that's very nice of you."

"We're neighbors," said Billy.

"Yes, I know," said Margaret. She lifted the lid of the Tupperware and was instantly overcome by the pungent perfume of rotting meat. She closed it quickly, but her reaction didn't register on her face. She had been warned to beware of Billy bearing gifts.

"They call that a housewarming present," said Billy, tossing a nod at the Tupperware. "I don't know why that is. It don't heat the place much."

"I think it's because it's a kindness," said Margaret. "And kindness warms the heart."

Billy turned this over carefully in his mind, examining it from every angle. "Home is another word for house," he announced at length. "And home is where the heart is. You heard 'em say that?"

"I have."

"So housewarming means the same as heartwarming," Billy decided with a nod and a raspberry. It had been a very satisfying exchange on an intellectual level. One by one, all life's questions were answered, in good time.

"You movin' in here?"

Margaret tossed the papers on the bed, put her hands on her hips, and looked around. "I've been wondering that myself."

"You wonder 'bout things, too?" said Billy.

"I certainly do."

Billy nodded, and raspberried thoughtfully. "Me, too."

"Right now," said Margaret, when silence threatened to engulf them, "I'm wondering if I'm up to it."

"Up to what?"

"All this," said Margaret, gesturing widely about her. "The place needs so much work. And it's a mess."

Here, Billy thought, Margaret was showing her feminine side. The place looked pretty cozy to him, and there was still room for a lot more stuff. "Is it?"

"And all these papers. It could take me a year to go through them."

Billy looked at all the various piles. "Not if you used a shovel," he suggested.

Margaret laughed, as if he'd said something funny. He liked her laughter. It sounded like the waves on the shore. "Not if you used a shovel," he said again, hoping for the same result, but the laughter died away. Apparently is was funny only once. But the smile that remained at the corners of her mouth was worth the trip. "He left the place to you, didn't he?"

"Yes."

"Funny how dead people can do that."

The thought had never occurred to Margaret. "Yes, I guess it is."

"He was your father, wasn't he?"

"Yes. He was."

Billy stood for a while, sorting and sifting his thoughts. He looked at the bundle of papers on the bed. "Me and Nate Gammidge was up here the other night. He was lookin' for papers."

"I know."

"Cal was here when we got here. She was lookin', too."

Margaret nodded.

"Got a few, she did."

"Yes."

"That much less you have to worry about," Billy deduced.

"I suppose that's true."

"Lot of 'b's on 'em."

"Were there?" Margaret was not condescending. In less than two minutes she had formed a favorable impression of Billy. She felt perfectly at ease with him, despite the somewhat abstract functions of his mental apparatus.

"She hit me with that typewriter." He nodded at the Underwood, which occupied the same place on the floor it had when he last saw it.

"No," Margaret cried, taking a step toward him. "Is that how you got this bruise?" She brushed a thick tangle of hair from his forehead, revealing the wound.

"I guess it must've been," said Billy. Here was a woman who acted just like one. She'd have the place neat as a pin in no time. Pity.

"Are you all right?" she asked sincerely.

This was another question Billy was often asked. And he always had a hard time answering. All right as opposed to what? He nodded in a circular, noncommittal motion. "She come to my place, too."

"That's what Professor Crisp told me."

"He did?"

"Yes."

Deliberative raspberry. "You know," he said, choosing his words carefully, "the Professor knows more from bed than most folks do standin' up."

The comment precipitated another cascade of gentle laughter. If only he could figure out just what made that happen.

"He certainly does," Margaret agreed.

"How's your mother?" said Billy. He wanted to know.

She sighed deeply and stared over his shoulder through the door at nothing in particular. Billy could tell from the look in her eyes that if he turned around there wouldn't be anything there.

Margaret considered the question. Her mother had been betrayed not only by her best friend but by her husband. On top of it all, she'd lost her first love. "She has a lot to deal with right now. But she's strong. I think she'll be all right." It was a wishful addendum rather than one born of conviction. "She's gone to stay with her mom and dad."

"Your grammie and grampa?" asked Billy. Relationships were important.

"Yes. Nanna and Papa, I call them. They live in upstate New York."

Billy nodded. "That's a long ways away."

"Yes. It is."

Billy looked at the typewriter and rubbed his head. The cool touch of Margaret's fingers still tingled there. It was an angel's touch. The thought reminded him of something.

"There's a new grave up at the cemetery this morning," he said, tossing a nod over his shoulder. "That him? Your father?"

"Yes. I buried him with his mother and her baby."

"I know 'bout them. Sometimes when I'm visitin' Henry Hopkins, Kilby Miller's up here diggin' graves. He likes to talk 'bout the people. He calls 'em the 'old people,' even if they was only babies. Like that one. There wasn't no name on his tombstone before, though," he observed. "There is now."

Margaret went to the door and leaned thoughtfully against the jamb as she stared out toward the cemetery. "Yes. I named him Oscar Bermann, Junior."

Billy knew by her demeanor that this was important. He joined her at the door. "No 'd's in that," he observed quietly.

On those rare days when the temperature exceeds fifty degrees in January, islanders call it "fool's spring," and that's what Crisp woke to the next morning. Either the unexpected warmth itself or its false promise of warm weather ahead seemed to unclog the sap in his veins and send it coursing through his limbs. He bathed, dressed, donned an overworn pair of tennis shoes that he dug from their place of hibernation, and capered down the stairs in a jaunty thirty seconds flat.

"Matty!" he called. She was too busy shuffling pots and pans to hear. "Matty," he repeated as he rounded the kitchen door.

"Land sakes!" said Matty, spinning and slapping a hand to her breast in a single motion. "You scared me half to death. I didn't know you were up." Her greeting turned abruptly suspicious as her gaze fell on the sneakers. "What on earth are you doing with those things?"

"I was just wondering," said Crisp with a twinkle in one eye and a prayer in the other, "what did you do with my bicycle?"

"Bicycle!" she cried. "Bicycle, he says," she muttered as she crossed to the cupboard where she kept his mail. "I was going to give you this yesterday, but things got a little, well . . ." She removed an envelope and held it out. As he reached to take it, she snapped it back. "I don't think I should give it to you, if you don't have sense enough to know you aren't going to ride any more bicycles in this lifetime, mister man."

"Why not?" he said with mild curiosity. "Besides, if that's for me, it's either a bill or a solicitation."

"Tell me you won't try to ride your bike," said Matty, holding back the letter tantalizingly.

"I won't," said Crisp. He wanted to get the game over with. He was hungry, and the smell of hot blueberry syrup was by far more tempting.

"Promise?"

Crisp prevaricated. "I was just kidding, Matty. Just a joke. I know I'm in no shape to ride a bike."

Misinterpreting his reply, Matty waved the envelope in front of her face like a Japanese fan. "It's just that I don't think bicycle riding is a dignified activity for a published poet. Do you?"

She gave him the envelope.

Crisp sank to a chair at the table, and he took the letter with trembling hands. It had been opened. He looked at Matty.

"Well," she said innocently. "Are you going to open it or just sit there looking foolish?"

Sweat beaded on his brow. In the course of his long life he'd been shot, stabbed, poisoned, abandoned, lost at sea, trapped behind enemy lines, imprisoned . . . and worse, but however profound the anxiety of those experiences, they paled in comparison to this. He fumbled a second longer, but, losing patience with insubordinate fingers, thrust the envelope at Matty. "Read it to me."

Matty removed the letter with a practiced hand and unfolded it a little more deliberately than necessary.

"It's from the *Atlantic Monthly*," she said over the reading glasses she'd propped on her nose. "I never heard of 'em. Have you?"

"Read," Crisp commanded, nearly choking on the syllable.

"Patience," said Matty teasingly. "You've waited this long, haven't you?" She'd hoped to savor the moment, but the look in his eyes suggested that her moments might be numbered. "'Dear Mr. Crisp'—that's nice and polite," she editorialized.

"Matty!" said Crisp, grabbing at the letter. Matty snatched it out of harm's way.

"I'll read. I'll read," she insisted, smoothing the letter. "'Dear Mr. Crisp, Thank you for your submission. Normally *Atlantic Monthly* does not accept unsolicited submissions, but one of our editors was so impressed by your poem that she insisted the rest of the editorial staff read it. I'm pleased to inform you that we have agreed unanimously to publish "The Bucket," if it is still available. We have enclosed a copy with one or two editorial suggestions for your consideration. Overall, it can't be improved. Please write me with your response at your earliest convenience.

"'Thank you for thinking of us. We like to encourage gifted young writers and look forward to receiving more of your work in the future. Yours respectfully, Danielle Allforth, Poetry Editor. *Atlantic Monthly*.'"

Crisp had lowered his head, and large, silent tears formed pools on the knarled and ancient knuckles he held up to his eyes. He stood slowly, left the room, and shuffled silently up the stairs.

"'Bout time," said Matty, unfolding the sheet that accompanied the letter. She read aloud:

The Bucket

These are the days that our minds have made
Here are castles for periwinkle princes
Ocean-going galleons of sea-shells
With gum-wrapper sails
And crews of colored stones
Who know no fear.

How easy to sail
Out of sight of land
In a mussel-shell boat
In a bucket of sand.

T HERE WAS NO ONE TO GREET WILLY WILEY when he
stepped off the boat, the last one of the day. His head still
unclear after a four-day drunk, he stood for a long time,
searching the crowd for his sister's face, but she was nowhere to be
seen. He didn't recognize any of the other faces, and they didn't recognize him.

He tossed the heavy black canvas seabag that contained all his
worldly possessions over his shoulder and plodded up the street
toward the run-down house by the cove, now empty, its windows
boarded over.

Whatever his part in Cailey Hall's death, the statute of limita-
tions had run out long ago.

Besides, it had all been an accident. He never meant to hurt anybody.

If you enjoyed *The Dead of Winter,* you'll certainly enjoy these other Maine mysteries from Down East Books:

A Show of Hands:
A Maine Island Mystery
by David A. Crossman

Retired NSA code breaker Winston Crisp retires to peaceful Penobscot Island, but with the discovery of the body of a young woman frozen in the ice of an abandoned quarry, he finds himself entangled in a murder investigation, haunted by a red-headed ghost, and the target of a killer with a strangely twisted mind. ISBN: 0-89272-398-X

Murder on Mount Desert
by David Rawson

In the town of Eagle Harbor on the "quiet side" of Mt. Desert Island, a Sheriff's Department patrolman, Jimmy Hoitt, follows the investigation of a hit-and-run death through high-speed chases, sniper attacks, and cliff-hanging suspense to its surprising conclusion. ISBN: 0-89272-363-7

Country Living, Country Dying:
A Witty Tale of Secrets Unburied
by Able Jones

When a skeleton turns up in the Bosky Dells, Maine dump one Halloween night, the quirky residents of this peculiar town all get involved in trying to figure out who left it there. ISBN: 0-89272- 378-5

> *. . . keeps the wheels spinning merrily, with macabre surprises*
> *at just the right intervals.* —PUBLISHERS WEEKLY

And for young adults:

The Secret of the Missing Grave
by David A. Crossman

Teens Bean and Ab are expecting to spend a normal, fun summer together on the Maine island where Ab lives, but things quickly become exciting as they encounter a haunted house, a secret tunnel, buried treasure, and stolen paintings from an exclusive Boston gallery. ISBN: 0-89272-456-0

Available in bookstores, or by calling Down East Books at:
1-800-685-7962